Praise for Deb Caletti's

# The Secret Life of Prince Charming

★ "Caletti's gifts for voice and for conjuring multidimensional personalities
are at their sharpest."

—*Publishers Weekly* (starred review)

"The author excels at getting to the heart of her protagonists' mixed-up emotions,
and her fans will not be disappointed."

—*Kirkus Reviews*

"A sure hit with both Caletti's and Sarah Dessen's legions of fans."

—*Booklist*

"Caletti gets her message across without being preachy in this charming read.
Quinn and company are real and vivid and really help the story to hit home. A truly
great read."

—RTBookReviews.com

"Caletti is a master of language and an astute observer of the human condition."

—*VOYA*

"A thoughtful, funny, and empowering spin on the classic road novel."

—*SLJ*

An ABA IndieBound pick

ALSO BY DEB CALETTI

# The Secret Life of Prince Charming

## DEB CALETTI

Simon Pulse
New York London Toronto Sydney

SIMON PULSE
An imprint of Simon & Schuster Children's Publishing Division
1230 Avenue of the Americas, New York, NY 10020
First Simon Pulse paperback edition March 2010
Copyright © 2009 by Deb Caletti
All rights reserved, including the right of reproduction
in whole or in part in any form.
SIMON PULSE and colophon are registered trademarks of Simon & Schuster, Inc.
Also available in a Simon & Schuster Books for Young Readers hardcover edition.
For information about special discounts for bulk purchases, please contact
Simon & Schuster Special Sales at 1-866-506-1949 or business@simonandschuster.com.
The Simon & Schuster Speakers Bureau can bring authors to your live event.
For more information or to book an event contact the Simon & Schuster Speakers
Bureau at 1-866-248-3049 or visit our website at www.simonspeakers.com.
Designed by Tom Daly
The text of this book was set in Berkeley.
Manufactured in the United States of America
10 9 8 7 6 5 4 3 2 1
The Library of Congress has cataloged the hardcover edition as follows:
Caletti, Deb.
The secret life of Prince Charming / by Deb Caletti. — 1st ed.
p. cm.
Summary: Seventeen-year-old Quinn has heard all her life about how
untrustworthy men are, so when she discovers that her charismatic but selfish father,
with whom she has recently begun to have a tentative relationship, has stolen
from the many women in his life, she decides she must avenge his wrong.
ISBN 978-1-4169-5940-3 (hc)
[1. Fathers—Fiction. 2. Interpersonal relations—Fiction.
3. Family Problems—Fiction. 4. Divorce—Fiction.] I. Title.
PZ7.C127437Se 2009
[Fic]—dc22
2008013014
ISBN 978-1-4169-5941-0 (pbk)
ISBN 978-1-4391-5927-9 (eBook)

For John Yurich,
who showed me
the real meaning of
the words that matter most

# *Acknowledgments*

My affection and gratitude goes to the usual suspects—Ben Camardi, Jennifer Klonsky, and all the fine folks at Simon & Schuster who treat my books like family. Special thanks, too, to Richard Hutton and Michael Caldwell of Vulcan Productions.

My deep appreciation also goes to a new force in books—the dedicated YA Web bloggers (thank you, Allie Costa, especially) who read and write and share their love of fine writing with a passion that's pure and catching.

Lastly (but always, always firstly), my never ending love and appreciation to my family—Mom, Dad, Sue, and all the gang. And to my kids, Sam and Nick, who make me so unbelievably proud. You've got my heart, always.

"Fathers, be good to your daughters
Daughters will love like you do
Girls become lovers who turn into mothers
So mothers be good to your daughters, too."
—John Mayer

"These are the things I tried to warn you about."
—Your Mother

# The Secret Life of
# Prince Charming

# Chapter One

When it came to love, my mother's big advice was that there were WARNING SIGNS. About the "bad" guys, that is. The ones who would hurt you or take advantage or crumple you up and toss, same as that poem I would once try to write for Daniel Jarvis. The wrong men—the psychopaths, cheaters, liars, controllers, stalkers, ones too lazy or incompetent to hold a job, to hold their temper, to hold you properly, to hold anything but a joint or a beer bottle—well, there were RED FLAGS, and you had to watch for them. If you were handling love correctly, it should go the way of those Driver's Ed videos, where things were jumping out at you right and left and you had to be on alert—a swerving truck, a child's ball rolling into the street. The important thing was, love was dangerous. Love was that dark alley you were walking down where your purse might be snatched.

Love was also an easy word, used carelessly. Felons and creeps could offer it coated in sugar, and users could dangle it so enticingly that you wouldn't notice it had things attached—heavy things, things like pity and need, that were as weighty as anchors and iron beams and just as impossible to get out from underneath.

"They ought to make people apply for a permit before they can say they love you," Mom said once. I remember this—she was in our big kitchen, holding a mug of coffee in both hands, warming her fingers against an image of Abe Lincoln embossed on ceramic, the oldest mug in the house, from when my father once went to Springfield, Illinois, home of our sixteenth president.

Mom was talking to me and Gram and Aunt Annie, who both lived with us, and the sound of cartoons was coming from the living room, where my little sister Sprout was sitting cross-legged on the floor in her pajamas.

"Yeah. Make a man pay fifty bucks and take one of those mental tests," Gram said. She was fishing around in the kitchen drawer as butter melted in a pan for scrambled eggs. "Quinn, help an old lady find the damn whisk," she said to me.

"Cynics," Aunt Annie said, but she did so with a sigh. "You're both cynics." She tightened the sash of her robe around her. She'd just started seeing Quentin Ferrill at the time. We knew him only as the Double Tall Chai Latte No Foam guy, who gave long looks at Aunt Annie when he asked how her day was going across the counter at Java Jive, where Aunt Annie was a barista. Looks that shared secrets, she had told us. "Looks that are trying to get you into bed, is more like it," Gram had replied.

The favorite lecture of some mothers was Don't Talk to Strangers or, maybe, Look Both Ways. My mother's favorite was All Men Are Assholes.

I tended to side with Aunt Annie that they were cynics. I was only seventeen—I wasn't ready to be jaded yet. I was just at the start of the relationship road, where lip-gloss-love ends and you're at that Y where if you go one way, you'll have flat, easy pathways and everlasting happiness, and if you go the other, the rocky and steep slopes of heartbreak—only you have no idea which way is which. I liked to think I was already heading in the right direction, determined to prove my mother wrong by making Good Choices. I was sort of the queen of good choices, ruled by niceness and doing the right thing. Good choices

meant asking that weird, solitary Patty Hutchins to your birthday party even when you didn't want to. Good choices meant
getting your homework in on time and being on the volleyball
team and sharing a locker with someone who played the clar-
inet instead of someone who drank their parents' Scotch. It
meant liking math because it makes sense and liking your family even if they don't make sense and driving carefully and
knowing you'd go to college. It meant taking careful steps and
being doomed to be someone no one really remembered at the
high school reunion.

I think "good choices" also meant *other people's choices* to
me, then. I could feel hazy and undefined, even to myself. Was
I going to be amazing, the best, the most incredible—win a
Nobel Prize in mathematics, achieve great heights, as Dad
would constantly tell me? Or was I going to be someone who
would only continue to stumble and flounder and search, which
is what I really felt would happen, since Dad's words sounded
as shiny and hollow as Christmas ornaments to me? Maybe I
would be simply *ordinary*. What would happen if that were the
case? Just ordinary? And how did you get to a place where you
knew where you were headed and what you wanted? I hate to
admit this, I do, but the fact was, if most of my friends wanted
hamburgers, I wanted hamburgers, and if the whole class kept
their hands down during a vote, I would not be the single raised
hand. No way. Too risky. When you went along, you could be
sure of a positive outcome. A plus B equals C. When you didn't
go along, you got A plus X equals a whole host of possibilities,
including, maybe, pissing off people and ending up alone. I
badly wished I could know my own truths and speak them, but

they seemed out of reach, and it seemed better to be sure of yourself in secret.

And in love? Good choices so far meant my boyfriend, Daniel Jarvis, whom I'd been dating for over a year. Dating meaning he'd come over to my house and we'd watch a video and he'd hold my hand until it got too sweaty. Teachers loved Daniel, and he ran track and was polite to my mother and went to church every Sunday morning with his family. Daniel was *nice*. Like me. He made good choices too. He bought that Toyota instead of the classic little MG Midget with the broken convertible top that he'd run his hands over lovingly. Toyota love was only responsible love—remembering to put the gas cap on, refilling the wiper fluid. Convertible love was fingertips drawn slow over the curve of warm metal.

My inner evil twin, the one who would say the things I didn't want to hear but that were the truth, would also say that *oatmeal* is nice. Second-grade teachers are nice. That Christmas present from Aunt So and So was nice, the little pearl stud earrings. My inner evil twin also knows that the kind of nice that appears in the phrase "But he's *nice*," that emphasis, well, it's suspiciously defensive. Sort of like when you buy a shirt you don't really like because it was half off and then say, "But it was a good buy." Justification for giving in to things we don't feel one hundred percent for. Maybe I just wanted to believe in love, even if I didn't all the way believe in me and Daniel Jarvis. Maybe what Daniel Jarvis and I had was half-off love.

With Daniel, there weren't any red flags, but there weren't any blue ones or green ones, either; no beautiful silk flags with gold threads and patterns so breathtaking they could make you dizzy when they blew in the wind. It was enough, maybe, not to have bad things, even if you didn't have great things. For example, my best friend, Liv, went out with this guy, Travis Becker, whom she was totally in love with until she found out he was seeing two other girls at the same time and had recently been arrested for breaking and entering. God. Then again, Liv is beautiful and I am not. Good choices are a little harder, maybe, when you have lots of options.

As for Mom, I'm guessing she began developing her favorite lecture somewhere around the time her own father (Gram's way-ward husband, the elusive Rocky Siler) left when she was two, and after her stepfather (Otto Pearlman, Aunt Annie's dad) did the same thing ten years later. She added to the running theme when she and my dad divorced after his affair with Abigail Renfrew, and perfected it sometime after her three-year relationship with Dean. Or, as we call him now, OCD Dean. He and his two horrible chil-dren moved in with us for a while after Dad left, before Gram and Aunt Annie moved in. Let me tell you, people of different values don't belong under the same roof. We named Dean's kids Mike and Veruca, after those characters in *Charlie and the Chocolate Factory*, Mike Teavee and Veruca Salt ("Da-dee! I want an Oompa Loompa *now*!"). It got so bad with them there that it felt like some kind of home-invasion robbery where the robbers decide to live with you afterward. Mom, Sprout, and me would go somewhere and leave them behind, and when we had to come back, Mom would sometimes drive right past our house. *We can't go in there*, she'd say, as if the building itself were dangerous, filled with toxic fumes, threatened by a collapsing structure. As if the problem was with the house and not the people in it.

My mother, Mary Louise Hoffman, is a graphic designer who used to paint and had shown her work at several galleries. She used to dance, too, which is how she met my father—they actually performed in a show together. It's hard to imagine her as this painter/dancer wearing swirling skirts and swoopy earrings; there's a picture of her from the time just before she met Dad—someone had snapped her in the middle of a cartwheel, only one hand on a deep green grassy lawn somewhere, her feet in the air. It seems odd; it seems like a different her, because her feet were so firmly on the ground after that. She was sort of the super-functioning head woman in our clan. Mom handled things—she could sign a permission slip at the same time she was steaming wrinkles from a blouse and cooking Stroganoff. But if you got her started on the man thing, she'd get a little crazy-extremist, super focused and wild-eyed both, like those anti- or pro-religious people, only without the religion part.

Most particularly, you didn't want to get her started on my dad. "Men" meant him, especially, multiplied by a gajillion. She tended to forget that he was my father, that he was her ex, not mine. And that I wanted to love him, needed for him to love me back because he hadn't been in my life always. Her constant reminders about why I shouldn't didn't help anything. Actually, they hurt her cause. Because every time I heard anything about him, or about "men," I put up a nice new stone in my mental defense wall of him. It's sort of like how you protect the little kid from the bully. You want to say, *Hey, every time you do that, I love Dad more,* but you don't say that. When your parents are divorced, there's a lot you don't say. And another thing you think but don't dare speak: *When you talk bad about each other, you're wasting your breath. I stopped listening years ago.* You stop listening when you figure out that the words aren't actually directed at you, anyway. That you're basically a wire between two telephones.

Anyway. I guess what I mean to say, what I should say right off, is that I knew good choices did not include stealing things from my own father's house. I knew that, and I did it anyway. I had to. Frances Lee, the half sister I never knew but know now, would say this about what we did: sometimes good choices are really only bad ones, wrapped up in so much fear you can't even see straight.

# Chapter Two

Sprout and I saw Dad every other weekend since he came back into our lives three years before. We'd take the train into Portland to visit him. From our home in Nine Mile Falls, Mom would drive us over the floating bridge to Seattle, where we'd wait on the wooden benches of the train station until it was time to board. I would bring my backpack to do homework on the ride, and Sprout would bring her hat, one of the ones Gram crocheted, putting little toys in it to take along—a pony with a mane and a miniature brush, or this small stuffed monkey she got in a Happy Meal, or three kinds of lip gloss and a mirror shaped like a heart. She would roll the lip gloss on throughout the trip and smack her lips together, admiring the shine in the mirror and sending small bursts of fruity bubble-gummy smells across the seat.

But that day, the day when I began to learn the importance of lifting things up and looking underneath, she had this power girl, a mini superhero in a skintight purple suit, whose red mask would light up when you pushed a button on her back. You have thousands of days in your life, if you're lucky, but not many stay with you. You remember objects, maybe, or a person or moments—that bike you once had, or that birthday party, or that neighbor boy, Kenny, who used to dress in army clothes, or the first-grade class hamster you brought home for winter break. But the days you remember are the big days, when life goes suddenly left or right, and this was one of those days. And so I remember that the power girl wore a suit of purple and black. Sprout would take power girl and dance her cheerily up my arm, flashing that mask.

"Sprout," I warned. "Quit it."

"She's dancing," Sprout said. "Girl's gotta dance." The mask flashed, on-off, on-off.

"She should be rescuing things," I said, because I was only mildly annoyed, really. Sprout (Charlotte, her real name) was eleven, six years younger than me; enough that I always knew it was my job to look after her. This meant that I couldn't pummel her for anything but her larger crimes. "Saving people. Performing heroic acts. Leaping across buildings."

Sprout took my advice and the power girl jumped from my shoulder to my knee. "Her name is Rosebud," Sprout said. She looked nothing like a Rosebud, with her pointy plastic breasts and wild black plastic hair and lethal plastic heels, but I kept quiet. "Rose. Bud," Sprout said as the tall evergreens outside the train window sped past in blurry fast forward. "Someday I'll just be sleeping and he'll come along and wake me up with a kiss," Sprout said. I looked over at her; she had her head laid back against the seat, her long black hair (which tangled like tree branches) in a braid behind her, eyes closed. Her lips were puckered, waiting. She'd done that conversational slipup, that thing you do when you forget that other people aren't following along with you in your head. I connected the absent dots— Rosebud, Rose Red, fairy tale, Sleeping Beauty.

"You better hope not," I said. "Any strange guy comes up to you and kisses you while you're sleeping, man, you call the police."

"He wouldn't be a strange guy," Sprout said as if this were obvious. "He would be *the one*."

"God, don't let Mom hear you say that."

"I *wouldn't*. I *know* that," Sprout said. She was ticked off at me, because when you're eleven, what makes you madder than anything is when people think you don't know things that you do.

She flicked me with her thumb and forefinger, the kind of small gesture in close quarters that *did* make me want to pummel her. "Don't," I said.

"Cruisin' for a bruisin'," she said, which is something Grandma would say when Aunt Annie walked out before she'd helped with the dishes. But Sprout didn't flick again. The power girl/Rosebud stomped around in her heels on the plastic train seat, and I went back to my biology homework. Cells dividing, one thing breaking up into two, two things breaking up into four. The blurred evergreens gave way to an expanse of water, a rocky shoreline under a gray May Northwest sky, two men in a boat, shingled houses. We were about halfway there. I erased a mistake, blew the bits of rubber dust from the page. I thought, *Four weeks until summer*. I felt Sprout's eyes on me. I looked over at her.

"You have such long eyelashes," she said. She made a curve in the air with her index finger. I smiled and wrote, *Cell division is a process by which a cell, called the parent cell, divides into two cells, called daughter cells*. Sprout fished around in her hat and pulled out her phone, which Mom insisted we each have for "emergencies." Sprout's was bright pink, and the emergency at the moment was the need to photograph my eyelashes. She held up the little camera lens very close to my face, and I heard the phone's own electronic version of a shutter snap. She looked at the result, showed me the picture.

"Big eye," I said. Sprout waved it around in spooky, big eye fashion. She then started taking up-close pictures of things while I finished biology. Close up of the knee of her jeans, the *A* on the cover of the Amtrak magazine, the scar on her right hand that she got when she fell off her bike. I pulled out the lunch Mom packed for us because she was convinced Dad would forget to feed us. It wasn't *forgetting* exactly, I thought, just that he got so wrapped up in what he was doing he sometimes didn't think about food until he himself was hungry. Then it was, *Wow, I'm starved,* and we'd get cheeseburgers and fries and onion rings and milk shakes and whatever else we wanted. And the milk shakes—he'd ask them to make us something that had never been made before. Half and half, or a mix of things. The poor fast-food guys didn't know what to do. Dad never liked doing things the regular way, even something as mundane as eating. So, okay. Maybe he didn't like doing parenting the ordinary way either.

### Dorothy Hoffman Siler Pearlman Hoffman:

*The first young man I ever was sweet on was Ernest Delfechio, back when I was fifteen. This was before Rocky Siler, even. My first kiss. Fifty years ago, and I still remember it like it was yesterday. It was by the concession stand at the high school football game, and he used his tongue. Holy moly! That was pretty racy, let me tell you. The times were different—there wasn't sex all over the television like there is today. People would never have talked about what Bill Clinton did with that intern. Ernest Delfechio's kiss shocked and thrilled me, oh boy. I was in such a tizzy afterward that I came home and went to my room and played Pat Boone's "Love Letters in the Sand," Ernest Delfechio's favorite song. I played it over and over again on my record player, thinking about that kiss.*

*My mother asked me, "What do you like about this young man?" I remember this, because I thought it was a strange question. What did I like about him? He liked me. All the other girls liked him. Take one look! That hair of his—he could have been a movie star.*

*I guess the real answer was that I had chemistry with Ernest Delfechio, and I had it with Rocky Siler, and Otto Pearlman, too. Let me tell you, you either have chemistry or you don't, and you better have it, or it's like kissing some relative. But chemistry, listen to me, you got to be careful. Chemistry is like those perfume ads, the ones that look so interesting and mysterious but you don't even know at first what they're even selling. Or those menus without the prices. Mystery and intrigue are gonna cost you. Great looking might mean something ve-ry expensive, and I don't mean money. What I'm saying is, chemistry is a place to start, not an end point.*

*Later I remember finding out that Ernest Delfechio hated Pat Boone. I'd heard him wrong. "Love Letters in the Sand"—it was his* sister's *favorite song.*

Sprout and I ate tuna sandwiches and apple slices and Oreo cookies. The train stopped and started again, stopped and started, which meant that Portland was coming up. I zipped everything back up into my pack, shoved the little plastic bags into the brown lunch sack and crumpled it up. The train eased and slowed, and the people on the train rose and shuffled and reorganized and filed out, same as Sprout and me. We would do as we always had done—walk outside through the wide hall of the station, where we'd search for Brie's black Mercedes by the curb. Brie Jenkins was Dad's girlfriend of just over three years, and she'd been in his life since he came back into ours. She'd meet us and bring us to Dad's because he always used the morning hours when he wasn't traveling to work on his book. I made the mistake of telling Mom this once.

"His *book*." Mom blew out a little puff of air from her nose and shook her head. "He can't meet you at the train when he sees you twice a month? You know how long he's been working on that book? Since forever."

"I don't mind," I said. I didn't. He got so excited about that book when he talked about it. *Gabriel Garcia Marquez has nothing on me!* It was the story of his Armenian family, told in magical realism. "And the book's really good. He showed me a little of it."

"Mmm-hmm," Mom had said. We were in the kitchen, me looking for a snack after the long train ride home, her opening a can of food for our old dog, Ivar. "Don't tell me. Something about his father, the diamond merchant. And his grandfather, who so believed in love that he turned into a stone after his third daughter married the old, fat, rich grocer."

His grand*mother*. And he wasn't a grocer, but a man who sold silks. But then, at her words, my chest began to ache; it felt like it was caving in on itself. I didn't say anything. It would have been at least eight years since she'd seen that same few pages of "new work" he'd read aloud during a party of Brie's friends a few weekends ago. Everyone had applauded, but Brie had seemed

ticked off. I closed the cupboard door. I didn't feel hungry anymore. Then again, smelling Ivar's food could do that to anyone.

At the train station that day, we stood on the sidewalk and
looked up and down for Brie's car. Taxis scooted in and away,
doors slammed, people waited at the curb, the luggage at their
feet sitting like obedient retrievers.

"She's late," Sprout announced. She was playing with the
end of her long braid, whisking it back and forth, back and
forth against her palm.

"She's never late," I said. "Your tooth, right here." I pointed
to my own tooth, in the place where Sprout's was brown with
Oreo. She fixed hers with the edge of her fingernail, smiled big
until I nodded my okay. I looked far up the line of cars—still no
Brie. I felt a little skitter of worry. Brie, tall, blond, beautiful,
who seemed both strong and fragile as glass, lived by the clock.
She had taken over her father's business when he died, a service
that escorted visiting celebrities when they came to Portland for
various events. Brie was never late because you couldn't be late
for movie stars and politicians. You couldn't be late for sultans
of other countries and rock stars who needed to get to a radio
show by nine forty-five exactly.

"She's late, big deal," Sprout said. She loved Brie, in the way
you love someone that you'll never in a million years be. Sprout
would try to be Brie for a moment anyway—she'd toss her head
back and say, "So . . ." in that same way Brie did. One train ride
home, I left the seat beside Sprout to sit somewhere else for a
while, because she'd used so much of Brie's perfume that I was
getting a headache. I came back, though, because when I looked
over at her, she looked sad. You could almost see the cool, con-

fident puffs of cotton blossom perfume marching away from her in determined avoidance, this small person with her hair coming loose in chunks from her braid.

"I'm going to call," I said.

"Don't get her into trouble with Dad," Sprout said.

"I won't," I said, though I wasn't quite sure how to go about that. He would probably be pissed at being interrupted. I heard the phone ring, that echoey *brrrrr* in a far place. No answer.

"What if she's not coming?" Sprout said. She held her hat close to her chest, her fingers through the holes of the crochet.

"Of course she's coming," I said, although I wasn't sure at all.

I thought about calling Mom, and just as that thought was working out whether to stay or not, I saw Dad's car, a little classic 1953 Corvette, white with red trim, that he kept in perfect condition. The top was down, and right there at the curb, three people turned to look at him. It's a weird thing about Dad, but people always notice him. He has this mane of black hair (which he wears in a braid, same as Sprout) and a beaky, Armenian nose, and he's tall and broad, and when you stop to think about it, not that great looking. Still, people are drawn to him, same as you're drawn to that orange rock shining underwater amidst all the gray ones. He's a performer in one of the longest-running juggling/vaudeville troupes around—the Jafarabad Brothers. Being a performer—maybe that's another reason why he has this charisma. He works on a stage, and maybe there's this piece of him that's performing whether he's actually on a stage or not. People's eyes go to him. They'll watch him picking out a grapefruit in Albertson's.

That day, he didn't notice everyone else's noticing, as he

usually does. He waved his arms toward us. "Get in, get in," he said. "Traffic . . . Who thought it'd take this long to get to the fucking train station? Aren't train stations supposed to be *close*? Aren't train stations supposed to be *convenient*?"

"Where's Brie?" Sprout demanded.

"Gone," he said. "Stick your stuff in the back." I heard a *pop* and the trunk opened. I tossed in my backpack. I saw a plaid blanket there, and a shopping bag full of some presents I recognized from Christmas with Brie's mom. The sweater she'd given Dad, still in the box with the snowman wrapping paper; dress socks, bound in their white strip of packaging. That they had come from JC Penney had seemed to embarrass him, which I guess I understood, since he was used to much more expensive places.

Sprout had squeezed herself half on my lap and half on the gear shift. I buckled the seatbelt around us both. "You okay?" I asked, and she rolled her eyes.

Dad told us a story about Thomas as he drove, something Dad said was hilarious, about Thomas and Dad being recognized in a restaurant by some fans, but it was hard to hear the details with the wind whipping around us. Thomas was one of the Jafarabad Brothers. Dad was the main guy, with the stage name "Anoush Hourig," Brother Anoush, whose name means "Sweet little fire," which Joelle, his wife before Mom, thought up. Dad's real name is Barry Hunt, and his other "brothers" are Siran and Ghadar, or, to us, Uncle Mike and Thomas. None are related, but Uncle Mike started the troupe with Dad before we were born, when he was first married to Joelle. "Ghadar" has been about five different people; the latest is Thomas, who used to live in New Jersey. The big joke is that the names are girl names in Armenian, but only Armenians know that, and they like being in on the laugh.

We got to Dad's house, which is right on the river, an angled two-story shingled house that looks like a fairy-tale cottage gone mad. Cobblestones lead to the front door and down to the river, and the fireplace is made from big rocks. We pulled into the drive, and when Dad cut the engine, Sprout let out a long groan.

"Get me outta here, I can barely breathe," she said. "Where has Brie gone? Did she go to LA to visit her mom? Did she take Malcolm or is he here with you?"

I got out of the car and let Sprout free. She was obviously more clued in than I was—I'd assumed Brie had gone on a business trip or something. But the questions meant something more to Sprout. You could tell by the way her eyes were darting around, searching for clues. These weren't the kinds of questions that were only information gathering—they were anxious ones, begging for reassurance. "I don't see her car," Sprout said.

Dad got out, slammed the door. He wiped a smudge on the hood with the sleeve of the white tunic he wore with his jeans. "No, no," he said. "Gone. Gone as in, gone, gone. Left. Sayonara. Nice knowing you, Barry. Thanks for the memories. . . ."

He opened the front door with his key, and we stood in the entryway. Sprout looked stricken. "What do you mean?" she said softly, but you could tell what he meant by just stepping foot inside the house. Malcolm was Brie's four-year-old, and he usually left evidence of his presence—tennis shoes by the door, plastic dinosaurs, Legos in the living room, a Ziploc bag of cheese crackers abandoned on the stairs—a trail of his activities same as breadcrumbs in a forest. But there were none of those things in sight—the house was clean. And it was quiet. There was no slam of a door or the pounding, running feet that we usually heard when Malcolm knew we'd arrived. There was no sound at all. It was so quiet, you could hear the kitchen clock *tick-tick-tick*ing.

"I can't believe this," Sprout said. Her cheeks were flushed. "She can't be gone." Her voice wobbled. I took her hand.

"Charles, these things happen. I don't want some big reaction on your part. If anyone should be having a reaction it's *me*." "Charles" was what my Dad called Sprout. No one on Mom's side called her that. It was another strange thing about divorce. Sometimes even your own name was different.

"Why did she leave?" I asked, but maybe I had some idea already. I was trying to work up some sense of surprise, but it wasn't what I was feeling, not really. I could pretend surprise out of politeness for Dad, but surprise was a lie. Brie was fifteen years younger than Dad, and he sometimes treated her as if she wasn't quite ready to be out in the world without his help. Maybe he had his reasons. Probably he had his reasons. But I'd hear her through the wall in the next room. "I run my own business, Barry," she'd say. "I'm perfectly capable of figuring out which skirt goes with what shoes."

"I don't know why she left," Dad said. We followed him to the kitchen, where the walls were covered in wood from an actual barn, a deep brown, cozy wood. He opened the refrigerator and took out a Coke. "And, frankly, I don't care. She's the one making the mistake. After all I've given her?" He popped the cap, took a long swallow. "She'll come running back, won't she, and then it'll be too late. You betray me? Simple. Good. Bye." He wiped his hand in the air as if Brie had just been erased.

"Will we ever see her again?" Sprout said. "Will we ever even *see* her?" Sprout's voice rose. She clutched that hat so tight in one hand, squeezed my own hand in her other.

"You *want* to? Charles, I don't get why you're all out of control, here. Brie never did anything for you. For any of us. She was a *taker*."

"You said to treat Malcolm like my *brother*. Brothers don't just disappear," Sprout said.

Dad looked at me and made his eyes say *Can you believe this craziness?* He shook his head. He looked at his watch.

"Come on, Sprout," I said. I let go. I didn't know what else to say. I didn't even know what *Come on* meant, or what place I was urging her toward. Just someplace else, I guess.

"I'm going upstairs," Sprout said. "I don't know how you could *do* this. Goddamn it." She would have never tried this at home. For some reason, at Dad's we were the Good Child and the Bad Child. Sprout turned into some little tyrant here that she really wasn't. Her back looked both fierce and dejected as she headed up.

Dad looked down at his hands, gave them an appraising look. He opened a drawer, took out a pair of fingernail clippers, and fit them over the curved moon of one fingernail. "Charles doesn't know how much she hurts me," he said. *Click.*

"I know," I said.

"I try and try, and you know, honestly"—*click*—"I don't know what I could have done different."

"Nothing," I said. "It was a little sudden. She's just . . . confused."

"*Very* confused." He put the clippers down and looked up at me as if we agreed more than we did. "Does your mother allow her to talk like that? A ten-year-old girl, with that mouth? How is she going to turn out? You'll help with dinner? Maybe something with chicken? Or we can go someplace."

"Sure," I said. Eleven-*year-old girl with that mouth*, I thought but didn't say. I slung my backpack over the back of one chair.

"I'm going to write for a while," he said. "You know Saturdays. The only day I've got. And once June hits . . ." June meant that the Jafarabad Brothers were on the road a lot. June meant that Dad "lived out of a suitcase," though I noticed that "I live out of a suitcase" is one of those complaints that is actually bragging in disguise.

"Okay," I said.

He turned as he headed out, as if he'd just remembered something. "How's school and all? College applications? Et cetera, et cetera?"

"The counselor at school said I should apply to Yale," I said. "Can you believe that?" I felt embarrassed to say it. Even the word itself seemed huge and made of ivy-covered brick.

He clapped his hands together, then gripped me in a hug. "I knew you'd be doing something fucking outrageous. My daughter at Yale." He released me, held my shoulders. His dark eyes bore into mine in a display of deep connection and utter confidence. "Golden child," he said.

I smiled. "It's really competitive. I don't even know if I want to go there. It's just something she suggested."

"Of course you'd want to go there," he said. "You are not just *anyone*. The Hunts have never been *average*. You deserve the best," he said.

"The best is expensive," I said. "Even with a partial scholarship—it's crazy expensive."

"Well, we'll have to talk," he said. He kissed my cheek, a big on-purpose noisy smack. I felt pleased and hopeful. This was the thing about Dad. He could make you feel so special. He went upstairs to his office, and I played a game of Masterpiece with Sprout to cheer her up, because it was her favorite. We sat on her bed in the room we shared at Dad's house, selling and buying treasures with paper money.

"Sprout, he hasn't done anything to you," I said.

"You're kidding, right? Christ Almighty, Quinn," she said. Another one of Grandma's favorite expressions.

"I don't know why you're always on his case."

"I don't know why you never see a bad thing he does."

We'd had this argument before, and it never went anywhere. And it would never go anywhere, as long as she kept listening to Mom. "He's a great dad, even if he isn't like other fathers. He's different, that's a good thing. He loves us," I said.

"Right. He talks to us, and it's like we're not even really there."

"That's crazy. Of course we're there. It wouldn't kill you to make an effort," I said as she rolled the dice and won a painting—the Jackson Pollock that looked like a square of crinkled aluminum foil.

She looked under the painting, at its hidden value. "Forgery," she announced. She wasn't supposed to tell, but she always did.

"Put it back. Go again," I said.

"I wish you'd open your eyes," she said.

*FRANCES LEE GIOFRANCO:*

*When I was in the fifth grade, I had a thing for Carl Davis. Everyone had a thing for Carl Davis, so I guess you can say I lacked imagination. We were still making those frilly-assed paper hearts for Valentine's Day in our class. Those big envelopes you stuff the valentines in. Mrs. Becker told us that we had to give every kid a valentine if we were going to give any, making sure some kid didn't get so rejected he'd shoot up a school later.*

*But I wanted to give Carl Davis something special. More than just one of those cards with the pukey-tasting red suckers stuck through two holes. I begged my mom to take me to Bartell Drugs so I could get him a present. You could tell she didn't think this was a great idea, but she was managing to keep her mouth shut. If you know my mom, though, you know she can't manage to keep her mouth shut for long.*

*So, we're standing in the pink-and-red aisle, you know, the one with the bears and the chocolate and the hearts and roses, those bizarre proof-of-love objects, and she says, "Frances Lee, why is it that you want to do this?" And I say, "Because I am in love with Carl Davis." And Mom looks at me, and she's very calm, and she says, "Frances Lee, I've been in over my head and in trouble and in need and in danger and incomplete, but I'd never been in love until I was forty-two and finally figured myself out."*

*And it wasn't meant to be mean or to kill my enthusiasm or anything, I know. And we did buy a big heart box of chocolates that the next day joined a deskful of presents for Carl Davis. She just said it to get me to stop and think. It did get me to stop and think. It still does.*

Sprout and I finished the game of Masterpiece and then played another. After a while, Dad popped his head in the door.

"Let's go out!" he said. "Let's try something totally new. Celebrate."

"Celebrate what?" I asked.

"Celebrate anything. Our life! The fact that we're luckier than ninety-nine percent of the population. Name the cuisine," he said to Sprout. "Name it. Something we've never had."

"Holland," Sprout said. She'd just done a report on it in her fifth-grade class.

"Dutch," Dad mused. "Do they have Dutch food? Dutch restaurants? Waitresses in clogs? I'm not sure we'll have much luck with that one, Charles. How about African? Pakistani? Korean? Afghani?"

"Afghan," Sprout agreed. "Like the blankets."

"Or the dogs with floppy ears," Dad said. He flicked Sprout's braid, and she reached up and flicked his in return. It was a small surrender. She needed him, too, even though she didn't like to think so. Everyone needs their dad. I was glad we were all friends again.

Dad bounded down the stairs, and we grabbed our shoes and followed. He opened another dark wood drawer by its iron handle, the one where he kept the phone books. He pulled out the fat lump of the Yellow Pages and slopped it open. His Internet use was still at the first-grade level. "Afghan, Afghan . . . Ha! Basmani. Over on twelfth. Excellent. I've heard it's got the best Afghan food. Buraani bonjon, qaabuli pallow. I love to say those words." He said them again, added a midair curlicue flair. "Sounds like I'm casting a spell. Buraani bonjon!" he said fiercely, and thrust his fingertips at us.

"Ribbit," Sprout croaked.

"Beautiful, it worked," Dad said.

We squashed back into the car and headed to the restaurant, the bottom level of a Victorian house, with tables outside and strings of lights hanging all around. Dad parked in the handi-capped space just outside the door.

"Handicapped," I said.

"No one cares," he said. "Anyway, people love it when I park my car out front. Brings in business."

The inside of the restaurant was candlelit, with orange walls and ceilings draped with fabric. Crowded, and humming with noise. That night, he was Dad at his best, when he drew you in and you had more fun than you knew you could have. Dad of energy and big ideas. One time, Dad decided that we'd go in a restaurant and order the first six things on the menu, no matter what they were. Another time, we had a Yellow Party, where we ate yellow food and dressed in yellow and then left in the evening to find a yellow Rolls Royce we could test drive. Another night, we ate six brands of frozen Salisbury steak din-ners to see which was best. At Basmani, Dad ordered more food than could fit on the table and told us stories about all the famous people he knew, and about the time the Jafarabad

Brothers had tried a trapeze act, but only until he'd broken his arm in two places. He told us about his father, the diamond merchant. How a diamond was the hardest and most perfectly imperfect substance on earth, an object of beauty forever, its crystals forced up from the depths of the earth by erupting volcanoes. He drank a couple of glasses of wine and flirted with the waitress, and we all laughed loud, and quiet couples looked at us with envy. Then we carried a stack of Styrofoam boxes full of food home again, and they were still warm when I carried them on my lap.

Sprout went up to bed and so did Dad, but I promised Daniel I'd call him as I did every night, so I stayed downstairs because there was more privacy there. I wouldn't have wanted anyone to hear all the passion and desire and sexual longing in our conversation. *How was your day? Fine, great. How was yours? Oh, pretty good.*

I took the phone from the cradle in the kitchen, settled into the big leather chair in the living room. Dad's living room was as creative and patchwork as the rest of the house—the ceiling was covered in squares of tin pressed into elaborate designs, which had been taken from an old bank in New York that was about to be demolished, and the rug was a worn Oriental one covering the floor, which was made of the sort of polished, bumpy wood you'd see on an old ship. The room was full of objects he'd gotten on his travels—a music box, an ancient globe, a red tribal mask—and there was a painting above the fireplace that Sprout hated, a naked woman in cubist style, with one pointed, triangular breast, one rounded, oblong one. Dad loved these things—whenever there were

visitors, he'd show them his objects, like a hunter in his trophy room. *I got this when I was in Africa. . . . I got this when I
met the artist in New York. . . .* I put my feet up on the fringed,
velvety footstool, got comfortable for the intelligent and stim-
ulating conversation that was coming. *So, what'd you do today?
Oh, track practice. Mowed the lawn. You? Train ride—did my
homework.*

I was feeling the tumbling irritation of boredom, and the
need to shake myself out of the kind of bad mood that would
lead to the inevitable *What's wrong? Nothing* conversation that
would be full of edges and politeness and something close to
cinched-in homicidal urges. I didn't know what my problem
was. Daniel was a great guy, and everyone told me what a great
guy he was. I tried to remember what I liked about him. He was
nice. That's right. He had good legs from running track. We both
liked math, and not many people understood that. He was . . .
My mind snagged. Well, he was clean. Clean in all ways. His
thoughts were as clean as his freshly showered hair. Which I
think I liked. I was pretty sure I liked.

I leaned my head against the high back of the chair, holding
the phone in my palm, and that's when I saw it. Something that
hadn't been in the room the last time we were here. It was a
small statue on a black square, a glass statue. It was a curve of
glass about ten inches tall, something that managed to look both
delicate and strong. I could see that there was a brass plate on
it, with some sort of writing, and I got up to see what it said. I
left the phone in the soft squish of the chair, squinted at the
words. *Humphrey Bogart,* I read. *Lifetime Achievement Award.
Film Artists Association of America.*

Okay, this was strange. Why would my father have a statue belonging to Humphrey Bogart? Why would it appear here suddenly? If he bought it somewhere recently, wouldn't he have shown it to us or told us about it? It wouldn't have been like purchasing a new pair of shoes or a garden tool not worth a mention.

I looked at it, and there was a part of me that did not want to touch it, did not want to do what I did next, which was to pick it up and look underneath. I think I must have already had the sense that something was wrong, that this object had no place here. That the reasons it was here were bad reasons, ugly ones. But I was curious, too. And so I held the bottom of the statue up close so that I could read the words taped on a tiny note at the bottom of the statue. *To Hugh Jenkins*, it read. *And to scotch on the rocks . . . Humphrey Bogart.*

Humphrey Bogart! *Jenkins.* I felt something heavy and dark in my stomach, some whirling mix of questions and the dread of their answers. It was Brie's statue. Something that had belonged to her father. So, why was it here? Maybe she had given it to Dad. A present. A going-away thing. A good-bye, something-to-remember-me-by thing. People did that, right?

But I had a stronger, whispered thought. One of those whispers that are less curtains fluttering in a breeze than lawn chairs being tossed across patios in a windstorm. I knew that Brie did not know my father had this. That Brie might never know my father had this.

I knew because I remembered another object in the room. A bust of a woman's head that I had always found slightly eerie, made out of some kind of clay, with initials scratched into the base. *A.R.* I knew those initials. *A.R.*, Abigail Renfrew.

Two things that belonged to women in his life. Was this a crazy thought? Was I nuts? That I thought there were maybe more things in this room that belonged to other people? Other women?

I did something else then, and I don't even fully know why I did it. It was a hunch, if a hunch is ever just that. I lifted up other objects and looked underneath. A globe, no, nothing. A paperweight, just a paperweight. A book end shaped like an elephant. Nothing. I looked with growing unease. And then, there it was. Just like that. A name scratched in the bottom of a tall, brightly colored vase. *Jane, age six,* it said. And there, too, under the red tribal mask, the name *Olivia Thornton*. Written with blue ink on a piece of masking tape in handwriting I didn't recognize. Under a mantel clock, its hands stopped at 3:30, one word, *Elizabeth*. I pulled the footstool to the mantel and lifted down the painting there. *I got this when I met the artist in New York. . . .* It was large and heavy, and I struggled with it. But there, tucked into the corner of the frame was a business card. *Joelle Giofranco,* it read. *Costume design and alterations.*

Inside, I felt as if something were falling and about to crash: He had taken something from every woman he'd been involved with. Isn't that what he had done? It was too eerie and disturbing not to have an explanation, right? What was the truth here? I suddenly wanted that, no *needed* that, more than anything else. I felt my breath in my chest and my heart beat as if a thing *had* crashed and landed just there beside me.

And, too, right then as my sister and father lay sleeping and I stood on a footstool with a painting in my hands, there was a softer, quieter realization: that the truth I wanted so badly was likely as hard and faceted as one of the diamonds Dad told us about—perfectly imperfect, formed somewhere deep within and existing there, until it was brought to the surface by volcanic eruptions and simple need.

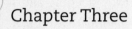

# Chapter Three

"Jesus, you scared me." Grandma minimized the computer screen in a flash, whirled her fluffy-white-haired head around. She looked guilty. She put one veiny hand against her pink sweatshirt. "You almost gave me a heart attack. Don't you know better than to do that to an old lady?"

Gram sat at a desk in our office/spare room, one of those spaces that collected everything that had nowhere else to go—Mom's sewing machine, Aunt Annie's weights, this huge "Leprechaun trap" glued to green Elmer's-and-glitter cardboard that Sprout had made in the first grade for St. Patrick's Day. I put my hands on Gram's shoulders, kissed the top of her head. "I just needed to work on a paper. Film studies . . . 'Phantom of the Opera as an example of Classic Horror Cinema.'"

"eBay," Gram said, tilting her head to the computer, which now held only the blue desktop with white clouds. "Don't tell your mom. Salt and pepper shakers shaped like chefs. Adorable." She looked at her wrist, but she wasn't wearing a watch. "Ten more minutes until the bidding's over. Can you come back?"

"Sure," I said. She waited with her hands in her lap. Stared at me intently. "I'm going," I said.

"It's just I get nervous when the competition's hot," she said.

I tried to call Liv, but she didn't pick up, and I left a message for Daniel to tell him I was thinking about him, because I felt guilty for not thinking about him. I went back into the office fif-

teen minutes later—Gram had left, so I settled into the chair. It
had been five days since I had seen the names under the objects
at Dad's house, and for those five days I had felt oddly fragmented, as if a piece of my mind was constantly at work on
something else. It was that sense you get after you've lost something—your car keys, say, and you've decided to give up looking for a while. You go on with other things, you make a
sandwich, pour a glass of milk, but there's still a part of you
going, *Maybe I left them in the pocket of my black jacket. Maybe I
dropped them down between the couch cushions. . . .* My mind was
doing some kind of indistinct nagging that I didn't want it to do,
some off-duty work it could have been paid time and a half for.

I typed a few lines of my paper; listless, have-to lines, flat
and uninspired lines. I looked up "1920 Horror Cinema" on the
Web. I switched back to the mostly blank page I was working
on, watched the cursor blink on-off, on-off. I swapped back to
the Web. I typed "Jafarabad Brothers" into the search box. I was
aware of the silver ring on the middle finger of my right hand,
two arms that made a circle and held a heart, a ring my father
had given me on my sixteenth birthday. I pushed enter and a list
of results came up—newspaper articles, reviews of shows, inter-
views. I clicked one at random. *Anoush Hourig began the troupe
just out of college, when he needed money to fund a round-the-world
sailing trip with a friend. The first show, at a campus dormitory, was
so financially successful that the sailing trip was cancelled.*

I knew this story. This was where Dad would joke that the
audience was so sloshed that they started throwing things, and
he and Uncle Mike had to run for their lives, empty-handed.
Financially successful? Broke, I thought he'd said. I read on:

*"That the audience members were severely intoxicated helped with tips,"* Hourig joked. *"One guy threw his wallet at us . . . We walked out of there with more money than either of us had ever seen."*

This was what you did when you were a performer, I guessed. You acted out a good story. Maybe you'd change it a little, depending on who was in the audience. Dad on a sailing trip? We could barely get him on a ferry. He was afraid of boats, he said, a fear instilled in him by his mother, after his diamond-merchant father was nearly lost at sea. I guess the main thing was to give a good show. Dad could keep you right there, listening and laughing, and maybe you didn't always think about exactly what he said until later. Maybe the details didn't matter, because you were just so entertained. Or maybe I had just remembered the story wrong.

I looked at all the search results, all the entries. Pieces of my father known and unknown. If I put my own name, Quinn Hoffman Hunt, in there, I know what I'd get. One entry, from the time I organized the food drive for Honor Society and it got written up in the Nine Mile Falls paper. One me, hundreds of hims. I felt the huge space between those numbers, the known and the unknown; I saw that space, and it looked like it stretched for miles.

### MARY LOUISE HOFFMAN:

*The first boy I ever liked was Sam Jaeger in the ninth grade. I should tell my girls about this. We had this class called Home Economics. Apparently there isn't a Home Economics any-more—my daughter Quinn once got stuck in some elective called Life Skills, but it wasn't the same. They balanced a check-*

*book, that kind of thing. But ours, you learned how to be a nice little housewife. The classroom even had all these mini-kitchens and sewing machines, and they taught us how to sew a pillow that looked like an animal and plan a meal that was varied in color and texture. We made a grilled-cheese sandwich using an iron, although I must say I never again made a grilled-cheese sandwich using an iron. You wrap it in aluminum foil; I still remember that. Anyway, boys who wanted to meet girls would take the class too, and Sam Jaeger was one of those. Now that I think about it, he was a perfect start to my romantic history, because he was a player. One of those guys who's sexy already at, what, fourteen. The ones you pray will never cross the paths of your daughters. Not thin and short and awkward, but aware of his body and knowledgeable about the way eye contact can make you want someone before you realize who they even are.*

*We had to plan and cook a breakfast in our group, which included Sam Jaeger and Renee Harding and Wendy Sylvester. Funny, girls named Wendy also sort of disappeared, same as Home Ec, haven't they? Anyway, who knows why, maybe because I was the only one with breasts, but Sam Jaeger decided to fix me with his long dark gaze of wanting. I didn't stop to ask myself if I wanted him back, because it was enough to have someone focus his desire on me. Me, who was so ordinarily unnoticed. I was sure those long looks were going to save me from my drab existence. Being saved—always a big romantic motivation. When you're young, you hope he'll save you with his excitement or his way out, and then, later, you hope he'll save you with his . . . Well, those things still, but maybe too you hope he'll save you with his money or his tool box, or his extra set of hands with your kids. You can want the saving more than you want the actual person.*

*Sam Jaeger gave me his phone number and kissed me and stuck his hand up my shirt on the last day of the trimester, after we fixed French Toast l'Orange and Southern Hashbrowns and Confetti Fruit Cup for the class. Then he never so much as looked at me again. He wanted me and then he didn't, and the only thing I could think of was how to get him to want me again. I called that number so many times and listened to his mother's voice saying hello before I hung up. I wrote him passionate, humiliating notes, as if love required some convincing. I went out of my way to cross his path and bought him bags of M&M'S, because he once said he liked them. And here's the part I try to forget but can't—I gave him the pillow I'd made in class. God. That was the most cringing touch—a dog, with pink felt patches for feet.*

*Maybe I won't tell the girls this, after all. You want them to know, but you don't want them to know.*

*My mother had always said, "Love is work." I made Sam Jaeger my full-time job without pay. Funny thing was, I never even really liked Sam Jaeger. He always bragged obnoxiously about his dad being a D.J., and he always smart-mouthed the teacher in a way that made you feel bad for her. That's the thing, see—"love"—it can be more about being wanted than wanting. Needless to say, he never saved me, either.*

"Qui-inn," Aunt Annie called from downstairs. "Phone for you."

I picked up in the hall, heard the polite click of Annie hanging up. Daniel's voice had an urgency I'd never heard before.

"Quinn, God. I'm looking forward to seeing you. Tonight, right? I'm going to see you tonight?"

I wondered what happened. Maybe he'd had a brush with death. Something extreme to remind him that life was short. Or that life was too long, maybe, when lived without some sort of passion. Maybe he'd fallen and hit his head. Maybe he dropped the hair dryer in the bathtub while he was in it. "Are you all right?"

"Yeah, I'm all right. I just miss you, is all. I just really want to see you."

"Wow," I said. I felt this little buzz inside, a hum. Something that attached itself to the word "want." "You're coming over after dinner?" That's what usually happened on a Saturday night. He'd come over after dinner; we'd watch a movie. When we first started dating, we tried going out with his friends from track or my friends from volleyball, but it always felt like trying to jam together a couple of jigsaw pieces that didn't fit. Pieces from entirely different puzzles, even, a snowy mountain cabin scene attempting to merge with an oversized image of Garfield the cat.

"Quinn, do you mind if we don't? Can we do something *different*? It's such a beautiful night. . . . School's almost out, summer's coming. . . . We can get a blanket, drive over to Greenlake or something. . . ." He laughed a little. The kind of laugh his minister wouldn't have approved of.

"Okay. Sure," I said. Definitely a brush with death. Or paint fumes. Or drugs. Whatever it was, I liked it. "Yes. You, me, tonight."

"'Yes' is a great word," Daniel said.

🌀 🌀 🌀

Sprout laid out the silverware, lining it up on paper towels folded in half, as Gram reached up into the cupboard for dinner plates.

"Why do we put spoons out when no one uses a spoon?" Sprout asked.

"Good question," Gram said.

"You always made us put out a spoon," Aunt Annie said to her as she took the milk out of the fridge.

"Hogwash. I don't give a rat's ass about spoons," Gram said.

"Mom," Mom warned. She opened the oven door, potholders on both hands.

"Oh, they've heard 'ass' before. Or is it 'rat' you don't like?" Gram said, and Sprout chuckled.

"Wait, go back to the spoon thing," Aunt Annie said. "Because I've always put them out because I thought I'd get in trouble with you guys if I didn't."

"Me?" Mom said. "What do I care about spoons?" She took the chicken from the oven. I handed her a plate for it.

"If you're still worried about getting in trouble with me when you're almost thirty, you got another problem than spoons," Gram said.

"Twenty-seven," Aunt Annie said. "Please. I don't need you prematurely aging me. And fine, from now on I'm doing whatever I want."

"It's about time," Gram said.

"Forget the spoons," Sprout said, and put them back in the drawer.

"Unless we're having soup," I said.

We sat down to dinner, passed around chicken and Mom's

old wooden salad bowl, and Sprout dropped chicken bits down to Ivar, who sat upright beside her chair, staring without blinking.

"Is Ivar looking fat to anyone else? He looks like he's gaining weight," I said. It was one of those moments you wondered if he could hear and understand you, and if you were hurting his feelings. Aunt Annie leaned back in her chair to look.

"Don't say fat, you'll hurt his self-esteem," Sprout said, thinking the same thing as me. "Say he's got more square footage."

Ivar was an old dog who until recently only laid around in the sunny spots of the house. Lately, though, he'd leave every weekday morning and we wouldn't see him again until late afternoon, when he'd plunk down exhausted on his pillow as if he were a Boeing employee returning home after a tough day. We didn't know where he went or what he did. Maybe he was like one of those guys you read about in *People* magazine, who have separate families in different locations who don't know each other exist. Maybe he had his own water bowl and dish somewhere else, and people who wondered what he did all night and all morning and on the weekends.

"Well, he ate half a bag of fortune cookies, remember?" Aunt Annie said. "Fortunes and all. 'You have an unusually magnetic personality.'"

"That was months ago, though," I said.

"Did you get your paper done?" Gram asked me. She shook the bottle of salad dressing so that the little bits of herbs swirled up toward the top.

"What paper?" Mom asked.

"'*Phantom of the Opera* as Example of Classic Horror Cinema,'" I said.

"Whore cinema?" Sprout said. Mom lowered her eyebrows in Sprout's direction. "I thought that's what she said." Sprout kept grinning as if her joke just kept on pleasing her.

"*Phantom of the Opera*—oh, I love that play," Aunt Annie said. "So romantic."

"Romantic?" Mom set down her fork. "You're kidding, right? Psycho guy obsesses over woman? Stalks and kidnaps her? Sure, you got candles and fake fog, but my God."

"You didn't feel sorry for him? Tormented guy, deformed face, shunned, in love with someone he thought he could never have? Come on, that cry of pain he gives didn't make you feel *anything*?" Aunt Annie's own fork was stuck in midair in disbelief.

"Instability isn't romantic. Tormented guys aren't romantic. This is exactly what gets us into trouble. Feeling *sorry* for them. Help me out here," Mom said to Gram.

"I never liked a man in a mask," Gram said.

"Masked—ha," Mom said. "A metaphor. Hiding his true self. Then, surprise! Surprise, I'm a psycho!"

"He *was* a psycho," I said. Come to think of it.

"Let's talk about spoons," Sprout said.

"I'm just saying, we mix up pity and love and then, boom. Trouble," Mom said.

"I would have picked the Phantom," Aunt Annie said. "Over the other guy. The prissy opera dude . . ." She looked at me for help.

"Raoul," I said.

"Over Raoul." She stuck her chin up at Mom, and you got a

sudden glimpse of how Aunt Annie must have looked when she was seven.

"Yeah, great. Good for you. The whole play is like making a romantic musical about some stalking boyfriend who kills his girlfriend in a parking lot. I loved the big dance number in that one called 'Restraining Order.'"

"You're too serious," Aunt Annie said.

"Something only said by people who aren't serious enough," Mom said.

"Girls, girls," Gram said. "I'll send you to your rooms."

"I give up," Mom said.

But she didn't give up. After we'd put away the dishes and Gram went back to eBay and Aunt Annie went out on a date with Quentin Ferrill, Mom sat alone at the kitchen table, a piece of blank paper in front of her, a red Sharpie in her hand. She made a list. A list titled "Warning!" Under that, attributes to be on the lookout for in a guy. *He has either a very low opinion about himself, or a very high one,* she had written. Under that: *He believes he's more special than other people. The rules don't apply to him.*

I stood behind her. I put my hands on her shoulders. "Mom, I love you, but you're losing it. Do you want to just lock us in our rooms and not allow us to date until a panel of experts approves the guy?"

"Excellent idea," she said, and chewed the end of her pen.

"We're not stupid."

Mom set down her pen. "It's not a matter of being stupid. You can be smart and *not know.* And you can know and *not care.* Sit down, talk to me," she said.

"I've got to go. I'm going to meet Daniel."

"He's not coming over?" She raised her eyebrows.

"He wants to go to Greenlake and walk or something."

"Well, good," she said. "I was wondering if the two of you ever *talked*. All those movies . . ." She took my hands. I could have guessed what was coming. The thing that she always said when she wanted to cover up extreme behavior on her part. "You'll understand when you have kids of your own," she said.

"Right."

"I was twenty years old when I met your Dad. That's only *three years* from where you are now. Three years! This could happen to you in no time. From that one point, my life veered off. You and Sprout are here because of it, and I'm grateful for that. But, Quinn, I just wish somebody would have told me. Somebody should have *said* . . ."

"They could make it a requirement at school. Relationships 101."

"I'm not kidding, they should," Mom said. "The most important decision you'll make, and no one tells you *how*." She let go of my hands. "All right. You've got to go, and I'm going to Lizbeth and Jack's for some dessert-champagne thing. She got promoted at REI. Now there's a twist of fate for you. REI, Lizbeth, who can't walk and bounce a ball at the same time, and who thinks a hike to the mailbox should be rewarded with a Ho Ho. You guys should stop by. Sydney's home for the weekend."

Lizbeth was Mom's friend since their days at the UW. They both ended up living in Nine Mile Falls, and Sydney, Lizbeth's daughter (a student at Whitman), and Evan and Charles, her twins, were like cousins to me. The small white line by my left eye was from the stitches I got falling off the trampoline they had in their yard. "Next time?" I said. "Daniel really wants to go to Greenlake."

"Okay. I understand. Hey, I love you, daughter."

"I love you, too."

"I've got to go figure out what to wear," Mom said.

I followed her upstairs. Ivar tried to shove ahead of us like he always did. To him, the starting gun went off the moment someone's hand touched the banister. Mom wore her old khaki shorts with all the pockets, a tank top dotted from spots of wayward bleach. Her hair was pulled back, making a too-small ponytail. There was a smudge of red on her forearm, from leaning on the paper a moment ago. I loved her. I did. But in that moment, right then, looking at that smudge, there was something about her that irritated me. Maybe it was her own ordinariness, the ways she came up lacking. The gray showing through her brown hair, her relentless insistence on wanting the best for us, her slightly bristly legs. But being irritated by her made me feel weirdly relieved; the hazy, hovering worry I'd had since seeing the objects lifted. I had a mean thought—it sat there in my head the way a crow does on a railing—cruel, entitled, mocking. *That's* why he left.

Daniel was definitely on uppers.

"Let's lie down," he said. He spread out a blanket he'd brought from home, a blue quilt with a fabric image of a girl in a bonnet on it.

"She can lie in the middle." I pointed down at the girl.

"Holly Hobbie," Daniel said. "My mom's had this blanket since she was a little." Which explained the white rickrack at the blanket's edges. Seventies-kid bedspread. He tested the fabric

with his palm, to make sure there was no dampness underneath. He sat down and looked up at me with a grin as shiny as
a new appliance.

"Why are you so happy?" I said. I sat beside him. He leaned
back on his elbows, looked up into the lacy trees over us.

"God, Quinn. Why not be? Why not be happy when this
day is so beautiful?"

I looked over at him, watched him for signs of dilating
pupils or sudden tremors. Daniel talked about his math test, or
how Evan McConnell was such an ass but how Coach Grayson
never noticed. He didn't talk about feelings or life or anything
larger than a moment. We'd laugh about Señora Little, the new
Spanish teacher, whom you'd feel sorry for if your capacity for
pity hadn't turned into frustrated contempt. Her lack of classroom control had turned every fifth period into a prison riot,
which she attempted to fix with altered seating charts and "new
rules" that lasted the day. Adam Seddell and Mitchell Hagen
would move her cactus around when her back was turned, and
Mitchell Hagen was a good guy who never got in trouble anywhere else. Sean Riley got expelled from the class after hitting
the donkey piñata with snowballs, became an office T.A.
instead, and now used his new position to excuse students from
fifth period. The principal had sat in Mrs. Little's class five times
that semester alone, but still students would ring up the class
phone as she taught, or set their own phone alarms to all go off
to "La Bamba" at exactly one thirty. Daniel would tell me what
happened in Mrs. Little's third period, and I would tell him what
happened in her fifth, but happiness and beauty were not things
we discussed.

I leaned down next to Daniel. I ran my fingers along his arm, the soft hairs there, and it seemed that maybe I could think about Daniel in a new way. Something about him had changed and I didn't know why. I put my nose on his sleeve, remembered his separateness from me, his internal life I knew nothing about. It seemed thrilling to me, the fact that I might not know or couldn't know. It made me feel like I wanted him, maybe for the first time, although maybe it wasn't really him I wanted, but just the chance to overcome some obstacle within him, to get him to hand over something he wasn't willing to hand over. Maybe desire needed mystery. Maybe desire needed something out of reach, some impossibility. Desire meant wanting, not having.

Daniel's shirt smelled flowery, sweet. It didn't smell like cotton and laundry soap. It was strong enough that I wrinkled my nose. "Did you get squirted by some perfume lady at Nordstrom's?" I said.

"What?" Daniel said. He brought his sleeve to his own nose. "I don't smell anything," he said.

We watched a slow jogger, a woman who did not lift her feet while she ran, but instead shuffled them close to the ground. Then, her opposite, a man made thin with tight, shiny nylon, speeding past on a bike with wheels circling in a blur. We watched a man and a wife and a baby, lifted from a stroller and placed on a quilt.

Daniel leaned in and kissed me then. It was a different kind of kiss, less distant and polite, more present. It felt like a part of Daniel was there in a way he'd never been before. I tried to be there too. I so much wanted to be there, to feel something you might call love. I tried to summon up that feeling, what I guessed it might be like, something big. It was a little like the time my dad took Sprout and me to a circus. Long ago, before he left, one of the memories that had stayed with me from when he lived with us. I must have been no more than nine. He was excited to go, and I can still remember trying to get there, too, to that excitement. I smiled and went along and clapped and tried hard not to feel what I really did, which was sad, because the elephant's eyes looked sad and the girls in sequins looked sad, and the trapeze artist rubbing chalk on his hands looked sad, yet still I was clapping and smiling.

I kissed Daniel, but part of me, the truthful part, was holding back. His lips slowly pulled away from mine, and his eyes were closed, but he looked happy. He looked almost surprised when he opened his eyes.

"Quinn," he said. I'm not sure who he was expecting.

"It's me, I'm here," I lied.

### ANNIE HOFFMAN:

*Hank Peters, freshman year of college—sort of proved that if a man likes himself more than he likes me, I'm in. Yeah, boy, I'm right there, laid out across the emotional freeway, ready for the Truck o' Love to run me right over. Ha. Um, he was* the *professor. Can you say "Daddy Issues"? No one in my family knows about this because they would* kill *me. Something about him made me sure that even his silence held some great weight of importance. He'd keep on with his class lecture when we were in his car making out. I thought this was weirdly sexy. "Alluuusions," he'd say, with his lips on mine. He'd transition into some talk of fine wines or music*

*I'd be sure to know nothing about. Then he'd check his looks in the rearview mirror before starting up the car again. He was constantly bragging about the writers he knew and the few things he'd published in literary magazines, the kind no one reads except the people in them. Heated love triangle. He, himself, and me.*

*We both were in love with him. And, of course, in the competition with him for his love, he always won. The big prize goes to . . . guess who. I always came up short. Are you going to be wearing that to dinner? he'd say. Or, How can we help you make a better decision than that? He couldn't like me better than he liked himself, he was just* incapable. *He wasn't built with the ability to see other people. I was just the warm breath on his own mirror. Which meant this was a competition I would always lose, which meant I would feel like shit in the end, which meant I would get what some fucked-up part of my psyche was after.*

*It's weird how much of a relationship isn't even really about him or you, but about some other, alternate world where you're working out your garbage from childhood. Love, as some walk through a mental junkyard, where you look for the broken carburetor that maybe will make your personal car run. Whichever parent you had the most trouble with, watch out—you'll be looking for that type, in some version or another. You've got to be so clear about what you're playing out. That, I know. Distant mother— bingo, you're suddenly into some unavailable guy with a girlfriend. Or you're going for the one who smothers you, because you're trying to get what you didn't have.*

*Understand your own story, is the point. My sister and I were magnets for impossible-to-please narcissists. I just walk around with the invisible target on my chest. Egomaniacs inquire within. And no wonder—look at Mary Louise and Barry, and then at Mary Louise's father, Rocky Siler. And look at Otto, that dick, and Mom. Otto, 50 percent of my genetic material, strutting around and talking with his notice-me boom. Telling everyone how he used to drive a freaking Rolls Royce. He'd flirt with a lamppost.*

*I liked Hank Peters for his superiority and then dumped him because he was always acting superior.*

Everyone was in bed when I got home, or I thought so at first. I went into the dark kitchen to get something to drink and gave a little screech when I realized someone was sitting at the kitchen table. It was Aunt Annie, just sitting there, drinking red wine out of a juice glass, the bottle sitting in front of her.

"What are you doing?" I asked.

"I thought you were home already. I thought everyone was in bed. I just got back from my date with Quentin."

"Must have been great," I said. "Drinking away the memories?"

"No, no . . . ," she said. "It was great. Really great." She was wearing a sparkly top and jeans, but her eyes looked tired. The curls she'd made in her hair were tired too, relaxing back to their old normal straight selves.

"Yeah?"

"He's got the greatest eyes. Did you see him in the magazine?" *Northwest Homes For Sale* magazine. Quentin Ferrill was one of those real estate agents who felt that their picture would send the clients flocking. I nodded. Annie had left the magazine open to his page, him and the six bulky, high-end homes he was selling, some photographed at sunset. "He's really into art, did I tell you? He used to teach at the university level, but didn't like academia. Real estate gives him more freedom. But those are the kinds of words he uses—*academia*."

"Smart, then."

"God, beyond that. I can feel like such an idiot, compared. He's always mentioning certain painters . . . The *Fauvre Style* . . ."

"Do you like that?" I was still trying to understand the half-empty bottle.

"I *love* that. I love everything about him. And he's different than anyone else I've been with. He is. Not so full of himself. More vulnerable. I just don't know what he feels about me. I mean, he asks me out, right? He looks into my eyes? But then I took his hand and he pulled away. What's with that? I don't get it. I don't get what's going on."

Ivar snored underneath the table at Aunt Annie's feet. "It's early," I said. "Maybe he's just . . . sorting out his feelings."

"Yeah," Aunt Annie said.

"I'm the wrong person to ask."

Aunt Annie didn't think so. Or maybe she was just in that place where you need someone, anyone, to tell you what you need to hear. "He must like me if he asks me out, right?"

"He wouldn't do it if he didn't like you," I agreed.

"I hate this," she said. "It was the best night I've ever had, but I hate this."

I went to the refrigerator to get some juice. Mom had worked more on her list after she'd come home. It was now stuck to the fridge with a magnet shaped like a watermelon.

*He's a loner. No one has ever understood him,* one line read. *He's jealous and watchful,* read another.

And then, the last line on the page: *You have a sense that something's wrong but can't quite figure out what it is.*

I went upstairs. The last thing I wanted then was to stop and think if my mother might be right.

# Chapter Four

The reporter's name was Hannah something, and Dad didn't seem to mind that she was practically the same age as Frances Lee, Dad's daughter with his first wife, Joelle. We'd only met Frances Lee once, when she and Joelle came all the way from Orcas Island, Washington, to meet Dad and us at an IHOP to discuss college. Frances Lee was wild haired and wore a bracelet of braided jute around one wrist. She had a tattoo of a mermaid on her ankle. Frances Lee seemed to me to be the visual equivalent of driving too fast—something you feared and wanted at the same time. It was strange to have someone like Frances Lee in your life but not in your life. She was my half sister, my father's daughter, and yet, to me, she was only a rumor. I picked up pieces of Frances Lee and tried to make a whole. Frances Lee was in trouble again. Frances Lee was *just like her mother.* Frances Lee gave Dad a figure of an upraised wooden middle finger that she made in woodshop class in high school. Frances Lee was a secret box in an attic that you weren't allowed to go near.

At IHOP that day, Joelle seemed surprised we were there, and the talk was all about how Dad should contribute to Frances Lee's education. What I remember is Joelle's batik dress and strawberry pancakes and Frances Lee slamming down a syrup container when Dad joked that Frances Lee studying child psychology was like a bank robber studying law. I also remember Sprout knocking over her water glass and Dad taking a long time to figure out who owed what on the check while

Joelle kept repeating, "Just give it to me," wiggling her fingers in his direction and blowing long sighs of air out through pursed lips, like ladies do in childbirth.

This reporter couldn't have been more than twenty-one, Frances Lee's age. Dad told us earlier that Hannah something was coming, and that she worked for the *Portland Courier,* which he said with a roll of his eyes. From his description, the *Portland Courier* was like our *Nine Mile Falls Press,* which specialized in the sports statistics for our high school athletes and updates from the Salmon Fest Planning Committee. Occasionally, they'd toss in a hard-hitting story on EDUCATION or POVERTY or THE ELECTION.

"You must be really talented," Dad said, "to have a job with a paper already. Quinn, can you get Hannah a drink? What, Perrier? Lemonade? Pepsi? Margarita?" He laughed.

Hannah laughed too, gathered her shiny blond hair in one hand and let it drop down again over her shoulder. "Lemonade? Thanks. Well, you know, my dad owns the paper. True story."

"Oh sure," Dad said. "Sure. But you should use the contacts you have, right? That's smart. That's only using your head. Perrier for me, as usual." He looked at me and smiled.

"You wouldn't believe how many people give me shit for it," she said. *"Stuff,"* she corrected herself.

"Jealousy," Dad said. "Look, you've got beauty *and* success. People are threatened by that. Let me show you around." Hannah Reporter stopped scratching her heel with the back of her toe and looked at Dad as if she was surprised to finally find someone who understood her. She kept her eyes fixed on him as they went into the living room.

"Cool room," I heard her say. "Very cool."

"I'm a cool guy," he said, and she laughed.

"Wow," she said.

"I got that when I was in Africa," he said.

I knew she was looking at the red mask, the one with the words "Olivia Thornton" written on a piece of masking tape on the back. Maybe she was even holding the mask in her hands. The wrongness of that made my stomach fall, the way wrongness does for most people. There had to be some explanation. Maybe he'd gone to Africa *with* Olivia Thornton.

"Wow," I heard Hannah Reporter say again. She must have excelled on the vocabulary portion of the SAT.

"Some of my most prized possessions are in this room," Dad said.

Sprout sat at the kitchen table, pen scratching on paper, writing a short story. She did this for fun sometimes—she'd get an idea and scribble away for hours. "God," she said. She'd been listening, too. She looked my way, stuck her finger down her throat, as Dad led Hannah out the French doors to the back deck.

"I love your hair," Hannah said to him.

"It's only been cut once, when I was two," he said.

"Really?" Hannah said. I wondered if her dad would have thought it was okay for her to come to an interview wearing shorts.

"No, but you can write that if you want." Dad laughed.

They headed outside, sat at the umbrella table that looked over the river. "'You can write that if you want. Ha-ha-ha-ha,'" Sprout said.

"Be nice," I said.

"He had his eyes glued to her boobs," Sprout said.

"Okay, that's not fair. That shirt's so tight, they're all anyone would look at."

"Shut up so I can concentrate," Sprout said.

God, she got weird over at Dad's house. I twisted a tray of ice, clinked cubes into tall glasses, the ice crackling and popping when I poured in the drinks. I carried the glasses outside, set them on the table.

"Quinn's going to Yale," Dad said.

"No way," Hannah said.

"I'm not actually sure where I'm going yet," I said.

"You must be really smart," Hannah said. She stirred her ice with the tip of her finger.

Dad held up his hands in front of himself, tipped his head down, as if bowing to applause. "Naturally . . . ," he said.

"The nut doesn't fall far from the tree," Hannah said.

"Acorn," I said.

Dad sipped his drink. "So, questions?" he said.

I went back inside. "Still staring at her boobs?" Sprout asked.

"Your attitude sucks," I said.

"*Your* attitude sucks," Sprout said.

"You don't even try," I said.

"You shouldn't have to try in a family," Sprout said. "You should just be able to *be*."

Sprout hunched back over her paper, one arm over her work like she was protecting it from cheaters. We did have to try, she didn't get that, because everything was still so new. You can't just expect things to be natural and easy when they're new. And Dad was still pretty new to us.

He came back into our lives mainly because of my eighth-grade heritage project, the last big deal of middle school. You had to make a family tree, pick a relative to study, trace his or her history, splay it all out on a trifold board, which would earn you "creativity points." Then, you had to give a presentation in front of judges (meaning Mrs. Wilkowski, the vice principal; Mrs. Lincoln, Kyle Lincoln's mom and Booster Club president; and Hailey Richard's dad, Brian Richards, who was some big shot at Cingular Wireless and who brought us all Cingular Wireless pins that read *Please Turn On your phones!*).

There's something sort of sadistic and voyeuristic about teachers making you do family trees. Family trees should be private matters. No one would ask you to show your family's medical records or list of dirty secrets, and yet it's all there, divorces and marriages and babies, the most private stuff. Or maybe it only seems that way to those of us whose trees have broken branches and sawed-off limbs.

I could study Gram, Mom suggested. I could study Gram's parents. Her father was a builder with hunched, uncertain shoulders who died young, and her mother, short and frail as a lace hankie, later married a man who drank. That's what we knew of him: He was A Man Who Drank. The rest of that tree was as fuzzy as old photographs, not worthy of memory or ink in journals. But Dad's family—even what I knew already was more vibrant and plot filled than any of the plodding folks in Mom's family. There was his Armenian grandfather, who sold silks and then came across a fortune buried under a plum tree;

his grandmother, who had a sixth sense so right on that she was called to service by a Russian czar on the imminent birth of his daughter. His father, the diamond merchant; his mother, who hopelessly loved them both. There were roots and branches there, and the branches were filled with flowers that would turn to lush, ripe fruit. He would have boxes of photographs, I was sure, snippets of songs, his father's ancient shoes, gold coins, love letters written in pen strokes delicate as spider's legs.

It was a reminder, is what it was. Of everything I could have had but didn't.

"This is crazy," Mom said. "How much of that do you think is even true? You want to open all that back up again? Because of a school project?"

But even Mom knew it was more than a school project. The need for a mom and a dad, for their love and approval and presence, it's such a deep need. Old and deep, like the need of oxygen for blood, blood for a heart. And a year later, the need was still present, even after my project on Gram's father, the builder Stewart Ewing, was completed. I'd used the only photograph we had of him and his wife, and I'd painted the Transcontinental Railroad (he crossed the country while laboring on it) across the back of the board, earning me a B, a mercy grade next to the solid A that Celia Harris got for her project on her great-grandfather, George W. Ferris, inventor of the Ferris wheel. She'd included a miniature battery-operated version of his invention, snitched from some Christmas scene—it was set in plastic snow, with two tiny plastic people below in earmuffs and scarves, mouths open as if caroling.

I called Dad after a week of fighting with Mom and three

days of near silence and cool politeness, which had finally disintegrated into a night of us both sobbing and hugging on my bed. *I don't want you to get hurt,* Mom said. *I don't want you to get more hurt.* I wasn't sure if she was talking about me or her. But she agreed. If I needed this, she needed this for me. Gram said she was going to have a parade now that the war was over, throw around some Styrofoam packing peanuts in lieu of confetti.

These were the things I remembered about Dad when he lived with us all those years ago: eating crab on newspapers at the kitchen table. Playing with his shaving foam. Riding next to him in a car, his legs hairy in shorts. Maybe a bike? Him cleaning gravel from my knees? Or was that Mom? *Beauty and the Beast* wrapping paper, his hands around a shovel as he dug something in the yard. It made you wonder (and worry), your memory. Like maybe you'd be ninety years old and all you'd recall of your life would be the hem of a skirt and beach sand in the cracks of a book and a birthday cake with frosting roses and the chicken pox.

But when I saw the real him again after almost seven years' absence, his presence came back to me. His smell, his voice, the light in his eyes—they were all familiar even though I hadn't remembered them. They were there again, and the feeling of that, its importance, its loss not lost anymore, was something I felt so far inside me that it was as if I felt it to the very edges of my cells, to the farthest reaches of their earliest memories. It was a connection a heritage project was supposed to make me feel but could never really make me feel, because this was not about cardboard and glue and Magic Marker but about the way you know things and recognize the people who do mean the most and will mean

the most to you in your life. Even his shirt, the shirt he was wearing that day, bought by Brie the week before—as he hugged me
against him, it seemed I had felt that fabric for years.

He told me then, Sprout and me, and Brie, too, who sat and
held his hand in her lap, that he never wanted to stop seeing us.
He never wanted this separation. That it had just gotten too
hard, there was too much fighting. It had been the best thing for
us, for him to back out. Did we remember coming over to
Abigail's house every weekend? The back and forth? We had had
some great times, he said. I had nodded and smiled but didn't
really remember the great times. Weirdly, I remembered only the
feeling of a strange place, my father in a strange place, and signs
of Abigail Renfrew. Red geraniums, when my mother hated red
geraniums (she said they stank); Abigail Renfrew's personal
items on the bathroom counter (a blue box of Tampax, a pink
bottle of Nair), when Mom kept hers tucked in drawers and
used a razor. Watching a National Geographic movie about tor-
nados while sitting on Abigail Renfrew's woven couch with cat
hair on it, and Abigail Renfrew asking if we'd enjoyed it as much
as she had. The way Abigail Renfrew's name felt when my Mom
said it when we were back home again. As if it were something
you'd pick up off the floor using a Kleenex.

Brie's eyes had been shiny with tears. She patted the place
next to her own on Dad's leather couch there, in the house on
the river, and Sprout sat beside her and looked up at her white-
gold hair. Dad had given up because he had thought it was best
for us, he'd said, and I believed him. Dad even had a term for
what had happened: "Parental alienation."

"Parental alienation" meant that Mom had turned us against

him, and not that he had turned us against him. It was a *campaign,* he had said. He didn't want to say anything bad about Mom, but it got so relentless that one time Sprout wouldn't even get in the car to go over. She had clung to Mom like Dad was some Nazi ax murderer—did we remember that?

Brie shook her head in that way people do when something is sad, sad. A shame. Something preventable, if not for the poor behavior of human beings. *But the truth rises,* Dad had said. See? The truth rises. He had pulled me close. He told us how perfect and special and wanted we were. Wanted—I felt it, too. He started to cry. Brie got up and made tea. She delivered him a cup and kissed the top of his head. The kiss was like a period at the end of a sentence. A paragraph completed, or a story. A good ending.

I watched Dad and the reporter, Hannah, outside. Dad leaned in toward her, on his elbows. She was teasing him, it looked like; she waggled her finger in his direction as if he were a naughty child. He grabbed her finger, pretended he was going to take a big bite. He raised his voice dramatically, "What big teeth you have, Grandmother," he said, and they both laughed.

"What big boobs you have, Little Red Riding Hood," Sprout said.

"You're the worst," I said.

"She'll be picking us up at the train station next week," Sprout said.

"Impossible. She doesn't have her driver's license yet," I said.

"Good one," Sprout said.

"Her mom could pick us all up," I said. I don't know why, but I was suddenly feeling on Sprout's side. My inner evil twin again. Anyway, we were insulting Hannah Reporter, not Dad.

"She could drive us in her Fisher Price Cozy Coupe."

"We could all make it move with our feet," I said. "Wait, here they come. Pretend we weren't just talking about them."

Dad had his hand at the small of Hannah Reporter's back, guiding her into the living room as if she might otherwise get lost.

"What are you working on?" she asked Sprout.

"A story," Sprout said.

"Charles is a wonderful writer," Dad said. "I'm also working on a novel."

"Really?" Hannah said, but she didn't write this down. "What's your story about, sweetie?" she asked Sprout.

"It's about a girl spawned from the devil," Sprout said.

Hannah's eyebrows went up, and her mouth opened like those dark tunnels trains go through. Sprout's story was actually about Ivar and the neighbor's dog, Tucker, who leave home and go on a trip. Stolen right from *The Incredible Journey*.

"Cool," Hannah said.

Dad walked Hannah to the front door. We could hear him: "The novel's based on my family history, told in magical realism," he said.

"Blah-be-blah-blah-blah," Sprout said.

The front door closed. He'd gone outside, where they were probably standing outside her car door. He was out there a long time.

"For God's sake, she's twelve," Sprout said.

"He's just being friendly," I said.

"If she becomes our new stepmother, I'm outta here," Sprout said.

*FRANCES LEE GIOFRANCO:*

*Before I started going out with Gavin, I met this guy, Terrence Vinnigan, who basically was just hot. Really great body. Nicest ass. Hard, round shoulders—they were like squeezing cantaloupes. I couldn't believe he wanted to be with me. It made me feel a little insecure. I'm not exactly a workout, pump-it, gym type. Give me a pint of coffee ice cream. But Terrence went to the gym seven days a week—after school, weekends—classes. Cardio Boxing, Power-Strength Lifting, Super Big Guy Strong Man 101. He drank protein shakes and had these serious-looking vitamin bottles with brown and green labels; you know, no Flintstones Chewables like the ones me and Gavin have as a side dish to our Fruity Pebbles.*

*I liked his body, I admit it, and he liked my potential. I guess he was going to shape me up too, so I could be a self-obsessed, freak-of-nature muscle mass like him. He started making these comments like, "We should start you out on little walks." He called them "walkies," isn't that adorable? As if that might make actual exercise cuter and less intimidating to me. He jiggled my butt. He brought me sushi, when I hate sushi. He was one of those guys you feel you have to try hard to be equal to—as in shape as he is, as intelligent, as whatever. The kind you're slightly uneasy around because you know that deep down, he feels you don't measure up. Gavin—he brings me peanut butter cookies. He hates sushi too. With Gavin, I relax.*

*Anyway, it all blew up in my face one day when I told Terrence I wanted to study child psychology, and he laughed and said that's what people did who had fucked-up childhoods.*

*It was a cliché, he said. You're going to counsel people on how to run their lives? I said, "What do you mean by that?" And he said, "You don't even see your own father. You have self-esteem issues."*

*And then suddenly, I realized he was right. I did have self-esteem issues. He was living, breathing, weight-lifting proof. He'd started to say things like, "Why do you wait so long before shifting into third? It's bad for your engine." "Why do you eat so fast?" Why do you everything, anything. And I just kept my mouth shut. He was always telling me how I felt and who I was, too. "You're just upset because . . ." "You're an overly sensitive person. . . ." He was wrong 85 percent of the time, but all that mattered to him was his own version of me. I'd tell him how I did feel, and he'd shove it aside like he knew me better than I knew myself. It was bullshit.*

*It was bullshit, and it was my dad all over again. He has a whole relationship with a you that's not even you. It reminded me of when I was a kid, right around the sixth grade. I'd put on weight and Barry, who has always thought he was Mr. Beautiful, was on this running kick at the time. He'd lecture me about carbs and shit and how I needed to be in control of food and not let it be in control of me, and he'd take pinches of me and say things like, "What do we have here?" Thank you very much. One more way I wasn't good enough for him. And he'd given me all this shit about what I was going to study in college too. You know, all the two times he happened to call me. He said that me studying child psychology was like an armed robber studying law.*

*Anyway, I decided to tell Terrence Vinnigan to take a*

*walk. I told him it was too bad you couldn't go to the gym and get a new personality. And I told my self-esteem issues to take a walk too. Gavin treats me great. He's there for me in all the ways that matter. I can be a bitch, my ass can jiggle, he loves me for who I am. You've got to have someone who loves your body. Who doesn't define you, but sees you. Who loves what he sees. Who you don't have to struggle to be good enough for. "He loves me for who I am"—a cliché, but one of the most fucking powerful clichés in the history of all clichés.*

*My mom thinks it's amazing that I found a great guy so early on. She says it wasn't until she was over forty and hit a "I won't take shit from anyone anymore" age that she started looking out for herself the way I do already. She's really proud of me for that. She says, "How do you do it, my girl?" And I say, "I'm learning from your mistakes, sweetie," and she knows I mean that in the best way possible.*

Dad worked in his office the rest of the day, and Sprout and I did homework. Later, Uncle Mike and Thomas came over to talk about the Jafarabad Brothers' summer show, and Dad made beef curry for dinner. Dad was a really good cook, though he didn't usually do it unless there was company over. He liked to make dishes that he could prepare right in front of guests, rather than something you shoved in an oven and forgot about. He liked to stir things up dramatically and flourish knives and juggle bottles of herbs and spices, same as he would in one of his shows.

Everyone sat down to eat, and Dad lifted a large goblet of red wine from his place at the head of the table. "To the Jafarabad Brothers' World Tour."

"The world's gotten pretty damn small." Uncle Mike laughed. He rubbed one eye with his fingers.

"Lift your glass, damn it," Dad said. "Our lives are more interesting than ninety-nine percent of the population."

"Barry, you're so full of shit," Uncle Mike said.

"The world?" Thomas said. "Wisconsin? New Jersey?"

I could almost feel Dad's face change before I saw it. "Fuck you," he said. "Fuck. You."

The room was suddenly quiet. Mike rubbed his thumb and index finger up and then down over the stem of his wineglass. "A joke, Barry," he said.

"I *like* New Jersey," Thomas said. He seemed a little stunned. I felt a sort of sick shame, either for Dad or about Dad, I couldn't tell which.

"You could still be juggling Coke bottles in your garage, if it weren't for me," Dad said. He stared coldly at Thomas, and then seemed to change his mind about the whole thing. Dad looked toward Sprout and me. "All right, then. To my family," Dad said. "Each and every one of you in this room."

We raised our glasses, and the weird and hollow clinks hung there in the tension of the room. Amidst the arm raising and elbows, Sprout knocked over the large bottle of Perrier in the center of the table, sending everyone scurrying for napkins. The strained moment passed, and we ate curry and Dad made Sprout read her story about Ivar and Tucker, which earned a round of applause. The dishes were piled in the sink. "Just put them in there for the maid," Dad said, even though we didn't have a maid, of course. After Uncle Mike and Thomas left, there was the smell of garlic and turmeric hovering around the house like a restless ghost.

Restless was how I felt inside too. I kept passing the living room and looking at that statue and those other objects, feeling a should I/shouldn't I push-pull. I wanted to confront Dad, but I didn't want to make him mad. Probably, it wasn't my business anyway. But why did it feel very much like my business? Why did I feel like one of those art films where time was chunked up and out of order and it was only somewhere near the end that all the pieces came together in a way that made sense? I wanted to understand things, really understand them, in some way that was deep and solid, and yet my own niceness required that I keep skimming along the surface. I brushed my teeth, decided to go to bed, backspaced on that idea, and set my toothbrush down suddenly.

I knocked on Dad's bedroom door but there was no answer. I listened for sounds of him upstairs, but all I could hear was the technological twinkling of Sprout playing with her cell phone ringers. I walked downstairs and heard the kitchen drawer open (the Useless Gadget Drawer, as Dad called it), the sound of plastic spatulas and potato peelers and once-used candy thermometers all clattering together. The drawer shut. The water faucet went on. Dad stood at the counter in his black silk robe with a dragon on the back and poured a measuring cup of water into a bowl. The dishes in the sink had been done.

"Chocolate craving?" I said. He was holding a telltale red box of brownie mix, head tilted back so that his eyes could see the small-for-him words of the directions.

"You caught me," Dad said.

"Brownies," I said.

"Brownies," he agreed, as if there may have been some dispute. He cracked an egg in with one hand. I saw that chocolate might not have been what he was actually craving—on a paper towel was a small hill of pot, which he'd stir in later, I knew. I'd seen this routine before, would sometimes also smell the burnt-grass-mat odor coming from the outside deck as he smoked, the orange rolling papers called Zig-Zag open on the counter.

He must have felt my eyes. "Those guys always get me so uptight," he said.

I didn't say anything. As part of my relentless trek along the road of good choices, I never drank or did drugs myself; honestly, I sort of looked down at those people. When I was friends with Sara Miller in the sixth grade (definitely not a good choice), we once downed a can of her brother's beer, and I guess she liked it so much she kept it up from then on. But I think she was just one of those people who drank self-destruction in her baby bottle. You've got a good life and you purposefully set out to mess it up . . . I never got that. Maybe I just never understood the point, the way other people seemed to understand the point. Some people understood the point so well, they made it a per-sonal credo, the law of their independent nation, but it just seemed stupid to me, and maybe even weak. Like the world was just too big and bright and real for you, and you just couldn't take it.

So, that Dad did this—it bothered me enough that I didn't know what to do with it. Inside, it felt as if someone had handed me something bad I didn't want—a switchblade, some poison in a bottle—and there it was, in my hand. The only thing I could do was to shove it in some drawer or at the bottom of a garbage can, pile other stuff over it. I didn't say anything when he folded the drugs into the batter. But I did say something else.

"How are you doing, Dad, with Brie gone and all?" I said. I

sat down at one of the tall chairs at the counter. Folded my hands in front of me and then unfolded them. I looked like I was giving him a job interview. I looked like Mom.

"Who?" he said. "Kidding! I'm *kidding*. God, you should have seen your face. Like this." He opened his mouth and eyes wide, wide open. "I'm fine. Of course I'm fine. You can't let any one person have that much power over you, okay, Quinn? Remember that. I didn't fail, here. I gave her everything I could give." He licked the spoon. "Hey, kiddo, I need to change the subject here for a minute, okay? We gotta talk about this whole college thing."

"Okay," I said.

"First, can I say that I think you're going to do great things in the world? Your intelligence, it makes you a very powerful person," he said.

I smiled. I liked the thought of that. I liked that he saw me that way.

"I've got to tell you, though, my philosophy on this. A person's education, well, I think they should own it, you know? Feel a sense of responsibility toward it. You see?"

I nodded. I wasn't sure I did.

"It's fine if that gets handed to you, but who cares about it then? Why do you need to work hard in school if someone just gives you a blank check? I just got to tell you, I don't believe in that. I won't participate in teaching those sorts of values."

I didn't understand where he was going with this, and then suddenly I did. "I don't have to go to Yale. I can go somewhere less expensive."

"It's not about the *money*," he said. "It's not about *not having*
the money. I'm talking about appreciating your education."

"But of course I'd appreciate my education."

"You'll appreciate it more when you're the one who has to
pay for it," he said. "We just need to get straight right now about
what I'm willing to do and what I'm not willing to do."

His point was becoming clearer and clearer. I felt creeping,
growing dread. In terms of college, I'd heard *Your dad and I will
work it out* enough times to know that Mom was expecting his
help. I pictured Mom writing checks, big checks, checks
weighty enough to make her shoulders hunch. "What *are* you
willing to do?" I asked.

"I'm not willing to pay for your own higher education,
and I'm not trying to be the bad guy here, it's a matter of *principles*. It's a matter of raising you to be the kind of person you
should be." He was still standing there with that fork. But
then he turned back around, conversation over. I wanted to
cry, but I didn't. I hate to cry. But my chest seized up in some
hot, heavy pain. I don't know what I was feeling, only that it
was too much.

The words that came next—they were out before I even
realized it. They shoved forward, rode a wave of what might
have been anger. "Did Brie give you that statue?" I whispered.

"What statue?" He plopped the batter into the pan. Scraped,
scraped the last gooey bits in.

"In the living room. The glass one. It wasn't there before."

He didn't look at me. He focused on that pan, opened the
oven door. "Right. The glass one? She gave me that a long time
ago. Long time. I never put it out before. It's kind of gaudy." His

back was curved, bent over. His hand was in an oven mitt. But his back was a liar's back—I could see the lie in that curve, I could see deception in the slope of his shoulders. I could feel it in the place between us—the lie filled the kitchen, all the air, squeezed at my own air in my lungs.

"Gaudy, don't you think? Little like Brie herself," he said. "Let me tell you one thing about your good old Dad. He's got a knack for finding crazy women." I felt an internal slap of injustice at those words. My mother, sane, measured, practical. He finally turned, and right then I felt something else between us. That lie about the statue—he knew that I knew. He was inviting me to it. He was asking me to join him in it.

After all these years of separation, there was nothing more that I wanted than that—to be one with him about something, to be let in and allowed to stay. I wanted that so much.

I felt the open door, the chance to have permanent membership in the club that was my father. And maybe it really was "parental alienation" in action then, maybe something entirely complicated as loyalty. Or maybe it was something much simpler, my own caution, that kept me at the threshold.

"You're lying," I said. The words felt brave. Maybe more brave than any words I'd spoken before.

"I always tell the truth to the best of my ability," he said.

### JOELLE GIOFRANCO:

*My feelings for Steven Devlin were a strange recipe—the wild, the tumbling, the dark and forbidden, folded in with my desire to nurture and make him muffins and have his babies and live in a cabin somewhere. The thought that*

*Steven Devlin would live in a cabin somewhere was ludicrous, naturally. A jail cell, perhaps. This was before Barry. Right before Barry. I met Steven Devlin in an anthropology class, where the professor had moons of dirt under his fingernails, as if he'd just returned from an excavation in the desert. Steven Devlin had raven-black hair. He was the kind of quiet that's sultry and that simmers. Remember Richard Gere in the old days?* Officer and a Gentleman *days? The kind of quiet that you can think he's thinking of all these deep things, the universe's secrets, his private torment, when he's likely only thinking about carburetors or lunch or breaking a lock. Listen to me—we have to be careful not to create a person in our imagination.*

*Steven Devlin was the sort who was always in trouble at school, barely graduated, conflicts with teachers, picked up by police for drinking and drugging. I don't know how he got into college, other than his parents probably paid his way in. I used to watch him turn in his tests, sauntering down the aisle, the low-slung walk of a coyote, and I'd picture us rolling passionately around on my dorm-room bed. He just looked so turbulent and dangerous and this appealed to me the way standing on a bluff in roaring wind does. Because you feel something, then, something real and large. He was a storm approaching. A walking, talking thundercloud.*

*He didn't disappoint me in the passion department. He was passionate all right, God, a great kisser, and once he ran right out in the middle of a busy street in the pouring rain to help a dog that had been hit. But he'd also disappear and get into deep depressions, and I'd cry and try to help him and it was all very dramatic. He didn't feel loved by his father, and I thought I'd show him what love was. If only he knew what love was . . . He had trouble with authority—he'd tell off his bosses and a teacher who failed him. He'd get upset, then disappear in the middle of the night. He had a terrible temper— his face would turn into someone else's when he got mad. That little muscle, you know, right here in your cheek? His would pulse with the force of his teeth clenching. He dislocated his arm once, throwing a book across the room.*

*A list of beautiful attributes, yes? Moody, depressive, deviant, terrible family relationships, drug use, and numerous previous sex partners? I felt something real and large, yes, that's true, but that something was pain. It ended when I found out that one of the places he was disappearing to was the bed of a thirty-five-year-old woman whom he babysat for. He was nineteen. I never told Frances Lee that part of the story.*

*I read somewhere later, years, that the boys who are delinquent in high school, the kind who are always in trouble, drugs, barely graduating, all of it, it's a huge indicator of a future sociopath. That's right. You are tempted to think,* Teenager, troubled. Part of the landscape. *But it's not part of the landscape. Not part of any normal landscape. This is who he is, who he will always be, and no amount of your love is going to change that.*

*In comparison, Barry's dramatics seemed mild. He just had a lot of girls around him all the time. Just. You see—I only turned the drama volume* down, *when I should have turned it* off.

I lay awake in the dark, in our room at Dad's house. When we first came back into Dad's life, the room had been used for Brie to work out in. There had been an exercise bike and weights and squishy green mats; a television with an assortment of videos beside it, with covers of women flexing muscles and running on the beach. But Brie had moved over for us, moved her stuff to the attic and gotten a membership in some gym downtown. Now the room had two beds and a dresser Brie had found in an antique store, with a big mirror in the shape of a shell. Brie had brought in a painter, who made a mural of two mermaids at sea. She kissed our foreheads when we went to bed, carrying Malcolm on her back as she headed to his room, his butt drooping low and his tennis shoes hanging on by just his toes. His room now held only boxes of books Dad had recently bought, with the intention of making a library.

I looked at Sprout's dark head, tucked snugly into her pillow. "Sprout!" I whispered. But there was no answer; just the in-out sound of her breathing.

I thought about Dad watering his flower baskets in his dragon robe. I thought about his holiday decorating—for Christmas, a huge reindeer and sleigh, inflatable snowmen, a ten-foot Santa with a puffy bag of air-presents over one shoulder. For Halloween, orange and black lights, an enormous spider on the roof, plastic bats hung on all the neighbors' mailboxes. I thought about how it felt to be around someone so much *larger* than you. I thought of his words: *I tell the truth to the best of my ability.* If the truth was like a diamond, then sometimes it might be too bright to look at. Sometimes, it would be hard to know whether it was real.

Maybe it was wrong, or maybe impossible, but I wanted the truth to be one thing. One solid thing. I knew what I had to do then. It was another one of those moments when I didn't know how I knew, or why. Just that I knew I had to call Frances Lee.

# Chapter Five

When I sat down in my seat for the train ride home, I saw that I'd missed a call from Liv. "Quinn, it's me," the message said. Her voice was breathless and worried. "Hey, give me a call. I need to talk to you. It's important. Love you . . ."

Liv and I had been best friends since we both started playing volleyball in the eighth grade, and I'd do anything for her, but when I called her back I was happy to get her voice mail: *You've reached Liv. Say something.* I didn't feel like talking, I realized, didn't want to hear about the latest crisis with Ben/Alex/Jason/Whoever. I felt the sort of low, vague pissed-off that could turn global. You know, where you get a paper cut and curse not only the paper but paper factories and the paper factory workers and pulp mills and trees. That's the thing about discontent—it's very flexible. It's perfectly content to invade wherever it happens to land.

Mom picked us up at the station, as always, her Subaru parked at the curb. We climbed in; Sprout's butt was barely on the seat before she told Mom about the reporter.

"Sheesh," Mom said.

I kept my mouth shut, stared out the window at the glassy buildings of the city, at the Space Needle and Lake Union in an oval in front of it, at seaplanes landing, at the packed freeway lanes heading toward the floating bridge toward home. I hated that Sprout did this—gave the FBI report on Dad and his crimes whenever we got home. Maybe she should bring a recorder, or a hidden camera in her shirt button. I didn't like this game, didn't like to give these little presents we seemed to give Mom after we'd been to see Dad. She would ask how it was, and somewhere inside you knew you couldn't say it was great, even if it was. You said, *It was boring.* You said, *Dad and Brie got in a fight.*

You didn't say he made you laugh until your stomach hurt, or that he bought you an Xbox and fifteen games (Sprout never told Mom about this either). You didn't say you saw him come up behind Brie and kiss her neck with happy passion when she was making slushy green margaritas in a blender, or that he bought so many wildflowers to plant on the shore down to the river that you had to go back to the store twice more just to bring them all home. You didn't say that you loved everything about Malcolm, even when he screamed and held tight to the banister like it was Good and his bed was Evil. You stuck to the small, nasty truths—that Dad seemed stressed about the upcoming show because he snapped at the car-wash guy. You knew you were offering something, holding out the chance for a satisfying, critical reply. *He treats that car better than the women in his life.* Or, *How nice that he can afford to get the car detailed.*

And even if it wasn't great, even if it was bad, you never said how bad it really was, either. You said, *Dad and Brie were fighting;* you didn't say you heard the *crickle-pop* of tires on the gravel road at two a.m. and that Dad wasn't there at breakfast in the morning. You said things were fine all weekend, but not that Dad was stoned and you all got in the car anyway. That he left the parking brake off later that night and the car ended up on the neighbor's lawn. Because one time you *did* say—you told about how he taught you to make him a gin and tonic or that you went on that boat ride with him and Uncle Mike and you ran out of gas and no, no one had a life jacket on. You told and you found out what happened—angry phone calls, a lecture from Dad about how what goes on at his house should stay at his house. *You don't have to be Mom's spy. Just because* she *thinks something, doesn't mean* you *need to think it too.*

It was best to keep your mouth shut. Don't offer the truth. The less said, the better, because there were a lot of people you had to protect. You had to protect Mom against her heartbreak and Dad against his wrongdoing. You had to protect yourself against feeling like a betrayer, a guilt-ridden thief showing off some jewels. You had to protect yourself, too, against the accusation that you were just like your mother. Which in a lot of ways you were. Which was, apparently, a bad thing. Both of them might be right—neither of them should know that.

All of this meant that you didn't say the things you really needed to say, either, about money and principles and college, things you would have to one day say, there was no getting around it. Just not then. Not until you were ready for days of upset and long conversations and bad feelings lying in the pit of your stomach.

"You okay, Quinn?" Mom looked over her shoulder to change lanes, snatched a glance my way.

"I'm fine," I said.

At home, I opened my backpack from the visit to Dad's and took the dirty stuff out. When your parents are divorced, you can also feel a lot like a traveling salesman.

After I unpacked, I went downstairs to cruise for mood-improving food. The list on the refrigerator had grown. *He presses to get involved very quickly. . . . He claims to know your feelings, perceptions, motivations better than you do. He says you're too sensitive, you're not seeing things right, or that you're wrong to feel what you feel.* In a different-color pen, and in her tiny, scratchy scrawl, Gram had added, *He's a dirty, rotten liar.*

Sprout must have gotten to my phone when I wasn't looking, because my ringers were changed again. She always thought this was hilarious. As I twisted open a bottle of Fresca, my phone sang some finger-snapping jazzy number some old guy over sixty would love.

"I've got to talk to you." Liv's voice was breathless again. Come to think of it, she was always a little breathless; maybe being beautiful was something you were always catching up to.

"I'm here," I said. I took a long, green, bubbly drink.

"Quinn, this is bad news, okay? I'm not even entirely sure I should tell you. I should wait, maybe, until I see you. I just thought, What would I want? You're my best friend."

I returned the bottle to the refrigerator, let the door slap closed. The Internal Department of Panic Control got to work. What could be that bad? Someone was talking about me, maybe. Big deal. Zaney? A friend I loved talking about me? Okay, that would be bad. Maybe it was Daniel. Daniel told everyone we had sex. Ha, Daniel would never do that.

"It's Daniel," Liv said.

No way. Just, no way. Daniel wasn't the type to hurt me. Of course, he wasn't the type to maul me, either, and last Friday he pulled me into his backyard and shoved me up against the house and kissed me with such hurricane energy that we knocked over a garbage can.

"I think he's seeing someone else."

"What?" The words sounded funny. Like they came to me underwater. Like they were unreal, and this was happening in some other place and time.

"Quinn, are you okay? Are you there?"

"Daniel would never do that," I said.

"I saw his car, parked in my neighborhood, and I thought, Hey, there's Daniel's car, and when I went over to say hi and ask him what he was doing there, I saw that new girl, Genevieve, what's her name, in his car. The one that came the last month of school? Who moves in the last month of school? I didn't even know she lived near me. I never even saw a moving truck."

"He was probably just giving her a ride," I said. But it felt like one of those stories you try out on yourself that you don't believe. "He gives people rides all the time."

"Quinn? I don't think you need to have your belt undone when you give someone a ride."

"Shit," I said. "Goddamn it. There must be an explanation." My chest felt squeezed of air. Thoughts shoved and pushed like people released from the train—Daniel, in my life, not in my life, a sudden absence, yanked. Loss, now anger. His tongue in my mouth, in her mouth. The smell of her perfume, what I now knew and maybe always knew was the smell of her perfume on his shirt, oh God, on me.

"Fuck you, good riddance. Quinn, you deserve better. I'm coming over. You want me to come over?"

"It's okay."

"I never liked Daniel, anyway. I didn't trust him."

"I just can't believe it." I sat on the arm of the living-room couch. I stared down at the straight little fibers that made up the carpet forest. But I could believe it, couldn't I? I had known, with that particular knowledge that likes to stay cozy and buried.

"*I* can believe it," Liv said. "He was nice, yeah. Too nice. Makes you worry, like those Jesus freaks into pornography, you know? Too much of anything is never a good thing, even goodness."

"I should call him," I said. It occurred to me suddenly that this was about him, too.

"You should *not* call him. What a coward, hiding out like a baby. He knew I saw. He knew it. And he hasn't called you yet? Cowardly shithead."

"I've got to go," I said.

"You deserve real goodness," Liv said.

Daniel picked up on the first ring. I didn't say anything, not even hello. He sort of sputtered and stuttered, like our lawn mower when Mom tries to start it after the winter. And like the lawn mower, when it finally got going, it had surprising power after lying dormant for so long.

"I fell in love, Quinn," he said.

That's when I hung up.

### BRIE JENKINS:

*I was one of these kids whose room was always clean, which, by the way, is* not *a trait Malcolm inherited! By the time I was in junior high, I had five-, ten-, and fifteen-year goals. I did, really—written down in my Rainbow Brite notebook. I still have it somewhere. My first serious boyfriend in high school wanted to be a doctor, and I think that's why I liked him. Larry Unstler. While all the other guys were smoking pot and talking about their cars, he was studying. He was a good guy—on the golf team, soft-spoken, real tall, long fingers that would pick out the lettuce from the sandwiches his mother made. He did sweet things, like bring me flowers, all that, a pie he made himself. I broke up with him because he was boring. I told him I'd go to Homecoming with him, then changed my mind after he'd rented his tux and everything, which was lousy and wrong and not the kind of thing I did. But it got to where I couldn't stand for him to touch me. He'd hold my hand and I'd just want to cringe. Those long, lettuce-removing fingers. When he touched me, I felt the way a slug must feel when you pour salt on it.*

*I didn't know what my problem was, because the next guy, Matt Mahnken—completely different story. I wanted him like I never wanted Larry Unstler. His father had run off and he lived with his mother; she worked and was so overwhelmed she never had time for him. She'd come home from work and go to bed, and sometimes no one even made dinner. His sister attempted suicide during our junior year. He was so sad all the time, big beautiful sad eyes, but my father thought he was a loser. I did his homework for him because he was failing a couple of classes, but wasn't that understandable with all that was going on at home? I made cookies for him, with uplifting, bolstering notes Scotch-taped on top,* I hope you have a great day! You're awesome! *things like that, and*

*I listened to his problems and bought him little presents and even made dinner a few times for him and his mom, before she came home. He'd always say,* I don't know what I'd do without you, *and that made me feel so good. He was* wounded.

*They moved away a year later. His mother got a new job. And I never heard from him again. Nothing. Not a word. It was like he'd dropped off the earth. And even then, my first thought was that something terrible had happened to him. They'd gotten into a car accident on the way to Denver. He'd gotten sick. His mother had gotten sick. His sister really did kill herself this time, and he was too despondent to write. I went into action—I wrote to him, researched possible phone numbers. I even tried to call some aunt I remember him mentioning.*

*I'd heard shortly afterward from a friend of his that he was fine—in a new school, almost failing again, but fine. It took me years to understand what had happened—basically, that he had found someone else to make him cookies, and that he would always have someone to make him cookies. I worried he'd die without me. I was sure he needed me, but it was maybe the other way around. And pity—people who inspire it in you are actually very powerful people. To get someone else to take care of you, to feel sorry for you—that takes a lot of strength, smarts, manipulation. Very powerful people.*

*It also took me years to stop putting some imaginary halo on Larry Unstler. The truth was, Larry was a good guy, but he was boring. The truth was, Matt Mahnken wasn't boring, but he was a bad guy. The truth was, they both were wrong for me.*

*I kept thinking that wrongness came in degrees of acceptabil-
ity, instead of that, rightness* is *or* isn't.

Daniel. My heart never leapt in desire at his presence; I never
imagined wearing white for him or living some long, entangled
life until our Silver Anniversary. But still, I felt then like my body
had been a building he'd just hit with a wrecking ball. Maybe if
I'd have dumped him it would have been different. Rejection,
though—it could make the loss of someone you weren't even
that crazy about feel gut wrenching and world ending.

"That asshole," Mom said. Rejection—it also demands that
the forces on your side assemble for action. It calls for all the
people who love you to gather, organize, and execute like a
good army.

Mom passed out bowls of ice cream as I tried to pull myself
together. The first bowl went to Aunt Annie, sitting cross-legged
on the floor. "He's too boring to even be an asshole, Quinn," she
said. "I never even noticed he was in the room until he spoke.
You were dating an end table."

Grandma was next. She sat on the couch in her robe and her
pink-slippered feet were propped up on the edge of the coffee
table. "You need someone with a little *life*." Grandma held her
fingers in the air. *Snap, snap, snap.*

Liv got bowl three. She'd come right over so fast that she
was still wearing the clothes she had on when she called—
Sunday night hanging-out pajama bottoms with penguins on
them and a tank top with pink hearts that one of her boyfriends
had given her for Valentine's Day: "I'm telling you, you've gotta
watch those Mr. Perfect, shiny-faced types," Liv said.

"It's the Jesus freaks who buy all the porno," Aunt Annie said.

"That's what I told her," Liv said.

Finally, Sprout got her ice cream. "Daniel was vomit," she said.

"Coffee ice cream, we're going to be up all night," Grandma said. The idea seemed to please her.

"Look under. Vanilla and butterscotch swirl, too," Mom said. "Every kind in the fridge. Honey, you're going to be fine. I know you don't feel like it, but you will. Us Hoffmans—we're strong women."

I hadn't wanted to cry until then. It was the thought of the Hoffman women that did it, the scattered and wrecked relationships that lay around like pieces of broken china—something beautiful once, now shattered and unrecognizable. My throat got tight. Tears gathered, but I put my palms to my eyes to stop them.

"Oh, honey," Mom said. She set down her bowl, squeezed in between me and Grandma on the couch.

"Ow," Grandma said. "You're squishing me."

Mom picked up my hand, gripped it hard. "I thought Daniel was foolproof," I said. My voice was small. It knew enough to be embarrassed, knew enough to hide.

"No one is foolproof," Aunt Annie said. She was hunting under the coffee ice cream for the butterscotch too, just like Grandma.

"We all make mistakes," Liv said. "And hey, Daniel was a small mistake! Look at me with Travis. I could have ended up in jail."

"That Otto gave me a run for my money," Grandma said.

"You just have to be careful," Mom said. She was holding

back, you could tell. You could almost hear her adding on to her list in her thoughts.

"Hey, Mom—all I got to say is O-C-D Dean," Sprout sang. This made me smile.

"Don't remind me," Mom said. "We got along fine when I didn't want to kill him."

"He alphabetized his underwear drawer. Fruit of the Loom before Jockeys," Aunt Annie said.

"My car was never clean enough. He always picked lint up off the floor mats like it meant my life was getting out of control," Mom said.

"Once I caught him looking in the microwave and staring at a little melted cheese like it was a terrorist. I wanted to sock him," Gram said.

"W. is in alcohol treatment," Liv said. W. was this guy she dated from a different high school who only went by his first initial.

"You never told me," I said.

"Too embarrassed. But now that we're confessing . . ."

"He was always having a crisis. Car accident, remember? Didn't he almost run over a crossing guard?"

"Not a crossing guard," Liv said. "Construction guy. Different orange vest."

"Is he the one who punched his boss? When he worked at Wendy's?" Sprout said.

"Were you snooping in on our phone conversation?" I asked. "Were you listening in while I was on the phone?"

"No," she said.

"Sprout," Mom said.

"It's just tempting," she said.

"Jack Xavier told me we needed to stop and get my coat pressed before we met his friends at a party," Aunt Annie said. "It was wrinkled. I took it off and scrunched it in a ball and said, 'You want to see wrinkled? Here's wrinkled.'"

"Jack Xavier was the biggest narcissist next to you-know-who," Mom said. Of course we knew who. You-know-who was Dad, and so was HIM and so was we-won't-say-who-I-mean and so was that-man-I-gave-all-those-years-to.

"Jack Xavier spent more time on his looks than a fashion model. He smelled like frou-frou water. He looked at his *reflection* in the microwave," Grandma said.

"Maybe we ought to look at a guy's response to our microwave from now on," Aunt Annie said.

"Really," Mom said. "The narcissist looks at his reflection in it, the OCD guy thinks you don't keep it clean enough, the Antisocial—"

"Puts his fist through it because it reminds him of his father," Annie said. She'd read all of Mom's books too.

"And the paranoid one would be jealous of the amount of time you spent cooking," Mom said.

"Were you using that microwave again? Is something going on between the two of you? I caught you looking right at its *clock*," Aunt Annie said. They cracked up. You could see the way they'd been when they were two younger sisters, like Sprout and me. "I hope you girls are paying attention."

"Just because he's good in bed doesn't mean you can live with him," Grandma said.

"Mom," Mom said.

"Oh, gross," Sprout said.

"It's shocking, the things we call love," Mom said.

"The best defense is a good offense," Grandma said.

"You sound like ESPN," Aunt Annie said.

"Daniel was vomit," Sprout said again. She was stirring her ice cream all up, into ice cream soup.

After a while, Mom eased herself back up and made tea and Liv asked if anyone wanted seconds. She was the only one who could eat more. After she was done, she had to loosen the drawstring of her penguin pants. She was the type of girl who could eat and eat and never gain an ounce, but you didn't hate her for it because you loved her so much.

"I feel like an alien might burst from my stomach," Liv groaned.

"God, that was good," Grandma said. Even her little slippers looked happy.

"Butterscotch swirl never lets you down," Aunt Annie said. She stretched her legs out.

"You don't need to hire a private investigator to check up on butterscotch swirl," Grandma said.

Aunt Annie sat up suddenly. "What?"

"I saw the phone book open on the table after you left the room. I saw the ads. 'Surveillance begins where trust ends.' Who uses a phone book anymore?" Grandma loved the Web.

Mom stopped midway back from the kitchen, abruptly halted her tea bag bobbing. She looked at her sister with a look I knew well. It was a look I probably first got when I had a crayon in my fist and was heading for the wall. "Annie, no."

"I was just *curious*. I would never do that. For God's sake, people."

"Why do you need a private investigator?" Liv asked.

"She doesn't need a private investigator," Mom said.

"Quentin Ferrill is giving Annie a run for her money," Grandma said.

"Like I could even *afford* a private detective," Annie said.

"If you need to pay a private detective to feel like you've got the truth on someone . . . ," Mom said.

"I *know*," Aunt Annie said. "I wouldn't do it! I promise." She sounded like Sprout. "He's just so freaking secretive."

"People are secretive when they have secrets," Mom said.

"Stay clear," Liv agreed.

Grandma looked at her watch. "Oh my," she said. "eBay time." She bolted from the couch, hurried her quilted-robed self toward the office where the computer was.

"Wow, an item must be ending soon," Annie said.

"I haven't seen her move so fast since she caught that kitchen towel on fire," Mom said. She sipped her tea.

"Thanks for making *me* tea," Annie said to Mom.

"Get it yourself," Mom said.

"Gram likes those salt- and pepper shakers that look like chefs," Sprout said. She was petting Ivar with her foot.

Annie leaned back against the couch. "She must suck at the bidding thing."

"Does she always lose at the last minute?" Liv asked.

"I guess so," Annie said. "Has anyone ever noticed that nothing comes in the mail? No packages from somewhere in New Jersey or Iowa? Nothing shoved so tight in the mailbox you can't get anything else out?"

"Yeah, we all remember your purse-buying spree," I said. "It felt like FedEx headquarters here."

"Nothing comes," Annie said. "We should have a kitchen full of mini chefs by now."

Mom sat down in the rocking chair, gave a few thoughtful rocks. "You're right."

"Highly suspicious," Liv said.

"I think it's great, personally," Mom said. "She hardly has any discretionary income. If she won all the time, she'd be into her Social Security check."

"How many chefs does a person need?" Aunt Annie agreed.

"One would be good because of Mom's cooking," Sprout said. "Ah-ha-ha."

"Let's get your mom one of those hats," Annie said. "The poofy white ones."

"Or cooking lessons," I said. Mom was actually a great cook.

Mom grabbed a pillow and flung it at Sprout, causing Ivar to flee as fast as Grandma had.

"You're all hilarious," Mom said. "Bunch of comedians."

## DOROTHY HOFFMAN SILER PEARLMAN HOFFMAN:

*I was eighteen when I got married the first time. In my day, you married the man before there was any hanky-panky, but it makes more sense what the young girls do now. Just because you're having fun right then or you want to go to bed with him doesn't mean he'll be a good father and someone you'll want to spend the next sixty years with. Rocky Siler was a looker, and at eighteen I wasn't thinking about what sixty years meant. That he might grow fat and snore and that I'd see his black socks pulled up high on white legs and that I'd have to one day maybe nurse him when he got his prostate out. I liked his shiny black hair and his dark eyes. Like a movie star's. He had big, strong hands. I didn't notice right then that I didn't even really know who he was, or that we didn't have the same type of humor. You've got to be able to laugh together. Anyway, I didn't nurse him through anything, because he ran off and left me with Mary Louise when she was three months old. I don't like to talk about it. That's water under the bridge.*

*Otto Pearlman, he was a looker, too, a lot like my father—he was a businessman, though I wasn't even entirely sure what business. Real estate of some kind, both of them. Otto was like my father in that he was the man of the house, and he never had nice things to say about women. Women were out to trick some man with money into marrying them. All they cared about was a big ring, and once they got it, the sex was over, la-la-la. You'd have thought those attitudes disappeared with Women's Lib, but you'd be surprised. You still have these big shots thinking they're so special and telling you how to dress because they're so afraid of your own power.*

*My mother always said, "Love is work," and I worked with Otto Pearlman. I wanted him to know I wasn't like those other women. It got to where I didn't have a voice, and I think even way back then, I liked my voice. I'd tell him what I thought and his temper would flare, and the way I saw it, he had a problem with his anger. He raised his hand to me, but it's nothing I like to talk about now. With him, I'd keep quiet and keep things nice until one day I realized that he didn't have a problem with his anger, he had a problem with mine. My anger meant I had power.*

*I had gotten so I trapped myself, though—with my*

*silence, with trying to be so good and ladylike, with the fact*
*that I had two babies and no job. Back then, that's what you*
*did.* He *was your job. I had no money of my own. But*
*Hoffmans have always been strong women. Even my mother.*

    *I started saving money in a sock until I had enough to*
*leave. I took my babies and left, which is not something you*
*did in those days. But let me tell you, if you don't keep hold of*
*your own power and strength, you're lost. Your own voice.*
*Your own money. You can get stuck somewhere you can't get*
*out of. You don't want to think about these things when you're*
*"in love." But I always tell the girls, you've got to keep enough*
*F-You money in case you ever need to leave.*

Liv went home, and we all got up and put our dishes away,
except for Grandma, who'd ditched hers on an end table in
her rush. I went up to my room. I was suddenly all alone, as
if the funeral was over and the people were gone and now it
was just me and the knowledge that someone had died.
Everyone else had done their job, and it was my job now to
do the moving on.

    I would miss . . . I would miss Daniel's hand. Holding a
hand. I would miss him sitting on the couch beside me on the
weekend. Wait—weekends. There would be no plans when
there were always plans! No more movies, no more filled
Fridays and Saturdays. No more nightly phone calls. No more
having the spot of boyfriend filled. I was used to having him
around, and now he wouldn't be. He'd had a place in my life,
like homework or volleyball practice. It was similar to the feeling you get when it's summer and there's no school or home-

work and there's this sudden space where school was. There was a sudden space where Daniel was.

Some kind of construction equipment, a bulldozer, was digging a deep trench in my internal foundation. God, it hurt and I hated to hurt. Hurting made me aware of bad choices, made me feel like I'd messed up, like I wasn't capable of proper functioning. It suddenly felt like Daniel was really and hugely important to me. Like maybe if I felt like this, I had really loved him after all. I decided I should write to him. Express how I felt. I took out a piece of paper. I'd write him a poem. I'd never written a poem in my life. I don't even like poetry. I wrote his name at the top. *Daniel.* I looked at all of the white space there underneath. I crumpled up the paper, threw it toward the wastebasket, and missed. I would call him instead. I would call him and tell him how I felt because maybe I had missed my chance at love by being too distant. We could have had something great if I'd have let it be great, instead of . . .

Instead of not really liking him, I remembered.

I needed to get myself together. I needed to take some action. God, I was one step away from pleading with Daniel for something I didn't even want! Liv had sobbed over Travis Becker. Aunt Annie had sobbed over Jack Xavier. Mom had sobbed over OCD Dean. I was not going to sob over Daniel Jarvis.

Rejection might make you feel small and crappy, and rejection might call for all those who love you to gather around and prop you up. But rejection could do something else, too. I felt some weird stirring of courage, or maybe just recklessness gathering, building from the night before when Dad put those brownies in the oven to now, when I refused to make Daniel Jarvis some altar I'd throw myself on.

I had the sense again of being an art film, of pieces of me in some confusing order. I wanted one truth, my own truth. A single diamond.

Mom wouldn't like me doing what I did next, and neither would Dad. But if the Hoffmans were strong women, that meant you did what you needed to.

Directory assistance.

"What city?"

"Orcas Island, Washington," I said. "Joelle Giofranco?"

"I have a J. Giofranco."

"Okay." My heart was beating, thudding away with some kind of guilty importance. Bravery was speeding through its phases right there while I held the phone—the wild moment of *yes,* the certainty of your own stupidity, the realization that you'd just assured yourself either terrible regret or great triumph, no in-between. It was late, and Frances Lee might not even live with her mother anymore, far as I knew. I'd have to explain myself to Joelle, a woman my father had been married to but whom I didn't know at all—a woman with whom he'd shared Christmas mornings, a bed, divorce papers with their signatures side by side.

"Hell-o."

I was struck dumb. I instantly understood what that expression meant then. Thoughts had completely vacated the premises. The idea of stringing words together in some meaningful way seemed like figuring out one of the mathematical equations that only mini genius Victor Wattabe and our teacher, Mr. Evanston, could solve.

"This is Quinn Hunt," I said. "Barry Hunt's daughter? I'm looking for Frances Lee."

"This is Frances Lee. *Who* is this?"

"Quinn?" I hated the question mark in my voice. As if I wasn't quite sure who I was, which was maybe the truth. Which was maybe exactly why I was calling.

"*Quinn*-Quinn, as in my father's daughter?"

"Yes," I said.

"Whoa, okay. This is sort of a surprise. Is Barry okay?"

"Yeah, he's fine. He's perfect," I said.

"And he'll be the first to tell you so," she said.

I smiled. "It's just . . . me," I said. "I was just hoping maybe I could talk with you."

"Thank God you're not calling to say he needs one of my kidneys," she said.

"I didn't think I'd even find you there."

"I'm home on break. But you almost missed me, because I'm just heading out. Friends, bonfire, cha-cha-cha. Can we talk tomorrow?"

"Sure. No problem." My heart was beating ridiculously. I felt like I was some twelve-year-old, calling a boy for the first time. But this was my . . . The word felt strange. The word belonged to Sprout. *Sister.*

"Phone number," she said.

There was a broad span of silence, because nerves had made me stupid. I was sitting on the other end of the phone with a pen in my hand, thinking she was going to give me her phone number, something which, of course, I had just dialed.

"*Your* phone number?" she said. "So I can call you back?"

"Oh, right," I said. My face got hot. I was blushing with weird-awkward humiliation. God, I was stupid. Stupid, stupid. I'd always been the older, capable one, the one who held Sprout's hand and told her what to do. I wasn't used to feeling so *young*.

Still, when I gave Frances Lee my number, there was something else besides humiliation that I felt. Some twist of hope. The sense that the velvet cord had just been lifted up, and that I would now be allowed through.

"Tomorrow," Frances Lee said, and then she was gone.

# Chapter Six

That morning, the last day of school of my junior year, I came downstairs for breakfast and saw that Grandma had snuck something onto Mom's list again. Underneath *He is in any way violent or explosive,* Grandma had written, *You feel you need to pay a private detective to get the truth about him.*

The list was getting pretty lengthy. Two pages now. Our fridge was looking like a self-help book. I left the house, walked into the kind of dewey-grass, sunny-sky day that made you feel like the summer had already promised you something. We had to be at school for only two hours, which seemed stupid. Two hours, and all that really happened was yearbook signing and locker cleaning, which really meant kids dumping stuff on the hallway floors, making the last day hell for some weary custodian. Two senseless hours—made you wonder if some rigid rule-freak was in charge over at the school-district office, someone who probably had thousands of those little KEEP THIS TICKET tickets.

I didn't see Daniel, or rather, I saw the back of Daniel's head once, and Daniel's car in the parking lot, but he must have been avoiding me, because the locker we shared was cleaned of his stuff; the pictures of his friends were gone and only the bits of tape that held them up were left. He didn't take any of the pictures of us, which meant that either he was being kind or cruel—giving me them, leaving me with them, who knew which.

There were too many endings—school over, Daniel over. Liv

came by with Zaney and Kerry, another friend of ours from volleyball, and tried to get me to come to Starbucks with them, but
I said no. I kept checking my phone (no call yet no call yet no
call yet), and I wanted to wait for Frances Lee by myself.
Waiting is one of those hard things best done in private. It's hard
enough to do a hard thing without an audience.

Ivar was home already, which was odd. He never got back
until three or four, but already at eleven he was lying on the
front porch, chin on his paws as if he, too, was feeling some sort
of loss. My appearance seemed to instantly cheer him, which is
a nice thing about dogs, because it instantly cheers you, too.
Dogs are a quickie self-esteem boost, for sure. He leapt to his
feet and swished his tail back and forth, back and forth.

"You're home early," I said. I looked down at him and he
looked up at me. It's not something I like to admit, but sometimes I forget he can't talk. I'll ask him a question and realize I'm
waiting for a reply. The funny thing is, he just looks back at me
patiently as if we'd gone through this a thousand times. *I can't
talk, remember?* Oh, yeah.

Ivar shoved past me on the stairs and raced me to the
kitchen and had a big, long, sloppy drink out of his water bowl
as I unpacked my backpack and waited for my phone to ring.
Another thing I shouldn't admit is how many times I actually
checked to see if the phone rang even though I knew good and
well the phone didn't ring. I had it right beside me and . . .
silence, and yet I kept flipping it open to see if I'd missed
Frances Lee. I even checked the settings to make sure I hadn't
silenced it accidentally, which made me think of Mom going
through the garbage, frantically searching for the IRS refund

check when she'd already put it in her purse to take to the bank. We can really freak ourselves out when something good's about to happen. Good can freak us out as bad as bad can.

It's amazing how much stuff you save, and I sifted through science notes and index cards from an English debate and daily math assignments and decided that my someday grandchildren wouldn't give a shit about any of it. All that work and effort and there it went, slid into the trash with the eggshells and coffee grounds. I kept my film studies paper on *The Phantom of the Opera,* an English paper about *A Farewell to Arms,* tossed pens that didn't work anymore and a dried-up highlighter, and wondered if I should just call Frances Lee back myself.

I heard the bus groan and creak to a stop out front, and a few minutes later Sprout flew through the front door, hauling a big paper bag full of school stuff, and her blue-and-green padded lunch bag and her backpack made of tie-dyed canvas. She was wearing Grandma's crocheted hat even though it was warm, and her braids stuck out from underneath. She wore red knee-highs with her denim skirt, and she could look like the kid with no friends, but somehow it all worked on her. Someday she'd probably marry a great guy somehow born from stuffy Republican parents who would disdainfully call her "the creative type." She'd drive them crazy with unmatched silverware and babies she'd name Grace and Beauty.

"Get ready, people, it's summer!" she yelled.

"No people, just me. Grandma left a note that she went to the dollar store."

"Cool. Maybe she'll buy more of those squirrel statues that have snow-globe stomachs."

"Or use-once-then-break screwdrivers."

"We still have that huge bag of straws she bought last time," Sprout said.

"When's the last time you used a straw?"

Sprout dumped her bag and was already looking for post–school satisfaction in the fridge. "True. Hey, maybe I'll use straws all summer."

"It'll be the Summer of Straws," I said.

"Some people have Summer of Love, but not us," she said. The fridge door closed, and now Sprout was hunting in the kitchen drawer. "Aha." The Bag o' Thousand Straws was tossed out. Sprout poked a hole in it with her thumb, plucked one out. She put a red-striped straw in her mouth and pretended to smoke it like a cigarette.

"Stop that or you'll ruin your lungs," I said, and then the phone rang. My heart thumped around and I started to immediately cushion myself against disappointment. My self-protection mode was on the default setting, so much so that it was like I was wearing a permanent emotional life jacket. Before I opened my cell phone I remembered the possibilities. It might be Liv. Maybe Zaney. Maybe Daniel, pleading for forgiveness. I peeked. Frances Lee's number! *Oh God, oh God, oh God.*

"Where're you going?" Sprout said. "Who *is* it, Quinn? New boy-friend! Man, you don't waste any time, do you?"

"Hello?" I jogged out into the hall, up the stairs. Shut the door to my room. I was panting. I needed to go to the gym or something.

"Quinn?"

"Yes, it's me."

"So this is weird," Frances Lee said. "You, me, phone. What, I've met you once?" Frances Lee was the type to get right to the point, I could see.

"Once, I know," I said.

"So, what do I owe the pleasure to? No, wait, that's wrong. To what do I owe the pleasure? Whatever, you know what I mean."

I paused. Why, exactly, *had* I called? What did I even want from her? "I guess I need answers to a few things," I said.

"Not something I'm exactly known for," she said. "Questions, yeah. Answers, not so much. Wait, can you hang on a sec? My mom's trying to come in and she's carrying all the grocery bags at one time. God, I don't know why she does that. They're hanging all up her arms."

"Sure."

The phone clunked down and I heard her voice in the distance. "Jesus, Mom. Here." And Joelle's voice, "You know I hate making more than one trip." There was the rustle of bags and the clunk of hard glass bottoms set on countertops, a few whispers I couldn't hear, and then Joelle's voice, sounding surprised. Sudden quiet.

"Okay, I'm back," Frances Lee said. "Answers, you were saying."

"I know this is strange." I stumbled. "I just, you know, Dad came back into our life a few years ago. I'm just trying to understand everything."

"Identity crisis."

"I guess."

"*That* I know about," she said.

I started to relax. I sort of liked her already. She reminded me of someone, but I didn't know who. "Something strange happened recently," I told her. "Just after Dad's girlfriend left."

"Is this the one named after a cheese? Or did he have one after her?"

"No, the cheese." I felt bad saying that. I liked Brie. "Brie," I said. "She was actually really nice."

I heard Frances Lee shout in the background. "Ma! Barry left the cheese."

"I think it was the other way around," I said. "She left him."

More yelling. "The cheese left *him*!"

"Not possible," I heard Joelle say. "Barry never gets left."

This wasn't exactly how I saw this conversation going. I didn't think I'd be having this talk with Joelle, too. Joelle, and the other women in my dad's life—they were, I don't know, *other women*. There was Mom and Dad, and even Brie felt like some sort of outsider we'd agreed to let in. It was strange to me that Joelle was, in a way, right here with me, a woman who'd had more history with my father than even my mother had. I felt like I was reading his diary. Maybe I'd find out more about him than I really wanted to know.

"After she left, something happened," I said.

"*What* happened?"

I twisted my ring around my finger. The one Dad had given me, with the arms holding the heart. "Something appeared in his living room. Something of hers. A statue. Something I'm sure she doesn't know he has."

"So he took it. Probably wants to punish her."

"But I think it's more than that, because I started looking at other stuff there, underneath things, and there were women's names on some of them. Certain objects. I think he took things from women. Maybe something from every woman." It sounded sort of crazy, said out loud.

There was silence as Frances Lee thought about this. "You think he stole something from every woman he's been with."

"Yes."

"And why would you think this again?"

"There were names on things. Women's names."

"Like some sort of freaky fucking museum. A woman-object trophy museum."

I hadn't thought of it like that. "I know this sounds nuts, and your mom probably just gave it to him, but is she missing a painting?"

"Hold on." The sound was muffled, a hand held over the phone to quiet her voice, but it wasn't doing much good. "Mom!" I could hear her shout. "Did Barry ever take a painting of yours?"

Joelle had disappeared I guess, but now her voice got loud again, same as an approaching siren that stops somewhere in your neighborhood. ". . . and he knows I know. Do you realize how much that painting's worth? Most valuable thing I had."

And then, a still muffled Frances Lee to Joelle again: "Why didn't you tell him you wanted it? Why didn't you call the police or something?"

"You don't call the police on your child's father, at least not for a painting."

"Fuck," Frances Lee said. But this was loud and clear, said to us both. She was back. "I guess the answer is yes."

"It's hanging above the fireplace," I said. My stomach felt heavy and sour, the way it does when you might get sick. I loved my father. I didn't want to betray him. There were pieces of me, big, screaming pieces, that wished I'd never made this call, that wished I'd never looked under that statue or behind that painting.

"Maybe that's a reason I always had to meet him somewhere else," Frances Lee said. "I've never been invited to his house, do you know that? I've never been in my father's *house*."

I didn't know what to say. Frances Lee was his daughter. There had to be a reason she'd not been allowed there, right? A reason that made sense?

"Well, we're going to want it back. You know that, don't you? We're going to want it back."

My hand was sweaty. So slick with sweat I was lucky I could hold that phone. Had I thought that far ahead? Because now what? Because, God, what had I set in motion? I pictured a blank spot above his fireplace. I pictured that blank spot being my fault. I pictured my father's reaction, my father's absence. No, I wanted to say. No. He was my father, and I needed him. No.

"Yes," I said.

"Can you bring it to us?"

Silence. I couldn't speak. I couldn't do that, I knew. I heard Joelle's voice again. "She can't do that, Frances Lee. You should know that more than anyone."

I wanted to cry. Maybe with relief. Maybe with that landslide of feeling you get when someone understands you. "I don't know if I can do that."

"Okay, sure. Maybe I can go get it. I don't know. We don't want him to know you told us, is that it? Is that right?"

"Yes," I whispered.

"Oh, Quinn," Frances Lee sighed.

"I don't want to hate him," I breathed.

"I know you don't. I know that. You don't want to hate him. But you do want to understand him."

"I guess."

"You kind of have to."

"I guess."

"To see yourself."

I didn't say anything. It seemed like we sat there on the phone for a long, long time. We sat there until Frances Lee sighed again and then spoke. "Let me just think about this, okay? Like, maybe we should get together or something. I'll call you."

"All right," I said.

She hung up.

My life, which for a day had felt on some edge of newness and change, abruptly slid back to being just the way it was. I wanted to lay down and sleep. I doubted I would ever hear from her again. But I had barely set my head on my pillow when my phone rang again. I almost didn't look. I had no room right then for Liv or anyone else. But I did look. I sat upright again.

"I've got an idea," Frances Lee said.

I went from despair to joy in about ten seconds. My heart swooped. "What?" I said.

"It's a little crazy."

"Okay." I was in the mood for crazy.

"We'll give it all back."

"Okay." I didn't exactly know what she meant.

"We'll do it together. Then we'll face the consequences. Together. You won't have to do this alone."

There was the sense of gathering again, some strength of forces. That something you feel when someone is right there beside you to pick up the other end of a heavy thing.

"It'll be some karmic trip," she went on. "Some act of karma. We'll go on a karmic quest. Pack it in my truck and give it all back. To the women."

"Starting with my painting," Joelle said in the background.

"Give back the stuff Dad stole," I said. "Go on some trip."

"Yep," Frances Lee said.

"We could just mail it," I said.

"You don't *mail* a quest," Frances Lee said.

"I'll have to think about this," I said. What I was thinking was, Mom would never allow it. No way would Mom ever allow this.

"Think about it and get back to me in twenty-four hours. I've always wanted to say that, 'Get back to me in twenty-four hours.' But actually, if we're going to do this, I've got to make plans. I told my friend Juan I might be able to help him move cross-country, and I've got to tell him yes or no."

"Okay," I said.

"There's only so many days of summer break."

"I'm still trying to imagine giving the objects back," I said. This wasn't just an empty spot above the fireplace—this was looting your own father's house. His *most prized possessions*.

"Wait, how much stuff is there?" Frances Lee asked. "There isn't, like, furniture or big shit, is there?"

"No. But I didn't look in the whole house. Maybe there's

more. I only saw five or six things. God, there could be a ton of stuff other places, I never thought of that. And these were the only things with names. How many more things don't have names?"

"We can't be responsible for his whole fucking life. We'll just do the few things you found. The five or six. Unless someone lives in Arkansas, or something. Mom'll get her painting, the cheese'll get her statue."

"How'll we know who they belong to?"

"Mom's known the guy forever. Do you have the names?"

"Yeah." *Jane, age 12. Olivia Thornton. Elizabeth . . . Abigail Renfrew. Abigail Renfrew!*

"So, we'll start there."

"I've got to figure this out," I said. What I'd have to figure out was what whopping lie I could tell to get away with this. I'd have to figure out if I could live with *all* the whopping lies I'd have to tell.

"Call me," she said.

"Thank you, Frances Lee," I said.

But she was already gone again.

My hands were shaking. I closed my phone and stared at it. I needed something, but I didn't know what. Something to drink. Food. An answer. I opened my bedroom door. Sprout was standing there with her arms folded.

"Boy oh boy, are you in trouble," she said.

Sprout followed me down the stairs and into the kitchen.

"Goddamnit, Sprout," I said.

"And I thought you had a new boyfriend," she said.

"Goddamnit, you know you're not supposed to listen in," I said.

"Good thing I did, is all I can say," she said. "Trouble is a-brewing." Gram's words again. Sprout had plucked off her hat, and her hair was all fuzzy-static on top.

"Find me some Fritos or something, I need to think," I said.

Sprout rummaged around in the cupboard, found those snack bags of chips that you need to eat three or four of to be sufficiently chip satisfied. "Here. And just so you know, you go anywhere with Frances Lee, I'm going too."

"We're not going anywhere," I said.

Sprout just laughed.

"Mom would never let us," I said.

"Mom would kill us. Dad would kill us. That just means we need a *plan*," Sprout said. "A plan that involves shading the truth."

"It seems so mean. Stealing from him. God," I said. "I don't know why I'm even considering this."

"Why is it that nice people can be so stupid and blind?" Sprout said.

I glared at her. "I told you, let me think about this." I tore open a dwarf-sized bag of chips with my teeth.

Sprout stopped, listened intently. "Ivar's in the bathroom. Ivar!"

"Someone left the door open," I said.

"Kleenex feast," Sprout said. She rushed into the bathroom, and a moment later Ivar came tearing out of there. Ivar was an old dog, but he had sudden bursts of criminal behavior, like a senior citizen who suddenly decides to rob a bank. He jetted out of the bathroom fast as a lightning bolt, with a flash of white Kleenex stolen from the garbage can clenched in his teeth. "Open up, Ivar. Open," Sprout said. She'd caught up to him, had her hands around Ivar's fierce little chin. Finally, reluctantly, he released his treasure.

"Gross," Sprout said.

"Who forgot to shut the door?" I said. I knew who, and I was looking at her.

"Who forgot to tell me about Brie's statue? It's what a good sister would have done," she said.

I didn't say anything, just munched my chips. She was right, of course.

### Abigail Renfrew:

*There is a song by the Eurythmics that begins, "Love is a stranger in an open car; to tempt you in and drive you far away." In love, I have traveled so far from who I am that at times I have not been able to see the barest outline of myself. It's not something I like to discuss, this self-betrayal. Only in my art do I tell my own secrets and the secrets I have kept of the men I have been involved with.*

*So, reluctantly: I met Michael Banks, quite apropos, in a college psychology class. He was different from the other male students in that he did not spend his weekends guzzling beer and finding this interesting as topic for discussion. He was more sensitive than aggressive. He couldn't even bear to kill a spider, or so he would repeatedly tell you. He cared about other people more than himself, and he would tell you that, too. Secretly, I thought him a little fussy. He abhorred*

*signs of real life—dirty dishes, hair in a sink—and he'd place*
*a Kleenex over his nose when something smelled unpleasant.*
*His reaction to my cat's litter box was that of someone who*
*had stumbled on a horrific crime scene.*

*I first appreciated, a great deal, the fact that Michael*
*talked about his feelings. But eventually I realized that I had*
*entered a whole land called Michael's Feelings, a land we*
*explored every corner of until the soles of my shoes were thin.*
*His feelings, not mine. Or, my feelings about his feelings. Or,*
*about me hurting his feelings, which I apparently did quite*
*frequently. I could hurt his feelings by blinking incorrectly. He*
*became upset once because of a dream he had where I had*
*betrayed him. He'd analyze a statement of mine to get the real*
*meaning behind what I must have meant, and this would go*
*on to the point where I didn't know anymore what I meant*
*and didn't care. And then the criticisms began. If I cared*
*about other people, he said, I wouldn't dirty that chair by*
*curling my feet underneath myself when I sat. I didn't offer*
*the juice bottle to him before I took a drink first, how self-*
*ish. I talked too long to a friend and made him feel ignored,*
*how insensitive.*

*It became a moral nightmare. His last girlfriend was*
*much more caring, he'd say, than I was. I didn't respond imme-*
*diately to his calls, so obviously I didn't love him. I didn't say*
*thank you when he brought over the blanket—was I always*
*so ungrateful? My relationship with him felt less like love than*
*a chronic condition.*

*I would like to say that I cured this condition with a*
*decisive break, but I did not. He had, after all, been so nice*

*when we met, and so why had he changed? How had this turned so horrible? I had wrecked things, I was certain. I wasn't handling it right. I was inexperienced in relationships. Or perhaps he was depressed—as a child he was relentlessly criticized. I was selfish. We needed more time together, perhaps, or less time together.*

*Many years later I realized that there was only one reason why he acted as he had, and that was because that's who he was. We were both having a relationship with his issues, not with each other. And because he was nice in the beginning did not mean he was a good man. Most everyone is nice in the beginning. Underneath all Michael Banks's sensitivity and unselfishness was a very insensitive, self-centered person. There was no mystery there. Only a person who was not what he seemed at first.*

*When I understood this, I created* The Stain. *It is a clay figure of a woman on her knees. Her head is bent down and her hands are on her chest as if trying to see a mark of some kind.*

*I wish, too, that I could say that I never again got in the open, dangerous car of that song . . . But it would be a long while before I moved from sculpting in clay to sculpting in metals.*

Grandma came home from the dollar store just before Mom was expected back from work.

"That Bernice Rawlings is a nutcase," she said. Bernice Rawlings, our neighbor, was a librarian at the Nine Mile Falls library. If you went there and asked her for a book about race relations, you'd somehow leave with *The Tormented Childhood of Marilyn Monroe.*

"Did she take our mail again?"

"Worse. She was hauling our garbage cans into her garage. She's got Old Timer's disease, I just know it. My God, we almost wrestled. I nearly had to grab that swag of flesh under her arm before she stopped." Grandma set her purse on the kitchen table with a clunk.

"What, no bags?" I said. "Use an oven mitt, for God's sake, Sprout," I said. She was surprising Mom by cooking dinner and I was supervising. This was usually my summer job, supervising Sprout, but I was guessing this would be my last year of it. I started the job when I was twelve.

"I'm not stupid. The oven's not even on yet," she said.

Grandma, I noticed, was sneaking out of the kitchen and hadn't answered my question yet. "I thought you went to the dollar store," I said.

She turned around, and her cheeks were flushed. Of course, she *had* just nearly wrestled Bernice Rawlings. "There was nothing of interest," she said prissily.

"No figurines of praying dogs? No Fourth of July hats?"

"I was tempted to get the Bible on CD for the house—Thou shalt mind your own business, and all that."

"Ooh, low blow," Sprout said from the sink. She was filling a pot with water for spaghetti, her specialty. Of course, spaghetti is everyone's specialty because it is pretty hard to mess up.

"Huh," I said. "Interesting." I remembered what Mom said, about secretive people having secrets. You don't go to the dollar store without coming out with something, you just don't. It's not exactly one of those places you go in and tell some salesgirl, *No thanks, I'm only looking.* At the least, you buy a pack of batteries and a picture frame.

Grandma's sneaky back was already making a beeline out the door. I didn't have time to think more about it, though, because right then Sprout lifted up the wrong end of the spaghetti package, the strands cascading and sliding out the hole in the bottom and onto the floor. We'd picked up the last of it just as Mom and Annie came in the front door.

"She asks for a no-foam cappuccino, which always pisses us off, because a *cappuccino* by its definition is espresso with *foam!*" I could hear Annie say. "You want no foam, then you want a cup of freaking coffee, okay? She wants it extra hot, and with one and a half packets of Equal, as if she's going to know the difference between one and two, and then she says it's too hot and wants it done again. Her life's so miserable that she needs to come kick a barista? Get her little boost of four-ninety-five power? Control in a cup. Wearing this little freaking tennis outfit, too."

"Man," Mom said. But you could always tell when Mom wasn't really listening, because it was like her voice had left the room. She poked her head in the kitchen. "Hi guys."

"Last day of school surprise!" Sprout shouted. Steam was coming off the pot, and Sprout's face was red and shiny from heat.

"Wonderful," Mom said. "Wonderful kids." She beamed, as if seeing our greatness for the first time. She gave us each a squeeze.

"You're in a good mood," I said.

"And why not? It's the last day of school and my kids made dinner," she said.

"Grandma went to the dollar store and didn't buy anything," Sprout said.

"She's being so fiscally responsible these days," Mom said. She sounded a little prissy too, just like Grandma.

Aunt Annie kicked off her shoes. "You never go to the dollar store and not buy anything," Aunt Annie said. "Batteries, at the least."

"That's what I thought," I said. "Remember when Grandma decided to start a business making hats?"

"And then she wanted to do that dog walking thing," Annie said.

"That would have been cool." Sprout said. She stirred with the old wooden spoon we'd had forever. It had burn marks all over it.

"Maybe she's starting a new business. Selling stuff on eBay, or something," I said. This would explain all her recent behavior. "Maybe she was at the dollar store looking for good stuff to sell for *three* dollars," I said.

"She should sell some of the hundreds of balls of yarn she bought to make those hats," Mom said.

"We've still got the flyers for the dog-walking business," Annie said.

"She walked Tucker a few times," Sprout said. "When Will Green was on vacation."

"I just wish she'd get off the computer every now and then," Annie said. "Give someone else a chance."

"You just want to investigate Quentin Ferrill. Cheaper to do it yourself," Mom said. She tore off the end of the French bread and took a bite of it.

"No, I don't," Annie said. Which meant, yes, she did.

"Sprout, you're cooking from now on. That smells fabulous." Mom sat in a kitchen chair. She really was in a good mood.

"One and a half packages of Equal. God, what a bitch," Aunt Annie said.

### MARY LOUISE HOFFMAN:

*Here's something I definitely never told my daughters, and never will. I had a one-night-stand in college. I don't even remember his last name. Brad. I would have been the first person to have said how stupid that was. The first. I went to a fraternity party (what a cliché) with my friend Nancy. I got to talking to this guy, Brad, and the next night we went out. It happened in his car. I've never told anyone, not even Nancy, who was my best friend then. I was too ashamed. I don't know what I was thinking—I wasn't. It seemed like one of those experiences you were supposed to have in college, I guess, was how I rationalized it later. God knows what could have happened. I was lucky. I was stupid. The sum total of things I knew about him: He was a business major. He liked Billy Joel. He skied. His brother had cerebral palsy. I remember that. Now, somewhere in the world there's a guy named Brad who shared this moment with me in a car. Maybe he lives in this city. Maybe he lives in Kansas, or Berlin. Maybe he remembers or has forgotten. Maybe he has kids he'd never tell either.*

*Again—you want them to know, but don't want them to*

*know. Too often in my life, love has been defined as "humili-*
*ation with occasional roses."*

    *We look down our noses at people who've made mistakes*
*in relationships. She's so stupid! How could she do that! Our*
*superiority makes us feel better. But I'd bet everything I have*
*on the fact that people who claim to have a perfect record in*
*love are either lying or have very limited dating experience.*
*People who say, I'd never do that! Some day, unless you are*
*very, very lucky, you'll have a story to tell. Or not to tell.*

That night at dinner, Mom discussed with Sprout all of the Parks
Department activities she could sign her up for that summer.
Pottery. Horseback riding. Swim team. Sprout kept catching my
eye, making hers big with *Do Something* urgency. I knew what she
was thinking. We had to keep the time open for Frances Lee. The
karmic quest could not be interrupted for a coil pot.

"What's going on with you two?" Mom said.

You couldn't get anything past that woman. "Nothing," I
said.

"Nothing," Sprout said.

Mom rolled her eyes. There was no way we were going to
pull this off.

"You're awfully quiet, Mom," Aunt Annie said to Grandma.

"Sore throat," Grandma said. She put her hand to her neck.
"Eck, eck."

Under the table where he lay, Ivar sighed through his nose.

Right then, every one of us had a secret. Every single one of
us in that kitchen.

# Chapter Seven

After dinner, Sprout came into my room, shut the door. She leaned her back against it and folded her arms.

"Well?" she said.

"Well, what?"

"I want to go on a karmic quest with Frances Lee. I want Brie to get her statue back."

She sat down, right there by the door. She circled her arms around her knees. She was wearing her pink bathrobe with the butterflies on it. On the collar she'd stuck a pin that had a picture of a dog in sunglasses.

"I've been thinking. This isn't an overnight trip. We don't know where these women live. Brie and Joelle—right there, that's a day."

"So, we do it when we're at Dad's. We're with him on those weekends anyway. We tell Mom we're with Dad. We tell Dad we're with Mom."

It had possibilities. "They don't talk to each other anyway," I said.

"The right hand doesn't know what the left hand is doing," Sprout said. Grandma always said this too, especially after she watched the news.

"Okay." My mind was clicking. I got a pen from my desk—sometimes I thought better with a pen in my hand.

"Don't write anything down. We can't leave evidence."

"You're right," I said. "The weekend with Dad . . . What if it takes longer? Plus a day or so? Who knows."

"He's taking us on a trip," Sprout said.

"She won't like it, but we'll tell her we feel we need to go. All those missed years, getting to know him, blah, blah."

"I can cry if we need," Sprout said.

"Subtlety is best." I sat down on my bed. I realized I was still holding that pen, and I tossed it back to the desk. My aim was bad and it hit this stuffed bear, Ariel, I'd had since I was little.

"He can take us to Paris," she said.

"Subtlety."

"Disneyland."

"Better."

"She always knows when something's going on," Sprout said.

"I know."

"Like she's got some Early Warning Detection System. I can't even think about doing something wrong and she knows."

This wasn't helping. "This isn't helping," I said.

"We just gotta be like spies, is all. Outsmart the enemy."

We only had a few more weeks with Dad before he was gone for the rest of the summer. He'd perform at local outdoor theater for a while before taking off on the "World Tour." Mom would know this. We'd have to leave soon, if at all. Maybe Frances Lee wouldn't be able to make it right now. I shouldn't be getting Sprout's hopes up, I knew that.

And what about the bigger picture? We were getting swept up in the energy of a Great Idea. But what about that pesky little concept of post Great Idea consequences? Alienating Dad forever, lying to Mom—none of it was in the realm of good choices.

"I've got to think," I said. "I've got to be the responsible one here," I said.

Sprout stood up. "I hate it when you do that," she said. Her arms were crossed, her eyebrows down in a fierce V. *"Hate."*

"Shh, for God's sake."

"I'm not a little kid," she said. I thought she even stomped her foot, but I might be remembering wrong. Her words were a foot stomp, anyway.

"Relax," I said.

"You treat me like I'm two," she said.

"Stop acting like it, then."

"I'm not acting like it, you're acting like it." We were starting the downhill slide into a serious fight, proof right there what a disastrous idea this could be. The insults had already degenerated into I-know-you-are-but-what-am-I territory, the vicinity of Nuh-uh, uh-huh. She could send me instantly to that place of fury I was in when I was eight and saw my favorite Barbie floating in the toilet, thanks to her.

And then, right then, my phone rang. Over on my desk. Like a referee blowing a whistle.

The fight was instantly over. Sprout's eyes widened. "Frances Lee," she said. The words sounded religious.

"Maybe she changed her mind," I said.

"Maybe she wants an answer," Sprout said. The phone rang again. "Get it, Quinn!"

I snatched the phone from my desk, looked at the screen. "Oh shit," I said. "Oh shit, oh shit."

"What?"

"It's Dad." Ring.

"He never calls," Sprout breathed. Ring.

"Oh shit." The phone rang again and stopped.

"He knows," Sprout said. She was there beside me now, on the bed. We were both staring at that phone like it might burst into flames.

"They wouldn't tell him," I said. But I wasn't too sure. I didn't know Frances Lee or Joelle, either. Maybe Joelle got pissed. I'd certainly seen my share of pissed with Mom and Dad to know how that went. She wasn't going to talk to him and then, *bam*, before you knew it, she was slamming down the phone after yelling at him.

"He never calls, Quinn. When has he ever called?"

I thought desperately. It seemed hugely important to find an answer. "He wanted me to bring my CD player that time. To go jogging. Remember when he jogged?"

"For, like, a month," Sprout said.

"He called then."

"We're doomed," Sprout said.

I stood and paced, the phone in my hand. I opened it and looked—no message. "No message," I reported.

"You gotta call him back," Sprout said.

"God damn it. I should never have called Frances Lee. Never." I punched in Dad's number. Fine. If this was it, this was it. Might as well get it over with. Worse case scenario, I could lie. Lying was beginning to seem like some friend I could always count on.

Ringing. Sprout stared her support my way. I paced around. *God oh God oh God.*

"Quinn!" he answered. "Quinn-y, Quinn, Quinn."

I squinched up my face in confusion, shrugged my shoulders Sprout's direction. What was going on? Dad sounded happy. Really happy.

"Sorry I missed you. I was in the bathroom," I said. Ha, lies were already rolling off my tongue.

"No problem!" Maybe he was high. He sounded cheery as a Christmas carol. "Hey, I had something I needed to talk to you about." I held my breath. It was some trick. His voice would turn nasty, and then he'd skewer me.

"Okay."

"About the weekend after next," he said. "You guys are supposed to come over?"

"Yeah." My chest tightened. I waited for the blow.

"I was wondering if we could reschedule. Remember when you were over last? That reporter came by?"

"The reporter for the *Portland Journal*?" My heart climbed from ground to sky in seconds. It was suddenly a seagull, doing a gleeful swoop. He didn't know anything about Frances Lee and Joelle. This was about Dad and that junior reporter. I could jump up and down. Sprout's jaw dropped, her eyes got big. She put her hands near her chest, pretended to grab big boobs. She looked as giddy as I felt.

"That's her. She took me to some party and I met this woman there."

"A woman?" I gave Sprout a confused face and she gave me one back. The boob-grabbing hands went back down to her lap. This was a little hard to follow.

"I met a woman at this party the reporter took me to. We talked on the phone a few times. . . . See, she's got three kids, but they're going away weekend after next, when you're coming, and I was just wondering if maybe we could postpone. You know, until I'm back from tour."

"You want to postpone?"

"I know how disappointed you must be, and I tell you, my heart is breaking over it, but she barely is ever away from those kids, and this would be a good thing for all of us, you know, if I started getting back into life again."

"It's no problem," I said. "That's fine, Dad."

"It's a sacrifice on everyone's part, I realize," Dad said. "I'm being a little selfish."

"No, it's okay," I said.

"A person's got to look after his own needs first, though, I realize, in order to be able to give to everyone else."

"We'll see you when you get back," I said.

"I'll miss you like hell," he said.

"We'll miss you."

"Tell Charles I love her," he said. "And you, too." His voice was large. Words of love seemed to seal the deal. They were the checkmark next to the item on the list *Call kids and reschedule*.

We hung up. Sprout turned to me; she put her hands on my shoulders. Bore her shiny, happy eyes into mine.

"We've been given a miracle," she said.

I called Frances Lee.

"Let's do it," I said.

The sooner, the better, she agreed. I gave her the names for Joelle to investigate. We'd make a driving route after that, Frances Lee said, if any of the women were even in the area. On the list would be Joelle herself and Brie, of course. And then Jane (age 6), Olivia Thornton, and "Elizabeth." I paused before I told her the next name, the last name, the name that was a betrayal of Mom. I thought of the bust of that woman left there in my father's living room, and I felt sorry for it, the way you feel sorry for a barn with a sagging roof, or a child's shoe abandoned in the street. You couldn't only finish part of a quest—a quest was something you did all the way.

"Abigail Renfrew," I told Frances Lee. "That's the final one. A.R. I know she lives in Portland too." I remembered her house. That cat hair on the couch. She was still there, I knew. "Mom saw an article in the paper about her recently."

"One less mystery," Frances Lee said, as if Abigail Renfrew was actually a good thing. I remembered what happened when Mom saw that article: "Portland Artist Makes a Splash in the Big Apple."

"'Local artist Abigail Renfrew's newest work has gained acclaim among New York gallery owners,'" she read. Her voice was the kind of strong and sarcastic that could crumple at any moment. "'Adding the subject of water to the female figures she's created in the past has added new dimensions to her already interesting work,' Dawson Edwards, owner of three Tribeca galleries said. 'The interplay between wave and human body is a primitive yet timeless theme we respond to at our basest level, and Renfrew manages these connections with both energy and integrity.'"

"Blah, blah, blah," Grandma had said.

"'The interplay between bullshit and bullshit is a commentary on the ephemeral nature of bullshit.' God, I hate phony crap like that," Aunt Annie said. "Look, it's a freaking wave going over a woman's body. Big deal." She stood over Mom's shoulder, poked at the paper with her finger.

"I don't think 'integrity' belongs in the same paragraph as

Abigail Renfrew," Mom said. But her voice had gotten wobbly, enough so that I could tell that she was at the edge of tears. Everyone else could tell, too.

"Oh, honey," Grandma said.

"It's a freaking ugly statue," Aunt Annie said. "She looks like she was carved out of a Tootsie Roll."

"After all these years . . . ," my mother said.

"It still hurts," Grandma said. "I know."

Maybe we could just drop Abigail Renfrew's head sculpture on her porch and run, I thought.

"So, we'll meet at the Portland train station? I'll pick you guys up?" Frances Lee said. "I assume you have a key, or something?"

"He's got one hidden." My heart started to thud around again at the thought. This was stealing. We'd be stealing things out of my father's house. Stealing stolen things.

"Think Robin Hood," Frances Lee said. She'd been reading my mind. "And figure out a way to tell your mom, okay? I don't want to be charged with kidnapping, or something."

"Sure," I said, but didn't mean. There was no way that was going to happen.

"I might have to bring my boyfriend, Gavin's, little brother, Jake. Fine with you? He needs a ride to Portland. Musician, car breakdown, the usual penniless performer crisis. The rest of the group's meeting him there. Can't get his stuff on the train, et cetera, et cetera."

"No problem."

"Weekend after next, then," she said. "I'll call you with some sort of plan."

"Great," I said.

"This is totally weird and therefore totally fucking awesome." Frances Lee chuckled. "What I Did On My Summer Vacation."

### Joelle Giofranco:

*Let me just say something else. People go on and on about safe sex, yes? Well, if you ask me, safe sex starts long before the condom—just after "hello."*

"We're in," I told Sprout. She was in her own room, sitting cross-legged on her bed, waiting, her sleeves pulled down over her hands to keep them warm. Her room had posters everywhere, barely any white space—animal posters with lion cubs sleeping and pandas in trees; a movie poster with cartoon penguins; another of Mick Jagger holding his crotch that she'd gotten from one of Aunt Annie's boxes up in the attic and that Mom opposed until Grandma told her to lighten up. Sprout had a habit of snitching band flyers off of telephone poles whenever we went to Seattle, so she also had advertisements for DEADBOLT PLAYING AT THE TRACTOR TAVERN! and SUMMER HEMPFEST! and FREE PRIDE WEEK CONCERTS, DON'T MISS OUT!

"No way," she breathed.

"Yes way," I said.

"I was so worried."

"Worry no longer," I said, although I had a feeling our worries were only beginning.

"I just love Paris this time of year," Sprout said.

"Disneyland!" I reminded.

"Oops, right."

Oh, God, what had I done?

*OLIVIA THORNTON:*

*In med school, as part of the required psychiatry classes, we had to take these tests. Psychological tests. The results devastated me. I've always been too sensitive. But according to mine, I "lacked personal insight." I read that sitting in class and I almost started to cry right there. I never forgot it because it was probably true. No, I'm sure it was true. I could understand science, the science of the body, but my own heart? I didn't know what I felt half the time. I was the kind of person who just went along.*

*I know I had a hard time being honest in relationships, even to myself. The very first serious boyfriend I had—Jerry Bannister. I liked him for the first couple of months because he was this great singer. He was in the college musicals, choir, all that, and it was exciting to see him onstage, doing this thing I know I could never do. I'm basically pretty shy. Even now—put two bones back together, no problem. Sing in public? Never. But the real Jerry—I don't know. Did I even like him? He had this mother that treated me like I was doing something criminal by being with him. And his mouth felt all large and gummy when we kissed, and I couldn't get over that. Wide and rubbery. My insides would clutch up when he leaned toward me. I kept turning my head when he wanted to kiss me, and he thought it was because his breath was bad. He chewed a lot of gum.*

*I couldn't tell him I didn't want to date him anymore, because he really loved me. He kept saying how lucky he was and all. He was talented and nice and I felt like something must be wrong with me because I didn't love him too. Maybe*

*I was being too picky. Maybe I didn't want to be close to any-one. Maybe I'd just be the type who couldn't feel love all the way or something. I couldn't tell what was wrong, but what was wrong was that it just wasn't right. Finally, I went on this campaign, when I look back now, this actual* campaign, *to get him to break up with me. It was like some part of me was acting in my own best interests, even if I wasn't. I tried every-thing without even being completely aware that I was trying everything—I acted indifferent, and then I was sort of mean to him, and then I accused him of seeing someone else even though I hoped he would. I was hitting him over the head with an emotional shovel and still he wouldn't let go of my ankles. That's what it felt like.*

*I finally did this awful thing and just didn't show up for a date. I kept picturing him waiting and waiting, but I couldn't go there and face hurting him. When he called, I didn't answer. It went on for days, the calling, until it finally stopped. One time I saw him coming and I actually ran and hid behind the library building. It was awful. I felt like such an idiot. Everyone always said how smart I was, but look at me. I was doing this big, bold thing becoming a doctor, but I wasn't brave enough to take care of myself.*

*I was one of those awful people you hear about who does things like that—maneuvering, disappearing. I couldn't listen to my own body, which was screaming this one word—AWAY. I felt guilty about doing what I needed to. Guilty about looking after my own best interests above someone else's. I forgot that wanting out didn't require certain reasons or a vote, or agree-ment, or the other person being okay about it. It was simply*

*enough to want out. If it feels bad, it's bad, and you have the*
*right to change your mind, even if that means someone's upset or*
*disappointed. You don't owe someone your life. Years from then,*
*after Barry, even, I finally learned that it was all right to say*
*something wasn't working for me when it wasn't working. The*
*world doesn't come crashing down when you speak the truth.*

I lay in bed reading *Catch-22*, Daniel's favorite book, a copy he'd given to me on my birthday. I didn't bother to read it before; I didn't know why exactly I was reading it then. Maybe now that Daniel was gone, it seemed more important to understand him than it had when we were together. I guess this was proving Mom right again, because she always made the point that you'd better get to know someone really well at first, or else you'd be spending huge amounts of time trying to figure him out later. Anyway, I don't know if what I was doing could be called reading, anyway. More like, Eyes Moving Across Words. I'd been over the last few sentences at least seven or eight times, and still, no part of what was written had made the full trip to my brain. I'd even turned the page once, as if the rest of the body parts were doing the reading thing without the participation of my mind. It was like those times you drive somewhere and after arriving, realize you don't remember a single part of the trip.

The problem was, I was having a weird sense of unreality about what was happening. Had I really called Frances Lee, a sister who wasn't a sister? Did she really suggest taking things from my father's house and visiting the women from his past? Had I really agreed? Two days before, if anyone told me this would happen, I would say that they were crazy. But now this was my life, and this was what was happening in it. Two days can change a life. Hours can, a minute.

There was a tap at my door. "Quinn?" Mom.

"Come in," I said.

She was in her robe—a thin blue one with white clouds on it. Her hair was pulled back and her face was washed clean of makeup. She smelled like soap. "I was just thinking about you," she said. She sat down by me on the bed. Her toenails were painted orangey-pink, as usual, but she never painted her fingernails. She always said that toes needed all the help they could get. "What're you reading?"

I showed her the cover. The title seemed suddenly like a little fate-joke. Like the times you turn on the radio and there's a little musical message, like God might be a part-time DJ. You just did horribly on a final, bringing you down a full grade, and there's some old song going, *"You can't always get what you wa-ant"* and you just go, Ha, real funny.

"Didn't Daniel give you that book?" she said.

"Yeah."

She was quiet. "Are you doing okay with all that?" she asked.

"I'm fine," I said. "It wasn't exactly meant to be."

"Still," she said. She looked down, made the ends of her robe tie meet. "I was thinking, too, that maybe it's getting harder for you, to look after Sprout in the summer. You'd probably like to get a regular job. Have more time with friends."

"It's okay. I really don't mind." Hey, if I worked at Red Robin, I'd never be able to just take off on a trip and steal things from my own father.

"I really appreciate you, do you know that? I don't tell you that enough." She leaned over to hug me. Her face was glowy from being just washed, and maybe from something else.

"You seem happy," I said. "Different happy."

"Do I?" She got this little tweak at the corners of her mouth, the way she did when she'd been caught. I don't know if this was how it was with other families, but it was how it was with ours. A tweak, a twitch, a slight smile. You knew each other so well that you heard the paragraphs that lay behind small movements.

I nodded.

"Things are good," she said. "I got a couple of new clients today, and it's summer. Everything's hopeful, you know?" She shoved her hands into her cloud-robe pockets.

"Which new clients?" I asked. I sat cross-legged.

"I came in here to ask about you," she said.

"Huh," I said. "Hmm."

"Don't 'huh' me," she said. "I had a good day at work. Period." A lawn mower revved to life outside, probably Tony's, our neighbor. "Okay," she sighed. Mom kissed my forehead, got up to leave. Her robe, her painted toenails, her clean, happy face—they made me pause for some reason before I asked what I did next. Soap smells and happy toes—they were calm and present. Maybe it seemed a little unfair to drag them and her back to a place she'd come a long way from.

"Did Dad ever take anything from you?"

Mom stopped. She was in the doorway of my room—right between there and here. "He took a lot of things from me," she said.

"Like an object," I said.

"An object? Why do you ask? Does he have something of mine?"

"No, he just had this thing of Brie's. It got me wondering, you know, like maybe there were things of yours he had too."

"A few things went missing when we split up. A person moves out, it gets confusing, what's coming and going."

"I was just wondering," I said.

"It's a funny thing to wonder, isn't it, Quinn?"

I kept silent. I could see her weigh this, whether to pursue, the decision to let it go.

"All right. I'm heading to bed," she said. "Good night, sweetie."

"Good night."

"Quinn?" Mom said. She turned back around. She bit at the soft part of her index finger. Tony's lawn mower sounded suddenly loud, practically under my window, then retreated again. "About the stuff going missing? I didn't spend a lot of energy over it. It seemed the least of the heartbreak at the time, you know?"

"I guess," I said.

Mom wrapped her arms around herself. "The most important things? He had already taken those."

# Chapter Eight

*ELIZABETH BENNETT:*

*I'm clearer now than I've ever been, and I have a lot of anger. I think a lot about regrets and what's been lost. It comes over me like a fierce wave. Mourning. Wasted time. Draining relationships, trivial upsets, years vanished, spent in heartbreak. I remember when I was maybe four, one of my earliest memories—I laid on top of this red padded toy box I had and folded my hands over my chest and closed my eyes and pretended I was dead. I laid there and imagined what it would be like for some prince to come and kiss me alive. I still remember how that padded vinyl felt, and the hard wood underneath the body parts too heavy for a half inch of foam—heels, butt, elbows—when I finally sat up again. It starts so young.*

*It starts so young, and I'm angry about that. The garbage we're taught. About love, about what's "romantic." Look at so many of the so-called romantic figures in books and movies. Do we ever stop and think how many of them would cause serious and drastic unhappiness after The End? Why are sick and dangerous personality types so often shown as passionate and tragic and something to be longed for when those are the very ones you should run for your life from? Think about it. Heathcliff. Romeo. Don Juan. Jay Gatsby. Rochester. Mr. Darcy. From the rigid control freak in* The Sound of

Music *to all the bad boys some woman goes running to the airport to catch in the last minute of every romantic comedy. She should let him leave. Your time is so valuable, and look at these guys—depressive and moody and violent and immature and self-centered. And what about the big daddy of them all, Prince Charming? What was his secret life? We don't know anything about him, other than he looks good and comes to the rescue. I told this to Andy, the real love of my life, and he said, "A guy wears a white suit like that, he's probably got a boyfriend on the side."*

*I went for Mr. Charming himself in high school. Barry Hunt was my first serious boyfriend. If you look up "charming" in the dictionary, you'll see that it not only has references to strong attraction, but to spells and magic. Then again, what are liars if not great magicians? I once looked at Barry's picture from then and I couldn't see what it was that was so magnetic about him. It's as if that quality can't appear in a picture, same as vampires can't be photographed. He broke my heart. I remember seeing this pamphlet not long ago in my doctor's office:* Living with Heart Failure. *Funny. But in a way, that's how I felt for a long time after Barry and I broke up.*

*I learned later about the wives, women, broken relationships, hurting children. And you think, these are the men we obsessed over. These are the men we gave ourselves to.*

*We should not give away a moment to anyone who does not deserve it.*

🌀 🌀 🌀

"Elizabeth is Elizabeth Bennett, Barry's high school girlfriend," Frances Lee said. "Mom's sure of it. She said it was always, 'I should have just stayed with Elizabeth and saved myself a lot of trouble.' Elizabeth this, Elizabeth that . . . Love of his life bullshit. Supposedly they dated throughout high school and she left him when she went away to college where he met Mom not long after."

"Okay," I said. I made a pace-loop around my room. Sprout sat on the floor in my room, arms around her knees, rocking back and forth. Mom and Aunt Annie were at work, but Grandma was in the office, and I was nervous about getting caught. Sprout's back-and-forth was as irritating as some wide-load truck driving fifteen miles an hour in front of you when you're already late.

"Apparently she's a writer or something. Lives in Vancouver, Canada, last time Mom heard. Barry visited her once when he was still married to Mom, so this is something she has a pretty good memory of."

"Vancouver," I said. I threw a pillow at Sprout and she stopped.

"Right."

"Okay." Three hours north of here, while Portland was three hours south. The thing about starting things is that you never know how big they'll get once you do.

"Mom didn't know who Olivia Thornton was. Her knowledge of his romantic life post your Mom is pretty hazy, so she's guessing this was sometime after her. But I did some checking, and there's a Dr. Olivia Thornton in Seattle. Orthopedics, and Barry had that back thing from performing."

I didn't know about his "back thing." I didn't know that there was a "love of his life."

"That's probably her, then," I said. I thought about the objects and their owners—Joelle's painting, Abigail Renfrew's bust, Brie's glass statue. A clock, a vase, a mask. I thought about all of the other objects in that room—an Oriental carpet, a footstool that was needlepointed with a hunting scene. A music box, an old Victrola, an antique black phone with a dial, a Royal typewriter with ivory keys, a globe. Was one of these things Mom's? Did they all belong to women with broken hearts?

"No luck with 'Jane, age six,'" Frances Lee said. "So, for now, how about we pick up the stuff in Portland, swing back here to give Mom her painting. We'll pick up Jake to take him to his gig, head to Vancouver to see Elizabeth Bennett. Down to Seattle for Olivia Thornton. Back to Portland for the Cheese and Abigail Renfrew, voilà. The whole thing is done in four-five days, and we can rest in our good deeds."

"Great," I said. Four or five days. Sprout and I were going to have to go on a "trip with Dad." I tried not to show my panic. I was still nervous with Frances Lee. Riding along with her ideas was a bit like getting into a rubber boat and riding down rapids. I just held on and tried not to seem afraid.

"Too bad about 'Jane, age six,'" she said. "Maybe your Mom knows."

"I'll find out," I lied.

"Perfect," she said. "Over and out."

The lies were accumulating, same as the *Warning!* items on Mom's list. After dinner that night, Sprout and I joined Mom outside in the warm, summery night; Mom stabbed the point of a gardening shovel into the spiky stem of a dandelion and pulled, tossing it onto a pile of already limp weeds that lay on the walkway toward the door. A game of kickball was going on down the street. The mean boys, Sprout called them. You could hear the yells of "Move in! Move in! Easy out!" which might have proved her right. Ivar sprawled on his side on the lawn, his tongue lolling out. One ear was flipped back accidentally, and the whole picture made him look sort of crazy and incapable and not fit for regular society.

Sprout was laying it on too thick before we'd even opened our mouths—she'd hauled the garden hose over to a small hibiscus that Mom had just planted, watering without asking, then offered to get Mom some iced tea. When I told Mom about the trip, her shovel froze midway. She stopped kneeling, set the shovel down, sat flat on her butt on the grass. Ivar took this as his cue to come over and smell her garden gloves. "You're kidding," she said.

"This is a good thing, Mom," I said.

She shook her head, did a little eye roll that meant *You have no idea.* "This really concerns me," she said. "I hate to say it." Which is something people say when they don't hate to say it at all.

"There's nothing to be concerned about," I said. "We'll be fine."

"We'll be fine," Sprout said. She was drowning that plant.

"I can just see you both wandering around lost while he's on the pirate ride," Mom said. "Honey, that's enough water."

Sprout moved the hose to a juniper, stood above it, and let the water spill on top. She stopped a minute to water her own knees and her feet in her sandals. "We're not going to be wandering around lost," I said. "We'll stick together."

"I need to call him and discuss this," she said.

"No!" I thought fast. I faked outrage. Maybe I really did feel a little outrage, for me and for Sprout and for Dad and the trip we might have taken if he *had* wanted to. Which, of course, he hadn't. "I can handle this. I'm almost seventeen. In a year I'll be going to *college.*" Might be going to college. If I could find a way to pay for it.

"Charlotte is not seventeen," Mom said.

Sprout stopped watering her toes. "I'm not a baby," she said.

"He's our *father,*" I said. "He just wants to take us on a trip. He didn't exactly get to do that when we were little."

I could feel it, the slide down a steep, gravelly trail, the way your shoes start to skitter and then you have to run, even if you don't want to run. Sometimes when you ran, you ended up safely at the bottom, but sometimes your feet came out from under you and you landed hard.

Mom didn't say anything. I could almost read all of her possible responses right there, in the throbbing of that muscle in her cheek. A physical Morse code—throb, stop. Stop, throb, throb.

"I always wanted to go to Disneyland," Sprout said. "Bad."

Mom's jaw tightened. "It's a shame I always had to work all the time to keep the family going, or else I could have taken you," she said.

I felt the clawing of guilt for this imaginary trip, and for the real Dad-bounty of Xboxes and a house on the river and dinners out; I felt the push/pull, light/heavy, play/serious of Dad versus Mom, which I knew did come in part because Mom was the one with all of the responsibilities (basically, the word "responsibilities" meant Sprout and me). I knew that, I did. I knew it was easy to play for a weekend but not for days at a time, when you had to make sure Sprout got her math facts learned and we needed plates and cups for the orchestra party and the emergency forms needed to be filled out and the yard needed to be cleaned of dandelions. I knew that—I'm not stupid. But I just didn't want to be reminded of it all the time, because there was nothing I could do about it, and it wasn't my fault to begin with. The funny thing about divorced parents is, they'll be the first to tell you it isn't your fault and the first to make you feel like a lot of it is your fault.

Sprout just kept watering that juniper, and I know that it (and probably most junipers of the world) never got that kind of attention before. I followed a crack in the cement with the tip of my tennis shoe, and then did it over again.

Aunt Annie came down the steps, hurried past us in her heels and tight jeans. "Late, late for a very important date," she said.

"You, Quentin, and the private investigator?" Mom said.

"I was being stupid. I completely trust Quentin. I'm a lucky woman."

"Have fun," I said.

Annie got in her car, beeped us a cheery horn good-bye. Mom sighed. "Look guys," she said. "I'm sorry, okay? This is just a bit of a surprise. I can understand you want to go." Mom's knees were still bumpy from sidewalk impressions. "God, okay. Fine. A few days, right? It's a few days. Nothing disastrous can happen in a few days, right?"

"We'll have our phones," I said. This always seemed to reassure her, which was kind of funny when you thought about it. That phone could be anywhere, for all she knew—a mountaintop, another state entirely—but if you had it, she felt better.

"You'll have to get me all the information. A full itinerary."

"No problem," I said. That could be a problem.

Sprout, like me, had almost seemed to forget we weren't actually going. "Teacup ride, teacup ride," she said, and spun the water from the garden hose in a circle.

"She's going to dump him. I give her three weeks," Zaney said, and sipped her slushy iced coffee. Zaney, Liv, and me had just gone to the movies and were now squished around a table for two at Starbucks. The movie was one of those where the man and woman seem to hate each other, which supposedly means they're actually in love. These were rival news anchors, and after doing every backstabbing thing possible, hurling every insult and plotting every evil, they fell into bed and discovered they belonged together. But Zaney wasn't talking about the characters in the movie. She was talking about Daniel and his new girlfriend, whom we saw on the way out of the theater. They'd been sitting behind us the whole time, and now I imagined both of their eyes on me in the darkness as I shoved popcorn into my face, or did other humiliating things I would have been careful about had I known they were there. It was amazing, when you thought about it, how much of love, before and after, was about avoiding humiliation.

"Two to three weeks," Liv agreed. "You can always tell who has the power by what movies they go to. If we'd seen them in some exploding bus thing, I'd have said he had a chance."

"Did you see what she was wearing? Very dominatrix," Zaney said. She took off the lid of her cup and stirred the slush with her straw. "A black laced-up vest?"

"Daniel plus slut equals bad combination. His parents will have a heart attack and have to give more money to the church," Liv said. "God, we fucked up. Here we take you to a movie to get your mind off Daniel, and he's right there sitting behind us."

"How could he do that?" I said. "Just move on to someone else without so much as a good-bye?" I said. I was finding out something: You could feel jealous even if you didn't even really like the guy.

"Someone shoves laced-up tits in your face, who has time for good-bye?" Zaney said.

"He doesn't seem like the same person," I said. Which was true. Which was maybe what happened after you broke up. Maybe he was the person he'd been all along and you never saw, or maybe he was becoming a new someone else, but either way, he was a stranger.

"How do you ever really know someone?" Liv said. She was eating the center out of a cinnamon roll and leaving the hard outside on her napkin, which just showed how smart she was.

"I hate that question," Zaney said. "It makes me totally paranoid."

"You're supposed to trust, but how are you supposed to trust if you don't know if someone's trustworthy?" Liv said.

"Maybe there's another way to get a full picture," I said.

"Hire a private detective, like your aunt?" Liv said.

"Your aunt's hiring a private detective? Cool," Zaney said.

"Maybe the only way to get a full picture is to ask around."

I was working my way toward confessing to them about my dad. "Ask a lot of people who know him."

"Then, *bam,* someone still surprises you out of nowhere. You never know what's in someone's head," Zaney said. "He could be secretly waiting for the right moment to steal your underwear. Or your mother's underwear." She'd made herself shiver. She was right—the question *did* make her paranoid.

"Trust should be used sparingly, like salt," Liv said.

"I like salt," Zaney said.

I waited for a nice pause that meant a topic change was allowed, but it never came. So I launched right in. "I never told you guys," I said. "I'm going on a trip. For my father." *For my father*—it sounded like I was doing him a favor.

"Don't tell me you're all going camping or something," Liv said. Now *she* shivered. Camping was one of her worst fears.

"We're not going on a trip *with* him. We're going on a trip *about* him," I said.

"Childhood home, all that shit," Zaney said. "My father made us go back to his old house in Michigan which is now a Dunkin' Donuts. He kept walking around by the apple fritters trying to figure out where his bed used to be."

"I'm going with my half sister to meet the women Dad's had in his life."

Liv set down her cup, hard. Since it was only cardboard, this didn't have a very dramatic effect. More like a little *plick.* "What?"

"To meet the women in his life," I said. There in Starbucks it did sound shocking. Like I'd just told them something dramatic and improbable—I was going to Hollywood to become an actress. I was actually the child of Romanian royalty.

"What half sister?" Zaney said. "I didn't know you had a half sister."

"What's been going on that you haven't told me about?" Liv said.

I told them about the objects. About Frances Lee. About our trip to "Disneyland."

"I know this is your father, Quinn, but what kind of guy steals something from all these women he's loved? It's kind of sick," Zaney said.

"There's got to be some kind of explanation," I said. "There's got to be. I want to know what it is."

"Why does there have to be an explanation?" Liv said. "Maybe he was just pissed. Post-breakup pissed. I kept a couple of CDs from Travis that I knew were his, and I didn't even like the music."

"I guess you're right. My mother has all these family photos that are my Dad's. What does she care about his German great-grandmother in front of a piece of farm equipment?" Zaney said.

"I just want to understand," I said.

"Sure you do," Liv said. "But maybe you should just *ask*?"

"Truth is slippery," I said. And Zaney clicked her cup against mine in agreement.

### ANNIE HOFFMAN:

*Just after college—this guy, Tony. Can't remember his last name. Starts with a* T. *He was really handsome in a crispy, news-guy sort of way. Those anchormen. You know, that smooth hair and Ken-doll face? He was funny, easygoing. Great job, liked to travel. He'd just gotten back from Italy, some sort of cooking trip he'd gone on with friends. But something felt off, you know? I couldn't put my finger on it. I thought I was being too critical, maybe. Maybe no one would ever satisfy me. Yeah, it must be me, right? He went to church every Sunday, maybe that was bugging me. I've never been very religious. He kept wanting me to go with him, though. I'd try to joke him out of it. Is that a crucifix in your pocket, or are you just happy to save me? Ha-ha. I finally gave in. He said I should take communion because it was Jesus's actual body. I mean, there's no way it's his actual body. We know it's not his actual body when those wafers are made in some factory in Wisconsin. I felt forced, and I've never liked feeling forced, so I spit the cracker into a napkin after, when he wasn't looking, which I'm thinking is the religious equivalent of not inhaling.*

*Anyway, one day he tells me he'll be a little late because he's going to confession. He goes to confession, like, three days a week. What in freaking hell is someone doing going to confession three days a week? Who even does that much wrong to confess? I didn't even know people still went to confession.*

*I started to realize that maybe something was seriously wrong, here. My hesitation was for a reason. I kept trying to talk myself out of my second thoughts when they were trying to help me. My advice? When it comes to relationships, second thoughts should be promoted.*

"Look at you," Sprout said. "Awkward phase." She held up a photo of me when I was about eight, that year when your teeth suddenly look too big for your face. She handed it over for

Grandma to see. They were both sitting on the couch, two boxes of photos between them. Grandma had a little stack of pictures tucked under her leg.

"You grew into those teeth just fine," she said.

"Right. My breathtaking beauty would come later," I said. Sprout made gagging noises. She was right. No one would look at me and use a word other than "okay." "What are you two doing?"

"Taking a trip down memory lane," Grandma said. "Now this I like." She moved the glasses that she wore on a chain around her neck to the end of her nose for a better look. She peered through them as if she were appraising some fine piece of art. "Mmm-hmm," she said. "Very nice."

"Who is it?" Sprout said.

"Let me see," I said, but Grandma was too engrossed to show me, or else she was losing her hearing. I leaned over her and looked. "Aunt Annie. Glamour Shot. I think she got it for some boyfriend for Valentine's Day."

"No way that's Aunt Annie," Sprout said.

"Love the feathers," I said. "And what's swirling around her? Fake fog?" But Grandma just looked down the length of her nose and then tucked it with the others under the leg of her sweatpants. Maybe she was making a scrapbook.

Grandma breezed through various school photos of mine, Sprout as a baby, Ivar and me before Sprout was born, she and Mom and Annie when we all drove down to the Oregon Coast. She stopped, though, at a photo of Annie taken on some beach. "Well, this is a good one," she said. There went the glasses again, the head tilting, as she looked at it from various angles.

"Back in the days of string bikinis," I said. Annie was wearing a tiny, shiny orange bathing suit made out of small triangles of wet-look leather. "Why bother with clothes."

"She might as well have stuck on a few cheese Doritos," Sprout said.

Grandma set it aside with the others. "Who's this?" I asked. It was one of those really old photos that are sepia toned and serious. A man and a woman stood in front of a heavy, velvety curtain.

"Some dead relative," Grandma said without really looking.

"Look at Mom and Dad," Sprout said. They stood on the steps outside a church, Dad in a suit, Mom in her wedding dress with her white veil back over her head. Her smile was wide. They gripped hands. Gram was off to the side, holding me, I guessed. I was about a year and a half old when Mom and Dad finally got married—I wore a little pink dress and black shoes. Behind Mom and Dad, I recognized Grandma Yvette, Dad's mom, who wore an elaborate hat. She had her hand on the shoulder of a girl in a dress that looked like it was made from sewn-together bandanas. I looked closely. Small round glasses. Braids. Willful eyes.

"Is that Frances Lee?" I asked.

"Who?" Grandma said.

"Dad's daughter, you know, with his first wife."

"Could be," she said. But she wasn't paying attention. It reminded me of the times she'd madly hunt through her recipe box when she had a serious craving for something chocolate.

"She looks like me," Sprout said, looking down at Frances Lee.

I took the picture from her. "Her face is a lot rounder," I said.

We sifted through a few more—unidentifiable babies and Christmas photo cards of people we didn't know we knew. Oceans and sunsets from some beach on some evening, something someone thought was beautiful for a moment but that was now only a mystery in a box.

"Ha-ha, two heads," Sprout said. It was me at Snoqualmie Falls, standing on the path that led down to the water, and some bald tourist just behind me. By the magic of Mom's photography skills, we looked surgically connected, his chin to the top of my head.

"Siamese twins not separated at birth," I said. "Why do I get all the ugly pictures?"

"Not all," Sprout said.

"Have you ever thought about all the photos you're in around the world?" I said.

"I went to Mexico once," Grandma said. "Puerto Vallarta. With Otto."

"No, I mean in other people's pictures. Like, we've got this bald guy in our box, and he's probably living in Maryland with his wife and out-of-control kid. And our elbows and heads and coat sleeves are in albums all over the world, probably."

"My elbow's been more places than me," Sprout said. "Speaking of going places. Guess who was home all day."

"You," I said. I thought this was a complaint because I'd gone out and left her alone.

"Besides me. Besides Gram. And not Auntie."

"That leaves Ivar."

"Bingo."

"Weird." Ivar heard his name. His ears perked up into two

triangles. He got up and sniffed around the table. If you said his name, Ivar thought that meant he was getting food. Daniel used to have a friend like that.

"He's been home *every day* since school's been out," Sprout said.

"Maybe Ivar's in junior high," I said.

Sprout petted Ivar's head. He shook it when she stopped, his ears making their *flapflapflap* sound. I set the bald guy from Chicago back in the box. I'd just about had enough of disjointed life flashes, when one more photo caught my eye. Mom, in a cap and gown. College graduation, I guess. Some guy, also in cap and gown, had just scooped her up it seemed—her arm was around his neck, her legs dangled over his arm, one high heel nearly lost but hanging from her toes. In her hand she was gripping a box, I noticed. It was the box that caught my eye, even more than my happy mother held by this young man on a day of celebration. It was an enamel box with a design on it, too small to see. But the colors were familiar. I knew that box. A music box, I'd bet. With Renoir ballerinas dressed in frothy white.

"Grandma?" I said.

"Some dead relative," she said, without looking up.

"No." I put it under her nose, made her look.

"That's your mom and Irving. What a nice boy. She dated him all through her senior year of college."

"Let me see," Sprout said. "Irving. I'm going to give Mom a bad time about dating someone named Irving."

"Nice boy," Grandma said. "Oh, he was crazy about Mary Louise."

"What's she holding?" I asked.

"A present," Grandma said. She was done with the conversation, but I wasn't.

"From you?"

"No," she said. "Maybe from Irving? Maybe from her dance teacher. It had dancers on it, I think."

That box—I knew it was that box—sat on a table in my father's living room. When you lifted the lid, a song played. My mother's box. She, too, had something that needed to be returned to her.

"Irving." Sprout chuckled.

# Chapter Nine

Mom's tan arms, her hands on the steering wheel, her yellow sundress—they all gave me a wrench of guilt as she drove us to the train station. A wrench of guilt that collided with nerves and energy and excitement. I'd barely ever lied to Mom, and even then, I'd eventually confessed. The time I went to Paul Sanders's party instead of to a sleepover at Liv's, like I'd first told her. Second grade, when I lost my lunchbox and said Zachary Judd had taken it. Halloween, third grade. Ate a bunch of my candy when I was supposed to only have two pieces at lunch. My conscience has always been very responsible.

I was expecting Hell Ride, one of those awful times in the car when it's dead silent, the silence loud with all that's not being said. When you feel trapped by vinyl seats and glass windows, when you stare at that little handle no one uses above the door, or at the cigarette lighter that also no one uses. You stare, and wish on that object for the miserable car ride to be over, but of course it goes on for thousands of miles, even when you're just going around the block.

But the ride wasn't like that, not really. Mom did her usual mini-freak-out routine of asking us again and again if we had things we didn't even really need (Pepto Bismol, for example, which I probably hadn't used since I was six), and then suddenly panicked because she hadn't reminded us to put on sunblock before we went outside, and to reapply after we went swimming. She placed our itinerary by the telephone, the one

I'd typed up on our computer after researching flights and a great motel for us to stay in right by Disneyland (I'd gotten us a pool and an in-room coffeemaker). Mom stuffed Sprout's old bathing suit in her bag as a spare at the last minute, the one with rainbows on it that Sprout wouldn't be caught dead in, even if she could get it to fit.

But when we got in the car, Mom didn't have that tight forehead, the stressed eyes, the constant temple rubbing that I would have expected. Strangely, she seemed light, that's the only way to explain it. Yellow dress, maybe, but also she just seemed easy—one arm out the window, hair blowing in the wind, a small smile at the corners of her mouth. She wasn't the Mom I was used to. I thought about Mom in that picture, with that guy Irving holding her. I thought about that other picture, too, of Mom doing the cartwheel, her feet off the ground. It wasn't a Mom we knew, but that I could see a tiny glimpse of now. That little smile. Maybe we should have gone on vacation more often.

I started to relax. This was all going to be okay after all.

Sprout had brought a little patchwork purse of hers, and it was over her shoulder in a serious manner when we got out of the car. Her braids looked determined, if braids can look determined. Mom took our bags out of the trunk. We were only going to be gone for five days, but we had an extra bag each, to hold the cold medicine and spare underwear and Kleenex and fruit snacks that we never needed at home and wouldn't need now.

Mom folded her arms and looked at us. "Well, look at you two," she said. She smiled. This was a different good-bye. It wasn't the rushed, hurry-hurry-hurry of our usual trips, of the almost forgotten backpack, the quick kiss. This was one of those mom-moments, where they suddenly remember the passage of time. Time was always a sudden remembering for moms, it seemed.

She hugged us long and hard, kissed our heads. When we hugged, she smelled like shampoo and the clean perfume she wore. I thought about that music box, her music box, in the photograph. It was a good, pure thing, there, that day. You could feel that goodness in the way she held it, a treasured gift, a loved possession, a happy present at a happy time. Given and gotten with the right kind of intentions. And now it sat on a table in my father's house, and the words around it were bad ones: *snitched* and *stolen*, *forgotten*; *anger*, maybe. *Retribution*, *heartbreak*. I thought about tears and struggle, the road to now, as Mom stood here with her small smile and yellow dress. And I felt something else then about this trip, other than guilt about lying to her. I felt a sense of right, of doing right, of putting things back where they belonged. There aren't too many times, I've realized, when you have that feeling that something is happening that's supposed to happen, even if you don't understand it completely. And I had that then, as we said good-bye to Mom and watched the back of her yellow dress as she returned to her car, and I had it still as Sprout and I walked into the train station and headed into a something unknown but a something true.

### ABIGAIL RENFREW:

*That song, by the Eurythmics. It also says that love is "a dangerous drug." It can seem "like religion." You can "stumble in the debris" of it. Love is many fine things, too, of course. Go to a hundred other songs to hear about that. But what I should speak to is the fact that a bad relationship is a powerful thing; yes, a dangerous drug. It can hook all the better parts of our nature until our own good can turn into a terrible and unfortunate quality. We want to be nice people. We do not want to judge unfairly. We want to work hard for the right outcome. We want to be kind to someone who might be hurting. We do not want to be quitters.*

*If things were once happy in the beginning of a relationship, we will do a lot to get that to return; we will go miles for a bread crumb, sometimes. We are certain it has got to be there, the good, if it was there once. It can be addicting, the need to get back to that good feeling; and then, like an addiction, the lengths you go destroy you. I'm thinking of Haden's father here, the man I married. After Michael Banks's fussiness, Trent seemed strong and masculine and mysterious. But what I wanted back had never really been there. He was a temporary illusion, a mirage of water after walking in the desert. I had made him up. And he could have killed me.*

*You've got to stop the ride sometimes. Stop it and get off.*

She had a green truck, a green pickup truck, and that was one of the first things we learned about Frances Lee. She'd met us at the Portland train station, and the truck was parked at the curb, right near where Brie's used to be. Frances Lee's truck had a backseat, and stuff was shoved under the front one in what was probably a speedy effort to clean up. I saw the white and yellow of a McDonald's bag, the fat edge of a textbook, a squashed orange-and-green Jamba Juice cup. She'd flung open both doors, and loud, garage-band music charged out.

"Toss your stuff in here," she said. This was Frances Lee's voice I'd known from our phone calls coming out of the real her, which seemed strange. I'd gotten more familiar with that voice, with dealing with her as a Person on the Phone, but now she was here, herself, in physical form. She looked different than I remembered. Every time I had thought of her, I imagined the way she looked that time at the restaurant. I saw the wild black hair and the dark outlined eyes, the braided jute around her wrist. Every time I talked to her, I saw her in that same long coat with the fur all around the collar and down the inside. But now her hair was shorter—shaggy, down to her shoulders—and she wore a white peasant dress with little mirrors on it and blue beads, and the tattoo of the mermaid was still on her ankle. Sprout was staring at it, hard.

We got our bags in the back and then Frances Lee stopped organizing things and looked at us. She put her hands on her hips.

"Well," she said. It was exactly what Mom had said, but it was a different kind of "well." Mom's was a thoughtful well, a pondering well. Frances Lee's was a "what do we have here" well. A "look what I've done now" well. A "I guess I'll have to make the best of it" well. In the comforting distance of our phone conversations, we'd forgotten that we were strangers, and I could see Frances Lee try to decide who we were to her.

Sprout hadn't said a word. She'd gotten stone silent and the great feeling of an important mission that I'd had earlier seemed to suddenly zap into nonexistence, filled instead with a sense of things having gone horribly wrong already.

"This is my sister, Sprout," I said.

"Charlotte," Sprout said, and held on to her purse primly, like an old lady at a dangerous bus stop.

"Cool," Frances Lee said. We all stood there for a minute. We were people at a party who all knew the host but didn't know each other, and in this case, the host was my dad, who was somewhere on the Oregon Coast, boffing some new woman with three kids. My father, who was completely unaware that his own three kids were about to set off on a trip to steal his trophies and meet his lovers. Frances Lee seemed a bit stunned at the reality that she'd created. "So, hey, I guess we'd better get going," Frances Lee said. She walked around to the other side of the truck and got in. I felt stunned, too. You put things in motion, and then you go, Shit, look what I put in motion.

Sprout got in the back with the bags and I got in the front, and when I slammed the door, the Buddha figure stuck to Frances Lee's dashboard shimmied and shook. The car rumbled when Frances Lee turned the key. It was a roar, really, some kind of sick exhale that spit out something black and nuclear from the tailpipe.

"You like this?" Frances Lee shouted over the engine and the metal clatter of the music, nodded toward the CD player she had duct taped to the front console.

"It's great," I said. I could feel Sprout kick the back of my seat.

"This is my boyfriend Gavin's brother's band. I told you about his little brother? Jake Kennedy? He needs to get to Portland same time we'll be there, so we'll pick him up at home and he'll come with us, okay? They've got some beginner-band Sunday-night gig, and he wanted to visit his folks on Orcas, yabbedy, yabbedy, ya. Gavin's paying for gas, is what we need to concern ourselves with, though why those parents just don't buy him a fucking car with all the money they've got, I don't know. I swear to God, Gavin's got to be adopted, because he is such a sweet guy and his parents are—" She twirled one finger beside her head.

Frances Lee looked over at me, and I looked at her, and I saw another tattoo, under her wrist. A small butterfly, which was nearly squished against the steering wheel.

"That's too bad," I said. I was feeling like I was about ten years old, walking in to a high school classroom. I felt the awkward humiliation you feel when you're carrying a lunchbox around people who've probably smoked joints. Frances Lee looked suddenly tired. She felt around on the seat beside her, then opened her ashtray and pulled out a cellophane package of cigarettes.

"Mind if I smoke?" she shouted. She was already taking a cigarette out of the package with her teeth. We had gotten on the freeway, and the truck was now thundering and shaking with the effort, and the Buddha was having a rubber-toy seizure.

"I'm allergic," Sprout shouted from the back. "Asthma." She had no such thing. She just hated the smell of cigarettes. If we were anywhere in public where she smelled smoke, she'd wave her hand in front of her face dramatically.

The cigarette hung dejectedly from Frances Lee's mouth. "Really?" she said. "Shit." She plucked it from her lips, held the cigarette and the pack in her hand. She paused, and then suddenly flung it all out the window, the cigarette, the package, all. Sprout kicked my seat again. They'd done litter pickup along the streets of Nine Mile Falls in her third-grade class. For two weeks, you couldn't drop a bread crumb without getting shit from her.

In the side mirror I could see that cigarette pack getting smaller and smaller in the distance. "I've been wanting to quit anyway," Frances Lee said.

No one said a word. The silence between us jangled and clattered, same as that garage band. I tried to think of something to say, anything, but my mind was a vast wide desert of dry, empty thoughts. Nothing came to me, nothing. Bands, cars, what? School, her boyfriend, Gavin?

"How long have you known Gavin?" I asked.

"Since forever. They've been our neighbors since I was, like, five. When I was eighteen, I looked up and he was gorgeous. God. I had an asshole boyfriend at the time. Gavin and me—inseparable ever since." She smiled at the memory of him.

"That's great," I said. Silence again. I was having some kind of conversational drought. Honestly, I was wondering where I was and how I got there. Frances Lee seemed to be wondering the same thing. She gave her head a little shake, some mental release of disbelief. She reached for the volume knob and turned up the music, maybe trying to fill the huge space of quiet between us.

We rode like that, and I stared at the cigarette lighter that maybe she did actually use, and then I looked out the window, watched the speeding cars and semitrucks, full of people, no doubt, who could actually carry on conversations. My own humiliation and awkwardness shriveled up my insides. We can be so large and then so small, and right then I felt like a tiny little figure sitting on that seat, with a whisper for a voice.

"Where am I going?" Frances Lee shouted. Which was probably a pretty good question.

"Oh, right," I said. I'd forgotten I was supposed to be leading.

"Exit 33," Sprout said from the back. "Coming up right after this one."

We led Frances Lee from the exit and down the winding road to the river, to the houses there. To Dad's house, with its curves and shingles, a mailbox with colored juggling balls on top.

"It's on the fucking water," Frances Lee said. "How nice is that." She'd turned the key and the engine shut off and there was sudden silence. Just the sound of birds being birds. She reached around on the seat again, realized she'd done in her cigarettes back on the freeway. "Shit," she said. A crow started to caw from one of the evergreens.

I looked at the house, which felt both full of Dad and empty of him. Three newspapers sat in plastic on his porch, yet a pair of his leather sandals was there too, and the wind chimes he'd hung up *chink-chink*ed in the breeze. His recycling bins were at the side of the house, with the green glass of his Perrier bottles showing from the top. *We can't do this,* I thought. I twisted my ring around my finger again. He had given me things, I remembered.

"You're honestly not telling me you're changing your mind now," Frances Lee said. For a minute I thought I'd spoken out loud, but then I realized I hadn't moved, and neither had Sprout. We just sat in that car, listening to the crow. Frances Lee didn't seem all that sure herself—she was still sitting there too, the keys dangling from the ignition.

And then there was the *cree-awk* of an old door opening, and Sprout was striding up the stone path, heading for the ceramic frog that sat there. She crouched down by it, lifted him up to expose what I knew would be wet earth and potato bugs and the silver key. The neighbor's orange cat appeared out of nowhere to wind himself around her knees.

"Come on," Frances Lee said.

She scooted from the seat and slammed the truck door and then my feet were on the stone path too, clomping up the wood steps to my father's door. Sprout was working the key into the lock.

"You're a couple of pansies," she said. Grandma said this whenever Mom and Annie hid their eyes at the scary parts of movies. Frances Lee looked my way and smiled. Sprout turned the door handle, and then we were in the living room. It was cool in there, the summer heat having been locked out. And quiet. The river beyond the dining-room doors sparkled, but the rooms themselves seemed diminished without Dad. Just rooms in a house.

They didn't seem like just rooms to Frances Lee. She whistled. "Wow. Pretty nice."

She walked around, surveyed. Walked to the fireplace. "Mom's painting." She stood before it, looked at the woman, the pieces of her broken up into triangles and squares, disjointed jawbone and breast and eye, twenty pieces, not one. I watched Frances Lee look at that picture, a daughter in her father's house, and felt the wrongness of separate pieces—a father, a daughter, two others, two mothers, all strangers.

She broke gaze with the woman in the painting, wandered

off. "What's all coming with us?" Frances Lee said. Her voice came from the kitchen now. Sprout was in there too. Frances Lee was checking things out, seeing this place where her father lived. We were both doing the same thing, probably. Trying to understand him.

"Just the few things in here," I said. I stayed there in the living room. I felt like a thief being in his house without his knowledge, and it felt less wrong to stay in only one room.

I heard the fridge door close. Sprout came back in and handed me a cream soda. I heard the click of a drink can opening in the kitchen, and then Frances Lee also appeared, taking a long swallow.

I pointed at the things, called them by their owner's name. "Jane, age six," I said, and gestured to the vase. "Olivia Thornton." I took the mask from the wall.

"Joelle Giofranco," Frances Lee said, and nodded her head toward the painting. "Let's get it down from here."

I stood on the needlepointed footstool, and Frances Lee stood on one of the kitchen chairs that Sprout hauled in. We lifted down the painting. It was so heavy, I couldn't imagine how I'd taken it down on my own that night. Sprout got some kitchen towels to wrap the small objects in.

"Have you thought about how entirely *pissed* Barry is going to be?" Frances Lee said.

I stopped what I was doing, wrapping the clock, *Elizabeth,* in an orange-and-pink striped towel. Frances Lee seemed sort of pleased with the idea. "I've thought about it," I said.

"He'll probably never speak to you again," she said. She seemed sort of glad about this, too. I wondered for a brief moment about all the reasons she was here. "Barry *hates* to be humiliated."

"I'm sure he'll forgive us eventually. We'll probably have a pretty awful talk," I said.

Frances Lee laughed. But it was a sarcastic, bitter one. "You're kidding, right? *Talk?* He never talks, as in you get to speak too. And he hasn't talked to me in three and a half years."

"Why?" I asked. I was beginning to think he had his reasons.

"I wrote a poem called, 'Tyrant Lizard Daddy.' It got published in the school paper."

I wanted to say, *Well?* I wanted to say, *We're obviously not the same people. Just because he stopped talking to you, doesn't mean he'd do the same to me.* But I didn't say any of that. I kept quiet.

"We're going to figure it all out later," Sprout said. She held Brie's statue, which was now cradled tightly in terrycloth decorated with leaves and pine cones.

"Fine," Frances Lee said. "You'll see." I hate it when people say, "You'll see." "You'll see" means that you're too much of an idiot to see a meteor coming. "Anyway," Frances Lee went on. "It's one of those times where this bad thing is a good thing, and when doing bad is the right thing. Fear can fuck up your eyesight like nothing else." I wasn't sure if I knew what she meant or not.

"I've got twenty-twenty vision," Sprout said.

But Frances Lee ignored her; she just looked at the woman in her mom's painting, set now against the fireplace hearth. "Why is it I know how she feels?"

Frances Lee went outside to get the large roll of plastic to wrap the painting in.

"Are you okay?" I asked Sprout. She'd gone from her silence

in the car to a strange, businesslike demeanor. She was worrying about Dad, I was guessing. And all of this would be my fault, I knew; this decision, whatever happened after. Dad never speaking to us again maybe; Sprout needing therapy for the rest of her life because of it. The words kept running through my head: *These are some of my most prized possessions.*

But Sprout had something else on her mind. "It just doesn't feel like sisters," Sprout said.

"I know," I said.

"It should feel like sisters," she said. "Not strangers."

"I know," I said again. She sat in the red velvet chair, holding the strawberry towel-wrapped package. She looked small there. She should have been thinking about Band-Aids and sprinklers and Sno-Kones, the things of summer. But she was thinking about damaged roots and broken branches. When your parents are divorced, your world is different from that of the kids whose parents aren't. It just is. In their world, moms and dads and kids go on bike rides together, and they all go on summer vacation. Dad cleans the gutters of clogged leaves; Mom knows how he likes his coffee. The big problems are being asked to clean your room and being treated like a child and the times the parents fight because Mom thinks Dad never listens. No one puts things in a suitcase unless they are going on a trip. No one watches their bags being handed over from one parent to another in a parking lot. No one knows the name of their parents' attorney. No one debates who they should get the field trip money from, or the check for school pictures, because each parent might get pissed because it's the other one's turn to pay. No one has to make sure both Mom and Dad are on the emergency contact form because each keeps crossing the other out.

No one feels they have to correct the wrongs of one parent to another.

Sprout held that statue, and I wanted to hug her. But I didn't. Because when your parents are divorced, you're really strong, too. People are always expecting you to be falling apart or in trouble or depressed or otherwise not coping. But you know better, because not coping is only an option for people who have everything. The rest of us have to get through, even if we don't do it perfectly.

And what Sprout said next reminded me of another thing about kids whose parents are divorced. Brief relationships are thrust upon us, relationships we're supposed to be game for. We're supposed to have good attitudes about the girlfriends and boyfriends and step-sisters and various kids—the boyfriend's monstrous seven-year-old; the girlfriend's slutty, bratty daughter who your father thinks is "so nice" but who goes to your school and you know she's done every guy there. The one you wouldn't want to get in an elevator with, but who now is going to accompany you on a spring-break trip to California because you should all "get to know each other." And too, there are the "grandparents," and someone else's uncles and cousins you're supposed to throw a Frisbee to at "their" family picnic, when you'd rather just sit on the grass and eat watermelon, the only food that doesn't seem casserole creepy and macaroni alien. You have to go to some house (not your house) with some relatives (not your relatives) on Christmas Eve, where they have ham when you always have turkey. Where they have Brussels sprouts and weird cooking you're supposed to compliment.

And sometimes, in spite of it being a slice of white smashed up with a slice of dark rye to make some sort of forced sand- wich, sometimes we do connect. Sometimes we actually even love. We touch down into another life like an insect on water, alight, and then, just as we drink and the drink is good, we're supposed to move on.

"This will all be worth it if we get to see Brie again," Sprout said.

# Chapter Ten

"What do you do when a father isn't a father? Hmm? Tell me, because I just don't know," Frances Lee said. "Wait, the seat's going to be hot." She tossed us each a towel to sit on. Mine said *Aloha!* and had a tiki hut and palm trees on it. Sprout's had Cinderella and those mice from the Disney movie, dancing around the hem of her dress. It seemed like a funny towel for Frances Lee to have. But maybe Disney movies are one thing most people have in common.

The objects from Dad's house were in the backseat with Sprout, all except for the painting, which was too large and had to be put in the open bed of the pickup. Frances had put so much plastic and tape around it that it could have been dropped from a high building and been fine, but still I worried when I could hear it slide and thunk after Frances Lee started back down Dad's road. I could see Frances Lee's eyes in the rearview mirror, watching Dad's house grow smaller behind her. I watched it too. I wondered if I'd ever see it again.

"If we don't go back, we don't go back," Sprout said.

"I'm not going back anyway, since I was never invited in the first place," Frances Lee said. She signaled to get back on the freeway, the truck's turn signal sounding frantic-fast. *Tick-tick-tick-tick!*

I seemed to be the only one who wasn't managing the who-cares-not-me attitude. My stomach was heavy, and I felt that press inside my forehead that meant too many feelings were struggling for too little space. Maybe I was going to cry. Maybe there was no way I was going to cry in front of Frances Lee and even Sprout right then. I loved him, that was the thing. I wanted him to love me. Sometimes it was hard to tell those two things apart.

We didn't talk for a long while, as Frances Lee drove back north to head for the ferry toward her home, our first stop. It was one of those times where there was too much to say, so you can't say anything. The job was too big, so we just rode like that, three separate planets with our own histories, spinning in silence.

"Never met a fried food I didn't like," Frances Lee said. We'd gotten to the ferry terminal in the early evening, and Frances had parked the truck in line with the others and then made a beeline to a fish-and-chips stand next to the dock. She'd cheered up as soon as she drove down the curved road toward the terminal, though I think we all did. The approach of the sea can do that, and so can the salty wetness of ocean air. That smell makes you feel that things are on the horizon, and I could feel the heaviness inside lift, too, when I saw the glinty white water, sparkly with sun. The sea seemed patient and endless and wise. It was a visual sigh of relief.

Frances Lee was practically skipping, carrying the brown bag already getting spotted with grease. I had that nagging feeling again that she reminded me of someone, only I couldn't figure out who. Sprout held the napkins and straws and the teeny packages of salt, and I carried the cardboard container of three cups of root beer, the crushed ice and soda sloshing against the sides. You could tell Frances Lee had done this before—the guy in the fish-and-chips stand knew her, and so did the lady in the ferry-ticket booth. She spread a blanket over the hood of the truck and we climbed up and sat cross-legged. Frances reached her arm into the bag and handed out the red-and-white checked containers of fries and fish.

"Now this is living," she said.

"That guy in the bread truck is staring at us," Sprout said.

"Take a picture, it lasts longer," Frances Lee said.

"He's actually a Hollywood scout in disguise of a hamburger-bun delivery man," I said.

"He's looking for a pair of great buns, ha-ha," Frances Lee said. She gave him a little wave.

"Oh God," Sprout said. "Don't wave!"

"He stopped, didn't he? Look, now he's pretending to read. We know you're not reading, sucker." Frances Lee dropped a floppy fry into her mouth. "When I die, bury me with a bunch of fries."

"Gross," Sprout said.

"I thought you were a vegetarian," I said to Frances Lee. "Or maybe you just eat fish."

"I'm not a vegetarian, my mom's a vegetarian," she said. "If you got that from Our Father, it's because he always gets Mom and me mixed up. He's sure we're either both the same or that she's turned me against him. He can't quite grasp the fact that someone might not like him all on their own for their own reasons." Another French fry, dropped in from above. "Wait, scratch that. He can't imagine anyone not liking him at all. Someone doesn't like him, something's seriously wrong with that person."

"Aunt Annie tried to be a vegetarian, but it only lasted a few weeks," Sprout said.

"I force myself to live in dead animal denial," Frances Lee said.

"Hey, I just bought it at Albertson's," I said. "I didn't *kill* it."

"Right," she said.

"Engines are starting up!" Sprout took a fast drink from her straw, started to grab up her food containers.

"We'll be fine," Frances Lee said. "We've got time."

But Sprout had leapt off the truck with a squeal and was already heading for the backseat. By the time we collected our napkins and bags and cups, Sprout was buckled into her seat and ready to go. We got back in too. Just at the very moment Frances Lee turned the key, the other cars started to move forward. A white paper from a straw was stuck to the bottom of her shoe, there on the accelerator.

You could know a family member so well that a single blink could tell you they were upset. And, yet, too, there was family so unknown they might as well be the guy behind the counter at Radio Shack.

Sprout got a little hyper on the ferry, leaning over the railing and going up to one deck and then down to another, her hair falling manic out of its braids so that there were only two little chunks still left in rubber bands. Frances Lee sat on a padded bench by the wide ferry windows, flipping through an *Island Real Estate* magazine. "Here's my house," she said. "It's got a pool. Wine cellar." She showed us a picture of a huge, chunky mansion.

"Holy moly," Sprout said.

We all picked out our houses and watched the water speed

past. After a while, you could feel the ferry shift from cruising to a slow lumbering. We'd passed the humps of the small islands of the San Juans, and now zooming toward us was the small dock of Orcas Island. The terminal building looked like a fishing shack, with the painted capital letters ORCAS on its front, and the white houses with red roofs offered something cozy and settled. We tromped down the narrow ferry steps and walked between rows of cars to reach our own. There was a sense of excitement at this arrival, it seemed—I felt it in the way all the cars and trucks were lined up and waiting, starting up their engines, as the men in their orange vests hooked fat ropes over the pilings black with creosote, and as the seagulls stood nearby and watched with practiced boredom.

We drove off the ferry and around the small town; we wound our way along wooded roads, punctuated with peeks of the sea. It was beautiful here; that was an easy thing to say, but it was true. Frances Lee drove casually, her elbow out the window and the radio off, and I could see Sprout in the back, face turned toward the window and watching everything we passed.

We turned down a dirt road and bumped past a pasture. An old gray horse looked up as we drove by, and Frances Lee raised her hand in a wave to him. "Hey, Harv," she said. "That's Harvey. He's Roy's horse. Roy's Mom's lover. Here on and off, but Harvey is here always." My secret inner conservative came out for a second at the words "mom" and "lover" in the same sentence, but Frances Lee acted as if this was the most natural thing in the world. She didn't say "Mom's boyfriend" (maybe that made it sound like they were sixteen and going to the movies), or "Mom's partner" (which maybe made it sound like they could plan a kitchen remodel but not a marriage), or "Mom's friend" (which maybe made it sound like they never had sex). But "lover"—that made it sound like all they *did* do was have sex. Maybe there were no right labels for love after you were a certain age.

The road turned from pasture to a messy garden of lavender and hydrangeas and sunflowers and daisies. There were the strings and new vines that meant green beans in September. A tiny blue shingled house sat on a lawn that was already browning from sun. Frances Lee shut off the engine. "So," she said. She seemed pleased with herself, but then looked over at us as if remembering that we were there—a couple of packages from FedEx, maybe, that had just arrived and she wasn't quite sure what to do with yet. The problem was solved immediately, though, because right then the screen door opened and out came Joelle, holding the collar of a jowly brown dog.

"They're here!" she said.

"Look what I brought you," Frances Lee said as she got out of the truck. We got out too, and I felt Sprout beside me, her hand slipping into mine. I squeezed it tight.

"All these girls," Joelle said. "Look at all these girls." She looked different than I remembered too, or maybe that was because the only image in my mind was that of a batik dress and bangled bracelets. Joelle was a lot older than Mom, with blond-gray hair that was long and curly and pulled back. Frances Lee looked like Dad, that was for sure. It must be weird to look so much like a parent you never saw. To have only the connection of your physical selves. Joelle wore a pair of overalls with a peace sign embroidered on the butt, which I saw when she came over and hugged Frances Lee. Next, her arms were around Sprout and then me, too, giving my back a pat, my shoulders a grip. She smelled like wood and dog and lavender and baking bread.

"And this is Grover," Frances Lee said, and the dog put his charcoal nose into her palm.

"Jake's asleep on the sun porch," Joelle said. "Some friend of his dropped him off. They'd been up north and driving all day."

"I'm gonna go jump on him," Frances Lee said.

"Leave him be," Joelle said. "You guys want dinner?"

"Fish and chips," Frances Lee said.

"I thought so," Joelle said. She leaned over the metal ledge of the truck, looked at her painting wrapped in cellophane bubbles. "So, she's finally back."

"Help me get it out," Frances Lee said, but she'd barely had the back open before Joelle had hoisted out the painting all by herself and was heading inside. She was small but strong, that was for sure.

We followed Joelle inside, into a house that was as jumble-cluttered as the garden. There was a dark floor and lots of windows and an old red velvet couch; pieces of modern art, vases of drooping sunflowers, stacks of books, lamps with beaded shades. A sun made from copper hung from a low beam. Something was cooking in the oven—the air was ripe with the smell of warm fruit. This was so different from our house, where things were in their place and books were on shelves and flowers were thrown away after they'd started to wilt. The funny thing was, it was more like Dad's house. A lot like Dad's house, only much, much smaller.

We walked through the covered porch, then. Frances Lee put her finger to her lips dramatically and pointed to a sleeping figure on the couch. *Jake,* she mouthed. I saw tousled black hair. I saw an arm flung over his head, marked with a tattoo of a sea serpent. Bare shoulders. Dark lashes against cheekbones. Dark lashes against . . .

"Stop staring," Sprout whispered. I glared at her. She wiggled her eyebrows up and down. Big deal, so he was gorgeous.

"You guys can have my room," Frances Lee said. "I'll sleep on the couch." She headed down a narrow hall and we followed. "Bathroom," she pointed. Painted green, a drapey glass chandelier hanging from the ceiling, a claw-foot tub. And then her own room—painted deep blue, a hundred yellow paper stars hanging from strings from the ceiling, quilted pillows everywhere, a big bed with a plump white comforter.

"It's beautiful," I said.

"Tonight, there'll be a surprise," Frances Lee said.

"You'll come back out for pie after you're settled? Or are you too tired?" Joelle shouted.

"Pie's great, thanks," I said, even though I felt a thousand years tired. Like I'd been awake for a thousand years, and that bed looked so good I wanted to sink in there and sleep and sleep. Fling my arm above my head. The curve of shoulders. Tan shoulders . . .

Sprout must have been tired, too, because when Frances Lee left us alone in her room with our bags piled in the corner, Sprout took off her shoes and flung herself onto the bed, burrowed into the covers.

"What a day," she said. This time, she sounded like Mom.

"Scoot over," I said. Ah, man. "We'd better not get too comfortable."

"I don't like pie," Sprout said.

"We have to be polite," I said.

"Screw being polite," Sprout said.

"Sprout," I said. But she didn't mean it, I could tell. She was just trying out the words. We lay there and watched the paper stars. A window was open, an old window with lots of panes, and the stars swayed and spun. I could smell the lavender outside the window. I could smell summer night coming.

"I'm going to lie here forever," Sprout said.

"What about going to the bathroom? Forever's a long time."

"Thanks for reminding me," she said. She popped up, disappeared down the hall, and came back a while later. "The cold is hot and the hot is cold," she reported.

"Good thing to know," I said.

We rested for a nice while, as night crept in and the windows turned light purple with dusk. We decided we'd better call Mom and let her know that we'd made it to "California" so she didn't do anything crazy and call the motel.

"Is your dad standing right there?" she said. This was always a big deal with divorced parents, it seemed, at least mine—as if the conversation they'd be having with you would be a lot different if either one was in listening distance. The presence of Mom or Dad in the background of our phone conversations was just another way to prove something to each other, I guess. If Dad was nearby when Mom and I were on the phone, Mom's voice would get icy, as if it were him she was talking to, not me. Dad himself would get louder and more jovial, as if to demonstrate all the fun she was missing out on—

too bad, her loss. How wrong of her to think bad of him.

"He's in the bathroom."

"Is everything all right?"

"Perfect," I said. "Long day from trains and airplanes. How's everyone there?"

"Fine. Grandma, though—the mystery continues. I surprised her when she was on the computer and she stood up so fast, she knocked over the chair. She said she was buying something too expensive and I just startled her conscience."

"She was probably bidding on a sports car."

"Vacation home, yeah. That's what I'm afraid of. eBay should come with warnings, like they have on alcohol bottles. Know your limit. Let me talk to Sprout."

I handed the phone over. Sprout listened, rolled her eyes at me. "No, my ears were fine," she said. "I chewed gum and I kept opening my mouth real wide like you said." Pause. "It's great. There's a pool. Dad's putting on his swim suit now. We're going for a quick dip." She wiggled her eyebrows at me to show off the fact that she could lie effortlessly and make faces at the same time. "Steak and baked potato. With the works. Okay. Love you too." Sprout flung one arm around me and then squeezed. "Mom says to hug you."

"A hug back," I said.

Sprout flicked the phone closed. "Mission accomplished," she said. She lifted her chin, in a display of *easy, no problem*. "Call me Queen of Liars."


It had gotten dark all the way, and the living room was lit with candles—candles everywhere, on tables and books and in the fireplace and on the windowsills. Joelle sat on the worn velvet couch with her feet on the coffee table, ankles crossed. She held a glass of red wine and was looking at the painting, propped now against one wall and sitting in a heap of wrapping. Frances Lee was in a fat leather chair; she'd changed into a long tie-dyed T-shirt and her hair was up in two clips shaped like butterflies. Her knees were up against her chest and the T-shirt was stretched over them.

Here's what I liked about Joelle. She patted the couch next to her, indicating for us to sit, as Frances Lee got up to cut some pieces of peach pie. Joelle did not ask us about school, or what grade we were in, or what we like to study, or any of the other BS I-don't-know-what-to-say-to-you questions. She treated you like you'd sat on her couch a hundred times before, so you felt like you'd sat on her couch a hundred times before.

"I spent nearly all the money I had at the time on that painting," Joelle said. "I barely ate for weeks after."

"I'd have rather had the food," Frances Lee said. "Burger King Whoppers, Kid Valley onion rings, skip the art." There was the small smack of Frances Lee licking a finger as she cut the pie. She seemed hungry almost all of the time.

"Vanilla malts," Sprout called back to her.

"Take one over a painting any day," Frances Lee said.

"Come on, Quinn, vote with me," Joelle said.

"It's interesting," I said, as I looked at the painting. I was trying to be polite. It was also disturbing—I'd always thought so. One breast was a triangle, one eye off in the corner of the canvas, boxed in a cube.

"She looks psychotic," Frances Lee said. She handed around plates and forks. Warm peaches, sugary crust. I cut the tip of the piece with the edge of my fork. It was some sort of fruity heaven.

"I'd been with Barry maybe seven, eight months? I was crazy about him, 'crazy' being the operative word."

"He hadn't started the Jafarabad Brothers yet, right?" I asked. I was feeling suddenly more awake. I could tell this was the start of the kind of conversation I had come for, the story of my father. It was right there, and I wanted both to hurry toward it and slow it down.

"He'd dropped out of school, was juggling in this summer vaudeville show that went from festival to festival. I sewed the costumes. I had no idea what I was doing. God, some of those outfits. I did this one for this singer. Bonita, something. Can't remember. It was a dragon. Big shiny green tail, and she couldn't even move. Had to inch her way off the stage."

"I thought he was in college when he started the show," I said. "I heard he did it to pay for a sailing trip." I remembered that article. The story I'd heard from Dad before.

"Can you imagine Barry on a sailboat for more than an afternoon? He hates the water. He practically has to get high before he sets foot in a swimming pool." I nodded. I knew she was right. "I had the idea to start the show. We were sitting around one night and I just started telling him how he had the kind of charisma and talent to hold a show by himself. Forget the singers and the old-fart ventriloquists. He could get a gimmick, make it big. Use his dark looks. Maybe team up with Mike, who wasn't nearly as talented, but who could play second string, yes? Can you tell I treated him like God? I perhaps haven't treated God even that well. I fell in love with Barry, and he fell in love with my adoration of him."

"Which all works out until you stop adoring." Frances Lee licked the back of her spoon. Sprout had completely polished off her pie. So much for hating it.

"I didn't stop adoring, that was the problem. I had plenty of evidence to stop adoring, but the more he didn't give me what I wanted, the harder I tried to get it. I kept putting coins in the proverbial slot machine, because that one time I'd gotten a small payoff. Putting them in, putting them in, hoping . . . By giving him this idea, by encouraging him, by sitting in on rehearsals and calling around to get bookings—I made myself necessary to him. And yet, always, *always,* he held back a bit, by being cool, being important, having other . . . *people* around always. Maybe we shouldn't discuss this," she said. She nodded her chin toward Sprout.

"If you mean we shouldn't discuss this because of me, I'm not a baby," Sprout said. "I can handle the truth. We're here for it."

Joelle smiled. "All right then, yes. I can see that." She took another sip of wine.

"Women, then. There were always other women around. I wondered who they were and why they were around and I told myself how confused I was when inside I wasn't really confused. I knew there was something he wanted to change about me— namely, that I didn't like his behavior. I knew that, I just didn't want to see. I started getting love confused with angst. Love meant upset. Love meant large, crazy feelings."

Frances Lee made the beeping sound of a truck backing up. "Warning, lesson ahead."

"Don't worry, Mom does it all the time," Sprout said.

"It took me years to figure out that upset was upset, and tumultuousness was not the same thing as passion. Love isn't drama," Joelle said. "Real love is *there,* not something out of reach."

"That's about twelve lessons," Frances Lee said.

"Hard earned," Joelle said.

"Now you've got Roy," Frances Lee said.

"Love with Roy is peaceful. I thought something was wrong, it was so peaceful. Then I realized that what was wrong was that for the first time, it was right. No big scenes, no crying, no clinging and plotting and scheming to keep him. It just *is.*" She set her wineglass down. The candles on the table flickered with her movement.

"And they all lived happily ever after," Frances Lee said.

"Don't knock it," Joelle said. "It's a hell of a lot better than feeling like *that.*" She gestured with her fork to the woman in the painting. "No wonder I spent all my money on her. The visual equivalent of me. That's about how disoriented I was. And I called that love." She shook her head at herself. "Let's hang her up now."

"Where are we going to put her?" Frances Lee asked.

"Somewhere where I can see her every day. To remind myself how far I've come."

"Great. We're going to have to look at that thing all the time? I'll have nightmares."

"Go get the hammer, Frances Lee," Joelle said.

*Dorothy Hoffman Siler Pearlman Hoffman:*

*Otto was one of these jealous men. Listen to me right now, a jealous man is a dangerous man. At first I thought I must be something pretty special—he cared so much he wanted me all to himself. Christ almighty. Truth was, in spite of what he showed other people, he was so insecure that the only way he was sure I'd stay with him was to guard me like a police dog, and to keep me small. It started out innocent enough. Did you notice so-and-so? Do you think he was handsome? The warning bells should have been ringing and clanging.*

*Pretty soon, it was him checking on me. Holy moly, I couldn't go to the mailbox without an accounting of my whereabouts. He called all the time, to see if I was where I was supposed to be, locked up in my little castle. I saw you looking at that man. Maybe I was looking both ways before I crossed a street! It got to where I didn't want to go out because I might accidentally do something to upset him. Once we went to go see a show and had a fight because he thought I found Burt Reynolds attractive. Who didn't think Burt Reynolds was attractive? He was a movie star! Otto would watch to see if I looked at some man in a magazine ad, or ask if some book I was reading had a racy scene. I was reading* Lust for Life *and he wouldn't speak to me.* Lust for Life! *About Vincent van Gogh, for Christ's sake! A classic! I didn't know what I'd done wrong. He just went all silent and moody. He criticized my friends, too. He worried about Rosemary, my cousin, whom I talked to every week. Do you tell her about me? I don't want you saying things to her when I can't defend myself. Rosemary is a gossip. She's not very smart. Rosemary was very smart, if you want to know the truth, though she's gone now.*

*He liked me to wear high heels for him, but not in public. He didn't want men getting the wrong idea. I looked like a whore. I acted like a whore. A man can create a whole iden-*

*tity for you, and you won't even recognize yourself. A whole picture that suits him. You don't draw a straight, firm line with a man—you start losing pieces of yourself, bit by bit. I finally went and got a job as a receptionist at a doctor's office, Dr. Galveston. I'd taken typing in high school, and I was good at it. Three days a week. When I told Otto, he had a fit. Anger, boy oh boy, you've never seen anything like it. A jealous man, I tell you, is a dangerous man. Dangerous. It was the beginning of the end. He couldn't stand that I had a little success of my own. He was holding me tight in his fist, and I'd wriggled free and gotten out into the world.*

*I felt this way then and I feel this way now: I was not put on this earth to be someone's possession. If I want to be in a prison, then I'll go rob a bank.*

Frances Lee was right about the surprise. When we turned off the lights, all of the stars hanging from the ceiling glowed in the dark.

"Magic," Sprout whispered. And then we just lay there in the darkness, quiet, watching the soft yellow lights sway in the night air. Sprout's breath was so hushed and regular, I thought she was asleep. But then, there was a small voice beside me.

"Are you awake?"

"Mmm-hmm," I said.

"Where are we?" she said.

I knew how she felt. "It feels like we've been gone a long time, doesn't it?"

"Weeks and weeks. I like Joelle, though."

"Me too," I said. It felt sort of wrong to like her. It felt like a betrayal of Mom somehow. But I did like her. She was comfortable and real, and her house was all cozy enchantment.

"It's weird she was married to Dad," Sprout said.

In a way, I could see them married more than I could my own mom and dad. "Their houses are sort of similar," I said.

Sprout was quiet for a long time. There was just darkness and spinning stars of gold, a crack of light under the door, the smell of night coming through the windows. Then she spoke. "Maybe he took that, too," she said.

### JOELLE GIOFRANCO:

*I want to rewrite that part of the Bible, I don't know what it's called, I'm not a big Bible person. Corinthians something. The one that goes, "Love is patient, love is kind," et cetera, et cetera. Not that there isn't good things in it. But I remember there's a part in there that says there should be no end to love's faith and endurance. And sometimes there should be an end. We need to call a halt and not persist in some grand hope of some grand love. Some people are not capable of love. Of maintaining a relationship. It's sad, but it's true.*

*So: Love is ease, love is comfort, love is support and respect. Love is not punishing or controlling. Love lets you grow and breathe. Love's passion is only good passion—swirling-leaves-on-a-fall-day passion, a-sky-full-of-magnificent-stars passion—not angst and anxiety. Love is not hurt and harm. Love is never unsafe. Love is sleeping like puzzle pieces. It's your own garden you protect; it's a field of wildflowers you move about in both freely and together.*

I was having a hard time going to sleep. I had gotten to that point where I was so tired that I wasn't tired anymore. I'd listened to the sounds of everyone going to bed, the dog flopping down to the floor, the quieting of his jingly tags and clicking toenails; a door shut softly. I heard the scrape of a chair outside against a cement patio, smelled cigarette smoke drifting, and then the back screen door sliding closed. The light filling the crack under the door was gone now. The house seemed to breathe in and out in rhythms of sleep. Even the breeze had stilled and the leaves on the trees had hushed. I had to go to the bathroom, but I was trying to talk myself out of it. I didn't want to get up and walk around this unfamiliar house, and it was so quiet that a flush would certainly wake people up.

I watched the stars and felt far from anything familiar. Liv and Zaney seemed almost like people from a long time ago, another life, and I hadn't thought about Daniel at all since I'd left. He was beginning to feel like a memory you weren't sure if you'd made up or really experienced, like the trip to Florida I'd taken as a baby and only knew through the stories I'd been told. I'd given up baby food on that trip, Mom had said, and though I know I was too young, I swear I remembered the scrambled eggs she said were the only things I would eat.

Talking myself out of the need to get up was going nowhere, that never works—it's one of those things you know but try anyway. I swung my legs out of bed and onto the cool wood floor. I was at the bathroom door, standing right there, before I realized what was happening. What my eyes were seeing. A naked guy standing at the toilet, his butt a white globe in the moonlight coming from the window, and then the sound of a sudden burst of sleepy peeing.

I must have gasped or done something else entirely humiliating because he looked at me then, gorgeous face framed in scraggly dark hair, arm with tattoo traveling down to hand holding penis, *oh God*, and . . .

"Oh shit," he said.

He reached for the door as I turned away, me in my Nine Mile Falls High Volleyball Team T-shirt and chaste white underwear that Grandma would have been comfortable in, and he in . . . nothing.

And that was how I first met Jake Kennedy.

# Chapter Eleven

"I heard you met Jake," Frances Lee said.

*Oh God.* "Oh God," I said. Everyone was in the kitchen, Joelle in a flowy caftan, at the stove, flipping several pancakes onto a plate that already held a nice stack of them. All the windows were open, and the air smelled like sizzling oil, frying bacon, coffee, and summer morning.

"What?" Sprout said. She hated missing out on things.

"Your sister saw Jake in his skivvies," Joelle said.

"No skivvies," Frances Lee said.

"Ha, he told me skivvies," Joelle chuckled.

"I guess this isn't going to be our secret," I said.

Jake walked into the kitchen then. "This is what I look like with my clothes on," he said.

"Kind of late for introductions," Frances Lee said.

"*You* didn't walk in on me peeing," Jake said to Sprout. Now he wore knee-length cargo shorts, a tight white tank top. Big white smile, too, that same tangle of hair, this dimple in his cheek that had to mean trouble.

"I'm Charlotte," Sprout said. Tattooed arm held out, arm connected to bare chest, bare chest easing down to naked ass . . .

"You left the door open!" I said. My face was hot. I was blushing, I knew it, which only made me blush more.

"Sell tickets next time, Jake," Joelle said.

"Big deal, you're not that much to look at," Frances Lee said.

She took a big jug of milk from the refrigerator; put it on the table, which was set for breakfast.

"Grab a seat, people," Joelle said. "You're getting on the road, you need a big breakfast."

"She's kicking us out," Frances Lee said. "She and Roy are going away for the weekend."

"Roy is my business," Joelle said, and set the platter of pancakes on the table. "And I'm very glad of that fact."

"Joelle, can I pour myself some coffee?" Jake said. "I need serious caffeine when strangers see me naked."

"Get over yourself," Frances Lee said.

Plates were passed; syrup, too. Frances Lee got up to get the roll of paper towels to share around. Grover sat by my chair and watched me eat, same as Ivar. Dogs are funny, the ways they're all similar and the ways each is different. Grover kept inching closer to me until he finally set his chin on my chair with such a sweet and hopeful look that you couldn't help but give him a bit of pancake. This was a better method than Ivar's, whose endless unblinking stare felt a little creepy-insistent and unsympathetic.

I didn't dare look at Jake Kennedy, who was cracking jokes and getting teased like the little brother Frances Lee seemed to see him as. The painting now hung on the kitchen wall, right across from the chair where Joelle sat. The fragmented woman gazed right down over Jake Kennedy, which I decided was a bad sign. If any guy was trouble, Jake Kennedy was. He was the kind of guy who would make my mother freak. Musician, tattoo, gorgeous when naked. Gorgeous when clothed. I didn't dare look, but I kept looking. He was a little grungy, actually, and he ate with a kind of messy energy that could have been bad manners.

But it was all sexy in a way I couldn't define. The opposite of *clean*. I could hardly breathe.

Joelle set down her fork.

"I've got a little favor to ask you all," she said.

"Oh, great," Frances Lee said. "'Little favor' never means 'little favor.' 'Little favor' always means 'big favor.'"

Sprout kicked me under the table. She agreed, I could tell.

"Now come on. You're going that direction anyway. I have something of your dad's that I'd like you to return."

"No," Frances Lee said. "I know what this is, and the answer's no."

"This is going to be good," Jake said.

"Not a painting," Sprout said.

"A little bigger," Joelle said.

"A lot bigger," Frances Lee said.

"Come on, Frances Lee," Joelle said. "I cannot keep that fucking thing out in the barn forever. And it scares Harvey."

"Don't ask this," Frances Lee said.

"It'd fit in the truck, no problem."

"What do you think," Jake said to Sprout. "One of those enormous lions people have to guard their gate?"

"Close," Joelle said.

Frances Lee snickered. "Yeah, he'd guard the gate, all right."

"Tell!" Sprout said. Joelle just sat and smiled. She seemed pleased with herself.

"Bob's Big Boy," Frances Lee said. "A *huge* Bob's Big Boy."

"Bob's Big Boy?" Jake said.

"Hamburger place?" Joelle said. "The little cartoon boy with the red-and-white checkered pants? He's holding a hamburger on a plate in the air? A little swirl of cartoon hair? He's adorable."

"He's fucking ten feet tall," Frances Lee said.

"Barry and some friends stole him from some frat boys his first year of college. Said the hardest thing was getting him in the elevator of their apartment building. He used to stand outside a Bob's Big Boy in Montana, or somewhere, they said. He'd fit in the truck just fine," Joelle said.

"Nooo," Frances Lee groaned.

"Frances Lee," Joelle said, in a way that finished things. So after we'd cleared up the breakfast dishes, we all followed Joelle to the barn. She hauled open the big doors, and Harvey ran to the farthest corner of the pasture. He stood there and watched suspiciously as Joelle hauled a plastic tarp off of a huge mound in the corner of the barn, revealing, as promised, an enormous, cheery cartoon boy in red-and-white checkered pants, his hair a soft-ice-cream swirl on his gigantic black plastic head. His arm was in the air, and a huge hamburger sat on a plate in his palm. Harvey started to pace.

"Harvey, it's fine, he's harmless. Quit your fretting," Joelle called to the horse.

"Harmless? He flings that plate with the hamburger and someone's gonna die," Jake said. He had a syrup spot on his shirt, and even that syrup spot was sexy.

"So you put it in the truck and give it back to Barry," Joelle said.

"Like it's that easy. Easy as mailing a letter," Frances Lee said.

"Did you take it from him?" Jake asked. "Like he took the painting? Because, frankly, I'm a little confused."

Bob's Big Boy smiled down upon us. Joelle wiped cobwebs off of him with her hand.

"God, no. I've told Barry for years to come and get this thing. What you get stuck with during a divorce, you wouldn't believe. I also had this really hideous raccoon coat of his that I finally just threw away because I screamed every time I accidentally touched it in my closet."

"Mom ended up with a set of place mats with the animals of Australia on them from her last boyfriend," I said. OCD Dean had gone on his honeymoon there.

"And those videos about the life of Pope John Paul," Sprout said. OCD Dean was a devout Catholic, except for the divorce and the living-together part of his life.

"Gavin's friend Ben? You know Ben," Jake said to Frances Lee. "His girlfriend gave him half a scissor in his boxes of stuff she packed up."

"Psycho killer," Joelle said.

"And a television set that didn't work. And an old turntable without an arm," Jake said.

"Break up and you're suddenly a convenient human Goodwill box," Joelle said. "Clean out your attic and leave me the junk, gee thanks."

"There ought to be some Web site called 'Crap from My Ex dot com.' You could trade the Crock-Pot you got left with for someone else's eight-track player," Frances Lee said.

"Her mismatched gloves for his left-behind Jockeys," Joelle said. "Love it. But for now, let's get this baby out of here. Sayonara, Big Bob. It's been fun, but you're going home."

❀ ❀ ❀

Big Bob attracted a lot of attention as he rode in the back of the truck, hamburger upraised. You could see the faces of little kids craning to look as we passed, and trucks blew their horns, and a motorcyclist gave us a thumbs-up, keeping his arm out for a good half mile until he disappeared from view.

Jake's gear was in the truck bed with Bob, and Jake and Jake's guitar rode with Sprout in the backseat; Jake liked to have the extra room to take his guitar out and practice. His presence made me feel strangely *here,* aware of him and of myself, as if there was a force of energy that flowed from him to me. Everything about him was on one of Mom's lists somewhere, wasn't it? My eyes were drawn again and again to the side mirror, where I watched his head bent down over his guitar, the serpent tattoo cradling the instrument's body. The music sounded completely different than it had on Frances Lee's tape deck, just his acoustic guitar, this tender strumming. Can you feel sentimental about something that never happened? Or that might happen but hasn't yet? Because that's what I felt then, riding in Frances Lee's truck. Jake's voice, soft and low, made everything seem important and full of meaning—EZ Storage places seemed full of meaning, and so did exit signs and flocks of crows and rest stops. Jake sang, and Sprout leaned her cheek against the window and Frances Lee drove with a smile and truck drivers honked and waved at Bob, and this was how we made our way to Elizabeth Bennett's house (mantel clock, hands stopped at 3:30), the second stop of our karmic quest.

We were traitors to Bob as we drove through the Burger King drive-through. Frances Lee gave our order through the little speaker, and Bob kept smiling way up there against the sky. The boy at the window in his paper hat leaned over to give us our bags.

"Is this some kind of joke?" he said. He scratched the place under his ear, looked upward.

"Is what some kind of a joke?" Frances Lee said.

"That guy in the back of your truck with a hamburger," the boy said.

"What guy in the back of my truck with a hamburger?" Frances Lee looked puzzled. She took her change.

"Right there! I'm looking at him!"

"What's he talking about?" Sprout said from the back.

"Dude, you should stop smoking that stuff," Jake said.

Frances Lee gunned the engine. The boy leaned down on his elbows on the take-out window ledge, raised his arm, and flipped us his middle finger.

"Sheesh, customer service," Jake said.

"Someone give me some fries, pronto," Frances Lee said.

### BRIE JENKINS:

*I moved through my five- and ten-year goals, checking accomplishments off my list as if they were household chores. I had a 4.0 average in college, worked for my dad, had money saved . . . But there was always some chaotic guy around. Except this one boy, though. Tim Phillips. I remember him. I think about him every now and then. This was in college. Right after the crush on the cowboy and just before I met Lincoln. Before everything (meaning, my life) seriously veered off my careful plan. Tim was just a great guy. And he didn't have issues, like he was abused in the past, or his father hated him, or his mother sent him away when he was seven to military school. I didn't have the urge to help him with my love. I just wanted to be with him. Being with him felt so good. I never had to walk on eggshells. It was just happy, you know? Just plain happy. Sort of simple.*

*Of course, Lincoln came along then and this whole nurturing thing kicked in, as if my past was louder than my present. I hadn't stopped to figure out what was going on in my head yet. And so I stopped seeing Tim then. I'd always taken care of my mom, just emotionally speaking, and then when Dad got sick . . . Lincoln came along and I followed, like a bear going to the river. He drank too much on our first date, and I saw how much he needed me. If a guy seems to need saving, call the Coast Guard.*

*Tim Phillips—he didn't need me. We were like salt and pepper—great separately, great together. Those early days with Tim—they were such fun. I wonder what happened to him. He just—see, I smile even remembering him.*

It got hot that afternoon, real hot. You could see wavy lines coming off the asphalt, and we had all the windows down and Frances Lee also had the air conditioner on, which she said wasn't really an air conditioner. It was some sort of vent that was spitting out lukewarm air and making a horrendous racket like a helicopter landing. The backs of my legs and arms were hot and sticky, and I kept taking pinches of my skirt and shirt and fanning them in and out for coolness. Sprout had fallen asleep and her mouth hung open and her hair was wet around her forehead, stuck down with sweat. Every now and then Frances Lee would exclaim, "Jesus," or "Jesus, it's hot," and Jake had lost his shirt somewhere back after we had eaten lunch. One arm was out the window so that you could see the fluff of his underarm hair. Sun fell in a triangle against his chest.

"Jesus," Frances Lee said.

"We've got to be getting close to the border," Jake said.

"Quinn, can you check the map? Do I need to make a turn off here somewhere?"

I'd been appointed official map reader due to my position in the front seat, and let me tell you, I wasn't the wisest choice.

"Upside down," Jake said to me from the backseat.

*Shit, shit.* I turned the map around, tried to get some sense of where we were. I followed the freeway with my finger. "A little bit more and then it connects to I-5 north," I said. I tried to fold the map back up along the creases, unfolded it, and tried again.

"Do you need some help?" Jake said.

I would have blushed if my face weren't already so hot. "I've got it," I said, and thankfully, I did. Wasn't there something on Mom's list about someone making you feel humiliated? Or was that just me making me feel humiliated?

"Oh, shit, guys," Frances Lee said.

Something in her voice made Sprout wake up. "Is everything okay?" she said.

"Shit," Frances Lee said.

"What?" I asked.

"Overheating," Jake said. "This stupid truck always overheats."

"This stupid truck is getting you to your next gig," Frances Lee said testily.

"We hope," Jake said.

"Goddamnit, Jake," Frances Lee said. "Shut up, would you?" It was the old "yell at a human when an object does something awful" move. Honestly, this new person who was my sister could sometimes be very hard to like. Frances flipped on her turn signal, setting in motion the frantic *tick-tick-tick-tick-tick!* The tires crunched in the gravel off to the side of the freeway. Cars whipped past, making their *shee-ooom!* sound.

"I have half a mind to leave you right here," she said to him. This seemed suddenly possible. The three of us (four, if you counted Bob) on the side of the road with our luggage beside us as the truck sped away in a cloud of dust.

"Is everything okay?" Sprout said again.

"It's fine," I said. I didn't know if it was fine or not.

Frances Lee turned off the engine. "We just have to wait a while until it cools off," she said.

"How long does that take?" Sprout asked. I heard her suck on her straw from her Burger King cup, making a reached-the-bottom dry slurp.

"An hour?"

I wanted to groan. I pictured a desert, those cow skulls lying under a cactus on dry clay ground. I licked my lips. No one said anything.

"Come on, people, it's not that bad," Frances Lee said. She was pissed. The kind of pissed someone gets when they feel responsible for the bad way things have turned out.

"Frannie, let me do the Coke trick," Jake said. I felt this mix of hope and dread at his words. He had a solution that would save us. The solution sounded illegal at best.

"Forget it," Frances Lee said. The dread part of the hope-dread equation got bigger. Frances Lee shook her head, opened her car door for more air. *Shee-oom!* Cars passed. Someone honked again, hooted out their window. Bob kept smiling up there in the back.

"It worked last time."

"You'll fuck up my engine," she said.

"Your engine is already fucked up," Jake said.

"Fine," Frances Lee said. She folded her arms. I finally realized who it was that she reminded me of. She reminded me of Sprout. Sprout's feistiness and certainty and sometimes irritating independence. Sprout, a little older, knowing her own mind even more than she did now.

Jake got out. He was carrying his Burger King cup, monstrous in size, big enough for Bob to drink from. Jake's back was shiny and slick with sweat. He flipped us a peace sign and that smile with the dimple in his left cheek. He lifted the hood and disappeared from view.

"You're sure about the asthma thing?" Frances Lee said to Sprout. "I could really use a smoke." I'd noticed a new pack on the seat that she must have brought from home.

"I'm sure."

Frances Lee got out too. I could see her making her way down the ravine by the highway, stepping carefully. She sat down on a rock, her back to us. A moment later, I could see the curl of smoke, and Frances Lee's head tilted back as she exhaled toward the sky.

"Quinn?" Sprout said.

"Yeah?"

"Are you wishing we were in Disneyland?" she said.

"A little."

"Me too."

I had a sudden panicky vision of the truck getting started again only to break down at Abigail Renfrew's. God, fate would never be that cruel, would it? The truck hood slammed back down again, and Jake reappeared. He crumpled the empty cup in one hand.

"Did he just pour his Coke in there?" Sprout said.

"I think so," I answered.

"Won't that fuck up her engine?" Sprout said.

"I think it is already," I answered.

Jake popped his head into the truck. "Hey, Quinn? Can you turn that key?"

I scooted over into the driver's seat. Jake leaned in my window as I turned the engine on. I was aware of his bare skin, the heat coming off him. He smelled salty-hot, tangy with sweat. I didn't know that could be a good thing. The engine roared alive, and Jake watched the temperature gauge on the dash. The arrow rose then rested on the low end of the half-circle display. It sat there solidly, without moving.

"Look at that!" Jake said. I could feel his breath on my cheek.

"Hooray!" Sprout shouted from the back.

"Great job, Jake," I said. I looked at him and smiled.

He sucked in his breath as if he was about to say something, then changed his mind.

"What?" I asked. I was expecting a warning—that the truck was bound to overheat again, or break down, that we'd never make it. I was ready, but not ready enough.

"It's just, you have really beautiful eyes," he said.

I think that for a moment the blood in my veins just stopped pumping and the synapses in my brain stopped firing and that everything that was supposed to be working suddenly ceased to work. I just sat there.

"Romantic moment," Sprout said. I didn't look at her, but I could hear that she'd wiggled her eyebrows up and down, same as Grandma or Aunt Annie or any of us would have done at a hint of this sort of attention. We would NOT have done it, though, with some guy standing right there, close enough that you felt his breath on your face. I wanted to kill her. I wanted to put my hands around her scrawny little neck.

"Don't you think?" Jake asked her. "Don't you think she's got beautiful eyes?"

"Eye *lashes*," Sprout said.

"Those too," he said. He was still looking at me, smiling.

"If we're all done discussing my eyes, maybe we'd better get going," I said. I somehow managed to sound offhand, as if my eyes had regularly and frequently been the subject of admiration and I was just plain weary about it. This was to cover up what was really going on inside right then—some joy parade with marching bands, banners, clowns in clown cars, whistles and trumpets, and spinning silver batons.

"Let's get this show on the road," Sprout said.

"Right," Jake said. He slapped the window ledge twice with his hand, stood straight as Frances Lee stubbed out her cigarette with the toe of her sandal and climbed back up the ravine to the car.

"Okay, car-mechanic genius. Just promise me what happened last time won't happen this time."

"A fluke," Jake said.

"What happened last time?" Sprout said.

"Don't ask," Frances Lee said.

We didn't. Sometimes (a lot of the time) you just really don't want to know the truth, right? We just kid ourselves, and don't mind so much. I scooted back over to the passenger side and Jake hopped in and Frances Lee put the truck in gear. I wasn't too hot anymore, or tired from driving, or even worried about reading maps and getting to Elizabeth Bennett's house. My insides were just too busy with their energized, excited thrum. My mother had warned against this, I knew. Being taken in by a guy's compliments. *We can fall for a guy because he seems to like us, not because we really like him,* she would say. *Flattery is not love.*

But, "beautiful"? The word used in connection to *me*? Could that even be real? Could that have really just happened? I glanced at Jake in the side mirror, and he caught me looking. He winked, and I turned away. *God oh God oh God.* I would force myself not to look. I would not ever again look in that mirror at him. My heart clutched up in some uneasy combination of humiliation, joy, and warning. But I knew one thing: I sure wasn't wishing I was in Disneyland anymore.

# Chapter Twelve

Elizabeth Bennett was expecting us. Frances Lee had called her last week, and she'd offered to have us over for dinner. We were running late, though, after waiting in an unexpectedly long line at the border crossing, and Frances Lee called Elizabeth to tell her as Sprout and I stretched our legs and walked around the Peace Arch in the center lawn at the border, a tall rectangular arch that looked like a huge bookend. It was easy to find the truck again in the long lines of cars—Bob was still smiling up there, with his cartoon-swirl hair still shiny and patient.

There's something about people in positions of authority that makes me feel like I've done something wrong even when I haven't done anything wrong. If a policeman is behind me, I'm sure he's about to pull me over. My guilty conscience is a full-time position, without even two weeks' vacation in the summers. Going through customs was the same. I had our birth certificates, taken from Mom's file cabinet drawer, but I was already concocting ways to convince him that we were indeed American citizens who were not smuggling drugs or guns or illegal aliens or those apples from the Apple Maggot Quarantine Area. I would smile in a way that he would know I was a nice person who would never do anything like that. I would greet him in a way that meant that we were perfectly open to having our car searched, no problem. My nonguilt guilt scrabbled around the whole time we waited, scratching at my moral side, which was indeed guilty of something—betraying my dad, lying to my mom. I could never commit a crime, that was for sure. I was wishing I could provide not only my birth certificate, but a passport and my birth parents, and my great-grandfather Aldo, the first American-born relative on my mother's side.

Of course, the customs guy did not think we were smuggling AK-47s or even fruit with stowaway fruit flies. We liked this customs guy, who asked if Bob was attempting to avoid the draft by moving to Canada. He waved us through for our day visit, gave Bob his own up-high wave.

"It's funny how Canada looks like Canada right away," Sprout said, and it was true—as soon as you crossed the border, you could tell you were in a different country. The road signs were different and everything was metric and the gas station we stopped in had food we didn't have at home—pickle-flavored potato chips, red plaid boxes of butter toffee.

The city of Vancouver looked different too, a city of tall green-glass buildings, columns of hundreds of shimmery panes of glass. Elizabeth Bennett, Dad's old high school girlfriend, lived on a houseboat on Granville Island, at the city's center. We joined the traffic on the Granville Island Bridge, cars and trucks inching along over a twinkling waterway on which little boats traveled back and forth, ferrying people from land to island.

"They look like bathtub boats," Sprout said, and she was right. You could practically pick them up in your hand and give them a squeak.

"This traffic sucks," Frances Lee said. "We're going to be later than I even said, and her husband already made it clear we couldn't come after seven thirty. Elizabeth had to go to bed early, he said."

"Control freak," Jake said.

"No kidding," I said.

"I ever have a husband who tells me when I need to go to bed, he'll be out on his ass," Frances Lee said.

"Maybe he's not too pleased that the children of his wife's old boyfriend are descending upon him to give her back an old clock. A broken old clock," Jake said.

"Well, she seemed to understand the karmic mission perfectly when I talked to her," Frances Lee said. "Are all the people in the city in this one place?" she asked. "Is there some rule in Canada that we all meet here at this time of night? Friendly mass get-together?"

I looked at the time on my cell phone. The ringer had been off from last night, and I saw that I'd missed three calls from Mom. Three, in the last . . . hour? All my panic neurons (or whatever they were) started to sway back and forth like those creepy underwater urchin things (whatever *they* were). Problem, definitely. Three calls in an hour meant cranked-up mother anxiety. I debated whether to check the messages. It was a quarter to seven, and we were still on the bridge, and it was not the time or place to have a private, calm-your-mom conversation. Better to not even know yet what disaster loomed on the horizon. It was a shame those Disneyland restaurants were so darn noisy that you could never hear your phone.

We inched along, finally making it to Granville Island itself, a tiny place of art galleries and restaurants painted in bright shades of yellow and blue and red, a public market, jugglers and musicians performing amidst crowds, the smell of just-caught fish and browning garlic and caramel corn in the air. Groups of people stopped to turn to look at Bob; some guy in a Corona tank top shouted a drunk *"I love you"* up to Bob, who was not impressed but still smiled politely. We got untangled from the tourist center, drove to the edge of the small island where a tiny group of houseboats huddled together at the water's edge. Frances waited for a huge RV with a license plate that read CAP-TAIN ED and a bumper sticker that said HOME OF THE BIG RED-WOODS to pull out. Captain Ed reversed, then pulled back in, reversed and tried again.

"For God's sake, Captain Ed, get it right, we're in a hurry here."

I craned my neck, trying to see who Captain Ed was, but no luck. We parked and Frances turned off the engine and sighed, and we all got out. I felt a sudden bout of nerves as we passed the PRIVATE! RESIDENTS ONLY! sign posted on the dock gate and made our way down the wooden planks, looking for her house number. The houseboats were all different—large, two-story geometric homes and small shingled cottages, all floating on the water and swaying with the waves made by passing boat traffic. Sprout carried the clock, with its hands stuck at three thirty. Jake had his shirt back on, and Frances Lee had brushed her hair. All we knew about Elizabeth Bennett was that she and my dad had gone to high school in Seattle together. No one else could quite compare to her in my dad's eyes, Joelle had told Frances Lee. Sweet, beautiful, good.

We reached houseboat number 6, and I knocked. I'd had Elizabeth Bennett's husband pictured all different—angled cheekbones, maybe; angry eyes. The kind of man who watches a lot of sports and then expects dinner. But he wasn't like that at all.

"You made it," he said. "My name's Andy." He held out his

hand. He had a thin, kind face and warm eyes, curly brown hair that was turning gray. He had a soft T-shirt on from some marathon you could tell he probably ran in. He had that sparse, lean, no-frills body of a runner. "Elizabeth is in here," he said, and we followed him through a hall lined with black-and-white photos into a living room that looked out onto the water. A woman lay on the couch, her head wrapped in a scarf, her knees in a blanket, which she kicked off to sit upright and greet us. Elizabeth Bennett was sick. Really sick. You could tell by the bottles of pills on the end table and by her bony face and hands and by the yellow cast of her skin.

"Fair warning, I look terrible," she said. It had been such a hot, hot day, but her feet had fuzzy pink socks on them. "So, I hear you're on a quest. And that you've got something for me," Elizabeth Bennett said.

### MARY LOUISE HOFFMAN:

*I want my daughters to understand that step one is avoiding the wrong men, but step two is finding the right one, if that makes sense. I used to think that finding the right one was about the man having a list of certain qualities. If he had them, we'd be compatible and happy. Sort of a checkmark system that was a complete failure. With Barry, when I was in my late twenties, I thought that list was made up of the things I liked in someone. Personal ad adjectives. Barry was fun, he was attractive. He was interesting and creative. Confident. Bigger than life. But those same qualities turned into other, really bad things—irresponsibility, disrespect, control; an endless and exhausting ego.*

*After Barry, I felt the key was basically to find someone who wasn't Barry. Barry's opposite. The list changed. Someone really responsible. Someone less blatantly cocky. Someone more measured and less wild. Someone with a conscience. Enter Obsessive Compulsive Dean. Loved for those qualities, only to find out he was so responsible, he wouldn't take home a paper-clip that had come from his office. So lacking in confidence that his insecurity could never be fed. So measured he couldn't make a decision between a blue towel and a red one without a list of pros and cons and who analyzed everything I said sixteen different ways. You could never just talk. To him, there was a* reason *you said that and in that way, and the reason usually involved some hurt feelings on his part. It was exhausting.*

*Dean felt there was a proper, efficient, twelve-step way of doing everything. He'd reload the dishwasher the "right way" after I or the girls loaded it. Everything had a right way. Choosing a path across a parking lot had a right way. Who knew? No one ever gave me the "Right Way to Do Everything" manual. I thought we all just had our own way. And con-science—his thinking was so black and white he thought I was going to hell for having premarital sex. It didn't cross his mind that throwing a water glass across the room at me when he'd found out I'd had premarital sex was not exactly heaven-bound behavior.*

*This was not a story I did or did not tell my girls—they lived it. One of the million reasons why divorce is awful—your kids have to suffer your current or future romantic catas-trophes.*

*I found out that a healthy relationship isn't so much about sense of humor or intelligence or attractive. It's about avoiding partners with harmful traits and personality types. And then it's about being with a good person. A good person on his own, and a good person with you. Where the space between you feels uncomplicated and happy.*

*A good relationship is where things just work. They work because, whatever the list of qualities, whatever the reason, you happen to be really, really good together.*

The clock had belonged to Elizabeth Bennett's grandmother. It had Elizabeth's name on it because her grandmother had labeled all of the objects in her home before she died, indicating who should get them. Elizabeth had been twelve years old then, but she knew enough to keep the little piece of tape where it was, with her name written in her grandmother's hand. She especially liked that, she said, her grandmother's ink loops of love.

Years ago, when Dad still lived with us, his mother, my grandmother Yvette, had been in the hospital in Santa Barbara. We didn't know her, really, but I'd gone with Dad to the hospital, and we sat on the top of the air conditioner, which made a long bench against one wall. Dad had brought an enormous bouquet of yellow balloons, her favorite color. We all looked up at the television during the visit, because there wasn't much to say. Dad had to tie the balloons to a chair because they kept drifting and blocking Grandma Yvette's view of the TV. Even the memory made me cringe with the discomfort of illness and strangers and too-big things that there aren't words for.

But this wasn't like that, not at all, even though Elizabeth

Bennett was so obviously sick. The room was cozy and clut-
tered—full of books and spinning shelves of movies and CDs,
quilts and pillows amidst the water glass and thermometer and
plastic bin of supplies from what must have been a recent hospital visit. Jake sat in a beanbag chair on the floor, Sprout sat
next to me on a little leather couch, Frances Lee was in a rocker,
and Andy had turned on some music and opened a window and
brought us pizzas. He made Elizabeth a milk shake; you could
hear the blender going on in the kitchen as we talked.

"I've got to tell you, this is a little double whammy from the
past," Elizabeth said. "I didn't think I'd ever see this again." She
patted the clock in her lap. "And Barry. Honestly, he's someone
I try not to think about."

"He talks about you all the time, according to my mother,"
Frances Lee said. "He always said you were the love of his life."

Elizabeth threw back her head and laughed. "You're kidding, right?"

"That's what he said," Frances Lee said.

"Did you hear that, Andy?" she shouted toward the kitchen.
"Barry thought I was the love of his life."

"I thought you said *he* was the love of his life," he shouted
back.

"Barry," she said, and shook her head. "Ah, he broke my
heart. God, the time I spent being torn up over him. You men
don't do this, do you?"

"Get upset over a woman? Hell yes," Andy said. "You think we
don't have these same problems? Of course we do." He'd reappeared and was now studying his CDs. He plucked one out with
his finger, interrupted what was playing, and put the new one on

instead. Some kind of relaxed piano replaced a jazzy guitar.

"Affirmative," Jake said.

"But you don't spend months and months in agony over some guy," Elizabeth said.

"Not over some guy," Andy said.

Elizabeth rolled her eyes at us, to show how exasperating he could be. "Anyway, all that romantic agony . . . And then you look back over who you wasted all this time on. I mean, I spent my whole sixth-grade year in pain over Harvey Kamada, who was the Whac-A-Mole game champ at Chuck E. Cheese."

"Sexy," Frances Lee said. Sprout laughed.

"That was *later*. When he was in his *twenties*."

"He had a future behind him," I said.

"Oh, he did. And then there was Dennis what-was-his-name in college, and I cried over him for months," Elizabeth said. "See? I don't even remember his name now."

"Susanne Renowski," Andy said. "Bawled my eyes out for three weeks straight because she dumped me. Sophomore year. She was the most important thing in my world then, and I care more about the mailbox now than her. Saw her at the twenty-five year reunion, and she's cleaning aquariums at the West Van Pet Mall."

"Terrence Vinnigan," Frances Lee said. "*I* dumped *him,* and still I cried for a week."

Elizabeth leaned back and sighed.

"Tired, babe?" Andy said.

"No, I was just thinking about Barry. You guys came all this way. Is there something you want? Were there things you wanted to know?"

"Just . . . ," I said. I wanted to say, *everything*. "The story," I said instead. Sprout nodded.

"Well," she thought. "We dated all through our senior year of high school, part of junior year, too, come to think of it. And we were serious. I thought we were serious. He was the first guy I thought I loved. Oh God, his mother hated me. She thought the sun rose and set on him. Don't laugh, but I pictured us getting married. Barry had this charisma, you know? I don't know how he ever graduated, because I don't think he ever wrote a paper himself. He was one of those people who always gets let off the hook."

"Meaning they never learn consequences," Andy said.

"Meaning the rest of us are suckers. We had fun together, though. He had big, crazy ideas that made you laugh. I'm feeling weird about this. This is your father."

I looked at her, her cheekbones two ridges against her skin. "We just want the truth, whatever it is," I said.

"All right," Elizabeth said. Still, she paused, maybe to sift through what she would say and not say. "Things started to fall apart when I realized Barry would lie to me about stuff. He'd tell me he'd be going out with a friend, and he'd be really going to some girl's party. He'd lie about . . . a lot of things. Sometimes it felt like everything. And then he started to put me down in little ways, hurtful things, telling me how he thought I laughed too loud or how great some other girl dressed or how my goal of being a writer was too far beyond my actual talent."

"Honey, I've been meaning to tell you, you laugh too loud," Andy said from over by the stereo.

"So basically, what he was like at seventeen is how he stayed," Frances Lee said.

I squeezed my fingernails into my palms, tight. I wished she wouldn't do that, crucify him at every turn. I wanted to learn more about him, I guess. Even the bad stuff. But I didn't want to go on the Slaughter Dad Road Trip.

"I have to say, though, that it was my fault too. Because I *let* him say these things. I'd keep my mouth shut, because I was afraid he'd get mad and leave. I took him back after other stuff happened, too, other girls . . ."

"Ouch," Jake said.

"Well, I thought love was supposed to be *unconditional*." She said the word as if it gave her a bad taste in her mouth. "And whose idea was unconditional love, anyway?" She shook her head. "Man, how dangerous is *that*? And why are we still taught it? It should go the way of hitchhiking and smoking in public places."

Right then, I had an internal snag of *wrong* at her words, as if she'd just stated the opposite of some well-known fact—that you shouldn't treat others like you want to be treated, or that you shouldn't help other people less fortunate. *Shouldn't* love be unconditional? Even though Mom had drowned us in warnings about making good choices, I still held the solid thought that love meant you gave it everything. Wasn't "unconditional" pretty much the same as "commitment"? What was love if it wasn't the permanent and forever resting place of our best intentions and whole-hearted generosity? Held-back love seemed like second-place love. Runner-up love. Not the full-out, give-every-thing, succumb, *fall-in* love that *real* love was supposed to be.

"Parents and children," Andy said. "Unconditional love should be there."

"Well, sure. Of course," Elizabeth agreed. She plucked at some fuzz on her pink socks before speaking again. "Of course. But otherwise? Unconditional love is like a country of two with no laws and no government. Which is all fine if everyone is peaceful and law abiding. In the wrong hands, though, you got looting and crime sprees, and let me tell you, the people who demand unconditional love are usually the ones who'll rob and pillage and then blame you because you left your door unlocked."

She was getting a little carried away, gesturing with a thin arm. She had things to say, you could tell, things to say still. She had set her scarf askew, exposing a patch of downy baldness on the side of her head. Andy noticed, came over, and stood behind her; he straightened her scarf and then leaned down to kiss her forehead.

"Love *should* have conditions," she said, more softly now. "And the biggest one is that you should be able to look in someone's face and respect what you see." She tilted her head back and looked up at Andy, and he took her face in his hands and kissed her again.

I felt a wave, a tsunami, of emotion inside. If you wrapped all love and disappointment and hurt and outrage and the desperate need for healing and for things to work out like they should—if you wrapped up all of that, that's what I felt. If you took those largest of things and put them into one person, that was me then. It was the cosmos stuffed into a glass jar, and the only thing to do with all that feeling was to force the lid down hard with the palm of your hand, hold your heart away in some place. Some place where it would be safe, safe and undiscovered.

*ELIZABETH BENNETT:*

*I had always had a little problem looking out for myself in love. I was afraid people would leave me. So I sort of clung on and did everything possible to keep someone around. I didn't have a hard talk with myself about who I was keeping around, what I was keeping around, as long as someone was around. Doesn't take a rocket scientist to figure out—my mom died when I was twelve, and my dad was pretty distant from us. I clung to people like human life preservers. I thought I'd die if someone left me. It's ironic, because now I'm the one who's leaving.*

*So I put up with bad behavior in the name of loving the way I thought you were supposed to love. Darryl, my long-term partner before I married Andy (whom Andy calls Public Enemy Number One), was moody and remote, and I did everything I knew how to keep him connected to me until I realized I'd finally better protect myself because no one else was going to, especially not Darryl. It makes me so mad—all those nights you spent hurting. You wonder later, all the stuff you hold in. The impact on your health, you know.*

*I met Andy at a grocery store. We were both buying gum. Really. We got into this silly, great conversation. Big Red versus Dentyne cinnamon. We reminisced about Chicklets, and those packs of little tiny Chicklets you don't see anymore. He told me about saving Bazooka comics for a magic kit that turned out to be a wand and a sad little pamphlet of tricks. I think we just wanted to keep the conversation going. We just talked and loved and laughed from that moment on.*

*I wasted all this time with the wrong people. And now*

*there's Andy, and I wish like anything I could still keep that*
*conversation going.*

Andy walked us to the door to say good-bye. Jake was the only
one brave enough to ask what I think we all wanted to know.

"Will she be all right?" he asked.

Andy rubbed his jawline with his hand. "No," he said.

Everyone was silent when we got back into the truck. The
light was twilighty-tender as we drove back through Granville
Island. Even the sight of Bob's big checkered pants in the back
of the truck made me feel like my heart could snap, as did his
cartoon hair against the backdrop of the setting sun. The colors
of Granville Island, the yellows and blues and reds, they were
bright on the way back through town in those moments of sunset, so bright I had to blink.

# Chapter Thirteen

We were staying the night at the Sandy Beach Resort, which was owned by Frances Lee's aunt Sandy, who was one of those people you called an aunt even when they aren't related to you. Sandy Beach Resort was actually eight small cabins in a half circle, with a barbecue pit and picnic tables in the middle, all of which sat at the edge of a rocky beach on Puget Sound. It was one of those places where families might come every year, Grandpa Ed and Grandma Eileen in one cabin; Uncle Brian and Aunt Jenny and their two perfect boys in another; Mom, Dad, and daughter-son and their dog, Scruffy, next door, all joining together in the evenings for hot dogs and games of Hearts and remember when–ing. At least that's what I imagined.

All those people, though, they must have had their family reunion on another weekend, because the place looked pretty empty—the parking lot held only a car with *Just Married* painted on the rear window, and a minivan with a baby seat in the back. Frances Lee parked the truck so that Big Bob would have a good view of the water.

Aunt Sandy gave Frances Lee the cabin key on its sea horse key chain, along with several foil packages of coffee and a cake she'd made us, set on a plate and covered in waxed paper. Her boys would be having some friends at the place for the week-end, so she hoped they wouldn't be too noisy for us when they came in later.

"Her boys—Chris and Michael," Frances Lee explained when she opened the door of the cabin and let us in. "Twin dumb shits. I always got stuck hanging out with them growing up. Mom thought I needed siblings. They tried to get me to drink beer when I was six. They told me they'd give me a dollar if I did. Totally out of control, not that Aunt Sandy ever saw it."

I guess even family that wasn't family had their problems.

"Hoodlums," Sprout said.

"Delinquent losers," Frances Lee said.

"Yeah, but did you drink the beer?" Jake asked. That's what I was wondering too.

Frances Lee ignored him, surveyed the small room. "Nobody better snore."

Sprout snored a loud pig snort and Jake joined in. I dropped our bags on the floor. There were two beds and a scratchy woven couch, and one chair with a scratchy woven seat. A table with a TV on it, one of those ancient, huge kinds with an antenna. Small kitchen, with an olive green Amana Radar Range, which sounded like something they used to give away on old game shows. Jake opened the refrigerator. "Hey, look," he said. It was completely empty except for a box of baking soda and a can of Coors. He held up the beer in his hand. "Frances Lee, I'll pay you a buck."

"It's all yours," she said. I expected him to crack the top right there and down it. He was probably a drinker and a drugger, girlfriends, sex . . . Guys who looked like that generally weren't exactly wholesome. Good looks too often meant, *I expect to be forgiven*. It was too bad his appearance made my eyes so happy—the rest of him would likely make me miserable.

Sprout emerged from the bathroom. "The counter has gold glitter in it," she reported.

"Fancy," Frances Lee said.

I finally got up the nerve to check Mom's messages while everyone got ready for bed. Two *Call me's*. And the last, more firm, but slightly guilty-sounding message: *I'm concerned about something here. Something you said yesterday. I'd like a call back right away.* Something I'd said yesterday? I ran through the possibilities. I'd talked to her for all of two seconds. I'd said it had been a long day. Well, whatever it was, she seemed to be fine about it now. No more messages, anyway.

I got into my big T-shirt, climbed into the creaky bed beside Sprout. I didn't know a mattress could have so many springs—I felt each one under my back. Frances Lee was outside, talking to Gavin on her cell phone. The windows were open, and we could hear everything she said.

"Love you, miss you, love you, miss you," Jake said loudly.

"Smoochie, smoochie," Sprout yelled from beside me on the bed.

After a while, Frances Lee came back inside, slammed the door. "Jesus, would you guys grow up?"

Her words stung. They stung me, anyway. We knew each other well enough to tease a little, but not to be pissed at that teasing. She seemed once again a person easily irritated, maybe even hard to get along with. Maybe Dad had tried. Maybe he tried and tried until he couldn't. I didn't know—we really didn't know each other at all. I wondered for a moment if this would be the last I'd see of Frances Lee. One trip, and that would be enough for us all. Everyone was quiet. But Jake had known Frances Lee longer than we had. He didn't seem particularly bothered. He'd put in the time required that allows you to make a smooth shift past a bad moment.

"They had a fight," he told us. He sang it. *"They had a fi-ight."*

"We did not have a fight," she said.

"For sure they had a fight. Frances Lee always gets bitchy when they fight," he said. He was lying on the couch, which opened up to a bed. The edge of his bed almost touched ours. His voice sounded lying-down. It was different than his upright voice. Huskier. Slower.

"Gavin can't understand why I'm taking five days out of the summer to do this," she said.

"I'm not sure I really get that either," Jake said. "Your dad has fucked up relationships. You visit his exes . . . It's a bold move. So, why?"

"He's a mystery," Frances Lee said. She looked over at us for help, but I didn't know what to say. I didn't exactly know why I was doing this either.

"You know him, though," Jake said.

"Knowing him isn't the same thing as *knowing* him. Even if you know him, you don't know him." I understood what she meant. Maybe we were the only ones who could understand that. "It's like grabbing at air," Frances Lee said.

"Hot air," Sprout said.

"Sprout," I said.

"She's always trying to get me to be nice when I'm just telling the truth," she said to Jake and Frances Lee.

"Your truth is not everyone's truth," I said.

"Your truth is not everyone's truth," Sprout copied in a brat voice. God, I hated when she did that.

"If you start this game, you're dead," I said.

"If you start this game, you're dead," Frances Lee said. Sprout cracked up.

"You know what you all sound like?" Jake said. "You sound like sisters."

We were all quiet then. For a long time. But it was a nice, pleased kind of quiet. A quiet you didn't want to break with words. Frances turned off the lights. She climbed into bed.

"Crickets," Sprout said after a while, and she was right. I lay there and listened to the *threeep, threeep*.

"I remember the first time I met you." Frances Lee's voice was soft from across the room.

"At the pancake place," I said to the darkness. "That restaurant."

"No, way before. You didn't know we met before then? He brought you over when you were maybe a year old. I was six. First grade, my teacher was Mrs. Silver, and that seemed funny because her hair was orange. But he came over, this was before we moved out to the island, and he had you in a backpack. He took us to a park. And I just sat there on the bench and you toddled around and he tried to get me to go play, but I think I already felt too old. Maybe that's just me thinking that now, but I just sat there, I know, and watched you plop down in the dirt on your diaper because you were just learning to walk. He'd put his fingers in your hands and stand above you and lead you around, and then he'd let go . . ."

"And I'd fall," I said. I tried to imagine it.

"Yeah, and I sat there on that bench and watched and then we left. And he put you in the car and you both went home. Sometimes you wore a red coat. And he started to do that every now and then, come and visit."

"I didn't know that."

"For maybe a year, on and off. And what I remember most was when he'd put you in the car. He had his red Corvette."

"Still has."

"I can't think of him with any other car. He *is* that fucking car. And he'd put you in there, and off he'd drive, and I always wondered, you know, where you went and what it was like there, and if he put you to bed at night. I wondered what your house looked like, and what your mom looked like. Then they got married, and I saw her, and she was pretty, but different than I imagined. Really young. And really pretty. And then he stopped coming over not long after."

"I didn't think we'd ever met," I said.

"Yeah. We went to that fucking park a lot. I didn't know why he stopped coming. My mom said that maybe it was hard for your mom. That it wasn't me, just adults having a hard time being adults. I tried to think of that young, pretty woman keeping him from seeing me, but it never felt right in my mind. And now I think that maybe he just makes a mess, and then he shuts the door. The mess is too big. Like when your room gets that way. You shut the door, and then finally clean it one day after you can't stand it anymore. But he never comes back to clean. Instead, he shuts the door and then sells the house."

Sprout grabbed my hand.

"I kept wondering what your kitchen looked like, and if you had a dog," Frances Lee said. "Where you went to school. He stopped coming over, but I didn't stop imagining."

I woke up in the middle of the night because I heard a car door slam, and then another, and then some loud laughter. I laid there and listened. "Steven, you're walking funny, you dumb shit," someone said, and they all laughed.

"Look at that," someone else said. "What the fuck is that?"

"I've had too much to drink," someone else said. "Because I'm seeing a fucking giant with a fucking giant hamburger."

"Jolly red giant," the first guy said again and laughed.

"I didn't know giants ate hamburgers," a third guy said.

"Kill it!" the second guy said.

"If this were the Bible, wouldn't I have a slingshot?" someone else slurred. "Is this the Bible?"

"Yeah, I'm God," said the second guy.

I sat up. I could see a form in the darkness, Jake, his head propped up on his hand.

"Big Bob," he whispered.

"He's in trouble," I whispered back.

Jake swung his legs out of bed. He was wearing a pair of shorts, that was all. I could see his lean and muscled back in the moonlight. I looked at the waistband-crinkle of his shorts. I wondered if there was a mark there, an indentation on his skin, under the elastic. I followed him as he turned the door handle silently and went outside. We were both in bare feet; I had only my long T-shirt on, and the air was cool from the sea, sticky and salty, as if you could put your tongue out and taste it.

Jake walked across the asphalt toward the four guys, who stood around our truck. I held back, felt a grip of uncertainty. One Jake, four guys, a confrontation. "Hey," he said. "Is one of you Steven?"

"Yeah." It was a what's-it-to-you "yeah." Steven was tall and blond, with straight hair and a clunky nose.

"I just wanted to warn you, the police were looking for you earlier. They were here when we came. Saw you on some surveillance camera?" Jake waved toward the roof of the Sandy Beach Resort office.

"Shit. I told you not to mess with that car," one of the other guys said.

"There's no surveillance camera," a male form of Aunt Sandy said. Chris or Mike obviously. But he didn't sound so sure.

Steven flipped his middle finger in the direction of the "camera." "Surveillance this," he said, and cackled.

The fourth guy hooted and laughed. Pulled down his pants and bent over, showed his butt to the Sandy Beach Resort office roof.

"We got to get out of here," Steven said. "Fuck man, they're looking for us. Mike, shit, pull your pants up, come on. Thanks, man," he said to Jake.

"No problem."

"Let's go to Carl's for a while," Mike said, zipping up his pants.

"It's like *1984*, man," Steven said. "Government is watching everywhere."

Jake and I watched as they piled into a four-door Honda Accord. A businessman's car. A car a parent bought, with some misguided hope for the future. "Dicks," Jake said. "You sleepy?"

"Not really," I said. I wasn't at all sleepy. Not even a little bit. More alert than maybe I'd ever been in my life.

Jake gestured for me to follow him. I caught up to him just past the barbecue pit on the lawn, and we walked down the prickly, wet grass toward the beach. We left behind the cottages with their yellow, humming porch lights, headed for the dark sea. We picked our way across the rocks in our bare feet, and small waves shushed in and out on the gravelly beach. Jake sat down, his back against a large driftwood log. He moved a snake of seaweed away so that I could sit too.

"You cold?" he asked.

"You must be," I said. I wasn't cold, not at all. I wasn't cold, and my feet didn't hurt, and I was happier than I'd been in maybe all of my seventeen years.

"No, I'm great," he said.

Our arms were touching. I had pulled my T-shirt down to sit on, but our legs were touching, too. I could feel heat and energy there, where we touched. It felt so strong that it seemed I might see something when I looked down—a band of blazing light, maybe—something besides just our skin touching.

It was quiet except for crickets and the sound of the sea. And then: "It's amazing what damage a person can do," Jake said.

I didn't respond. He'd been listening, too, to Frances Lee before we'd gone to bed. But he didn't know my father. I knew more about him, didn't I? Or was it possible that some people, with less information, can know as much, more? That without the small hindrances and details of love, they possessed clarity?

"He's not all bad," I said.

"Do you have to be all bad to be bad?" he said.

"Do you have to be all good to be good?" I said.

Jake thought. "I think you can be mostly good and still be good. And bad enough to be bad." He grinned at me. White teeth in the dark, that dimple in his cheek. God, I felt like the hairs on my arms were standing on end. I didn't feel anything like this with Daniel. Never. Nothing close. These feelings shouldn't have been in the same country, let alone the same person.

The beach made me brave, the night did. His skin lying against mine did too. "Are you speaking from experience? Bad enough to be bad?"

Jake laughed. "You're kidding, right?"

"Hmm," I said.

"Me? Can't even take two cookies instead of one without a guilty conscience."

"No way," I said. It sounded like me. Just like me.

"I think you've been making assumptions about me," he said.

"Wild women and parties," I joked, but didn't joke. "Or is that, wild parties and women?"

"I'm not sure who you're describing. Maybe a couple of friends of mine." He laughed, but I could tell he meant it.

"Tell me then. What I should know," I said.

"I wore a dress shirt once to a wedding when I was six and never did again. Music makes me feel alive. I can't watch any-one drink the milk from their cereal bowl—"

"I hate that too."

"I don't know why, it makes my stomach . . . Bleh. I was

voted 'nicest boy' in junior high, don't laugh. 'Most likely to join a commune' in high school, though I still am not quite sure what they meant by that. I like to go fishing but don't like to catch the fish, and can't stand public displays of cheery, all-in-fun humiliation—anything involving me wearing a costume, no way. I wear my Hawaiian shirt on the inside. Your turn."

He sounded kind. He sounded shy. He sounded like the Daniel I thought Daniel might be but wasn't. Nothing like I guessed he'd be. "Okay," I said. I thought for a moment. "I love the smell of a new eraser, those pink ones. I once ate half a can of Play-Doh, when I was three. I love Tator Tots and hate Christmas carols."

"'Jingle Bells'?"

"*Hate.* Nicest? Everyone says I'm *too* nice. My niceness is almost a bad habit. Someone could hit me and I'd worry they'd hurt their hand."

Jake laughed. "Oh man."

"I know," I said. "And math. I love it. Especially the Fibonacci series, the golden ratio . . ."

"Sound like fantasy books," Jake said.

"No . . . How do you explain? They're math sequences, sort of, equations discovered long ago, that have been found in nature and art and all kinds of places."

"They don't have anything to do with those awful story problems, right? 'Uncle Ted is on a train going twelve thousand miles for sixty-five minutes. If he travels for three more hours, what did he have for breakfast?'"

I laughed. "No. Just a series of numbers, a pattern, that appears in nature all the time. A weird amount of all the time.

An it-can't-be-an-accident all the time. The number of flower petals in all varieties of flowers will be a Fibonacci number. Those little sections in the spirals of pinecones and pineapples and sunflowers—a Fibonacci number. Shells. Even the numbers in DNA."

"That's amazing."

"And the golden ratio—it's an equation, a proportion, that's seen everywhere. The solar system, the pyramids, Renaissance art, the rise and fall of the stock market, and the growth of populations. The human body. It's almost eerie."

"Some kind of proof of the God-nature-universe mystery, maybe. Discovery of some truth."

"Exactly—that's exactly what I like about it." I felt so pleased, my insides glowed. "There can be a mystery, but then there's good reason behind it. Evidence for belief."

Jake reached down into the sand. "Look," he said. He set a shell in his open palm, traced the spiral with the tip of his finger. He handed it to me. "Memories of the Sandy Beach Resort and the search for truth."

I took the shell, held it tight in my hand. I could have kissed him then, I wanted to. He was so close; his lips were so near mine. The skin of his shoulder was against my own.

"Look at you, now you *are* cold," he said. He was right—I hadn't even noticed. Goose bumps ran up and down my arms. I hadn't noticed, but he had. He stood. Held his hand out to help me up. I took it, stood too.

"I've been hurt by girls. I'm not really hot to have it happen again," he said.

"I get that," I said. But I wasn't sure I got that. I didn't know exactly what he was telling me. I wished I had Aunt Annie around to ask.

We made our way back to the cottage. On the porch, under the yellow light, Jake whispered my name. "Quinn? The thing you most need to know about me? You're not the only one looking for something true," he said.

*BRIE JENKINS:*

*Lincoln's mom insisted we get married in the Catholic Church, and so we did. We had to take marriage-preparation classes. I liked this idea. If we could put a checkmark next to "marriage preparation," we could know that we were being responsible and conscientious and our marriage would succeed. The big message there was, "Love is a decision." It wasn't a feeling, they said, but a choice you made and stuck to. Meaning, you didn't change your mind. No matter what. Good times and bad, sickness and health, et cetera. I liked this, too. Feelings didn't follow a five-year plan, but a decision could.*

*Lincoln had a lot of sickness. Emotional variety. I read every book to try to understand him, because that's what the magazines said to do. If you were a good wife, you tried to understand him. You listened, empathized. You let him know you were there for him and always would be. You did everything you could to solve the problem. I would have gotten an A for effort.*

*But a major piece of the "sickness" was that he was spoiled and just not a very nice person. He was always first in his mind. He resented my dad for having cancer, because this took time away from him. He resented my morning sickness because it meant I couldn't make his breakfast. No amount of listening was going to change that. It's like listening to a two-year-old. Lincoln was sort of a two-year-old in a man's body. He left before Malcolm was born because he said he was the only one I didn't take care of anymore.*

*I know now that if love is a decision, it should be stuck with not out of some sort of cement-and-chains obligation, but because the choice was a good one. A solid one. Love is a decision that should be made for the right reasons and kept for the right reasons.*

I slept badly. I was trying not to worry about Mom's messages, which meant I was worrying a lot. And I was aware, too aware, of Jake's presence. I had placed the shell under my pillow. I dreamed of a girl in a patchwork dress at a wedding. I dreamed that I was trying to get home on a plane, trying to get to the airport, but that I wasn't going to make the plane because I was sitting in the audience of a circus, and the show wasn't over yet. I dreamed that I couldn't see because I was wearing sunglasses, but when I took them off, I still couldn't see.

I was the first one awake. I lay there for a long time, the shell in my hand, until I couldn't stand being the only one awake any longer. I threw my pillow at Sprout.

She opened her eyes. "You're cruisin' for a bruisin'," she said.

Frances Lee made coffee from one of the foil packs and picked at the frosting of the cake. "Olivia Thornton awaits, people. It's tribal mask day. Get the lead out," she said.

Jake brushed by me as he came out of the bathroom. "Good morning," he said.

"Good morning."

He folded the bed away, and we all packed up. We snitched bits of cake and brushed our teeth and then we were ready. Jake opened the door and Sprout shoved her way outside.

"Oh no," she said from the porch.

"What?"

"Ah shit," Jake said.

I walked out to join them. "Goddamn it," Frances Lee said.

Big Bob looked like an enormous mummy in the back of the truck, wrapped and covered in endless loops of toilet paper.

"Hoodlums," Jake said.

Sprout took out her cell phone and flipped it open. She aimed, and then snapped a picture.

"Abominable Snowman, with Cheeseburger," she said.

We stopped for breakfast on the way. The same sort of pancake house in which I had first (not first) met Frances Lee. She and Jake ate one of those breakfasts that have everything—bacon and sausage, pancakes and eggs. Sprout had a strawberry waffle with a snowplowed circle of whipped cream around its edge. I had French toast, decorated with a round glop of whipped butter and an orange slice. After breakfast we called Mom again. It was time for damage control. Sprout and I stood out front, where there was a newspaper stand, a cigarette machine, and a candy dispenser filled with some sort of bumpy red nut item. Sprout pushed the buttons for Camels and Marlboros and Salems.

"Your mom's not here," Aunt Annie said. *Thankyouthankyou-thankyouthankyou,* I thought.

"Can you just give her the message that we're doing great?" I couldn't believe my luck. "She called three times yesterday. I was beginning to think she couldn't let us out of her sight for five minutes."

"I told her the same thing. She was freaking out about your dad changing into a bathing suit when your dad hates the water. 'He doesn't own a bathing suit. I know he doesn't own a bathing suit.' She wanted to call the place you were staying, but I told her she was acting like paranoid stalker parent."

*Shit, shit, shit.* I watched Sprout, Queen of Liars, over by the candy machine. She stuck her finger in and out, in and out, of the little silver door. "Tell her . . ." *Shit.* "We made him buy it. In the motel gift shop." This sounded lame. You could feel the weird disbelief-hesitation pause that sat between Annie and me, the telltale hover that came post-lie. "For tanning purposes," I added.

"Okeydokey," she said. Now she sounded doubtful. "Will do."

Change of topic, quick. "How's everyone there?"

"Bizarro. I finally asked your grandma about all the time she's spending on eBay, and she just stared at the bridge of my nose and said, 'It's none of your beeswax.' Couldn't even look me in the eye. And I hate when people say 'beeswax.' It makes me think of Kendall Greene from the fourth grade with that yellow stuff in his ears." I could hear her shiver. "And then your mom. She's just been sitting in the rocker by the window, listening to music. Shakes her head like she's having some conversation with herself she just can't believe. Ivar lays there at her feet . . . He still hasn't been out."

"Mom's freaking needlessly," I said. I watched Sprout turn the little silver handle of the candy dispenser. She didn't put a quarter in but cupped her hand underneath the hole, just in case.

"No, this isn't just you guys and your dad. She seems pleased with herself. I asked her what was up, and she just said, 'Nothing. I already told you. Nothing.' That kind of thing drives me crazy. She just sits and smiles and shakes her head."

"She just sits and does nothing but listen to music and stare off?"

"You'd think she was in love, but we know that can't be it," Annie said.

"She probably won the lottery and won't tell any of us," I said.

"No kidding," Annie agreed.

Sprout made a little excited squeal. She turned to show me some disgusting bumpy red nuts in the palm of her hand. The candy people must have done a reasonable thing and were trying to give them away. I could see Frances Lee bend her head down on the steering wheel. She did this every time she started the truck since Jake had poured the Coke in. I think she was praying to the mechanic gods. "Well, can you just tell Mom that everything is fine? She doesn't need to keep calling."

"Will do," Annie said.

"How're things with Quentin Ferrell?" I asked.

"Quentin Ferrell is an asshole," Aunt Annie said.

# Chapter Fourteen

"Upside down," Jake said.

"God," I said. I turned the map around, studied it. "It's a straight shot south."

"Three hours to Seattle, this I know how to do," Frances Lee said. She went to school at the University of Washington. "We'll be at Olivia Thornton's house by late afternoon. I've got to warn you, she didn't exactly sound thrilled about this. I think the only reason she's letting us come by is because she wants the mask back."

"Hey, if she's a bitch, we've got a ton of TP in the back," Jake said.

"True," Frances Lee said. "It's just too bad we never found Jane, age six."

"I know it," I said.

"But tomorrow we get to see Brie," Sprout said. Brie and Abigail Renfrew—the last two women on our list. I didn't want to think about Abigail Renfrew. It was one thing for Dad to betray Mom with Abigail Renfrew. It was another thing for Sprout and I to do so. Besides, thinking about Abigail Renfrew now—I was sure it would send some sort of psychic informational waves to our mother, and we'd already had one near miss. I swear, Mom had some sort of batlike radar. You couldn't get anything past her.

I looked in the side mirror at Sprout. She had a little pad of paper and was writing intently, her head down.

"What're you doing back there?" I asked.

"Nothing," she said. She looked pleased with her own secret. Aunt Annie was right—that kind of thing *does* drive you crazy. When people say "nothing" when they're obviously doing something, it makes you much more interested in finding out. Same as when a person starts to say something and thinks better of it. If you knew what the "nothing" or "never mind" was, you probably wouldn't care less, but the not knowing made you care a great deal.

"What?" I asked. "What are you writing? Another story?"

"None of your beeswax," she said.

I held back from leaping over the seat, grabbing up the paper, and reading it out loud, which is what I wanted to do. It was the sort of desperation-fury that came with a game of keep-away. This was how you could feel when things were held back, things you needed or just wanted.

I turned back around. Who cared what she was writing? And just like keep-away, when you walked away from the game is when someone would decide to give you the ball. "I'm writing down some things about our trip. To remember," Sprout said.

"Cool," Frances Lee said. "Great idea." I felt some twist, a sense of being shoved into my place, which was a different place than I'd ever been. I looked around from the new ground I was standing on, and wasn't sure I liked what I saw.

I snuck a glance back at Sprout for any sense of smugness, but she just wore the same little smile she had before as she bent over that pad of paper. We drove with the windows down, passing outlet malls and lumberyards, and the yellow and green fields of the Skagit Valley. Frances Lee made fun of passing cars. *"'I'm proud of my honor-roll student'? Why don't you ever see ones*

that say, 'I'm proud of my C-plus student'?" And made her feelings
clear about a few things. "How can they undo a planet? Pluto's been
a planet for, like, ever. All those Styrofoam models you made as a kid?
And now it's a great big 'never mind, you idiot suckers.'" After a
while, Jake click-clicked the clasps of his instrument case, lifted
out the guitar, and began playing. I watched him as my hair
blew around my face; I saw his long fingers bending to the neck,
strong fingers strumming. I thought about hands, all that they
do in a lifetime—plant seeds in dirt, grasp hammers, hold
babies, give pills to a loved one. I thought about Jake's own
hands, what they'd already touched—beach sand, number 2
pencils, cool sheets, sudsy shampoo, steering wheels, and
Christmas wrapping. And what they might one day touch. A
hand, the curved space of a hip, smooth hair warmed by sun.

Jake whistled. "This place must have some views."

"She's a doctor," Frances Lee said. She turned off the truck,
jammed down the parking brake with her left foot. The address
had led us to a glassy, angled condominium building at the top
of Queen Anne Hill in Seattle. We climbed out of the truck. You
could see the city stretched below from the street. Big Bob had
the best view from up there.

"Did I tell you I'm giving up music to go to med school?"
Jake said.

Sprout carried the mask, and we walked through the doors
of the building. There was a small TV set in one wall that was
part of a security system. We all crowded in so that we could fit
on the screen. Sprout held the mask up to her face. She was a
very short medicine man with braids.

"Hooga-hooga," she said. Jake gave her rabbit ears.

"Okay, troops, disperse," Frances Lee said, and we did. She pushed the bell to Olivia Thornton's apartment, and in a moment, the door buzzed and we entered the lobby. We took the elevator up to the seventh floor; when we got off, there were four identical doors around a square floor.

"Let's all knock on a different one," Sprout said, but before we could cause any more trouble, door number two opened and a woman with shoulder-length blond hair appeared. She wore tight jogging shorts and a tank top and held a bottle of water in one hand.

"Barry's kids?" she said.

"That's us," Frances Lee said. "We spoke on the phone."

"I just got in. The place is a bit of a mess . . ."

The apartment stretched out in front of tall glass windows that looked across at the city, framing the Space Needle artfully just to the left of center. The furniture was creamy beige on white carpets, and tan marble blocks held other African art— tightly woven baskets, sculptures of tribal figures in black stone. Mom would love to have the "mess" she meant—a few envelopes and magazines on a counter where she'd dumped the mail, a couple of suits in thin dry-cleaning bags over the couch. She picked these up, moved them to a dining-room chair upholstered in tight black leather, and before she'd even set them down, her mind caught up to what her eyes saw.

"My mask," she said.

Sprout handed it to her and she held it, looking down at it as it looked up at her. And then, in this clean and ordered place, a messy, unorderly thing happened. Olivia Thornton started to cry.

*ABIGAIL RENFREW:*

*Yes, love is a danger, a drug, and Trent, Haden's father, became dangerous when I first began experiencing success with my art. His refusal to come to my first show was akin to throwing shards of glass into a garden. He said he didn't know what I expected of him. What, after all, was he supposed to say about statues? They looked like statues, what else was there? A week later, he punched his fist through a wall, just to the side of my face. The next time, it was not the wall.*

*There was nothing ambiguous in his message. In order to get what you want from me—love, decent treatment, my financial support—you must do what I want. And not do what I don't want.*

*There was no room for me with Trent to be successful, intelligent, vibrant. I made a statue, then, of a woman with her mouth gagged and her eyes blindfolded and her hands behind her back. But I destroyed it. Even I could not bear to look at it. Even through art, I could not tell this secret.*

"I *hate* to cry," Olivia Thornton said once she stopped, once she'd gotten herself a cup of tea, and us a drink from her refrigerator, which was stocked with so many bottles of juice and soda and water that they were a glass-bottle forest on the shelf. I could see the rest of the food (a pair of grapefruits, anyway) shoved to the back. She confessed that she'd been so nervous to meet us, she bought a little of everything so we'd have something we liked. I could picture her in the store, her cart so full that the bottles shuddered like wind chimes when she turned a corner.

I knew what she meant about crying. I hated it too. I always worried that if I started I might never stop. Like maybe tears were a separate thing from me with a power of their own—to bring me to some dark place I'd never make it home from.

We sat down on the creamy leather couch, and Sprout sat on a window seat with the Space Needle and the curved arc of the sound behind her. A ferry was crossing, making a ballroom glide across the water. A schooner passed, with proud double masts.

"I don't usually fall apart in front of strangers," Olivia Thornton said. She smiled, and little wrinkles appeared by her eyes. I decided I liked Olivia Thornton. She had a direct gaze and kind hands and vacuum-cleaner tracks on the carpet that made you feel like she was someone who tried very hard to be the best person she could be.

"Here we come, a bunch of people you don't know, handing you some object from a past life," Frances Lee said.

"It was a bad time in my life," she said. "I've got to confess, this is a little strange for me. Barry's kids and all. And you said you were half sisters? I thought Barry said he'd been married once before."

"Once?" Frances Lee said.

"Maybe I made a mistake," Olivia Thornton said.

"Twice. My mom before that," Frances Lee said. She wove her fingers together, looked down at them. "He said once?"

Olivia Thornton rubbed her arms as if she were cold. "I must have made a mistake," she said. But you could tell Olivia Thornton was not the type to be careless with details. "Can I ask, what made you decide to do this? To find the owners of these things? All these women?"

"It's a little strange," I said.

"It's a little . . ." Olivia Thornton paused. "I don't know what it is, actually."

"Karma," Frances Lee said. "Doing the right thing, et cetera, et cetera," Frances Lee said.

*"Information,"* Sprout said.

Olivia Thornton looked at me, and I nodded.

"Well, I've been thinking a lot about this since you called. But this is something"—she held up the mask—"this is something that means a lot to me. I got it on a trip to Africa with a humanitarian group when I was twenty years old. When I got home from that trip, I knew I wanted to be a doctor. Barry always denied he had it. He told me I must have lost it when I moved. I was always losing things, forgetting things, remember?" She cleared her throat. "The mask—it was a symbol for me. My own strength and purpose. That thing I'd grab, if there ever was a fire."

I looked at the bookshelf on the wall across from where I sat. Medical books, spy thrillers. A photo in a frame—Olivia Thornton and a boy with her smile, wearing a blue cap and gown. Another photo—a baby on a blanket, with a goofy smile, a diaper on his head. It occurred to me about Dad, that the women in his life were very nice people.

Jake sat forward. "So, I don't get how he always knows," he said. "He takes the thing that means the most."

"Believe me, Barry would know," Frances Lee said. "Just like he knows what to say to really jab you."

"Oh, and I'm sure I *told* him about the mask," Olivia Thornton said. "You've got a lot of material things. But there's only those few you have an actual *relationship* with. They're the ones that have a story."

"You hold them more carefully, too," I said. I thought of my own ring, weirdly. The way I set it in a safe place whenever I had to take it off.

"True, I guess," Jake said. "My mom saves all of her old house keys in a box. Back from when she was a kid, even," Jake said.

"A jar is just a jar except when it was in your kitchen growing up. An umbrella is an umbrella, except when the man you love stood under it during a hailstorm when he asked you to marry him," Olivia said, and sipped her tea.

"How did you and Barry meet?" Frances Lee asked.

"My office," she said. "He came into my office. He'd injured his back. He asked me out, right there. He's very charming, your father. I told him I'd have to cease seeing him as a patient, and he said it was easier to find a doctor than a woman you might want to spend the rest of your life with. That's what he said, 'a woman you might want to spend the rest of your life with.'"

"Gag," Sprout said.

"Oh, exactly, but I fell right for it. He crooked his finger and I followed. I was such an *idiot*. God, I'm sorry—that sounds cruel."

"We *want* to know what happened," I said.

"There was always a little imbalance. Where you're the one that loves more? Not a good thing. I gave the gifts, I said 'I love you.' But it was exciting for me. To be around the show, the performers, backstage. All the people he knew. He was playful and fun but had this certainty, this *power*. The limelight followed him wherever he went. Wherever. You just wanted to be around it."

I knew about that. It was true. You could go to the grocery

store and feel proud of who you were because you were with him. Things were bigger with Dad. It felt so good. Somehow, you were never ordinary, the way you were in your regular life.

I felt a pang, thinking about it. All that I could lose and didn't want to lose, in spite of everything.

"I took a summer off from my practice to go with him," Olivia Thornton said. "I can't believe I even did that. I should never have done that. But then the next year, he told me that the 'brothers' had decided against bringing partners—too distracting. No partners at rehearsals, either. He called me one night from rehearsal. But it sounded wrong. You know how different places sound the way they're supposed to on the other end of a phone? A mall sounds like a mall. A party sounds like a party, a car, rehearsal . . . But this sounded like a house. A really quiet house. A trying-to-be-quiet house. And then, all at once, there was a shout, a woman's voice, *'Jane, no!'* and then a crash. I still remember that voice. And he told me Mike had just knocked over a ladder, but I knew Mike had not knocked over a ladder."

"And that was that," Frances Lee said.

"Oh, no, it was far from that. Far. I went into all-out panic. I convinced myself that maybe Mike's wife *was* on the set. I couldn't look at the truth. I did what I could to make him want me. He loved to tell people I was a doctor, but I think he hated that I was a doctor—he always complained that I was too serious about my work. It wasn't *feminine*. So I took fewer patients. Cooked—I'm not a cook. Dressed the way he liked."

Frances Lee groaned.

"Oh, I know. I do. This is not easy to confess. But I tell this story because there's something I want *everyone* to be aware of.

People need to understand this. I started getting headaches, migraines. A terrible pain in the base of my neck. Stomach problems. I got very sick. Listen, headaches, a ball in the pit of your stomach, tightness in your chest—these are not signs of true love, and if I'm being honest, I had those 'symptoms' from the beginning. I was *always* anxious with him. Here I am, a doctor, and I'd forgotten something hugely important."

Olivia Thornton took a sip of her tea then. She looked at us intently. "The body knows. Okay? Even when we don't know, the body knows. And sometimes, often, its knowledge is superior to ours. It's the one thing I'm completely sure of. Body knowledge—it's the purest kind. It does not succumb to the mental edits and little erasings that the mind is so fond of. You want the truth, go to the body. *Listen* to the body. It screams, when necessary."

Frances Lee worked the key into the lock of the apartment. A brick building, in the University District of Seattle. We'd scraped the top of Bob's head getting into the underground parking garage. *Ouch*, Frances Lee had said. Frances Lee went to school here, and we were spending the night at the apartment of her friend, Riley, who was away on vacation. As we stood at the door, I felt tiredness hit, as if it had waited politely for the right moment to show itself. God, I was tired—an *inside* sort of tired, where it's not just your body that needs rest, but your mind and your thoughts and your feelings, too. "We're supposed to feed the cat and water the plants," Frances Lee said as she turned the key upside down and tried it that way.

"I'm allergic to cats," Sprout said.

Frances Lee groaned.

"Kidding," Sprout said.

Frances Lee opened the door, and the cat appeared, mrow-ing and winding itself around her legs. "Warning, I'm a dog lover," she said to it. Riley's apartment was absent of nearly everything but a pile of clothes and a big-screen TV. One couch. One bedroom with one bed and a computer on a desk, a mud-dle of papers around it.

"Riley's got his priorities straight," Sprout said. She clicked on the television, and a bunch of guys in football uniforms had a beer at a bar as a table full of cheerleaders looked on. "Hussies," she said, and clicked it off.

"He said the couch makes into a bed," Frances Lee said. She dropped her bag, looked in the fridge. "You guys aren't going to believe this," she said.

"What?" I went into the kitchen, and Jake and Sprout came too. A single can of Coors sat in an otherwise empty refrigerator.

"It's a sign," Sprout said.

"I wish signs were easier to read," Frances Lee said. "What do two cans of Coors mean? God sends signs in beer cans? Has it occurred to anyone else how Barry finds these really great women?"

"I know it," I said.

"I was thinking the same thing," Jake said.

"And then proceeds to treat them like crapola," Sprout said.

Sprout flung herself on the couch, and just as she hit the cushions, something tipped over an edge inside of me. Just, over, like that. Maybe it was only because I had reached the overload mark—after being with each other for three days straight, packed in a car, in a bed, in elevators, in restaurant booths and gas station bathrooms, anyone who might have said anything might have been doomed, most especially someone as easy to flatten as a little sister. Or maybe, this image of my father—I kept trying and trying to hold it, to keep it real, but it was like a reflection on water, and Sprout kept running her hand through that water, breaking up the pattern, making it impossible to see. She kept on doing this, again and again, and I wanted her to stop. She really needed to stop that, though maybe, too, the vein of magma under the earth's surface had just finally reached the point of boiling, the point where the earth rose and shifted and changed forever. I didn't want Jake to see us argue, or even Frances Lee, but what came next was out of my mouth before the guards of self-control could step in.

"Why do you hate him so much?" My voice sounded tight as violin strings.

She was like a happy little windup toy suddenly scooped up into someone's palm. She stopped squirreling around on the couch. She beamed lasers from her eyes.

"Why do you love him so much?"

"He's our *father*. He loves *us*." She was an idiot if she couldn't see this. Stupid and childish.

"'Father' is a word. 'Love' is a word. It doesn't mean that something actually *is*."

"Well it *is*. He's not perfect, I know that. What have we seen? He's not good with women. He's not good at relationships. So?"

Frances Lee made a little snort of disgust. "*So?* He eliminated my mother and me from his personal history. Olivia Thornton didn't even know about us. You don't eliminate people you love."

Jake slapped his thighs with his palms and stood. "O-kay. I'm outta here. Dinner. We need dinner. I'm going to go hunt a bison or something and drag it back to the cave."

"Make sure he has extra cheese on him," Frances Lee said.

There was silence. The door closed behind Jake.

"He's not good at *any* relationship," Sprout said.

"Maybe with his *plants*," Frances Lee said.

"Even his plants are just another way of showing off," Sprout said.

"Yeah, you're right. He doesn't have a relationship with them, either. Have you noticed that there's no person-to-person thing here, only a person-to-object-that-makes-me-look-good?"

I ignored her. I glared at Sprout. "You're just protecting Mom. You sound just like her."

Sprout crossed her arms. "You sound like *him*. Why do you act like he's been so good to you, when he hasn't? You give him more loyalty than you give Mom, who's always there for you."

The magma rose, rose. I could feel some crackling fire of anger inside, the kind that could spit sparks. The kind that could do something horrible if I let it out all the way—grab her and hit, pull her hair until she screamed. That anger was so deep it *was* the veins of the earth, hidden, but a real fact of its structure, capable of doing immense damage at the slightest quake.

"He's there for me," I said. Sparks could fly, sparks could catch on things and destroy them. Veins of the earth could open and crumble buildings with the force.

"You want to know what I hate? Do you?" Sprout's voice rose. "I hate the way he's been to Mom. I hate the way he's been to me. But what I really hate? I hate the way he's been to *you*."

"He's good to me." I spit the words.

"You try to talk to him and tell him about your life, and he changes the topic back to him. You say, 'Here's what happened at school,' and he says, 'When I was in school, I was the most popular kid . . .' blah, blah. You say, 'I scored seventy on the math PSAT,' and he says, 'I never used anything I learned in math in real life.' He treats you like a *servant*. 'Quinn get my this, get my that . . .' And you just do what he asks. He cuts you down all the time. *All the time.* 'Well, you have brains, Quinn, that's the important thing. Anyone can have beauty.'"

"That's sick," Frances Lee said. "Fucking sick."

"I'm not listening to this." Goddamn her!

"'Maybe you're just a late bloomer, Quinn.' 'Your mom never was that good looking, either.'"

I hated her then. *Hated.* I felt a fury I didn't even know I could feel. "SHUT THE FUCK UP!" I yelled.

"I hate that the most, because you just take it," Sprout said. "Like you don't even hear it. Like you don't even *feel*."

"Get away from me," I said. "Get away." I made a lunge for her, and she ducked. I ended up with one of her braids in my hand. She yelled out in sudden pain.

"You're beautiful, and he doesn't even know it!" she cried.

I let go then. I felt as if my heart stopped. I'm not sure I was breathing; I think the cracked earth stopped spinning. If there were diamonds below the ground, or only the fury of molten rock, I couldn't tell. There was just stillness and darkness. "He doesn't even see how beautiful you are," she whispered.

I went to the only place I could go to escape. Into the bedroom of Riley, some guy I didn't know, who had a picture of a basketball player on his wall and a box of Cheerios by his bed, the flaps open. A pile of guy stuff in a tumbled ball on the floor— athletic socks, jockeys, a towel and a bathing suit with Hawaiian flowers on it, both likely still damp; there was the smell of damp things left too long with other damp things. I laid down on Riley's bed, put my face into Riley's pillow with the green pillowcase. I could hear the sound of a baseball game from the park across the street—the *pink!* of a ball against a metal bat, a crowd cheering. I was there for a long time, until there was a tap at the door, and Frances Lee ducked her head in.

I kept my head there, on Riley's pillow. I shut my eyes tight against her words. Frances Lee came and kneeled beside me. She put her hand on my hair. She had opened the Coors—her breath had the bright-sour-yellow of just swallowed beer. She stroked my hair.

"He *has* given me things," I said.

"I know," she said.

I sat up, because I remembered something. Frances Lee sat cross-legged, the tattoo of the mermaid facing upward. I'd remembered my ring, given in a small white box on my sixteenth birthday. He'd made a cake, with Snow White on it. I held up my hand, to show her. "He gave me this," I said. "When I turned sixteen."

Frances Lee sighed. "Oh, Quinn," she said. And then she held up her own hand, pointed to a ring in a stack of others, a gold ring with a small garnet in it. "My sixteenth birthday." And

I couldn't help myself, then. I saw and I saw and I saw clearly, but I hated that I did. I hated it, and I started to cry, and I hated that I did that, too. Tears gathered out of nowhere, a sudden monsoon. It may have been years and years worth of tears. Tears from a whole life, there all at once, after waiting so long.

I laid down on that bed and cried, as Frances Lee rested her cheek on my back, staying there beside me until I was through.

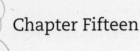

## Chapter Fifteen

Jake came back with two big square boxes of pizza, with a stack of napkins balanced on top, and a bottle of Coke.

"Everybody is friends?" Jake asked, and I nodded, but my insides still felt hollowed out. I was exhausted in a way that felt like years and years exhausted. Eons exhausted. It hurt too much to look at Sprout. She knew the worst things, and that somehow made me feel ashamed. We sat in a circle on the floor, pizza slices in front of us on the pizza-box-top table.

I tried to eat. Jake was telling the story of when he and Gavin were seven and ten and staged a death scene for his mother to find. They had sprawled out in twisted poses on Gavin's bed, with ketchup splurted all around. The only problem was, she was late coming home. They had to keep popping up to look out the living room window to see if she was coming yet, and they made a mess in the hall. She got mad at them and made them clean everything up and told them that death was not a joking matter.

"Which of course we say now every time anything gets too serious. 'Death is not a joking matter,'" Jake said.

"I'm going to try that when I get home," Sprout said. "Freak out Mom." She wasn't looking at me, either.

Frances Lee lifted up another piece of pizza with a long string of cheese still stuck to the cardboard box, and that's when my brain did that amazing thing brains do—made some kind of connection that it must have been working hard on without my knowledge. "Jane," I said suddenly.

"Jane?" Frances Lee said.

"She said, 'Jane.' Remember? Dr. Thornton. What she heard on the phone, 'Jane, no.' Jane, age six."

"It's not a woman . . . ," Frances Lee said slowly. "It's her *kid*."

"Okay, wait," I said. My brain was doing the other thing brains do—once they get going, they don't stop. Put the right nickel in, and you get a thousand others, pouring down Las Vegas riches. "I know who this is. I know who the vase belongs to. We met her." I snapped my fingers, trying to make the name come. I looked at Sprout for help. "Woman with a kid? We went to the zoo with them. The girl wet her pants and we gave her an extra pair of yours that Mom had packed in case you got cold. God, what was her name?"

"I don't remember this," Sprout said.

"It was probably when Mom and Barry weren't speaking, because I don't remember a woman with a daughter," Frances Lee said.

"Heather," I said. Jackpot. "Heather something."

"Heather Grove," Sprout said.

"Oh my God, how did you remember that?" Frances Lee asked.

"I thought it was the most beautiful name I ever heard," Sprout said.

"That's amazing," I agreed.

"I named my sock monkey Heather Grove. That one Grandma made," Sprout said. "With the red butt."

Jake cracked up. I didn't feel like smiling, but my smile didn't seem to know that.

"What are we waiting for?" Frances Lee said. "World Wide Web, watch out."

### HEATHER GROVE:

*Boy crazy, is what my ma called me. Friends at school too. I was. Chris Vallarta, fourth grade—from that point on, boys were what you might call the color and excitement in life for me. Fifth grade, Brian Robinson. Sixth grade, Gary Andresen. I'd choose one to be interested in the first few days of class. Usually just the cutest.*

*I want to say I grew out of that, but I didn't, not for a long time. If there wasn't a guy to like, a guy on the scene, I felt bored and restless. It made things way more fun and interesting. And when I had someone to like, things felt like I could settle back a little. Safe, maybe. Boyfriend, yeah, I had one, even if that meant I might be always on the lookout for someone better to come along. I'm not gonna lie, I was.*

*I always had someone. Always. I think now that maybe boys, men, were some sort of putty in my own cracked cement, so to speak. They filled in gaps. My own gaps, gaps of time and . . . in-between-ness? Gaps of aloneness. Gaps of same-old, same-old. I had "friends" around, guys, to fill in for the times I wasn't "in love." I didn't even like them all that much sometimes. It was just a person who was there to be the focus of the moment. Having a "relationship" made me feel better. It wasn't so much about the actual person, but about feeling more alive and okay.*

*After I got divorced, and then after Barry, it was like I got hit on the head. I could see suddenly how there was this chain of relationships, and how they hurt my daughter and me. I brought bad people into our lives. I hadn't brought the right people in, I brought whoever was around in. I have a lot of regrets. You got to be careful, where you go to fill need, where you go for safety. What looks safe can be very unsafe. When you ask people to rescue you, you just give them an invitation for them to control you. I finally decided that there would be no one else unless it was a good thing for my daughter and me and not about empty places.*

*You see the personal ads, and all the match sites and singles groups—we hunt down another person like we're in the wilds and it's our food. Have to have it. Maybe we all get that anxious feeling that comes with in-between-ness. When we're alone and drifting and things seem bland and gray, when we worry we'll be alone forever. So, we fill the space with someone else, and with "love." It's a lousy job for love to do. Don't get me wrong—a good relationship is a beautiful thing. When it's right and you're ready and it's not some advertisement that keeps you busy until the real movie comes back on.*

*Listen, when what you want is a relationship and not an actual person, get a dog.*

We found four Heather Groves. One owned a horse ranch in Montana. One was in Michigan, and she painted fantasy oils of wizards and dragons using lots of black and purple. She had written that she was "A Professional Role Player," whatever that was, causing Frances Lee to say that she and Dad would be a perfect match. There was a Heather Grove selling her car in Tennessee, and another Heather Grove in St. Petersburg, who'd run a marathon, who'd been a member of the Franklin Elementary PTA, and who had a website of her jewelry design.

"Try that one," Frances Lee said. "He likes artist types. And runner-dancer-athletes."

Jake clicked. Enamel jewelry, et cetera, et cetera. Various pictures of necklaces and rings. *Visit my website often!* it said. As if the site were a living room no one had to clean. "Let's read her bio," Jake said.

"That's her," I said. All you had to do was look at her picture.

"That's definitely her," Frances Lee said.

The woman was blond and pretty, the sort of woman with wrists as delicate as the handles of china cups. She'd have a leafy, whispered voice. "'Heather Grove uses her training in the ancient art of jewelry . . . blah, blah, so on, so on . . . ,'" Frances Lee said.

"Ha-ha. Look at this," Sprout said. She wasn't paying attention. She waved around some papers that were on Riley's desk. "Oooh, Riley."

"Keep out of his things, Sprout," I said.

"Riley's got a girlfriend," she sang. "Riley's got *lots* of girlfriends."

She stuck the papers in front of my face. Lots of small pictures of women, profiles of ages and places and interests. They were all mostly dressed and behaving reasonably well, so I didn't snatch the sheets from Sprout. "Get those out of my face," I said.

"This has got to be her. Look, she grew up in the Northwest," Frances Lee said.

"We found her," Jake said.

"Check this one out," Sprout said. "Oooh-la-la. Jeez, she's as old as *Mom*. Maybe Riley likes older women. Check it out, Grand Canyon cleavage," she said.

We ignored her. "See if there's contact information," Frances Lee said to Jake.

"Ah, ha-ha," Sprout cackled. "Is this supposed to be a sexy look? Because she looks like she's sleeping." Sprout poked the paper right under my nose.

"Sprout, knock it off," I said.

"What time is it?" Frances Lee said. "No, too late to call Florida now."

"We can call her in the morning," I said. "We can't meet her in person, but we can at least talk to her on the phone."

"We can mail her the vase, anyway. This is fantastic. I feel like we've done it. Found them all," Frances Lee said. "Vic-to-ry." She did a little dance.

"Quinn?" Sprout said. Her voice was small. I was ready for some hilarious trick on her part, a sudden yell of "Riley's soul mate!" or something else. Some great big funny joke to snap me back to a good mood.

"Do not," I warned. "I have no interest in seeing any more of Riley's potential love interests."

"Quinn, you might want to see this one," she said quietly.

Maybe I was setting myself up, but something in Sprout's voice made me turn from where I was bent over the desk and look down at the paper she held in her hand. My eyes followed to where the tip of her finger lay. "Oh my God," I said.

"Someone you know?" Jake said.

"Oh my God," I said again.

It was Annie, in that photo Grandma must have found for her, Annie in the wet-look leather bikini on the beach. Annie was here, in some college kid's apartment, taken from the same computer on which he'd probably written some Poly Sci 101 paper. Who knew where else she was. In some sixty-year-old's basement, next to his Radio Shack computer and *Playboys*? On the hard drive of some freak who kissed only one girl—in the sixth grade—and who lives with his mother?

"Who is it?" Frances Lee said.

"It's our aunt. She lives with us. Annie," I said.

"That is too hilarious," Frances Lee said. "What are the odds? Ah, ha-ha," she laughed. Then she looked at us. She made her face serious. "Maybe not hilarious. Not at all funny. Zero funny."

I took the sheets from Sprout and flipped to the front. Riley had done a search for women ages eighteen to thirty, within twenty-five miles of his zip code. Personal ad, in *Hot Singles Times*. And God, there was Annie. Our Annie, right there with all of these women who didn't seem like real women. Women who didn't seem like they had jobs and favorite cereals and *nieces*. Women who made themselves pieces and parts, breasts and legs and invitations. Women who maybe kept the same secret Annie did, who didn't let on when they gave you your change at the bank or made your nonfat vanilla latte or *came home* that they advertised themselves to anyone who'd look, because they were—

"Desperate," Sprout said. "It feels desperate." She sounded sad. Like she might cry.

"Lots of people do this, gang," Frances Lee said. "So, she's lonely and wants to meet someone. It's not some sort of crime."

"My cousin met his wife on eLust," Jake said. "They're very happy."

"Anyway, it's really hard to meet a nice prisoner these days," Frances Lee said.

Before I knew what I was doing, I had socked her arm, the same as I would have done to Sprout. She socked me back. Sprout socked both of us.

"Watch who you're socking, girly," Frances Lee said. "Both of you girlies."

In spite of the bad feelings I was having right then, all the bad feelings of the last few hours, about Dad and Sprout and Annie, I felt this small twinge of . . . *pleased.* I knocked my shoulder into Sprout's.

"I'm sorry," I whispered to her. She knocked her shoulder back into mine in reply. Forgiveness can be a long, complicated thing, involving confessions and Kleenex and promises. Or it can be this—simple, with the unspokens already known and understood.

### JOELLE GIOFRANCO:

*Can I just say one* more *thing? Ask for the best for yourself, ladies.*

It had gotten late, and the lights were all off in Riley's apartment. Frances Lee claimed the bedroom since she was the oldest, and we didn't argue. The cat, whose name we didn't know but whom Sprout named Big Dust Bunny (or BDB, for short), slept in there too, with Frances Lee. Sprout and I shared the pull-out bed, and Jake had arranged the couch cushions on the floor; he balanced on those with one of Riley's blankets. His feet dangled off the end.

"I've never felt so tall. I feel like a basketball player," he said.

It was dark, except for the circle of white from a streetlight outside. A siren screamed. A door slammed down the hall. Riley's refrigerator made a steady appliance-snore.

I lay awake. It was true, what Sprout had said, about not feeling. But something had changed, and the feelings arrived now the way a season does, with surprising suddenness, melting things and pushing up new growth. In some ways, I understood why they called it heartache, because your heart actually does ache, but then again, so does the rest of you. It perhaps should be called entire-person-ache. I felt the leaden sense of loss. I thought about objects, about what Olivia Thornton had said. About jars and umbrellas, about a certain umbrella in a certain hailstorm. I thought about rings on your sixteenth birthday and a shell given on a beach at midnight.

Objects. Objects had weight. Memory and meaning could cling to them, like the smell of laundry soap to a pillowcase. That wooden bowl in your parents' kitchen, the one where they put the keys and the single paperclip and the found marble— it's the bowl that's *always* held the keys and small lost things. It's not just a bowl, it's *home,* and so is that big platter edged with flowers that the turkey goes on. A dried corsage, brown and crunchy and past-tense except for the pin with its pearly tip still bright and sharp, stuck through a thick stem of green floral tape—it's all of your junior-high years. A mask, a clock, a painting—all pieces of yourself that you most want to hold on to. Long-kept objects were past moments where things felt sweet and right—a shell, curved and white, so full of hope still that it almost feels warm to the touch. To take them would be an act of cruelty. A hunter's trophies.

Objects could be false reassurance, too, couldn't they? Artificial proof of love, a memory that was maybe better than a reality—a ring, smooth against the base of your finger. In a white box on a small mattress of cotton. Handed over like diamonds.

Maybe I dozed, I don't know. If I did, it was the weightless, surface dozing that's only imitation sleep. You still feel awake, and if anyone told you different, you wouldn't believe them. I still lay on that pull-out couch, the rod where the bed folded right behind the small of my back. The windows were still dark, and not much night progress had been made. I stared at the bumpy texture of the white ceiling, which I could see in the light of the streetlamp from the window. I tried to force my mind into some state of bored-sleepy-confused, but it wasn't working very well. I flung one arm out from the covers; let my fingers dangle in midnight air.

Sleeplessness is a land with its own inhabitants, and it was there that I met him once again. Fingertips, against mine. I didn't need Aunt Annie to translate this. I found his hand with my own.

"Let me hold you to sleep," Jake said.

And it was like this, my arm dangling down, his reaching up from where he lay on the floor, that I finally rested.

## Chapter Sixteen

"That fucking cat slept on my face," Frances Lee said in the morning. She was in the big T-shirt she used for sleeping, but the faces of the Grateful Dead guys were on her back. You could see the stitching where the tag was, right at the base of her throat.

"Backward," Sprout pointed.

"What?" Frances Lee looked down. "Oh, man. Dress Yourself 101. I got hot in the night with that fur ball lying on me. I swear to God, he was trying to suffocate me. Some payback for the fact that his precious Riley is missing. He's never coming back," she said to the cat, who was *mrrrow*ing and circling the kitchen. "He's left you forever to go be with another, much better cat."

"Glad to see that Frances Lee woke up on the right side of the bed this morning," Jake said from the floor.

"Get me coffee," she said.

"I would do that, but I'm paralyzed from the waist up," he said. He made a lot of *ow, ooh, ow* noises, sat up. "Good morning," he said to me.

"Good morning," I said.

Frances Lee caught my eye. Raised her eyebrows in the way that said *oh-inter-esting*. She had disappeared her arms into her shirt and was scooching it around the right way.

"It's Brie day, it's Brie day, it's Brie day," Sprout sang. She appeared to be the only one who had a good night's sleep. "Hey, wait. Your phone's ringing."

My heart did a drastic, jump-off-a-roof plummet. I listened. It was a far-far-away sound. "Jingle Bells." Coming from my backpack.

Jake caught my eye. See, he knew this about me now. The Christmas carols. "Very funny," I said to Sprout. "You're hilarious. Go get it for me."

Sprout was still young enough that she would obey my command without thinking. It made me feel a little guilty, but not enough. She handed me my phone. I tried to stay calm.

"It's gonna be Mom," Sprout said. God, I hoped not. "We can tell her about Aunt Annie in the classifieds."

"We can't tell her that," I said.

"Of course we can. It's our duty. You love each other, you look out for each other," she said.

"You love each other, sometimes you mind your own business." I jabbed her foot with mine to remind her of why else we couldn't say anything about Annie. *Disneyland?* I mouthed. Sprout put her hands to her mouth as if shocked by what it had nearly done. I flipped open the phone. It wasn't even Mom. "It was only Liv," I said.

"Whew," Sprout whispered.

I listened to the message. "Just Liv, needing me to call her back," I reported. "Something important to tell me." Not about Daniel, she had said in her message, but I didn't repeat this part out loud. Daniel's name did not belong in the same room as Jake did. Sometimes different people could feel more like different lifetimes.

"Wait," I said. "The important thing has to do with someone who lives with us. Why does she have to be so mysterious?"

"Uh-oh," Sprout said.

"You don't suppose Liv was looking for a woman age eighteen to thirty?" I said.

Liv's message went on forever. Met some guy, et cetera, et cetera. I wasn't even really listening until she said what she said next. "Oh, and Quinn?" she said. "Weird thing. I was at a movie last night and my phone was off, but your mom called me, like, five times. She wants to know where you are."

There was no answer when we tried Heather Grove.

"Her machine," Frances Lee said. "Do I leave a message?" I shrugged, but Frances Lee was already talking. "Heather Grove? This is Frances Lee Giofranco. I'm Barry Hunt's daughter. I believe you used to date him. I just wanted to let you know we have an object of yours. Something that we'd like to return to you."

"Sounds like we're holding it hostage," Jake said. "'We have an object of yours.'"

"A million dollars in small bills and the vase won't get hurt," I said.

"Has anyone ever noticed that when people think something is real funny and that something is you, it doesn't feel especially funny?" Frances Lee said.

"*I've* noticed that," Sprout said.

"Frannie needs lo-ove," Jake said.

"If you hug me, I'll kill you," she said.

He walked his scraggly self over to her, draped one arm around her shoulder. "You are my friend, you are special," Jake sang in his husky morning voice. Mr. Rogers never sounded so good.

"You are my friend, you are special to meeee!" Sprout joined in beside me from the bed. She was bouncing on her knees.

"Not so loud," I said. My nerves were edgy enough. My own phone sat beside me—it seemed not entirely impossible that it might suddenly transform from a small bit of friendly metal to my own raging mother in the flesh.

"Somebody shoot me," Frances Lee said.

I did the simplest thing. As we were packing up to leave Riley's apartment, I sent a text to Mom to tell her we were fine, that we'd see her tomorrow at the train station. And then I turned off the phone. We had only two more days before we came home, and there was no way she could find us. We needed to finish this trip as we had planned. I would stonewall. I would shut my inner Venetian blinds and hope for the best. I decided I'd better get Sprout alone as soon as possible to tell her what had been going on, but then I changed my mind about that, too. Let her enjoy the rest of this trip. Let her enjoy Brie Day, especially.

"I'm so excited I can barely stand it," Sprout said as we headed for the truck.

"Front seat, you," Frances Lee said to her. For a second I thought Frances Lee was trying to be extra-nice to Sprout since this was a special day for her. But then she winked at me. I climbed in the back with Jake. He reached out for my fingertips and held them. My fingers felt like they had been on a long, long journey and had finally reached home. It was the kind of happy that felt like an arrival.

"So gang, our last official full day of our karmic quest. Today, Portland and the cheese. Tomorrow, Abigail Renfrew, and then we take ol' Big Bob home. You guys get the train, Jake makes it to his gig, and I head back to the arms of my ba-by."

"Poor Gavin. What a sucker," Jake said.

"Of course, I could just let you out here, Jake," Frances Lee said.

"Gavin's the luckiest guy on earth," Jake said.

Frances Lee turned the key.

"I can hardly wait to get there," Sprout said.

There are a few things you don't say to automobiles and appliances at certain times, lest you ignite some Freaky Friday–type moment of fate-altering disaster. "I can hardly wait to get there" is one of those things that should never be spoken as a key is turned, as is "I've never had a problem with this car yet" or "Everything's going my way today!" But it was too late, and so of course the engine did not kick and rumble to life but instead only made a sick, groaning sound, something like *ruh, ruh, ruh.*

"Goddamn it, goddamn fucking shit-ass car," Frances Lee said. "I told you, Jake, I told you."

Jake let go of my fingers, leaned over the seat; his back was long and lean, white T-shirt stretched across his shoulders. "Give it a minute, Frances Lee," he said. "Wait a second and try again."

"Don't tell me to wait a second and try again," she said, and then waited a second and tried again. *Ruh, ruh, ruh.* Frances Lee let out another stampede of swearing. Sprout folded her hands in her lap.

"Be patient, Frannie. This is what happened before."

"Don't tell me to be patient," Frances Lee said. Her voice filled the car the way a very large man would. "When you're the one who poured that Coke in and fucked up my engine."

"It was fucked up already," Sprout said quietly. She looked out the window as if at the scenery that would be passing had we been able to go anywhere. I could see her worried expression in her reflection in the glass.

"Count to ten, Frannie," Jake said.

Frances Lee counted to ten, which was really a counting to five. But when she turned the key, the engine rumbled alive just as it always did, maybe even stronger, as if to prove that the sick *ruh, ruh, ruh* actually belonged to some other, lame engine.

"Man," Frances Lee exhaled. Jake looked over at me and grinned. I grinned back, relieved.

"I keep having this horrible thought that we're going to get stuck at Abigail Renfrew's house," I said.

"Look, the truck's fine now," Frances Lee said.

"You don't like Abigail Renfrew?" Jake asked.

"Hate," I said.

"Barry and she were . . . When their mom and he . . . ," Frances Lee said.

"Oh," Jake said. "So. Yeah. It'd suck to be there any longer than you had to."

What would suck would be somehow missing our train home, freaking Mom out beyond the point of rational, having to stay with Abigail Renfrew or something. But I didn't say any of those things. We *had* to make it home. Home—that house in Nine Mile Falls where my family lived—it seemed like a faraway place, somewhere foreign I had once visited a long time ago. Home meant no Jake or Frances Lee, no sitting in this truck with its now familiar hot plastic seats and Buddha wobbling on the dashboard and floor mats with ridges that the bottoms of my

feet knew. Home meant big, dark unknowns. Secrets told. That
was the thing about secrets—they didn't too often stay that way.
Secrets always wanted out.

"I guess you always imagine the worst," I said.

"Don't worry. Fate's not so obvious, anyway," Jake said. "If
that's what you think *would* happen, that's not what's *gonna*
happen."

"Yeah, we'll be hit by a semi instead," Frances Lee said.

"I'm going to pray the whole way that the engine makes it,"
Sprout said.

"If you get God to listen, tell him I need new tires, too,"
Frances Lee said.

We were back on the freeway heading to Portland, so Bob got to
act like the mayor in a parade again, waving his hamburger at
the crowds, who were honking and shouting to him.

"I've kind of forgotten what it's like to drive without a ten-
foot cartoon in the back," Frances Lee said.

"Someone's going to honk because you left your coffee cup
on the top of the car, and you're just going to smile and nod,"
I said.

"Phone," Sprout announced. She was right. It wasn't even
my phone, but still my heart lurched at the sound—a tiny, electronic Latin beat, attempting minuscule cheer way down
between Frances Lee's seat cushions. She felt around for it,
swerving a little as she did.

"Whoa," Jake said, he looked at me and made his eyes wide
and fake afraid, and I nodded back with the same eyes.

"Hel-lo," she sang. Listened, listened. "Yeah, yeah I did. So, weird story, I know," she said. She tilted the phone toward her chin, mouthed, *Heather Grove.* Someone honked, but it was a long, angry *beeeeep,* an automotive yell that had nothing to do with Big Bob friendliness.

Frances Lee was telling our story, driving with her elbows and making exaggerated facial expressions so that we could have some idea of what was happening on the other end. "We need to get your address to send the vase," she said. Her truck veered slowly over the line, and Sprout gave a little squeal. "Pen." Frances Lee gestured toward the glove compartment, causing the truck to wander to the right again. She almost took out a big old car full of silver-haired old people, with the license plate MIZ JUNE. Sprout fished around inside the glove box— Fritos bag, envelopes, proof of insurance with coffee cup ring on it, French-fry bag, another French-fry bag, parking stubs.

"For God's sake, Frannie, pull over before we get killed," Jake said.

"So we can get your address, and uh, shit!" Frances Lee said. She swerved back into our lane, followed Jake's advice, and took the next exit.

Sprout looped three pens around in circles on an envelope before she found one that worked. "Okay, ready," she said.

Frances Lee repeated Heather Grove's address, and Sprout took it down. She stuffed everything back into the glove compartment. "We were hoping to hear a little about it, you know, how you met Barry," Frances Lee said. "What happened between you . . ." Frances Lee signaled *tick tick tick tick!* pulled into an Arco station, yanked the parking brake, and turned off the engine.

"Please start again. Please start again," Sprout said.

"If it doesn't start again, at least we're alive," Jake said.

"That must have been really hard," Frances Lee said. Listened, listened, listened. "Uh-huh. She probably won't even remember, even if you always will."

Jake took my hand again. Squeezed. My heart was so happy. It made me feel like I could live at the Arco station for the rest of my life. We could stay right there, in the truck, my hand in his. People could bring us CornNuts and Red Vines for dinner.

Frances Lee talked to Heather Grove a little while longer. I rolled down my window and smelled the smell of gasoline and hot asphalt, and the odor of mustard and slick magazine pages coming from the propped-open door of the mini mart. And then Frances Lee said something that made my heart break, sad as it was just happy, there with Jake's hand in mine and an old Volkswagen pulling in to a pump and a crow picking at a bread crust in the parking lot.

"Did you know about me?" she asked.

Jake stared out his own open window then, at the gas station island with its paper-towel dispenser and blue paper towels folding out from the bottom. Squeegees and buckets of soapy brown water and blue paper towels to wipe your windshield with were better to think about than Frances Lee's voice right then. It sounded split open, the way a piece of fruit is, laid bare in two halves.

"No, from his *first* marriage," she said. "No, *twice*."

After a little while, Frances Lee hung up. "Fuck," she whispered.

Frances Lee felt around for her cigarettes, which weren't there. We were quiet. Even Sprout just made the ends of her braids dance with each other in silence. We sat there a minute, until Frances Lee cleared her throat, sighed. Made her voice cheery as crepe paper and game-show hosts. "Pop quiz. Why did Barry and Heather not live happily ever after?"

"She wasn't good enough," I said.

"Very good," Frances Lee said. "Anyone else?"

"Mean to her," Sprout said.

"Excellent."

"He had one on the side," Jake said.

"A's for everyone," Frances Lee said.

"He's getting predictable," Jake said.

"Here's the story," Frances Lee said. "Recently divorced and she just wanted a relationship really bad. White picket fence, yeah, but also someone next to you at the movies. Someone you can share your too-big steak with and what that sleaze Victoria said about you to your boss. Wanted that more than anything. Only problem, Barry wasn't exactly Prince Charming. He didn't like all the time she spent with her kid. Jane, age six, who had made her that vase for Mother's Day in kindergarten. Well, she had a relationship, all right. Just, it was shit."

"I feel sad for Jane, age six," Sprout said.

"Collateral damage," Frances Lee said.

*HEATHER GROVE:*

*Those questions you have? Whether he's the one, whether you feel about him the way you should, or whether the relationship is going okay?*

*When you're not sure whether you're in love with someone or not, the answer is not.*

※ ※ ※

Frances Lee and Sprout wandered around the false brightness of the mini mart. I could see Frances Lee's head cruising around in the aisles, and the bright bits of orange from Sprout's shirt.

"This is beginning to feel like my life," Jake said. "Do you know what I mean? Like tomorrow we'll get up again and go to another Denny's before heading to some other woman's house."

"I know." I did know.

"I've never eaten so much meat in my life." He was referring to the Denny's and Denny's look-alike restaurants' Grand Slamish breakfasts that he'd always order. Eggs and pancakes with bacon/sausage/Canadian bacon and every other breakfast meat known to mankind.

"More meat than most families eat in a week," I said.

"My real life doesn't feel like my real life anymore," he said.

"I know."

And just like that, he leaned over and kissed me, and my arm was around his neck and it was a little like that time Mom decided to barbecue and we couldn't start it and then Grandma came along and poured on this stuff in a metal can and almost set the house on fire. Jake's breath, his sudden lips, his smell, taste of coffee and milk and Jake-ness—it was sudden fire, and my body was alive when it had been sleeping. Maybe whoever wrote that stupid *Sleeping Beauty* had a kiss like this once, because I did feel awakened; I would have gotten on the back of Jake's horse now if he'd had a horse, and let him take me anywhere. Anywhere—and it was me who had my hands on him, who wanted to feel his thighs through his jeans, the place where the edge of his T-shirt met skin. I didn't understand why I hadn't been kissing Jake every single day since I was old enough, why I couldn't have had that kiss every single day, and every day from now on. Once you are awake, truly awake, you don't want to go back to sleep again.

There was the rap of knuckles on glass.

"Break it up, kids," Frances Lee said.

I was embarrassed, but I wasn't. That kiss was so good that the evening news could have been there filming, and so what.

"Wow," Jake said. He was looking in my eyes, and my eyes were awake now too. The me I could tell he saw—she was someone I'd never seen before. She was brave. She walked toward the things she wanted. Maybe she was even beautiful; I saw that there in his eyes.

"Kissy, kissy," Sprout said.

*OLIVIA THORNTON:*

*You've had kisses that make you cringe? Kisses that make you want to run? Body knowledge and all? If you listen, a kiss tells the truth.*

"Brie is very beautiful," Sprout said. "And kind. And she smells good."

"Great," Frances Lee said. "I'll be sure to sniff."

"One time she made these cupcakes with little pirate swords in them for Malcolm. Some mothers might have thought that was dangerous, but she knew that the cool factor was bigger than the danger factor," Sprout said.

"Did one cupcake challenge another to a duel?" Frances Lee said.

Sprout wasn't listening. It was one of those times where the telling is more important than the give-and-take of actual conversation.

Jake held his guitar; I couldn't see his face, only his head of dark curls. He was playing something slow that made you think of new grass and the necks of babies. I wanted his breath again, in my mouth. It was a kiss that didn't have a place. A kiss of Daniel's belonged in the kiss department, but this kiss was wild and borderless. It was fantastic and frightening. I understood something for the first time—I saw the wide land of love, which stretched out far with infinite possibilities of jagged peaks and cool rivers. I saw the trip I was embarking on, across ground that was both timeless and well traveled, and completely new. And I had nothing on my back, really—just a few handed-down tools. There were no certain maps or powerful weapons to protect myself should I encounter danger. There was only the unknown landscape ahead, and me, standing before it with my heart in my hands.

# Chapter Seventeen

"Malcolm has very shiny hair," Sprout said.

"Shiny is nice," Frances Lee said. She'd been very patient. For the last hour into Portland we'd heard about everything from the time Malcolm shaved off his eyebrows with Brie's razor, to the color of Brie's toenail polish (Taste of Mango). Being back in Portland made my chest tighten. The hard parts were here. Brie and our recent, suddenly dropped past; Abigail Renfrew, my mother's enemy; my father's house, empty of his token objects. The nice thing about being on the road is the temporary illusion that you will always be on the road.

"Sometimes he smells like jam," Sprout said.

"I got to warn you right now. I don't like sticky, noisy children," Frances Lee said.

I only knew Brie when she lived with Dad, in Dad's house, surrounded by Dad's things, so I was surprised to see her own house. It was large, with angled, contemporary windows and clean lines, more like her statue than Dad's shingled, ambling home. Brie's house knew where it was going.

"Check the address," Sprout said. She seemed doubtful, too, that this was where Brie lived. It was maybe a case of that weird out-of-place sense you get when you see your teacher at Safeway.

"We're here. Let's go," Frances Lee said. She meant, *Let's get this over with.* When we talked about Brie before, Frances Lee had said, *I've seen her picture,* as if that told her everything she needed to know. She added young and blond together and got stupid.

"Remember what I said about becoming a doctor?" Jake asked. "I'm going to be a . . . What does she do again?"

Before anyone could answer, Malcolm flung open the door and headed right for Sprout, until he saw the rest of us behind her and froze. He suddenly had the face of a little businessman nervous about the deal.

"Malcolm!" Sprout shouted. She put her arms around him and lifted him up and his tennis shoes were hanging somewhere near her knees.

"I remember you, Charles," he said rather formally.

"You better remember me," she said. "You got so big." And she was right. He was taller, but it was something more. He looked like a boy, not a baby. It had been only a few months, but you could see muscles in his arms, not just squidges of baby fat. "You have a big-boy haircut."

"I was coloring," he said.

"Oh, cool." She set him down.

He looked at me as if I were the grilled cheese sandwich and not the potato chips. But then he said, "Quinny, Quinn, Quinn." Like Dad did sometimes.

"Hi, guy," I said as Brie rushed down the hall to the open door.

"You're here!" she said. She looked like summer—golden haired and happy, barefoot, and in a dress the color of the sky. "God, I didn't even hear you drive up, I was drying my hair. Malcolm, you know you're not supposed to open the door!"

"They've got a big man with a cheeseburger," Malcolm said.

"I see that," Brie said. "A story I want to hear." Brie held out her arms and Sprout went to her, hugging her shyly. "Charlotte, my God, look at you. You look so grown-up."

"I was coloring my dog," Malcolm said.

"Ouch," Jake said.

"You got a dog?" I asked, but Brie only rolled her eyes and shook her head to indicate an ongoing issue. "Don't ask," she said.

"We're getting one," he said. "Mom said."

"I said we'd *think* about it," she said.

Malcolm gave a nod, as if this proved his point. We made introductions, followed Brie in. Jake wiped his shoes on the mat even though it was a dry, warm day.

The house was all shiny wood floors and soft, pillowy furniture; Malcolm dive-bombed into the center of one couch when we walked in, as if this is what was required of the host. We'd agreed to spend the last night here, to give Sprout some time with Brie, and so Brie showed us Malcolm's playroom, laid out with air mattresses and sleeping bags. Some heaven-smell of warm garlic and butter was coming from the kitchen. I remembered this now about being with Brie, although I hadn't thought of it in that way before, *Being with Brie*. The way everything just worked. The way there was dinner and order, but only enough order, not too much. The kind of order that lets you relax because everything is going fine. The kind of order you feel safe in—there are no sudden crises of potholders on fire or abruptly being out of the one ingredient that can't be done without, or of parking brakes being left off in a car that makes an escape and ends up on the neighbor's lawn. Even with Malcolm in the house, there were Band-Aids and fish crackers and calm scooping up when there was screaming.

I had always thought of this as *Being at Dad's,* not *Being with*

*Brie* until now. But feeling this again, I realized its absence. Since Brie had been gone, there'd been a certain unease at Dad's, that feeling a dog must have when he paces around trying to find (but not finding) that place to bury his rawhide. Some anxiety of being not one place or another. Some sort of emotional equivalent of the crackle that separates the radio stations.

"I *need* a dog," Malcolm said. "They help you grow up."

"You're doing a beautiful job of growing up, all on your own," Brie said. "Pass Momma the bread."

Malcolm handed the basket to me, and I handed it to Jake, who smiled at me and passed it on. Jake was on his second plate of pasta.

"You must be, what, eight now?" Frances Lee said to Malcolm. She kept a straight face, but Sprout grinned as she twirled pasta around her fork. She'd taken her hair from her braids, and it fell down her shoulders in wide, wavy lines. Frances Lee had taken her shoes off. She'd relaxed enough to take a nap upstairs before dinner but was still walking such wide circles around Malcolm that it seemed like she thought babies and children might be catching.

"I'm four." Malcolm was so proud that his eyes were starbeams.

"Five," Brie said. "In two weeks."

"On my birfday," Malcolm said.

"I thought seven, eight, for sure," Jake said.

"Finished," Malcolm announced. For little kids, the end of dinner is always very sudden.

"Salad," Brie pointed. He ate a couple of bites. "Why don't you get some books and maybe Charlotte can read with you."

He shoved back his chair, and Brie caught it before it tipped. She watched him disappear up the stairs. "Okay, so, chatter, chatter, chatter. He doesn't stop. And I never got to thank you for bringing my statue back. I'm not sure if I can express how much it means to me—it was one of my father's most treasured possessions. So, to have it back, and to know, I don't know, that maybe we don't have to be cut off from each other forever?" She rubbed the top of Sprout's arm.

"We were surprised. Just, suddenly you guys weren't there anymore," I said.

"I wanted to talk with you, spend another weekend with you, have the chance to say good-bye, make some sort of plan for moving out. But Barry, but your dad, he wanted me to leave right then. I told him I couldn't do it anymore, the relationship, and an hour later my car was packed and Malcolm and I were driving down the driveway, and Malcolm was crying because he hadn't even eaten and I had no idea where I was going to go." Brie put down her fork. Closed her eyes for a moment, as if seeing herself there. "God. I had to kick the poor renters out. But I was lucky I had this house."

"Barry's not the sentimental sort," Frances Lee said. "Unless he's playing the Barry Being Sentimental role, and then he'll even cry. Otherwise, you cross him, it's over. You'll get silence. He'll pretend he's forgotten you, because anyone who doesn't see him the way he sees himself is just not worth remembering."

"I don't want to bad-mouth him," Brie said. "You're his kids, plus one." She smiled at Jake, who missed it because he was buttering another roll.

"We want truth," Sprout said.

I could feel Jake's foot, then, reach out and touch mine. We met eyes. They made some sort of promise. Truth, at least.

"Truth, then." Brie told us how she met Dad when Malcolm was just a couple of months old and her father had just died. "At that point, I was in caretaking *overdrive*," she said. "Father, baby, husband. If someone needed me . . . I met your dad when some friends and I went to a party he was at. He sat with me and had a drink, and he juggled a wine bottle and salt- and pepper shakers—" She laughed.

I laughed, too. Maybe it's hard to understand, but I still liked to hear about his good parts.

"But then he got serious. He told me this story, you know, how he had these kids he couldn't even see, and how it just broke his heart. He got tears in his eyes."

"Oh, man," Frances Lee said.

"And I was just *there*. He had me."

Sprout looked down. She just poked at her pasta with the tines of her fork.

"I don't get it. What is it with women and guys like this?" Jake said.

"We love a pathetic loser who needs a mommy and sociopath bad boys," Frances Lee said.

"Maybe it's a problem with strength," Brie said. "You want to feel strong and capable, so you take care of some guy who can't take care of himself. You don't feel so strong, so you get with some guy who feels powerful," Brie said. "Tough guy. Bad boy. Makes you feel safe."

"Those guys are pricks," Jake said. Inside, I grinned a little. His appearance screamed *bad boy*. But Jake was more than a two-word description.

"Some guy in tight jeans and a cowboy hat . . . Cigarette

hanging out of his mouth?" Brie said, and pretended to fan her-self. "Oh, God. I was nuts for this guy in college who was like that. Something about the way he smelled like cigarettes when we kissed, and the weird part was, I hate cigarettes."

"Vicarious rebellion," Frances Lee said. "Good girls being bad the only way they know how."

"I don't know," Brie said. "I think the bad boys hit us in some I'm-all-alone-in-the-forest place. We see the *bad* and we think *strong*. He'll protect me, all those times I've felt small."

"He won't take shit from anyone," Frances Lee said. Her fork waved in the air like it was one tough fork. "Me Big Jock. Me Protect Woman. Me Get Big Scholarship Even If I'm Stoo-pid."

"Kyle Simpson," Sprout said.

Kyle Simpson was a football player who'd been in my Spanish class. She'd heard me talk about him—he was one of the guys who terrorized Ms. Little and whom the girls loved. A superjock who dumped anyone who didn't have sex with him, and who drove a minivan. A minivan he'd put racing stripes on and drove like a sports car.

"Kyle Simpson," I agreed.

"Great, but someday he'll punch out a cop and won't be able to hold down a job," Jake said.

"So true," Brie said. "Maybe our evolution hasn't caught up to us."

"Evolution." Frances Lee looked doubtful.

"We've got some physical reaction, some gut instinct that a guy like that will protect us. But that kind of protection doesn't even work in the world anymore."

"The Western is dead," Jake said.

"Exactly. The truly powerful now—"

"Computer geeks," Jake said.

"A guy who knocks out someone's teeth and barely graduates—you hook up with him, and you're going to end up more vulnerable than you could ever imagine. No money, no real relationship. God forbid you marry the guy and have kids, and then you've just bought yourself a lifetime problem. Trust me, I know about this." She pointed her manicured finger in Sprout's and my direction. "You feel attraction to some guy like that, you better ask yourself some serious questions."

"*I'm* not going to do it," Sprout said. "I hate cigarettes. And cowboys are just okay."

Everyone laughed. Sprout's cheeks flushed. She hadn't meant to be funny, but decided to be pleased about it anyway.

"Why can't you find both?" I said. "You know, strength. But someone with—"

"Integrity. Integrity is what makes you truly safe," Brie said.

"Okay, integrity."

"I don't know. I haven't been able to find it yet," Brie said.

"Gavin has both those things," Frances Lee said.

"Lucky," Brie said. "Lucky you."

"But, still. Cowboys are more than okay," Frances Lee said. "Right, Brie?"

"Musicians are better," Jake said.

"Oh, God, musicians," Brie groaned.

"Wait a second. Musicians with integrity." Jake smiled.

"And college degrees," Brie said. She waved her fork again, at him this time.

"Of course," Jake said. "School of Business. UW. Next fall."

"Really?" I said.

"I believe in a backup plan," he said.

"Wonderful," Brie said.

"Moooom," Malcolm yelled from the other room. "I can't carry all these!" We heard the sound of books sliding and dropping.

"Charlotte, you'll be reading until midnight," Brie said.

"I hope he has *Curious George*," Sprout said.

"And that bear that pulls the button on the mattress," Frances Lee said. "I love him."

"Corduroy," I said.

"Yeah, that's right!" Frances Lee said.

Brie stood. She leaned forward, her palms on the table. "I am so happy, I could just hug you all. I knew I missed you, but I was trying not to feel how much," she said.

"Moooom!" Malcolm yelled.

"I'm sorry you were hurt," Sprout said.

"Me too," I said.

"I'm sorry *you* were hurt," Brie said.

"He shouldn't have treated you like that," Sprout said.

"I'm to blame too," Brie said. She came around the table on her way to help Malcolm. She kissed the top of Sprout's head, squeezed my shoulders. "I thought he was drowning," she said. "And I've always been a very strong swimmer."

### DOROTHY HOFFMAN SILER PEARLMAN HOFFMAN:

*My own grandmother told me something I never forgot. She died at ninety-something—old. Probably because of that glass of red wine she drank every night. We thought she was a bit of a boozer, but now they say it's good for the heart. I was a young woman, so this was a long time ago. She was talking about marriage, but it's true for any two people. She said a marriage is like a well-built porch. If one of the two posts leans too much, the porch collapses. So each must be strong enough to stand on its own.*

*I've thought about this over the years, and I've seen many a porch collapse. To know that you can stand alone, to know that he can too—it seems very good advice.*

Sprout read a stack of books to Malcolm. Brie asked if we'd like to watch a movie and then apologized because all she had were G-rated ones about fish and lost dinosaurs and toys that came alive. Jake put in a cartoon movie about two race cars that loved each other, and we sat on the couch with Frances Lee, and soon Malcolm migrated over, snuggling beside Frances Lee and leaving the big squishy chair for Sprout to squeeze into with Brie. Brie and Jake got up to make popcorn midway, and Malcolm fell asleep against Frances Lee before the race cars married, and Jake held my hand and didn't bother to hide it.

Before bed, I was brave and checked my messages. There was just one. *Motels don't have gift shops,* Mom said. *There are no Hunts at the Candy Cane Inn. I'm going to call your father.*

I turned off the phone again. I tucked it way down deep inside my bag, under my extra jeans and the just-in-case sweatshirt. I could put this in another compartment in my mind; I was good at that. That was one thing I learned on this trip, how good at that I actually was. It was easy, really, to hide away the things you didn't want to look at, and easier still to turn one thing into something else by the simple force of your will.

That night, on air mattresses on the floor, I could feel Jake waiting awake as I was, listening for the sounds of others asleep.

I was so tired, and here at Brie's house I almost felt myself drift alongside Sprout and Frances Lee, but Jake's awake-energy kept me awake too. No one had to say it—it was our last night together.

I could see his body scoot toward me on the floor, same as Malcolm when he decided he wanted to get closer to the TV. Jake stopped in front of me, elbows on the floor, chin in his hands.

"So," he whispered.

"Business school," I said.

"Yep," he said.

"In Seattle," I said.

He nodded.

"Just over the bridge from Nine Mile Falls," I said.

"That's right."

He leaned over to kiss me then, and the amazing thing happened again, this whole body tingle of satisfaction and pull. There was nowhere else I wanted to be. Nowhere. My whole life, all of me, the past me, the now me, the future me, felt wrapped up into being right there, right then.

"This doesn't have to be over," Jake whispered.

They were the best words I'd ever heard.

*BRIE JENKINS:*

*Character matters.*

I was beginning to realize that pancakes meant you cared enough to make pancakes, because in the morning, there was the warm smell of batter frying in oil, and Brie in her stylish warm-ups, standing by the stove as Malcolm watched Sunday-morning cartoons. We sat around the table again, and I had this family feeling. As if we were all family, version two, revised edition. A thin wisp of sadness mingled with the smell of breakfast in the air. Family visiting, family leaving. Sprout ate slowly and carefully, cutting her pancakes with the edge of her fork. Brie brushed away our offers to help with the dishes. She knew we had to get going. Today we had to make it to Abigail Renfrew's, back to Dad's, to the Portland Avenue Café to drop off Jake, and finally to the train station by early evening.

We stood outside on the porch with our bags. The sky was heavy and gray, promising summer drizzle. Malcolm ran in airplane circles on the grass, dropping and rolling. Then he sensed the mood, came and wrapped his arms around his mother's waist, his knees already dewey green and grass stained.

Brie hugged Frances Lee and Jake, and then me. "You've gotten so lovely, Quinn," she said. She swallowed. "I'm really proud to have been part of your life." Her eyes were shiny with tears.

"Thank you for everything," I said. "Everything."

Brie gathered up Sprout's hair in a ponytail and let it fall again. "And you," she said. "I just can't get over what a young woman you've become, Charlotte. You've changed so much from that little girl I first met."

"I'm going to miss you," Sprout said. Tears had fallen, rolling down her cheeks. Brie wiped them away with her thumbs.

"You come and see me," she said. "Anytime."

They hugged once more and Brie kissed the top of her head, and then Sprout walked to the truck with her head up straight. I saw Malcolm's back as he zoomed inside again, little jeans

flying up the stairs. But Brie still stood there on the porch, giving a last small wave as we left.

"The cheese stands alone," Frances Lee said, but it sounded
sad, not mean.

Sprout sat with her hands folded in her lap, staring out the
window. After a while, she finally spoke. "From now on, I'd like
to be called Charlotte," she said.

# Chapter Eighteen

"I thought I'd never hear from you," Liv said when I finally reached her.

"I've been a little busy," I said.

"Don't worry. I'm dodging your mom the way I used to dodge that creepy Harvey kid in the fourth grade," she said. "How are things going with the secret sister?"

"We're in the car now," I said.

"I expect all the details tomorrow," she said. "What's all that honking?"

"I'll explain later," I said.

"All right, well, I just thought you'd like to know that someone in your family is having a little fun for themselves," she said.

I shut my eyes against the gray clouds, the raindrops falling on the glass, against Frances Lee's one working windshield wiper. I hated for Annie to be humiliated.

"Go ahead," I said.

"You'll never guess who was in my sister's yearbook."

I opened my eyes again. The freeway. A billboard ad. Asphalt shiny and dark black from rain. "Yearbook?" I was confused now. Liv's sister, Hailey, went to Nine Mile Falls Middle School. She played the French horn in the band and wore braces and glasses, neither of which Liv ever needed.

"Ivar was in my sister's yearbook!"

"Ivar?"

Sprout, *Charlotte,* turned around to look at me, her face scrunched with worry. "What's wrong with Ivar?" she said.

"He's got a whole page to himself," Liv went on. "His picture, some dweeby poem a kid wrote underneath it. About a poor, lost dog who needs food and finds a home at Nine Mile Falls Middle School. I asked Hailey, and she said he comes in the morning and stays all day and kids give him their lunches because he bends his head and looks so hungry. He's become something of a mascot."

"That little sneak."

"What an actor. I told her that it looked like Ivar, and she said it couldn't be. No tag, all that . . ."

"The little bone with his name on it got caught on a couch cushion he was trying to rip up," I said.

"I know Ivar when I see Ivar," Liv said.

"That explains what he does all day."

"And where he goes after school."

"What!" Sprout screeched. *Charlotte* screeched. "Tell me!"

"Ivar's been conning the middle school kids into giving him their lunches," I said.

"I *knew* he was getting more square footage," she said.

"All these kids are giving up their food for poor, sad, hungry, homeless Ivar, who's actually got his own plaid pillow and basket of dog toys," Liv said.

"What a little liar," I said.

"A liar who knows how to use his puppy-dog eyes," Liv said.

"Fun's over, mister," I said.

*ANNIE HOFFMAN:*

*Hank Peters, Jack Xavier, we did the "I love you," thing before I even knew who they really were. I love you, oh, I love you, too, smooch, smooch, happy, lovey-dovey, whatever. But what*

*does that mean? Who is he? What is it that you're even seeing,
let alone loving? You're seeing the way they make you feel. But
you may not be seeing how they treat other people, or the way
they always talk about themselves, or the fact that they want to
start their own business but have never had a job that lasted
more than six months. You've got to take your time. Even
though, when you feel that good, the last thing you want to do
is take your time. For me, love's been a freaking* speed trap. *Go
fast, get caught, pay the fine. Here we go again.*

*What I should have said . . . Who* is *he? What's he
doing here, with me? Better question—who am* I? *What am*
I *doing here? What is it that I'm calling love?*

There are times for certain things, it seems—for loss, for things
going right. When Mom made OCD Dean move out, it was time
for things to fall apart—her car, the furnace (in November, too),
shingles from the roof in a windstorm. And in my sophomore
year I had a brief time of luck—a great schedule, friends in
every class, essay questions I knew the answers to, a
Department of Motor Vehicles guy who passed me on my driver's test even though I drove up a curb.

But then, those days with Frances Lee and Jake and
Charlotte—it was a time of secrets and of secrets splitting open.
Grandma and her rabid shopping; Annie and her advertised need;
Ivar, even. Me, mine. As we drove down Abigail Renfrew's gray-
drizzled street, I knew my time of secrets was nearly over. Dad
and I, we would have to face that moment I was both strangely
wanting and dreading—where we looked at each other and *saw.*

And Mom—I knew I would have to confess this trip, but I

still hoped we would hold this one piece away from her. I hoped Mom would never know we'd been here, in this neighborhood of fat elms and lilacs, suddenly familiar. Tidy brick Tudors with leaded windows and arched doorways. Cars parked along the street and lampposts—actual lampposts, with curved iron arms and round bulbs—

"Sprout, do you remember this?"

"Charlotte," she said.

"Do you remember this?"

"No."

But I did.

"You okay?" Jake asked.

I nodded. I wasn't sure. "Here," I said. "That one." It had a decoration on the point of the roof, an iron cone, like a little party hat with a spiral on top.

"The address says 245," Frances Lee said. "That's 248."

"That's it, I know that's it," I said. I remembered that roof. I remembered those stairs, turning in an L-shape toward the door. Dad had waited there, for me to hurry up. The house looked so much smaller than I'd remembered. There were geraniums in a box.

"O-kay, if you say so," Frances Lee said.

"Do you want to wait? We could just drop off the sculpture and head out," Jake said.

"No," I said. My guilty conscience had already rewritten this script, giving me a role I'd feel more comfortable playing. I could be the messenger of Abigail Renfrew's wrongdoing, Mom's bitchy foot soldier, icy semi-stepchild.

We rang the bell. Summer had turned cold. Frances Lee

held Abigail Renfrew's sculpture. The strange head with hollow eyes and smiling mouth looked as if it were horribly confused and trying to hide it. Where I used to see only one expression on it, I now saw a hundred feelings. Fear was there, too, and hope. Grief.

I had been right about the house—Abigail Renfrew opened the door. There she was, in front of us. If I thought Abigail Renfrew's house seemed smaller than I imagined, she herself was much smaller too. It's funny how big people can get in your mind, how large and powerful when their wrists are thin and their shoulders narrow. She was pretty. Memory, I guess, can also make people uglier. She wore jeans and a white T-shirt; her hair was brown, layered, long and loose, her hands filled with silver rings. She was dabbing at that white T-shirt with a wet towel. A red splotch on her chest was widening instead of disappearing. The real Abigail Renfrew—she just seemed like a woman.

"Salad dressing," she said as a greeting. It was an apology. "It's stained, I'm sure. Life imitating art." She looked at us, but no one responded. "I once made a statue by that name. I think I may be a little nervous."

"We seem to have that effect on people," Frances Lee said.

"The past has that effect on people," Abigail Renfrew said. "Come in. And thank you." She took the statue from Frances Lee and put it on the first available surface, a hall table. "Self-portrait back with the self. Do you mind if I change quickly? Now, it just feels all . . . wet. Blech."

"No problem," Frances Lee said cheerfully. Too cheerfully, I thought. I gave a small, ungenerous smile that conveyed irritation hidden behind against-the-will patience. A look can do all that. A look can do more.

We sat down, and I was overwhelmed with a then/now collision. We sat on a wide brown corduroy couch (didn't remember), across from a maroon leather bench studded with metal buttons (did remember). Tall sculpture of a woman under a waterfall (didn't remember), carpet of diagonal colors (did remember); bookshelf (did), fireplace (didn't). And then Abigail Renfrew was back again, in a black tank top with an open white dress shirt over it. She offered iced tea all around, and everyone said yes except me.

"What's with the bitchy attitude?" Frances Lee asked when Abigail Renfrew went to the kitchen.

"No bitchy attitude," I said. Bitchiness was not something I generally did or did very well, but I could summon it for a good cause.

"I would never have recognized you two," Abigail Renfrew said to Charlotte and me when she returned with the drinks. "I don't know if you remember, but you actually used to come over here."

"Oh, I remember," I said. Frances Lee hit my foot with her shoe.

"I was pretty little," Charlotte said.

"You'd play with my cat." Abigail Renfrew sat down on the leather bench across from us. We sat and looked at each other from our opposite couches. It reminded me of when we were kids; we'd stand in our backyard tree fort staring over the fence at Kenny, the little boy next door, and he'd stand in his tree fort staring at us. We'd just look at each other in our forts until Kenny decided to throw sticks at us.

I wondered then if Abigail Renfrew thought of me in the same way as my mother thought of OCD Dean's kids, particularly his daughter, Brenda, who displayed her irritation at all things that were my mother—Mom's cooking, Mom's clothes, Mom's conversation, Mom's basic presence in her life. Brenda, whose favorite dinnertime talk was the "Good Old Days" featuring her own mom and dad. This was usually some story that began with "Remember the time you and Mom did such and such" and ended with "the most fun time ever," the moral being that such fun would never be had again. *Brenda is hurting,* Mom said for a while, until she ran out of self-help books. Then it was *Brenda needs help.* Then it became *Brenda is a hellish little monster.* If this was how Abigail Renfrew thought of me, I wasn't sure I minded.

"Well, I guess I should thank you for bringing back my sculpture," Abigail Renfrew said. She didn't sound too sure.

Frances Lee heard the uncertainty too. "Hopefully, you *wanted* it back," she said.

"Oh, I did. Absolutely. I knew he'd taken it. A symbolic act . . . It's a little hard to look at, though, honestly."

*Like your past behavior,* I wanted to say but didn't.

"It reminds me too much of my past behavior," she said.

I felt the slap of shock, worried for a moment that I'd spoken out loud. We'd had this moment, Abigail Renfrew and I, where our thoughts had intersected, but she didn't even know it. She just went on, took a drink of iced tea with a lemon slice in it. "Past behavior, terrible decisions. Hurtful acts. A painful time. A painful time for a lot of people."

I looked up at her and didn't like what I saw. Her eyes looked kind. It was going to be hard to hate her if she was nice.

"Dad and 'a bad time in my life' have been used a lot in the same sentence, I've noticed," Frances Lee said.

Abigail Renfrew sighed. "Well, you can see it in that woman's face. I made that piece then, as you probably guessed," she said. She looked over her shoulder at the sculpture on the table. "She looks *haunted*."

"Not exactly a happy smile," Jake said.

Abigail Renfrew made an elaborate shudder.

"Happy smile, hurt eyes," Charlotte said. She looked over at me.

"Contradictions and falsehoods," Abigail said. "But . . ." She stood. She walked over to the other statue, of the woman under the waterfall, tapped it with her finger. It had a completely different feeling—a sigh. Relief. The peace of water rushing down on a face that welcomed it. "If you can finally speak your own truth, you're free."

Jake picked up my hand. Truth again, but coming from Abigail Renfrew. A part of me didn't want to squeeze Jake's hand in confirmation of Abigail Renfrew's words. And yet this was Jake's hand, and the truest thing about truth was that it needed to be seen no matter what it was and no matter how it came to you.

"Your work," Frances Lee asked. "Does it mean you got there? That woman is obviously much happier."

Abigail Renfrew laughed. "Got there? I've learned that it's all about the 'getting there' and not too often about the 'got there.' If there even is a 'there.' I'm forty-three and still mostly a work in progress."

Abigail Renfrew said nothing more about my father, or her and my father, or my mother and my father, or us, and maybe that was just as well. We were finished with our business with her, and what was between us was left in that strange echoey place of things unresolved and unspoken. Instead, she showed us her studio before we left, a converted garage space in her backyard. There was welding equipment and tubs of clay, sculpting tools and tables with small model figures. More works in progress, more pieces of women, becoming.

### ABIGAIL RENFREW:

*At the root of every large struggle in life is the need to be honest about something that we do not feel we can be honest about. We lie to ourselves or other people because the truth might require action on our part, and action requires courage. We say we "don't know" what is wrong, when we do know what is wrong; we just wish we didn't.*

*Art lets us tell the truth, but even art can be something to hide behind.*

*I did not want to acknowledge the fact of my abusive marriage, or my subsequent involvement with Barry, whose damage to me was as deep. I considered myself to be autonomous and informed, and yet my relational life was material for the variety of talk show I did not even watch. There is a surreal quality, a nagging sense that this is not one's life. These are not, after all, the outcomes you imagine for yourself. We are supposed to have loving parents and a happy marriage and a house with pictures on the mantel, and when we do not have these things, there is a film of shame. It hurts, yes, but maybe even more than that, it feels shameful.*

*Because it is so difficult to face, one makes a lot of excuses. Love "distorts and deranges"—the Eurythmics again. It is human nature, as well, to seek reason when there is no reason. It can become astonishingly convoluted. He abuses because he had a bad childhood, in spite of the fact that there are endless individuals who have bad childhoods and still have a measure of self-control. Who are even kind and gentle. "Insecurity" is not a good enough excuse for bad behavior. Excuses soften the outrage you should feel until eventually you've lost the capacity for appropriate outrage altogether.*

*But, finally, I had to open my eyes. I had to stop keeping secrets. The truth, thankfully, is insistent. What I saw then made action necessary. I had to see people for who they were. I had to understand why I had made the choices I did. Why I had given them my loyalty. I had to make changes. I had to stop allowing love to be dangerous. I had to learn how to protect myself.*

*But first . . . I had to look.*

Back in the truck, as we sat in front of Abigail Renfrew's house, after Frances Lee's door had been slammed shut, and then Charlotte's had and then Jake's and mine, Frances Lee turned and faced us all. "Congratulations, my friends. We have now concluded the karmic quest." And then she turned her key.

Didn't I tell you? There are things you don't say straight to fate's face.

*Ruh, ruh, ruh.*

"Fuck," Frances Lee said succinctly.

*Ruh, ruh, ruh.*

She leaned back hard against the seat, ran her hands through her hair, and sighed dramatically. Jake looked at me and gave his head a small shake, and I rubbed my forehead in response. Then Frances Lee leaned forward again.

*Ruh, ruh, ruh.*

Jake reached for his backpack, unzipped it.

"If anyone checks right now to see what time it is, you're dead," she said. *Zip,* back up again. "I'm aware we all have places we need to get to today. Very aware."

"We just need to wait," I said. "Waiting worked before." Hopefully, we just needed to wait, and hopefully not for too long. Our train would be leaving in just a few hours. "Besides, you guys said this would never happen. Didn't you say it wouldn't?" My voice sounded slightly pleading. "We wouldn't get stuck here because if you expect it, you get something else, right?"

"Yeah, but *I* was expecting to get hit by a semi," Frances Lee said.

Charlotte got out her notebook and pen, plucked the cap off with her teeth, and held it there. For a while there was no sound except the soft scritch of pen on paper and someone's dog barking in the distance.

"Anyone want music?" Jake asked.

"No," Frances Lee said.

"What are you writing, Charlotte?" I asked.

"Shopping list, what do you think? I'm writing what it feels like to be stuck in a truck with two sisters and a guitar player after visiting my father's former peignoir."

"Amour," I said. "A peignoir is one of those lacy top things."

"Amour, who cares? Point is, we're stuck."

Frances Lee bammed her palm flat against the steering wheel. Frances Lee did have a bit of a temper.

*Ruh.*

"That's not good," Jake said.

*Rrr.*

"Come on, come on, come on," Frances Lee said.

*R.*

"Frannie," Jake said.

The truest thing about truth was that it needed to be seen no matter what it was and no matter how it came to you.

"I know, okay? I know," she said. "You fucked up my engine with that Coke."

*It was fucked up already,* I mouthed to Jake, and he nodded. He brought my hand to his lips and kissed it sweetly. *Oh,* I told my heart. *Hold on.*

"God, Jake," Frances Lee said. Frances Lee really liked to blame people when she was pissed.

"Frannie," Jake said softly. "I think it's over."

*R.*

"Yeah." She laid her head on the steering wheel. In the side mirror, I could see Charlotte's profile bent over her notebook, and Big Bob's shiny checkered pants. It seemed polite to give Frances Lee a moment of silence, even though someone was pushing a foot down on my own internal panic accelerator. I was working my way toward *What now?!* from the fact that we were in a bad way, up a creek without a paddle, royally screwed, plus some, when I saw Frances Lee's shoulders moving up and down, up and down. She was either laughing hysterically or . . .

"Frances Lee?" Charlotte asked. The pen cap clicked back onto the pen.

"I don't know what to do," Frances Lee cried.

"We'll figure something out," I said. Hot water, really hot, dire straits, in a pickle. However it was that you could be in a pickle . . . We were in a *very big pickle*. Big as the one in Big Bob's hamburger.

"We're never going to . . ."

Charlotte put her hand on Frances Lee's back and patted.

"And my truck . . . ," she sobbed. "I can't afford to fix this thing. I can't *afford* this . . ."

She cried her desperation into the steering wheel. There was only one thing to do. I hoisted myself over the seat, Jake giving my butt a helpful or self-serving nudge on the way. I landed in front. I put my arm around her. Charlotte unbuckled her seat belt and scooted over next to us.

"Fucking *money*," Frances Lee said.

"We can help you," I said.

"We'll hold a bake sale," Charlotte said. "We'll say it's for the PTA."

"Or one of those car washes. Where the girls wear those tiny shorts and wave signs to bring in pervert old guys," I said.

Frances Lee's shoulders stilled. If shoulders could smile, hers did then.

"Magazine drive." Her voice was small down there by the steering wheel.

"We'll buy *Dog World* for Ivar," Charlotte said.

"Now that he's learned to read at school," I said.

Frances Lee started to laugh. I could feel Charlotte's arms

around me, her fingertips reaching toward Frances Lee's shoulders. Frances Lee sat up, leaned in to us. She might have had a temper. She might have been unpredictable and occasionally cranky. She might have had a tendency to blame others when she was frustrated. But I think I loved Frances Lee.

"Sisters," Charlotte said.

The word was large, so large. Bigger than it had been before. Family, too, a bigger word. That felt like a good thing. An essential thing. There was power in numbers.

"Sisters," Frances Lee said.

"Sisters," I said.

"Sisters," Jake said. Charlotte shot him a look. "Sorry. I just wanted to be part of things."

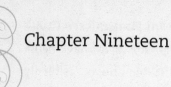

# Chapter Nineteen

We sat there together for a while in the front seat, until finally panic turned into a full-fledged bully—the kind that pokes you in the chest with one finger, and then does it again and again before finally shoving you hard to the ground. What were we going to do? There was no solution, none. We needed help. I climbed over the seat again, into the back. I kept looking at that brick house, its flat front, the leaded windows, the walkway. There was something I couldn't get to, beyond that fortresslike surface. Frances Lee was leaving desperate messages for Gavin. If she could reach him, he could bring a friend's truck. A two-and-a-half-hour drive each way.

We'd never make it to the train station on time. Unless Gavin called in the next few minutes. Unless he called right back and drove real fast . . .

"He said he might go out on the boat with Nate," Frances Lee said to Jake.

"Frannie, you can't hear anything over that engine. I had to read lips for three days after we went with Nate," Jake said. "What about Joelle?"

"Away with Roy for the weekend. I think they're up in Canada."

We sat in silence. And then, just right then, another little phone song rang from the front seat. "Gavin!" I said.

"That is *not* my phone," Frances Lee said. "I do *not* have the song that the farting warthog sings in *The Lion King*."

"'Hakuna Matata,'" Jake said, and before the words were out of his mouth, I had flung my body over the seat—*No!*—and grabbed Charlotte, too late.

"Hello," she said.

"No!" I said, again. Her phone never rang. *Never!* God, how could I have forgotten the pink emergency phone?

"Hi, Mom."

I groaned. "Don't tell her where we are!" I shout-whispered.

I could hear Mom's voice all the way in the backseat. Either Charlotte hadn't yet discovered the volume controls, or Mom was yelling. *"Your father's not answering his phone! I checked Quinn's cell bill, and there's all these calls to the islands! Joelle Giofranco?"* Charlotte's eyes were wide. She looked stunned. *"If someone doesn't tell me what is going on right now, I'm calling the pol—"*

Charlotte snapped the phone shut. She held it tight to her chest.

"Why did you hang up? She could help us," Jake said.

"I didn't know what to do," she said.

"Give it to me," I said. I grabbed it from her and shut it off.

"What is going on here?" Frances Lee said. "I heard Mother Hysteria."

"A little problem," I said. Frances Lee looked like she might strangle me. I took a big breath. "We never exactly told Mom we were going on this trip."

"She thinks we're in Disneyland," Charlotte said. "Well, she *used* to think we were in Disneyland."

"You have got to be fucking kidding me," Frances Lee said. Jake squinched his eyes closed as if to guard against oncoming pain. But Frances Lee just shook her head and sighed a *Dear God, what next?* sigh.

"Your mom doesn't know where you are," Jake said. "She just knows you're not where you said you'd be."

I nodded.

"And you're here at your dad's former peignoir's house?"

I nodded again.

"You're dead," Jake said.

"If we can just make the train like we said . . . ," Charlotte said.

We sat in silence. The rain had stopped, but it was getting steamy in the car. We rolled down the windows. The air smelled like damp earth. The sun had inched out, and the wet grass blades and tree leaves looked sparkly white. I was making frantic bargains in my head. *Just, oh God, please let us somehow move from Abigail Renfrew's front yard.*

"Jake, call one of the guys in the band to pick you up. At least you can make your gig," Frances Lee said.

"They won't be coming in for a few hours. Anyway, you think I'm just going to ditch you people? No way," he said.

"You came all this way with us just to get there," I said.

"Yeah, but it turned out that the trip wasn't about the 'got there.'"

"Musicians with integrity," Frances Lee said. "What's the world coming to."

"I'll redeem our reputation by bashing hotel room furniture when I get famous."

"That's a relief," Frances Lee said. She leaned her head against the car seat.

I sighed. My head was throbbing with the ugly pulse of complications. We were not going to be saved, I knew. "We don't have any choice," I said. "We've got to go back in there and ask Abigail Renfrew for help."

"Quinn, I know you'd hate that, but I think you're right," Frances Lee said.

"She's kind of nice," Charlotte said.

"They're all nice," Jake said.

"It's easier to be shitty to someone who'll take it," Frances Lee said. "Remember, you don't have to be *nice*." She poked Charlotte's chest.

"Ow," Charlotte said.

"Let's get out of this blasted truck and get some help," Frances Lee said.

*Slam, slam, slam, slam.* Big Bob grinned and waved his cheeseburger, newly cleaned from rain. I wondered who I was supposed to be with Abigail Renfrew now that I couldn't be a bitch.

We hadn't even left the side of the car/carcass yet (Frances Lee was just tucking her useless keys into the pocket of her jeans), when the front door of Abigail Renfrew's house opened.

"You're still here," she called to us. "Is everything all right? Of course everything's not all right," she said. She walked down the path in her bare feet. "My God, look at who you have in the back."

"The car died," Frances Lee said.

"Oh, dear God, no. What to do? I don't know, let's see. Actually, I have no idea." Abigail Renfrew reminded me of Mom then. She always narrated every thought in a crisis. "Okay. All right. Wait. I'll call Haden. Of course! Haden knows everything about cars."

"Definitely call Haden," Frances Lee said.

"He'll be right over if I ask," Abigail Renfrew said. It wasn't bragging—just more thought narration.

"Haden," Frances Lee said. "Boyfriend?"

"Oh, no," she said. "No. Son. My son. I've sworn off men until I can be trusted with them. Until a panel of experts approves, I'm refraining, lest I continue to be a terrible role model."

"You sound like my mom," I said. I guess it was an offering. An offering, but the truth, too.

Abigail smiled. "Let me get Haden."

### FRANCES LEE GIOFRANCO:

*You've got to go beyond the fact that you like his ass in those jeans. To get this right. Stop and think and lift up the big rock of your past and look at all the creepy shit underneath.*

*I don't know what's going to happen with Gavin and me. We're young, I'm not stupid about that. But I do know I've stopped to look at the pieces—my dad, my mom and dad, my mom, me and both of them.* Their *parents. What I have with Gavin is not made up of old stuff, some psycho merging of our fucked-up family trees. It's new. It's good. It's whole on its own.*

*And I know something else. Sometimes "two" can feel very lonely. Sometimes it can feel very crowded. But with Gavin, two is just the right number.*

Abigail and Charlotte and Frances Lee were inside, making lunch and waiting for Haden. Jake and I sat outside on those brick steps, where Dad had once stood holding Charlotte's hand, urging me toward some new life I wanted no part of. Now here I was, on those same steps, sitting next to a boy whose dimple should have meant trouble but didn't, who leaned in and kissed me again. Who knew a kiss could make you so happy? Who knew it was a whole new place the two of you could visit, a land that was just yours?

"I'm going to miss seeing you every day," Jake said.

I brushed his curls off his forehead. "I'm going to miss seeing *you* every day," I said.

"I never would have guessed that Frances Lee would have a kind, beautiful, smart sister." Jake smiled. I could see why this was so powerful. This feeling. To have someone see you in ways you had never been seen before—it was like one of Malcolm's coloring books, an image made of black lines now filled with blues and yellows and greens. It felt so full when you don't always feel very full. I could understand how it could cause you to take someone's hand and follow them into a dark forest where there might be monsters and giants and witches. But I believed Jake's eyes were sincere. Jake's eyes were good eyes.

I told him so. It got us kissing again, kissing interrupted by Charlotte, who bounded out of the door.

"Lunch is rea— God, you two are getting sickening," she said.

Frances Lee was looking at Haden's ass as he bent over the truck. Haden was close to Frances Lee's age, and it was true that he looked great, really great, from behind. I knocked her with my elbow. *Gavin,* I mouthed. *Who?* she mouthed back, and smiled. She winked at me, a confirmation of Gavin-love.

"I'm afraid there's nothing I can do," Haden said. "Last Rites, maybe? Other than that, you need a new engine."

Three hours left. We couldn't even catch the real train if we wanted to now.

"Okay, okay," Abigail started narrating again. "What can we do? You said this Gavin could come in the morning with a truck, right? You could stay at my house. Or I could drive you home. In my two-seater, no. No. And we've got this rather large man with checkered pants to consider. What are our options? You have to call a parent. There's no other way, of course. Your mother," she said. She looked suddenly gray.

"No," I said.

"No," Abigail said.

"Or their father?" Haden said.

"You've forgotten? Definitely not," Abigail said.

"Definitely not," I said.

"Right. Definitely not," Haden said.

Before I knew what she was doing, before I could stop her, I realized that Charlotte had taken out her phone again, that little pink savior to be used only for emergencies and for taking up-close pictures of parts of me. I reached out to grab it, but a call from this phone right now was akin to usage of that red phone in the president's office. Mom picked up on the first ring.

"Mom?" Charlotte said.

And then she handed the phone to me.

*ANNIE HOFFMAN:*

*Sometimes you've got to make a mess before you can clean up.*

I sat alone on those brick stairs, with the little pink phone folded shut. All of the biggest, worse phrases had been used. *I'm so disappointed in you. I am ashamed of you.* And the worst of all, when she found out exactly where we were, *How could you do this to me?*

There was no way, *No way!* she would let us stay the night in that house, with that woman. She would come and get us, *now! Right this minute! How could that woman let you into her house!*

*One more thing, Mom.* I had to say.

*What do you have to tell me? It better be an apology. A very big apology.*

Well, it did concern something very big.

*We need a truck,* I said. *We've got a ten-foot-tall cartoon character we need to deliver to Dad's front lawn.*

# Chapter Twenty

While waiting for my mother to come, tiny Abigail Renfrew ate half a box of Mystic Mint cookies that she'd offered to us. She also ate an ice cream sandwich, and nearly half a bag of Fritos. She ate like this when she got stressed, she said, which must have meant that her life was pretty peaceful before we showed up at her door. Her eating reminded me of the way people buy out the grocery store when they know a storm is coming.

The drive to Portland from Nine Mile Falls usually takes about two and a half hours. Mom arrived in two hours flat, and in a nice, new truck with roomy front seats and backseats. Hopefully, she didn't steal it, because doing ninety-five in a stolen truck would have gotten her into a lot of trouble. We saw her pull up, two large round headlights screaming down the street. Weirdly, though, the doorbell didn't ring for a long time. She was sitting in her car for a while, hopefully not downing anything alcoholic.

Finally, when the bell did ring, Abigail rubbed her shoulders as if she were freezing, and then got up from the kitchen chair she was sitting in to answer the door. I got up to follow her. Frances Lee stopped me and took my hands.

"God be with you," she said to me.

"Ha," I said.

Abigail opened the door and from behind her, I could see my mother standing on the porch, wearing jeans and a raincoat even though it was summer and the slight drizzle of the day had stopped. Her hair was slightly wild. I'm not sure there was anything underneath the raincoat, and from the look of her hair, it was possible she had just showered when Charlotte called, grabbing the first thing she could throw on. From where I stood, though, I could smell that she had just squirted herself with perfume, and this made me sad. Like perfume would pull it all together and make her a worthy opponent, or maybe just more in control than how she felt. A squirt of perfume is a shot of manufactured confidence, which is probably why it's so expensive and the bottles so fancy.

Mom opened her mouth. Abigail's hand was still on the doorknob, as if in an act of self-protection. Mom just looked at Abigail Renfrew with her mouth open, but nothing came out. Her face twisted up as if she might cry. And that's when Abigail spoke.

"I'm so sorry," she said. "I am so, so sorry."

And then, Abigail Renfrew was hugging my mother, and my mother was hugging her, and it seemed so unlikely, the most improbable thing, that I blinked. I really wasn't sure I was seeing what I was seeing. But that's what was happening. They were hugging each other, a big, long hug full of no-words words.

They separated, and then my mom said, "We're like those old men who served in the war together," and Abigail said, "I know." And my mom said, "War injuries," and Abigail said, "Yes."

"I've wanted to apologize for so long," Abigail said.

"He never did," Mom said.

"Barry—'Love is never having to say you're sorry.'"

They both laughed, then, and even though I didn't get their joke, I could feel the biggest exhale then, a life exhale, a universe exhale, the release of something huge and burdensome. That brick face of the house, what I couldn't get to behind it—maybe it was some realization that Frances Lee wasn't the only one who blamed the wrong people when she was angry. I don't know why we sometimes have such a hard time blaming the one who is really at fault, I just know that we do. It's easier sometimes to blame someone else entirely, than a person we love. Sometimes, too, it's easier, way easier, to blame *ourselves*. But my father, Barry Hunt—his body count was beginning to rise, and finally, it was just too hard not to see.

"So I've got this crazy idea," Mom said. "I saw the hamburger boy out there. Let's go tonight, take care of the deed. All of us. There's some sort of symbolism here, even if I can't quite figure out what it is."

"I'll get my shoes," Abigail said.

"You," Mom said to me. "Serious, *serious* talk coming your way. Where's Sprout?"

"Charlotte. She wants to be called Charlotte now. She's hiding from you in the living room."

"Charlotte Margaret Hunt," Mom called.

"You know I hate my middle name," came a voice from the living room.

"It's your grandmother's middle name, show some pride. Now get out here."

Frances Lee appeared behind her, Jake too.

"You're alive," Frances Lee said to me.

"This is Frances Lee, Mom, my sister. And this is Jake."

Mom turned her eyes toward Frances Lee. She put her hand

to her mouth. She looked like she might cry again. "I haven't seen you in so long—you're a woman now. You have Charlotte's eyes," she said. Her voice was wobbly. She hugged Frances Lee, who hugged her back. "And you have your own eyes," she said to Jake, who laughed, and she hugged him, too.

"I guess we'll all have a chance to get to know each other on the ride home," Mom said.

"Not Jake," Frances Lee said. "You'll get a ride back with your drummer? You still have time to make the show."

"No," Jake said.

"No? What do you mean 'no'? We dragged your sorry butt all around to get you there," Frances Lee said.

"I've got it handled," Jake said. "Fritz's brother is filling in. He's better than me, anyway. I want to see that ol' Big Bob gets home." He looked at me, and I smiled. If I knew Mom, I'd just extended my lecture substantially.

"I hope all of you are stronger than you look," Mom said.

### JOELLE GIOFRANCO:

*I grow green beans in my garden. The one thing I know about harvesting them is that you have to train your eyes to see the beans. At first it all looks like leaves, until you see one bean and then another and another. If you want clarity, too, you have to look hard. You have to look under things and look from different angles. You'll see what you need to when you do that. A hundred beans, suddenly.*

"So this is where your father lives," Mom said. The two head-lights of Mom's stolen truck were blaring on Dad's lawn. Big truck, big headlights; it was practically daylight out there with those. She just sat there, looking. You could see the river beyond, silver in the moonlight. The wind chimes swayed in purple-blackness, the sound of spells and night magic. I saw Dad's abandoned shoes again there on the porch, evidence of his restless urge to be anywhere else as soon as possible.

Mom shut off the engine, and it all went dark as if the stage lights, too, had been switched off. Frances Lee rode with Abigail in her car behind us, and they also sat in darkness. The house was lit only in moonlight now. You could hear the river's steady *shshsh,* a cricket, the slight rumble of a plane overhead, its red lights arcing across the sky.

"I'll help with Bob," Jake said, and made a courteous exit.

"You never said where you got this truck, Mom," I said.

"It was running with the keys in it," Charlotte guessed. "You hopped in."

"It's a friend's," she said.

"A friend's," I said.

"Will Green."

"Our neighbor, Will Green?" I asked. Secrets—I guess Mom, too, had been keeping them.

"Tucker's owner?" Charlotte asked.

Mom nodded. "Something's happened," she said. "Even your father's house doesn't look the same as I thought it would."

"Happened," I said.

"I can't believe I'm saying this," she said.

"Saying what?" I asked.

"I've fallen in love," she said. She seemed in shock.

From the backseat, Charlotte groaned.

"No, you don't have to worry," Mom said. "Not at all. That's just it. It's some kind of miracle."

"What kind of miracle?" I asked.

"It's good. It's actually *good*," she whispered.

I did what Jake did to me. I took her hand. I kissed it. I would be so happy for her. So, so happy. Her eyes were shiny with tears.

"I keep crying. I can't stop. Because I just can't believe it. It's *good*."

Abigail had some experience moving big pieces of art, and art he may not have been, but big he was. She had placed a blanket underneath him before we put him in the new truck, and this made it easier to slide Big Bob out. A little too easy, because he came out at a nearly uncontrollable speed once he got started, like a kid on one of those giant carnival slides, riding down on a burlap bag.

"Whoa!" Charlotte screamed.

"Slow down, big man," Jake said. There were many hands scrambling to catch him, so he didn't fall. We had to scootch, scootch, scootch him across the lawn. We worked together, hauling the edge of that blanket. Mom and Abigail Renfrew, Frances Lee and me, Charlotte, Jake. Family was even a bigger word than I imagined before, wide and without limitations, if you allowed it, defying easy definition. You had family that was supposed to be family and wasn't, family that wasn't family but was, halves becoming whole, wholes splitting into two; it was possible to lack whole, honest love and connection from family in lead roles, yet be filled to abundance by the unexpected supporting players. That's what I felt, then—full. I didn't even know a person could feel so much. When you let it, when you let family be unlikely and abstract and singular and spacious, those who can't give love, who are simply unable—they're dwarfed by the magnitude of those who can.

There was some discussion about displaying Big Bob dramatically, a floodlight shining on him maybe, or placing him in an inconvenient locale, but it was decided to just leave him quietly. This was not about acts of revenge, only about returning things to the people to whom they belonged. Objects, memories, responsibilities. When we got him in his place, there was the relief of the exhale again, the release of something huge and burdensome.

We left Bob there, in the center of the lawn, under the moonlight.

# Chapter Twenty-one

*MARY LOUISE HOFFMAN:*

*You always hear that you'll know when it's right. I've even told my daughters that without really experiencing it myself. Before, I always asked, Is this it? Is this the right they meant? Is this the knowing?*

*But it's true. You do know. And you don't have all those questions. You just know. All this time, they were right.*

We were too jazzed from our own personal victories to stop for the night, so we said good-bye to Abigail and drove home. Abigail and Mom exchanged phone numbers. They had some talking to do. There were few cars on the road, and riding on the freeway brought that sleepy blanket-weight feeling of night. Charlotte fell asleep, but Frances Lee and Mom talked during the drive. Green exit sign past green exit sign, town through town, Mom told Frances Lee what she remembered of Frances Lee as a little girl, her seriousness, her fearlessness, her strength. The time they'd gone to the beach and she'd run straight into the water. The time, when I was still small, that Frances Lee announced she'd be bringing me back home with her. And then, she told Frances Lee about our growing up, Charlotte's and mine. She filled in the lines of Frances Lee's imagination, as I laid my head on Jake's shoulder and finally fell asleep myself, just over the state line.

This time, Frances Lee and Jake stayed at our house, and

Jake had his skivvies on when Grandma walked in on him in the bathroom the next morning.

"Holy moly," we heard her shout.

Gavin picked up Frances Lee and Jake in the morning; he drove over in his station wagon. I didn't know there were station wagons anymore, the kind with three bench seats like Mrs. Brady drove. He had an air freshener in the shape of a hula dancer, a bumper sticker that said, MAKE COFFEE, NOT WAR. Gavin was an older version of Jake—a bit larger, the start of a beard—and he and Jake greeted each other with that shoulder slap–shoulder slap–hug maneuver that guys who loved each other did. Gavin lifted Frances Lee right up off the ground when he saw her. He took her face in both his hands and kissed her long and hard, which made me realize that a great kiss must run in the family.

"Wait," he said when they separated. "Mint. Toothpaste."

"I quit," she said.

"You're kidding," he said.

"Nope. You happy?"

He kissed her face all over, big noisy smooches on her eyes and cheeks and neck. "Happy," he said into her skin. "Happy, happy."

Frances Lee's backpack was over her shoulder. It was weird now, to have to say good-bye. We'd just found each other.

"You," she said to me. "You," she said to Charlotte, who stood there in her rainbow nightgown. "Me. Sisters. Love."

We all hugged good-bye. "Thank you for everything, Frances Lee," I said.

"Now that you're here, how about not going away again?" she said.

My throat got tight. I thought I might cry again. "How about you not going away either," I whispered.

"Stop being mushy," Charlotte said. "None of us are going away anymore."

"What I did on my summer vacation," Frances Lee said. "Family reunion."

Jake held me for a long time. I rested my cheek against his chest.

"It's an ending that's a beginning," he said.

"Whoo-eee, what a hunk," Grandma said at dinner. "I'd have said I was going to Disneyland, too, if it meant spending five days with him. Forget Frontierland." She dug into her lasagna with bulldozer gusto.

"I'm still trying to decide on jail time versus some form of torture," Mom said. She got up to get the milk. "And you two better understand that if you pull something like this again . . . You just better not pull something like this again."

"Can you get the napkins while you're up?" Aunt Annie said.

"Five days with a hunk, and I'm only getting a weekend with a couple of ladies from the senior center, going to the outlet malls," Grandma said.

"You're going to have a wonderful time," Mom said from the kitchen. "It's great you're finding new friends and getting out."

"What ladies from the senior center?" Charlotte asked. It was the first I'd heard of them, too.

"Helen and Louanne," Grandma said.

"I thought you said Louise," Aunt Annie said.

"Louise," Grandma said. "Pass the salad."

"Grandma's made some new friends. We've hardly seen her over the past few days."

"A girl's got to have a little fun," Grandma said, and snapped her fingers twice.

Ivar sat under my chair and looked up at me with his soulful brown eyes. "You, you've been having too much fun, you sneak."

Grandma knocked over her glass. There was a sudden clatter of silverware and glass. It was a good thing Mom had those napkins right there. There was a flurry of mopping and setting things right. I gathered up the soggy napkins and splattered knives. I figured I'd better start the torture now.

"I've just got to say," Aunt Annie said. "And I know your mom will kill me. But I think what you two did was really cool."

"Annie," Mom said.

"It takes a lot of courage to really look . . . Wait." Annie stopped. "*What* is going on here? Speaking of *look*. Neither of you will look at me. You've been avoiding my eyes since you got home. Or is it just my imagination?"

"Your imagination," Charlotte said into her plate.

"This is ridiculous," Aunt Annie said. "You can't tell me what's going on?"

"I don't think you'd want us to say," I said. "Maybe we should talk about this later."

"Talk about what later?" Mom said. "We've had far too many secrets from each other the past while."

"Agreed," Aunt Annie said.

"Agreed?" I said.

"You found out about the private detective, right? Just say it. I confess. I hired a private detective to snoop on Quentin Ferrill. There."

"Oh, Annie," Mom said.

"I'm embarrassed. I didn't want anyone to know. After I went on and on about how great he was? He had a woman on the side. And not only that? He had a guy on the side too."

"Whoa," Mom said.

"There. Everyone knows. How did you find out, did you see the pictures? The bill? I spent an entire month's salary. Okay, more like two. I'm an idiot. And if you give me any lectures about secretive men . . ."

"I have nothing to say," Mom said.

"There, are we fine now? Can I have a little eye contact?"

Charlotte looked at me and I looked at her. We were arguing with our gaze. Charlotte decided that she was the winner.

"We saw you. In *Hot Single Times*."

"I need to be excused," Grandma said.

"We came across some ads. Your picture was there."

"*Whaaaat!*" she yelled. Her eyes were wide and horrified. "Are you sure it was me?"

"Definitely you," I said.

"I did not place any ad in *Hot Single Times* or any other paper, other than two years ago when I had to sell my Datsun!" Annie cried.

Grandma was having a hard time trying to get her chair pushed back away from the table—one of the legs was stuck on the carpet, and she was trying to wedge herself from the small space to get free.

"Hold on a minute there, missy," Mom said.

"I need to use the lavatory," Grandma said.

"Mom! Did you put that in there for me? Tell me you didn't put that in there for me," Annie said. She'd clasped her hands together, prayer-style.

"I didn't put that in there for you," Grandma said.

Annie exhaled.

"I put that in there for me," she said.

"Mom!" Mom shouted.

"With my picture!" Annie shouted.

"Mine weren't that great," she said.

Charlotte started to laugh. I did too. "This is not funny!" Annie said.

"eBay?" Mom asked.

"Who the hell wants all those doo-dads?"

"I want me a *man*," Charlotte said, and we both cracked up.

"Buy It *Now*," I said, and Charlotte started to hold her stomach.

"Girls," Mom said.

"I can't believe this. I truly can't believe this," Aunt Annie said.

"All this time? No eBay?"

"I've got my own handle," Grandma said. She used to have a CB radio in the old days. "LustLady35."

"Oh my freaking God," Annie groaned.

"That picture with the feathers got me the most action," Grandma said. "Two from Hot Singles, one from the Stranger Personals . . . You gotta keep your options open."

"You're writing to these guys, and they all think you look like Annie?" Mom said.

"I sent my real picture to this one old fart on eBliss. Albert," Grandma said.

"And you keep saying how bad *men* are," Charlotte said to Mom.

"Yeah. You better include grandmas and dogs," I said.

But Mom wasn't listening. "Albert," she said.

"He's into river rafting and moonlit walks on the beach," Grandma said.

"I want my picture off of there *now*," Annie said. "Now, like *yesterday*."

"All right, all right," Grandma said. "Maybe I'll end up liking this Albert. I'll find out next weekend."

"Helen and Louise . . . ," Mom said.

"Who wants to spend the weekend shopping with a couple of old bags?" Grandma said. She snapped her fingers twice again.

"Oh, Mother," Annie groaned. "Why?"

Grandma settled her napkin back in her lap. She decided she wasn't finished after all. "You know, I got to thinking. About French fries."

"French fries," Mom said.

"You know when you get a bag of French fries and you're so hungry, you eat them really fast?" Grandma said. "Scarf them down? I didn't want that for my life. When you've gotten to the bottom of the French-fry bag and you realize you haven't really tasted any."

✿ ✿ ✿

*DOROTHY HOFFMAN SILER PEARLMAN HOFFMAN:*

*I realized something about my life and the choices I've made with men. Maybe it's the same with the choices I've made as a whole, because if you look in my closet you'll see what I'm talking about. I have pants I've worn only once, because they show a little sock. Too short. They were a good bargain. Or that blouse that itches, but I can't throw it away because I didn't get it on sale. There's that dress that makes me feel like I'm a sofa in an old bat's living room. I don't know why I bought it. The music in some of those places, you'll buy anything.*

*My point is, there's only a few things there that I like all the way. One hundred percent. My soft blue dress. My lounging pants. Had them for years, and they're still what I reach for when I want to be comfortable. Everything else I like maybe 50 percent, or 75 percent, or 15 percent. And it's been the same thing with men I've been with. I was married twice, and I didn't feel 100 percent either time. Fifty percent maybe. Sixty-five percent.*

*This is what I know. Don't settle for 40, 50, even 80 percent. A relationship—it shouldn't be too small or too tight or even a little scratchy. It shouldn't be embarrassing or uncomfortable or downright ugly. It shouldn't take up space in your closet out of a guilty conscience or convenience or a moment of desire. Do you hear me? It should be perfect for you. It should be lasting.*

*Wait. Wait for 100 percent.*

That night, I knocked on Mom's door. She was sitting on her bed, reading. I handed her the music box.

She looked up at me, surprised. "He did have it."

I nodded.

"It was given to me a long time ago. When I wanted to be a dancer."

"I know."

"I'd almost forgotten this about myself. That I wanted to dance." She held it tenderly. She opened it, and it began to play. "Oh my God," she whispered.

"Now it belongs to you again," I said.

"Quinn, thank you," she said. "Thank you. Really."

"Everything's where it's supposed to be now," I said.

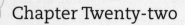

# Chapter Twenty-two

Within two days of getting back, I got the call from Dad that I'd been dreading. He was Zeus, King Triton, God. His fury was so dark, I held the phone away from my ear. We had betrayed him, he said. He should be calling the *police* right now. We had stolen from him. We were mocking him. After all he'd done for us . . . I was no better than Frances Lee. We were crazy, like our mothers.

I was so upset, my insides heaved with grief. I felt like I needed soft foods, and to drink from a straw. I tried to call him, but he wouldn't answer. I'm ashamed to say that I cried apologies into my messages. The strength and awareness about Dad that I'd gotten on the trip seemed to have left me; instead, I felt like a baby who'd been abandoned on the hospital steps. I begged him to see me. If we could just sit down and meet . . .

A few days later, he called. He would be in Seattle the next day. He would see me for dinner. That hip new Ethiopian place on Queen Anne.

It was Grandma's birthday, but I would have to skip the celebration. I had to see him. We needed to talk. If we could just sit across from each other and *talk* . . .

There was a downpour that night; the streets were shiny and black, and you could see the angled streaks of rain in the light of the streetlamps. I found the restaurant, packed tight between a Starbucks and a small gallery, its awning dripping water in steady streams. I looked in the window, trying to see if Dad was there, but I could only see my own reflection. When I went in, the restaurant was full, and we had to press inside—me and, ahead of me, a couple in wet coats, the woman drying her hair with one hand. The walls were deep blue, with ceiling-to-floor tribal masks painted on them, varying versions of the one we had returned to Olivia Thornton. I could see Dad at a window table, and he, too, was just arriving, removing his leather coat and handing it to a waitress. She was laughing at something he said, and he briefly touched her elbow as he maneuvered to his seat.

I felt sick inside, but ready, too. I wanted to be brave and honest. I wanted to reach out to him so that we could understand each other.

"Well, look who's here," he said.

He didn't get up. I sat across from him. "Dad," I said.

"The best thing to get is the special. Little of everything, on one large plate. You've eaten Ethiopian before, I take it?"

"No," I said.

"Never?" He looked stunned. "Whoa. Where've they been keeping you?"

The waitress was back in a moment with his drink, a martini with three olives on a skewer.

"Extra olives," she said.

"That was the fastest martini in the history of martinis," he said to her, and smiled. She had dark hair pulled back into a ponytail, and shy eyes. She laughed again.

"Wasn't she fast?" Dad said to me. And then to her again, "Are you always this good, or did you know I just finished a performance and needed this martini pronto?"

"You're an actor?" she asked.

"Something like that," he said.

"That's amazing," she said.

He ordered our dinner, popped an olive into his mouth, and chewed with satisfaction. He looked over my head toward the door, as if hoping for more interesting company. I felt my courage slipping. I felt like I was disappearing as I sat in that chair.

"You had a show tonight?" I said.

"Next week," he said.

I ran my fingers along the edges of my napkin. "Dad. I know I have some explaining to do." He sipped his martini. The words poured out. My feelings, my confusion. My need to know him. His face was blank. He didn't say anything. Not a word. I started to feel angry at that nothingness. I could feel the heat of irritation hurling forward.

"So?" I said.

But he just looked at me with that wall. Like my words weren't good enough to reach his ears. The anger was building and building into fury. My voice rose. The words were out before I could stop myself.

"I think you were really wrong to take those things," I said. "I think you treated those women like shit." I didn't even know what I was saying. This wasn't going how I had intended. I felt full of rage, but he just sat there. God, I wanted to hit him, throw something at him as he just sat there in cool silence and stared nothingness back at me.

My eyes bore into his. But his—they were flat and hard. They didn't even see me. His eyes were like the glass on the restaurant's window. I couldn't see anything there but my own reflection.

The food arrived. "Look at this!" Dad said. "Well, I sure

hope they appreciate you here, sweetie," he said to the waitress.

"Not really," she said.

"When's your birthday?" he asked.

"January twenty-eighth," she said. "You going to give me a present?"

"I might," he said. "But you're an Aquarius. I *knew* you were an Aquarius. Me too."

She set down the food—a huge circle of bread with various mounds of stuff on it. Brown lumps, black ones. A knoll of orange, a strange heap of yellow. I couldn't eat—I knew that.

"Enjoy, Mr. Aquarius," she said, and he laughed.

The waitress left. Dad ripped off a chunk of the bread, dipped it in the brown glob and stuffed it into his mouth.

"Dad," I said. I heard pleading in my voice. But he just chewed that bread, a big ball in his cheek.

"Dad." I wanted to cry. I wanted out of there. I grabbed my coat off the back of the chair. I could leave right then, and he wouldn't even care.

He swallowed. "Oh, by the way," he said. "Did I tell you I'm getting married?"

A few days later, our things arrived in a box.

"He kept the video games," Charlotte said. "And the Xbox. But look." It was our tube of toothpaste, half-used. Our toothbrushes.

"I can't stand this," Mom said.

School started again. My senior year. Ms. Little in Spanish Three, another two semesters of her whiteboard being pelted with Skittles and en masse slamming of books at exactly one thirty. I applied to Yale, but I also applied to the University of Washington, where Jake went. Where I could live at home and better afford to go. Liv got a new boyfriend—an exchange student from Britain whose name was Giles and who had an accent that had snappy, stylish edges. I saw Daniel every now and then at school, and it was hard for me to think we'd ever been together. He seemed so wrong to me now. I saw Jake on weekends—we'd walk around Greenlake, or lay on a blanket under a tree on the university campus, and it was Jake who was right for my eyes, and for the rest of me, too. Jake was seashell right. Real and absent of show—just himself. More beautiful because of that.

I'd see Frances Lee and Gavin in Seattle on the weekends also, and I'd bring Charlotte along. All of us would go bowling or hang out at Frances Lee's new apartment, and Gavin would teach Charlotte how to do tricks on her skateboard in the apartment's parking lot. We went to Joelle's house, too. When the old horse, Harvey, finally died in October, Joelle held an elaborate funeral, and we ate dinner on hay bales. We had carrots and apples, because Harvey liked those. Jake played sad songs on his guitar until Frances Lee said we'd better liven things up or she was leaving.

Albert would drive up to see Grandma on weekends, and they would go to the movies or for a walk holding hands. Albert had lied about the river rafting (water frightened him), but it was all right because Grandma had lied about the skydiving.

Charlotte got a poem published in a children's magazine, and Aunt Annie became a manager of her store; like Abigail Renfrew, she'd sworn off men until she could be more trustworthy.

Will Green would come over often with his dog, Tucker, who sniffed Ivar politely and laid in whatever spot of sun he could find. I saw them outside once, he and my mother; Will sat on the lawn, plucking pieces of grass and teasing her. My mother was laughing, and then she stood suddenly, as if on a dare. I didn't know she could still do a cartwheel. She was so graceful, too. One hand was on the ground, her feet in the air. Whenever they hugged, my mother closed her eyes and smiled and gave a sigh, like Will's arms were a good place to rest.

I wrote Dad a long letter, which went unanswered. I still wanted him in my life, needed him, in the primal way you need food when you're hungry, or a hand in the darkness when you're scared. I felt a constant, low-flying desperation, the kind you feel when you are trying, trying, trying to get something you will never, ever get. Something that's being withheld, just shy of your grasp. Maybe I didn't know how to dislike someone I loved. Maybe I didn't know how to love someone who kept causing so much pain. I guess I was inching and crawling my way toward Elizabeth Bennett's words about unconditional love. That it was a dangerous thing without heavy doses of mutual respect.

I decided, finally, to go and see him. To attend his show, to meet him afterward. I still believed in "one last try." The more he shunned me, the more I needed him not to shun me.

So I went to a show of his, (ironically) at the Music Box Theater in Seattle. I went alone. I sat in the plush chair on the aisle, next to a woman with a bulky coat; her heavy arms kept pressing into mine. The curtains parted and my father was there, his thick dark hair in a braid down his back, his energy filling the room, dark eyes flashing his playful grin. He tossed a chair to Uncle Mike, who tossed it back—and then another and another, so fast it seemed impossible, and the audience was gasping and laughing with him. I loved him, every minute he was on that stage, but the thing about love is that without its protections, without its boundaries and a close and careful watch, you can hand yourself over, little by little, pieces of yourself given up, until before you know it, you are standing like one of his admirers in the crowd when the show is over. Your need will be so bare it will hurt when exposed to mere air. You'll tremble at his power when he stands before you. You'll stand there, with the noise of the crowd around, and his name being called, and little shoves from people trying to get past, and you'll wait for him to make a decision about you—yes or no.

And when he sees you and he does not reach out, does not reach out but purposefully turns away, when he decides you are not good enough to love, when he does not see your goodness, your beauty, you will have a choice. To be devastated, or to let the truth in, finally, *finally,* all the way, all the way, all the way, until it fills you with its own strength, with its own knowledge—that love is light and not darkness, that love that is not good is not worthy of you, that love can only truly be given by those who are able, those with hearts of quality and with careful hands.

My father, as I've said, had a way of drawing people toward him. Same as his mother, my grandmother, who was said to have powers of magic (at least, she could get the landlord to forgive the rent, could get grown men to hand over their best watches simply because she asked for the time). He brought people in, and I'd seen him do it. He'd turn on this *something*, this energy; he'd toss them a lightning bolt of flattery and the things a person most needed, and people went to that as if they'd been put under a spell. Maybe we all just want to feel special, even for a little while, to be fooled for a bit into feeling something besides the truth of our own ordinariness.

I know about my own ordinariness, I think most people do, and I am okay with it. I am not the most, the best, the fastest, the greatest, but I am enough. Regular and enough, with my own simple but clear voice that I am learning to hear, and my own feelings I'm learning to accept. Beautiful enough for the good people who really care about me. But for Dad, ordinary was unthinkable. It was a crime, an evil force, kept far from his vulnerable center. NO PARKING signs did not apply to him, nor did lines, nor did past failures, or women and children not suitable for perfect storylines. The reason he took things from women, all things, but objects too, was because he wanted to. He wanted to, and so he did. He was a hurricane, a tornado, the powerful sea, God. But I had stopped thinking so. I was ordinary, and I pulled back the curtain and saw a man there, not Oz.

I would probably never be forgiven for it.

*In the summer of my seventeenth year, I learned something about truth—that truth has an urgency. It forces itself up sometimes, disregarding your need not to look, brought to the surface by that part of us that looks out for our own safety and well-being, if only we'd listen.*

*And I learned a lot about love. If you added up all the years of knowing—Mom's and Joelle Giofranco's and Olivia*

*Thornton's and Elizabeth Bennett's and Abigail Renfrew's and Brie's—even Grandma's and Aunt Annie's and Frances Lee's—you would get hundreds of years of knowing. And now I add my own piece to theirs.*

*Sometimes you think you've found love, when it's really just one of those objects that are shiny in a certain light—a trophy, say, or a ring, or a diamond, even. Glass shards, maybe. You've got to be careful, you do. The shine can blind you. The edges can cut you in ways you never imagined. It is up to you to allow that or not. You are the protector of yourself.*

*The most basic and somehow forgettable thing is this: Love is not pain. Love is goodness.*

*And real love—it's less shiny than solid and simple. It's the stuff of sunflower spirals and seashells, where there is beauty and mystery, but where there is logic, too. You do not need protection from it. It is not about lies that someone else tells you or that you tell yourself, but about the truth. Real love is clear. It's as uncomplicated as that shell. It's as timeless.*

*When you find it, if you find it, pick it up. For all the right reasons, pick it up and hold it close.*

*—QUINN HUNT*

TURN THE PAGE FOR A SNEAK PEEK
AT DEB CALETTI'S NEXT NOVEL:

# The Six Rules of Maybe

You could tell something was different about Juliet the moment she stepped out of that truck. She was wearing a yellow summer dress and her hair was pulled back so that you could see her cheekbones and her straight nose and the blazing eyes that used to make all the boys crazy in high school. I don't know how to explain it, but she seemed smug in some way I'd never seen before. Like she had this satisfying little secret. Like something had been decided by her and her alone. She held her head as if she were the period at the end of her own sentence.

We knew Juliet was coming home; we just didn't know she'd be bringing someone else with her, or several someone elses, depending on how you counted. Hayden's dog, Zeus—he was one of those people-like dogs; he listened hard and looked at you with knowing in his eyes, even if two minutes later he'd decide to zip around the living room, slightly crazed, ears pinned back, taking the corners around the furniture like he was in his own private race with lesser dogs.

When the truck door slammed outside, Mom looked out the window and gave a little *It's her!* squeal and we hurried outside. The afternoon was just right warm—a May day that could have been a role model for all May days, and the air smelled wet and grassy because Mrs. Saint George across the street had turned her sprinkler on.

The truck was one of those old kinds with the big wide front that could slam into a tree and still come out smiling its chrome smile. Juliet stepped out and she was all sunbeams in that dress. She was wet grass, and summer, and sunbeams, same as that day was. The thing about sunbeams, though . . . Well, it might sound unkind. You've got to know that I loved my sister very much even if our relationship was complicated (and, anyway, aren't *love* and *complications* basically words partnered forever, like *salt* and *pepper* and *husband* and *wife*?). But a straight shot of sun directed at a mirror can set things on fire. Juliet and I had learned this ourselves when we were kids one August day on the sidewalk in front of our house. When I was seven (and, honestly, nine and twelve and fourteen), I'd have held that mirror toward the sun for days even if nothing had happened, just because she'd told me to.

Mom ran across the lawn to hug Juliet like she hadn't seen her in years even though it had only been five months since she'd been home last, three since Mom and I had gone down to Portland, Oregon, where Juliet had gotten her big break singing four nights a week at the Fireside Room at the Grosvenor Hotel. When you saw her onstage in that sapphire gown, her head tilted back to show her long throat, smoke from some man's cigarette circling around her like a thin wisp of fog in some old detective movie, you'd never have thought she'd come from tiny Parrish Island. Tiny and *inconsequential* Parrish Island, where the only important visitors were the pods of Orca whales that came every summer. You'd never have thought Juliet was a regular girl who had graduated from Parrish Island High School only the year before. Barely graduated, I might add, almost flunking Algebra II had it not been for the tutoring of her younger sister, thank you, although Mom would say Juliet had never been a regular girl.

The driver's side door opened, and that's when Hayden got out. I thought he was having a nice stretch before he got back in and went home, a friend doing a friend-favor, maybe. He was about twenty-three or -four, tall, with easy, tousled brown hair. He wore Levi's with a tucked-in white T-shirt, and his jeans had a big wet spot on the leg, spilled coffee was my guess, which he was blotting with napkins.

And then he looked up at us. Or at me, because Mom didn't even notice him. Usually I was the invisible one in any group, but he was invisible along with me then. Mom was clutching Juliet to her and then holding her away again so that Juliet's fiery eyes could meet Mom's blazing ones. So his eyes met only mine, and mine his, and right then my heart shifted, the way it does when something unexpected begins. There are those moments, probably few in a life, where *before* and *after* split off from each other forevermore in your mind. That was one of those moments, although I wouldn't realize it for a long time afterward. I saw something very simple and clear there, in his eyes—that was the thing. Honesty. But with the kind of hope that was just this side of heartbreak.

He smiled at me, went around to the back of the truck. I guess anyone would have noticed the way he looked in those jeans. Of course I did. In the open pickup bed there was a big dog waiting to be let out. He was the sort of large, energetic dog that made Mom nervous. A sudden dog, and Mom didn't like sudden things. She mistrusted squirrels and birds and men and anything that had the capacity to surprise. If she ever got a dog, she'd say, it was going to be one of those white and fluffy ones, like Ginger, the Martinellis' dog, who looked the same as the slippers Mrs. Martinelli wore when she went to get the mail. You could put a dog like that into your purse like a lipstick and take it anywhere you wanted it to go, like women did in New York or Paris. A lipstick with a heartbeat that might pee on your checkbook, in my opinion, but this was Mom's dream, not mine. I liked a dog you could lean against.

The dog jumped down and made a galloping leap toward Mom, and the guy in the Levi's lunged for his collar and said, "Zeus!" in a way that was both emphatic and desperate. Zeus, it would turn out, was actually a very well-trained dog—he'd do anything for Hayden. Zeus would look at Hayden in the complete and adoring way you privately wished and wished and wished that someone, someday, might look at you. But Hayden was a good dog father and knew his boy's limits—meeting new people turned Zeus into a toddler in the toy aisle, with the kind of joy and want that turned into manic jumping. Zeus leaped up on Mom, who was horrified to be suddenly looking at him eye to eye, and she held him off with a palm to his tan furry chest. She looked down at her clothes as if he might have made her muddy, although the ground was dry and she was only in her old cargo pants and a tank top, her hair in a sort-of bun stuck up with a pair of chopsticks.

It was then that Mom realized that Juliet had not descended alone from the heavens. She looked surprised at the unexpected visitors and the facts in front of her: this truck, not Juliet's ancient Fiat convertible; this lanky, excited dog; this lanky, somewhat tousled and tangled guy grabbing his collar . . .

And that's when we saw it. We both did, at the same moment. It caught the sun, so shiny and new was the gold. A wedding band. On the guy's finger. We both did the same thing next, Mom and me. We looked at Juliet's left hand. And, yes, there was one there, too. That same gold band.

My mother put her hand to her chest. I heard her gasp. And then she breathed out those two words, the ones I was feeling right then too, that multipurpose, universal expression of shock and despair.

"Oh fuck," my mother said.

DEB CALETTI is the author of *The Queen of Everything*; *Honey, Baby, Sweetheart* (a National Book Award finalist); *Wild Roses*; *The Nature of Jade*; *The Fortunes of Indigo Skye*; *The Secret Life of Prince Charming*; and *The Six Rules of Maybe*. She lives with her family in Seattle. You can visit her at debcaletti.com and become a fan on Facebook.

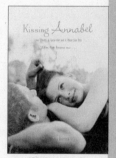

# SimonTEEN

Simon & Schuster's **Simon Teen** e-newsletter delivers current updates on the hottest titles, exciting sweepstakes, and exclusive content from your favorite authors.

Visit **TEEN.SimonandSchuster.com** to sign up, post your thoughts, and find out what every avid reader is talking about!